SOMEHOW, THEY HAD MADE

Vessel Commandof the Sauron Fleet F
slightly in the comm
effect of jump to we   cleared,
Diettinger realized he could make out more details
of the bridge than he might have liked. Fire had
blackened a third of the room, while smoke still
drifted lazily in the red glow of the combat lights.

Somehow, they had made it. In Diettinger's mind
was an image of the Homeworld as they had jumped.
Firestorms and mushroom clouds pockmarked the
land. Even the seas roiled as the Imperial ships
sought out the undersea cities. A great red wound
ran along the main continent of Lebensraum as the
Imperial assaults split the planet's crust, while in
the space above, the bright lights of the homeland's
hopelessly outnumbered fleet pulsed as each ship
died. All but one.

"Position, sir," Navigation announced.

"Speak."

"Byers Star system. The moon is the only settled
body. Local name: 'Haven.' An old CoDo relocation
colony, Imperial since the Terran Exodus. We're
really on the fringes, sir. Files show no Imperial
presence in this sector for almost a decade."

Baen Books From Jerry Pournelle

Falkenberg's Legion
Prince of Mercenaries
Birth of Fire
High Justice
King David's Spaceship
Fallen Angels (with Larry Niven and Michael Flynn)
Go Tell the Spartans (with S.M. Stirling)
The Children's Hour (with S.M. Stirling)

Created by Jerry Pournelle

War World, Volume I: The Burning Eye
War World, Volume II: Death's Head Rebellion
War World, Volume III: Sauron Dominion

WAR WORLD, VOL. I: THE BURNING EYE

Copyright © 1988 by Jerry Pournelle

A Baen Books Original

Baen Publishing Enterprises
P.O. Box 1403
Riverdale, N.Y. 10471

First printing, July 1988
Second printing, June 1989
Third printing, December 1991

ISBN: 0-671-65420-9

Cover art by Keith Parkinson

Printed in the United States of America

Distributed by
SIMON & SCHUSTER
1230 Avenue of the Americas
New York, N.Y. 10020

DEDICATION:

For Jim Baen,
who invented the whole idea.

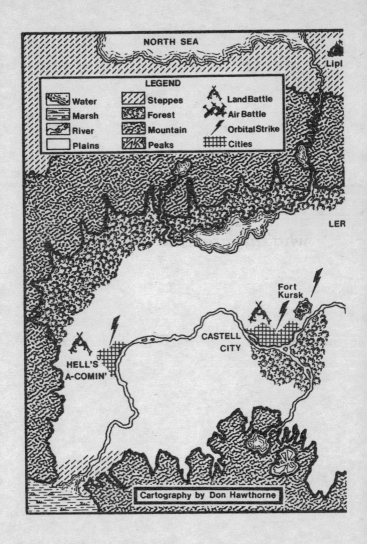

LEGEND

- Water
- Marsh
- River
- Plains
- Steppes
- Forest
- Mountain
- Peaks
- Land Battle
- Air Battle
- Orbital Strike
- Cities

NORTH SEA

Lipl

LER

Fort Kursk

CASTELL CITY

HELL'S A-COMIN'

Cartography by Don Hawthorne

A MAP OF THE MOON
HAVEN
AT THE EQUATORIAL REGION CONTAINING
THE SHANGRI-LA VALLEY
(BYERS' STAR SYSTEM)

ap's Yurt

MONTOVGRAD

The Citadel

"Fomoria" Downed

Fort Fornova

FALKENBERG

REDFIELD SATRAPY

Hamilton Castle

NOVY FINLANDIA

Chronology

1969 Neil Armstrong sets foot on Earth's moon.

1990 Series of treaties between the United States and the Soviet Union creates the CoDominium. Military research and development outlawed.

2008 First successful interstellar drive tested. Alderson Drive perfected.

2010 Habitable planets discovered in other star systems. Commercial exploitation begins.

2020 First interstellar colonies founded. CoDominium Space Navy created. Great Exodus begins as adventurous leave Earth to settle on other planets.

2032 Haven discovered by Captain Jed Byers.

2037 Universal Church of New Harmony given license to found settlements on Haven.

2040 CoDominium Bureau of Relocation begins mass out-system shipment of convicts. Colonization of Sparta and St. Ekaterina. First convicts arrive on Haven.

2048 CoDominium sends a consul general to Haven.

2060 Beginnings of nationalistic revival movements.

2072 Bureau of Relocation authorized to operate within Siberia, Russian Turkestan, Khazakstan, and Georgia due to "minority problems" in the U.S.S.R. Many shipped to Haven.

2079 Sergei Lermontov becomes Grand Admiral of CoDominium Space Navy.

2103 Great Patriotic Wars. End of the CoDominium. Exodus of the Fleet.

Table of Contents

PROLOG

DISCOVERY

CDSS *Ranger* was not a happy ship. It wasn't that there was anything wrong with her. *Ranger* wasn't new, far from it—she'd been one of the first exploratory ships built after the discovery of the Alderson Drive made star flight possible—but she was well maintained. Captain Jed Byers saw to that. No, Allan Wu thought, that wasn't the problem. It wasn't even the food. That was getting pretty monotonous after ten months in space, but Allan had been brought up on rice and whatever could be found to cook with it. He didn't need variety, he simply wanted enough to eat, and *Ranger* provided that, even if the rest of the crew made jokes about Purina Monkey Chow.

It wasn't the ship. It wasn't even the crew, not really.

The problem was that they weren't accomplishing anything. No one was going to get rich on Ranger's discoveries, least of all Allan Wu, and Allan needed the money.

It was Captain Byers' fault. Byers was fine at running a ship, but he didn't know beans about negotiating with the Bofors Company and the CoDominium. None of the systems he'd been given the right to explore had inhabitable planets. That was to be expected, habitable planets were rare, but the systems hadn't anything else either. One did have an asteroid belt with plenty of carbon, and even water ice—but no inhabitable planets, and no gas giant in the whole system. No place for merchantmen to get cheap hydrogen fuel. Belters could live without planets, but they couldn't live without *some* trade with Earth. Byers could file claims, but Bofors wasn't going to pay any bonuses for that find.

Probably not for the one coming up, either. Allan frowned and stared at the computer screen. It didn't tell him anything he didn't already know. A G2 star four light-years away and some twenty parsecs, over sixty light-years, from Earth. Not that the distance mattered so much. There were star systems nearly that far that could be reached in two Alderson jumps. Not this one. "It's a bear to get to, and there's nothing when you get there."

"You can't know that," Linda said. "We know there are planets—"

"At least one planet," Allan agreed. "Maybe more. Pity the bloody telescope fritzed, we'd know more about that planet. I think it's a big one."

"A gas giant and a Belt," Linda mused. "And a habitable planet, green, about—what? Point 7 A.U. out—?"

"That would do it," Allan said. "Riches in plenty. But it's pipe dreams."

"We still have to go look," Linda said. "And maybe we'll get lucky." She grinned, and Allan caught his breath as he always did when she smiled. He wondered if he'd ever get over that, and hoped he wouldn't. "Read the contract lately?" she asked.

"Which one? Mine, yours, or ours?"

"Ours." She patted her stomach. "Just in time, too. Mother will be pleased . . ."

"HEAR THIS. PREPARE FOR ALDERSON JUMP. SECURE FOR ALDERSON JUMP."

Linda shuddered and began strapping herself into the seat in front of her console.

"I saw that," Allan said. "Still worried about jumps?"

"Well, some. Aren't you?"

He nodded slowly. No one had any information on the effects of the Alderson Drive on pregnant women or their unborn children. "Damn, I wish we weren't going on with—"

"Don't be silly," Linda said. "Two more jumps can't matter."

"Sure," he said, but he didn't believe it. Alderson jumps had unpredictably unpleasant effects on healthy adults. They couldn't be good for children. Allan didn't care about the child, or at least could convince himself that he didn't, but the thought of something happening to Linda turned him to jelly.

"ALDERSON JUMP PLOTTED. INITIATING COUNTDOWN."

Allan checked his straps, then looked to be sure Linda's were properly fastened. All correct.

"STATION CHECK. BIOLOGICAL SECTION REPORT READY FOR JUMP."

"BIOLOGY READY AYE AYE."

"Biology," Allan snorted.

"Sounds nicer than waste disposal."

"ENGINEERING REPORT READY FOR JUMP."

"ENGINEERING READY AYE AYE."

"SCIENCE SECTION REPORT READY FOR JUMP."

Allan touched a switch, and his computer screen went blank. He glanced at the status lights on his console. "SCIENCE READY AYE AYE," he reported.

"QUARTERMASTER SECTION REPORT READY FOR JUMP."

The station check continued. Then the speakers said, "ALDERSON JUMP IN ONE MINUTE. ONE MINUTE AND COUNTING."

"Science section," Allan said. There was contempt in his voice. "If I was a real scientist, I'd be investigating things. Why does the Alderson Jump rack people up?"

"Nobody knows that—"

"Exactly. I should be finding out—"

"STAND BY FOR JUMP."

There was a moment of silence, and the universe exploded around them.

Allan hung limply from the straps. He felt drool run down his chin, but for the moment he was too sick to care. His thoughts spun wildly.

For a moment—

For a moment he had known everything. He was
sure of it. During that moment, when he, and Linda,
and CDSS *Ranger* had ceased to exist in the normal
universe, he had known, known with utter certainty,
how planets formed, how the universe began, why the
Alderson Drive worked. Now he couldn't remember
any of it, only that he'd once known.

It was a common experience. Probably half the people who had made jumps had felt it at least once. It was
also an odd experience, because no experiment ever
devised had measured the time a jump took. To the
best anyone could measure, it took literally no time at
all. Yet during that zero interval, humans had thoughts
and dreams—and computers went mad, so that it was
routine to shut down all computers except the ones
needed for the jump, and to have those on timers set to
cut power as soon as the jump was made.

"Linda?" he croaked.

"I'm fine."

She didn't sound fine, but at first it was hard to care
about her or anything else, and after he began to recover from jump lag he had work to do. He started the
powerup sequences on his computers.

"All right, dammit, so what do we do now?" Captain
Byers demanded. He reached into a sideboard and took
out a bulb of scotch whiskey, popped the top, and
squeezed a shot into his mouth.

"I'm looking," Allan protested. "Look, it takes time.
First I have to establish the plane of the ecliptic. That
means I have to find more than two planets, or wait
long enough for one to move."

"Yeah, I understand that," Byers said. "I don't suppose it will hurt your search if I mosey on over to the
gas giant?"

"Not a bit," Allan said. "I was going to suggest that.
It looks interesting. Hey—"

"Yeah?"

"Moons," Allan said. "The giant's got some. Ten anyway. They'll be in the ecliptic plane."

"Well, hell, of course they'll be in the ecliptic," Byers said. He looked critically at Allan, then shook his head.

"Sir?" Allan asked.

"I keep forgetting," Jed Byers said. "Not your fault. Mine."

"Captain, I don't understand at all," Allan Wu pleaded.

Jed Byers shrugged and reached into the cabinet. "Have a beer?"

'Well, thank you, sir—"

"By way of apology," Byers said. "Look, you can't help it if they deliberately crippled your education."

Allan frowned. "Captain, I—"

"You've got a Ph.D. from Cornell, and you're a licensed scientist," Byers said. "That what you were going to say?"

"Well—"

"And it don't mean beans," Byers said. "Not your fault. Look, nobody knows anything nowadays. It's all in the computers, so there's no point in knowing anything, right?"

"Well—it's not worthwhile memorizing facts," Allan said. "It's easier to learn where to find them—"

"Where to find them. In the computer. Ever think the computers might be wrong?"

"Sir?"

Jed Byers sighed. "Look, maybe I've had too much to drink." He eyed Allan carefully. "No recorders. Maybe you got one built into your teeth—the hell with it. Look, Dr. Wu, there was a time when 'scientist' meant somebody who knew something, who thought for himself—"

"Yes, sir," Allan said. "I know, and I don't measure up. I know that; I was just telling Linda. They don't let us do real research—"

"Maybe it's worse than that," Byers said. "Think on

it, laddie. The CoDominium Treaty is supposed to stop the arms race, right? So if the CoDominium powers abide by it, everybody else has to, or one of the little guys might get ahead of the CoDominium. Only one problem. *Any* scientific discovery is likely to have military value. Better to stop it all. So tell me, if you were in CoDominium Intelligence, how would you stop scientific discovery?"

"Well—"

"Get control of everybody's research budget, every country and every company, not just the U.S. and the Sov world, all of them, Swiss and Swedes and the other neutrals. Put your people on the editorial boards of all the journals. Take over in the faculty and administration of the big universities. Elementary stuff. But how can you stop people from thinking? And putting what they think into computer networks?" Byers laughed bitterly. "When I was a kid—Wu, do you know how old I am?"

"No sir—"

"Older than God. I've heard you say it," Byers said. "Oh, yeah, *Ranger's* wired up pretty good. And I know her. I took her out on her first run—"

"Sir? But that was—"

"A long time ago. Yep. Making me old enough to remember when 'scientist' meant something, which is the point. When I was a kid, we used to think the computer networks would end censorship forever. How can you censor on-line communications? Hah. You don't. What you do is corrupt them." Byers swigged hard at the bulb of scotch. "Think about it. Control research, control publications, and feed false data into the system. Know what Planck's Constant is? No? Look it up in your machine. Maybe you get the right answer. Maybe you don't."

"Sir—" Allan was interrupted by three chirps from his comcard.

"PLANET DETECTED, POINT SIX THREE AU FROM PRIMARY."

"Hey, a good distance," Allan said. "Maybe we're lucky after all. Sir, if you'll excuse me . . ."

"Excuse hell! Doctor Wu, go find out if we're rich, and be quick about it!"

Five minutes later Allan knew the worst. The planet was barren. So was the only other one in the Habitable Zone. There couldn't be any life in the system.

"That's the story," Geoffrey Wu said. He signalled to the waiter for another platter of pot stickers. "A new planetary system, with a gas giant. No Belt, though."

"I suppose that's why I'm buying the dinner," Bill Garrick said. "Pity. But how'd you end up coming to an expensive school like this?"

Jeff grinned and fished in the pocket of his tunic, found a pink slip of paper, and laid it on the table. "No Belt, but there was something else."

Garrick looked at the check and whistled.

"Peanuts," Mary Hassimpton snorted.

"Yeah, well maybe to you, Miss Imperial Banks, but not to Dad," Jeff said.

"Lighten up, Mary," Garrick said. He drained his Chinese beer and lit a pipe of borloi.

"You're still grinning," Elayne van Stapleton said. "And you've got money. Tell us about it."

"Now who's turn to lighten up?" Mary demanded.

"Aw, let Elayne be," Bill Garrick said. "Somebody's got to study. Why not her? So, Jeff, where did the money come from?"

Jeff grinned even wider. "Well, none of the real planets were of any use, but they found a good planet after all. It's a moon of the gas giant."

"Oh, for heaven's sake," Mary said.

"Yeah, I heard about that," Garrick said, "Haven, right?"

"Right. Not what Captain Byers named it, but it's official now that the Holy Joes bought it."

"So. Your old man did all right after all." Garrick

took the check and held it out to Jeff. "So you pay for the Peking Duck."

"Well, all right," Jeff said. "But I tell you, nobody ever got rich—not real rich—from selling out to Garner Castell."

HAVEN

Description

Haven is the official name given to the second moon of the fourth planet in the Byers System. It is unusual in every way. Byers IV—generally known as the Cat's Eye—is located far outside the normal habitable zone for a G2 star; but being approximately 1.3 Jupiter masses, the gas giant provides sufficient radiant energy to keep much of Haven marginally tolerable.

Haven's rotation is unusual, since it is locked tidally with the Cat's Eye, but in the synchronized pattern of Mercury rather than always presenting the same face as does Earth's Moon. The planet is somewhat smaller than Earth, and has a much thinner atmosphere. Due to its proximity to the Cat's Eye there is great seismic activity. During the period of formation, the tidal forces resulted in unusual patterns of vulcanism. Haven is a jumble of high mountains and deep rift valleys. Most of the mountains are high rocky peaks similar to the Andes mountains in South America on Earth.

The only temperate area is in the equatorial zone, which climatically resembles northern Scotland. Due to the thin atmosphere the only nearly comfortable area of Haven is a single deep rift valley in the equatorial area. The valley is locally called Shangri-La after a similar place in a novel of the 20th Century.

Like all life discovered so far, the indigenous plants and animals of Haven have biochemistries similar to those of Earth, but evolution has produced some un-

9

usual proteins. Needless to say, life native to Haven is extremely hardy and proved quite dangerous to the early settlers, as indicated by names such as "shark's fin," "hangman bush," "land gator," "dragon," and "wireweed." Efforts to reseed Haven with Earth plants and animals have been only partly successful.

Early History

Discovered in 2032 by Captain Jed Byers in CDSS *Ranger*, Haven was considered interesting enough to be reserved for study by the Cal Tech/MIT University Consortium until Captain Byers, in conjunction with Science Officer Allan Wu, brought suit demanding payment for discovery of an inhabitable world.

The University Consortium challenged the claim on the grounds that Haven was not an "inhabitable world" within any sane definition. One particularly telling quote came from Allan Wu's own diaries: "It's not precisely a niche for life. More like a loophole." The challenge was sustained in lower courts, but the CoDominium Council held that Byers was entitled to payment. The University Consortium set about raising the money, but failed to do so within the time limits set by the Council. It was widely rumored at the time that CoDominium Intelligence, assisted by the Bureau of Relocation, was instrumental in preventing the Universities from acquiring the needed funds.

Shortly thereafter, the wealthy Universal Church of New Harmony paid the requisite fees, including the discovery bonuses, and was given license to establish settlements.

The New Harmony expedition was led by the Reverend Charles Castell, son of New Harmony Church President Garner Bill Castell. The younger Castell's personal heroism and devotion caused the settlers, including a minority not members of the Church, to appoint Castell mayor of the first settlement and to name it after him.

The first settlement was composed of fewer than one

thousand members of the New Harmony Church. They were followed by twelve thousand immigrants sent by the Bureau of Relocation. Most of those were not Church members, but had no choice but to work with and for the original inhabitants. Qualifications for full Church membership (which was a requirement for voters in Castell) were never relaxed, but a form of junior membership was instituted.

The next wave of settlers brought by Bureloc arrived unexpectedly. The attempted revolt of the iron miners of northern North America was suppressed by CoDominium Marines, and two thousand miners, mostly without families, were deported to Haven. When they discovered the strict laws prevailing in Castell they founded a rival town, which they named Hell's-A'Comin'.

In 2048 the CoDominium sent a colonial governor (consul general) to Haven, and Bureau of Relocation resumed mass shipments of involuntary colonists. An attempted rebellion of the New Harmony Church in an uneasy alliance with the miners of Hell's-A-Comin' was easily put down by a battalion of CoDominium Marines. The Reverend Charles Castell, Mayor Fineal Naha of Hell's-A-Comin', and nine other rebellion leaders were hanged. A CoDominium Navy base, surveillance and power satellites, and other amenities were established, and Haven enjoyed a brief economic boom.

This was followed by the discovery of shimmerstones in the mountains. These rare gems had become extremely popular among Earth upper classes; one particularly fine stone was sold for 3 million CD credits at an auction held in 2057. Prices today are somewhat lower, but a single stone can make a prospector wealthy for life.

Following widespread unrest within the U.S.S.R., in 2072 the Bureau of Relocation was authorized to operate within Siberia, Russian Turkestan, Khazakstan, Georgia, and other areas with high concentrations of ethnic undesirables.

A brief Introduction to the CoDominium Worlds
by Arthur Jenson
Appleton Century Crofts
Third Edition 2090

From *Crofton's Encyclopedia of Contemporary History and Social Issues* (3RD EDITION)

The Bureau of Relocation is second in authority only to the Bureau of Internal Affairs within the CoDominium administration. Bureau of Relocation agents operate as a quasi-police force, being responsible for removing subversives, troublesome minorities, habitual criminals, and anyone else classified as a malcontent.

The Bureau has its own fleet of ships for transporting deportees to the resettlement colonies. Most are ex-Naval transports or passenger ships, generally in poor condition due to lack of funds for adequate maintenance.

Critics of the Bureau have pointed out that its agents are frequently unselective about whom they deport. There have been numerous legal cases arising from the deportation of individuals for inadequately defined "political" reasons. Also, debtors, hobos, gypsies, chronic substance abusers, and other comparatively harmless types have been picked up in Bureoloc "scoops." They are frequently deported by overworked magistrates, who have neither the time nor, in many cases, the inclination to make detailed background searches on anyone "recommended" for deportation.

In its favor, the Bureau is both understaffed and underfunded for a task that would be impossible to carry out even if it were several orders of magnitude larger. The increasing minority problem throughout the Soviet Union and the southwestern and northeastern United States has made both CoDominium powers much less particular about the methods used to "administratively contain" the situation. Coupled with the growing demand of both corporations and colonial governments for more "warm bodies" to develop established colonies, this has driven the Bureau of Relocation to use methods of transferring large numbers of minority-group deportees that in other cases might be considered to constitute criminal negligence.

Further Bureau of Relocation abuses outside the Sol System have been extensively documented. Many colonial agents openly barter their deportees to planetary governments, private companies, and wealthy individuals. Often transportees are sold into "indentured status" that is slavery in everything but name.

Even those deportees who escape such a fate are frequently charged for their transportation costs by unscrupulous agents and arrive at their destinations with little more than the clothes on their backs. It is not unknown for families to be broken up, with wives and daughters being privately auctioned to brothels or wealthy colonists. Complaining husbands and fathers have been known to be "spaced."

There is almost universal agreement about the extent of the Bureau's offenses. Unfortunately, nobody has yet proposed a more workable system for ridding Earth of its surplus population and the growing number of malcontents openly hostile to the CoDominium.

The current Director of the Bureau of Relocation, Samuel Webb, has described the situation concisely:

"Any and every abuse of this department can be corrected by the simple application of more funds. Give me the budget, and I'll give you results that will make everybody happy."

In view of the increasing reluctance of the Grand Senate to fund even Navy appropriations, it is impossible to be optimistic as of this writing about the possibilities of Bureloc reform. A vicious circle seems far more probable: abuses, opposition, more political deportations arousing more opposition . . .

DREAM VALLEY

Edward P. Hughes

The yurt lay like an abandoned toy on Haven's vast northern steppe. Orfan Judeiks peered out of a window in the slave quarters. Snow had sifted through a break in the outer pane. It lay frozen in the double-glazed gap.

Orfan stirred the *pups* over the charcoal burner, wishing the Cham all the benefits of his yurt's ineffective double-glazing. The pipe gang would be back soon, cold, and expecting their supper. The Cham should try preparing it in a chilly, draughty kitchen.

Once in a while Orfan regretted the maneuvering with which he had secured the kitchen billet. The comparatively comfortable job had set a gulf between him and the pipe gang which some of the slaves found difficult to stomach.

Orfan sighed. Six months previously, when a Roosky judge in Daugavapils had sentenced him to five years interior exile for stealing bread, Orfan had scarcely heard of this moon Haven. Bureloc scouts had picked him up wandering on the outskirts of Kazan, and within two months he was a kitchen slave on the prison world! And Haven was a far from comfortable place.

Overhead, the glass-fibre onion domes creaked in the wind, fractured seams leaking warmth into the chill air.

A cluster of muskylopes wandered into Orfan's field of vision. The beasts were part of the herd the tartars kept for milking. The beasts were never permitted to

16

stray far from the yurt. God alone knew how they endured the everlasting cold.

Orfan craned his neck to catch a glimpse of the candy-striped world overhead. Hadn't some schoolteacher once explained to him how a brown dwarf radiated heat? He shrugged. Profitless to speculate on such astronomical mysteries. Somewhere up in the sky, close to Cat's Eye, was a magic hole invented by an American called Alderson. If you were lucky enough to find that hole, you could step through it and find yourself back in the solar system—and able to erect a finger to the Bureau of Relocation!

Orfan stirred the *pups* pensively. What right had the Rooskies to scoop up civilized Balts along with their half-wild tartars to dump on a freezing world out among the stars!

He shivered. Cold weather could be fun. He recalled frost fairs on a frozen Dvina. But Baltic winters lasted only six months. Here on Haven, they went on and on.

The door banged. A gust of air from the passage chilled his ankles. Lisa Grinbergs, assistant scullion— and pretty enough to stop the chief scullion's breath— entered the kitchen.

She put her back to the door. "Is supper ready? The pipe gang will be here in a minute."

He put down the ladle and sidled towards her. She was his assistant scullion by dint of some keen haggling with the tartar chef. She was also a native of Riga, and considered herself a cut above Daugavapils yokels. But, the rest of the slaves were grown adults, and Lisa was just two months his junior. Orfan loved her with a passion only sixteen-year-olds can feel.

She allowed him to put an arm around her waist and cup her breast.

"Did you hear what I said, Orfins?"

Only Lisa, among the slaves, used the diminutive.

He nodded. "Supper's ready."

She peered into the steaming pot. "*Pups* again? No meat?"

He flourished a fist. "Remember you are talking to the monkey—not the organ grinder! Give me a knife and let me out there among those muskylopes . . . !"

She turned up her nose. "Pooh! You wouldn't hurt a fly!"

The outer portal slammed, rattling the kitchen door. Lisa dashed for her broom. The pipe gang would track melting snow all over her clean floor . . . !"

Old Maksis arrived first, shivering. Bent and shrivelled, the man was too old for lifting lengths of glass-concrete piping. Too old, too, to dig trenches in frozen tundra. Too old, in fact, for any kind of physical labor—if only the slave masters would show a spark of humanity! He had taught mathematics at Riga University before Bureloc snatched him from a city park during one of his absent-minded spells.

Orfan thrust a ready-warmed bowl and spoon into the old man's hands. He ladled out beans. Maksis cracked icicles from his whiskers, warming his cheeks over the dish.

Orfan pushed him gently away. "Shift, Maksis! You're not the only one who's cold."

Skinny Elmer Parn came next, bending over the cauldron, eyebrows shedding droplets. He cooed, "What peautiful peans!" Being Estonian, Elmer used English with the Letts, and being Estonian, he couldn't say his 'b's.

Crippled Michel Tasvin from Jelgava followed. Then the Roosian, Golikov, round eyes in a round peasant face, watching his bowl fill. Then one-time fishwife Eva Abolins . . . then Kujucs, the wrestler . . . then Bella Buksum, the beautiful . . . then . . .

Orfan Judeiks sighed. To be a slavey to the slaves of creatures lower than slaves must be the absolute nadir. Was it possible to sink lower?

After they had eaten, he piled the pots in the sink. This was the best part of Haven's 87-hour day. The Cham had ruled two work and two rest shifts a day. Slaves and masters were both striving to reconcile Terran clocks and human circadian rhythms to a new world's rotation period. For ten hours now, the yurt could rest or sleep, as it pleased. There were no chairs for slaves, so they sat in a ring on the floor. By tacit consent, Old Maksis got the spot next to the stove.

"Tell us about the hot river and your dream valley, Maksis," prompted gaunt Felix Anders, who acted as keeper to the dim-witted Tromifovics. They had all heard about the old man's river and valley a dozen times already. But, with talk one of their few recreations, topics tended to be squeezed dry. Chess had once been an alternative, until someone had stolen their pieces. Now, if they tried to play chess with paper men, only the draughts won!

Old Maksis sucked a strand of his whiskers. "You may scoff," he told them. "But I've seen it. Not the valley—you can't get through the mountains to see that. But the evidence is there to feel. The river comes out of a cave, warm to the hand. The sea ice is melted for half a verst."

Red-headed Voldemars Pics sniffed. "Sea ice, *vatsajs?* You must have been far to the north. Salt water doesn't freeze here."

The old man cackled. "Wait until winter, laddie. You'll see hot tea freeze, then!"

Rita Purins, who worked as hard as any man in the pipe gang, ceased combing her hair to ask, "But, *vatsajs,* how do you know that the river comes from the valley?"

The old man leered at her. "Didn't I see the clouds? A sky clear as a bell all round, but clouds over one spot in the mountains."

Rita dismissed his answer with a wave of her hand. "Okay—so how come you're the only one who's seen this river?"

Old Maksis appeared confused. "But . . . I've been here longer than any of you." He scratched his head. "At least, I think so. They used to let me go out with the muskylopes. Then Codo built this place for the tartars, and they don't herd muskylope any more. Those lazy scuts won't do a hand's turn while they can get free food and lodging."

They all nodded. Tartars were layabouts. And no one could understand why the CoDominium was so willing to support them.

Usually taciturn, Vasily Bugovics asked, "Where exactly is this river of yours, *vatsajs*?"

Old Maksis gestured vaguely westwards. "Oh—over that way. Three or four days ride."

"Haven days?" queried Bugovics. None of them had yet become accustomed to a day split into two work and two rest cycles.

The old man snorted. "Earth days, of course. We decided our own sleep times 'til Liplap came along with his new rules."

Cham Liplap had brought more than arbitrary division of Haven's day, but it was little use grumbling about a tyrant's ways.

Vasily Bugovics elected to remain obtuse. "And riding on what, *vatsajs*? A Bureloc lander?"

"Heh heh!" The old man cackled. "On a muskylope, my lad—if you were able to sit one!"

They all laughed, being aware that Maskis wouldn't perform for long without some appreciation.

They were awaiting the next sally, when the door was kicked open. One of Liplap's baggy-trousered ruffians entered. He pointed at Orfan, speaking in Roosian. "Chingiz wants you."

Liplap the Chingiz, Grand Cham of Novy Tartary-on-Haven, was chief of the exiled nomads. Bunkered in their plastic yurt, Liplat and his stalwarts bragged endlessly about sweaty exploits on Terra, while relying on a Codo reactor for creature comforts. But when the Chingiz crooked a finger, everyone—nomads and slaves—jumped.

Orfan got to his feet. The Cham's supper had gone in hours ago. The tartar chief probably required entertainment.

Orfan said, "Me?"

The Cham's messenger flourished a curved blade. "Yes, you, *tovarische*. *Scoro!*"

Orfan went quickly.

The tartar stayed behind to see if there was anything left to eat in the slaves' pot.

Orfan sped along the corridor towards the tartar section of the yurt. He took his time going through the airtight door which prevented warm air blowing into the slaves' quarters.

The Chingiz sat on a pile of cushions in his audience chamber. Around the walls squatted his favorite male courtesans. No woman was ever permitted in this room, Orfan knew. Tartars believed that the harem was the place for the animal-that-talked.

He halted a respectful distance from the Cham, bowed his head, and waited.

"Scullion!" Liplap used English, since Orfan's own language was beneath his dignity, and Roosky too superior a language for conversation with a slave.

Orfan looked up. He responded in the same language. "Sire?"

"Take off your clothes, lad."

Aware of the Cham's exotic tastes, Orfan had come prepared for the worst. It seemed he might not be disappointed.

He decided to make a production of it. He removed his coat. Then his shirt. Then his undershirt. Then the pyjama jacket he wore under his shirts. Then he pulled off his vest. He folded each garment, piling them neatly beside him on the floor.

Someone snickered.

He took off his boots. His top pair of socks. His under pair of socks. Then the socks which were little more than a knitted sleeve linking the holes at heel and toe. These, too, went into a heap beside the discarded garments.

A wizened ruffian at the Cham's elbow hid a grin behind a dirty hand.

Orfan then removed his trousers. Then the trousers underneath. Then his pyjama bottoms.

Someone giggled. Even the Cham smiled.

Finally, Orfan removed his long johns and stood naked.

The Chingiz clapped his hands. In a corner, a drummer commenced to thump out an irregular beat.

"Dance for us?" suggested the Cham.

It was an order. Orfan capered, ignoring the drumbeat. He knew what the Cham wanted. He hopped up and down to make his penis wag. The drumming continued, relentless. Orfan grew warm and sweaty.

At a sign from the Cham, the drumming ceased. Orfan stood panting.

Liplap pointed. "Can you make *that* stand?"

Orfan dreaded suggestions of this kind. He looked down. "I . . . I think not, sire."

"Try!" urged the Cham.

Orfan tried. Before an audience, it refused to respond. He desisted. "I'm sorry, sire."

Liplap contemplated him. "Can you stand on your hands?"

Orfan knew that unless he provided some kind of entertainment voluntarily, worse might be demanded.

"I can cartwheel, sire," he offered. Cartwheeling had been one of his accomplishments during his spell with a circus. The Cham had not seen any of his gymnastics.

"Cartwheel, then," agreed the Cham.

Orfan cartwheeled. Back and forth in the center of the chamber. Forth and back, careful not to trip over a casually extended leg. In circles, mindful of the limited space. Clockwide and widdershins. Facing the Cham, arse to the Cham. God damn! Why couldn't they take up scrabble instead!

Liplap clapped his hands. "Enough!"

Orfan collapsed, like an unstrung marionette.

The Cham stared around the chamber. "You desire more, gentlemen?"

They shook their heads. Hadn't the Chingiz already said "enough"?

Liplap fumbled in a purse dangling from his ornamental gold belt. He drew out a gold coin, big as an overcoat button, and threw it to Orfan.

"We prefer television, lad. Go back to your quarters."

Orfan stooped, grabbed the coin and his clothes, and backed from the chamber. Thank heavens they hadn't wanted an obscene exhibition. He dressed in the anteroom, clutching the coin all the time. The yurt boasted no shops . . . but people might be bribed with gold!

Lisa was awake when he returned to the kitchen. The other slaves sprawled about the floor, snoring. Her pupils gleamed in the light from the corridor.

"Are you okay, Orfins?"

He showed her the coin. "It was easy tonight. I made them laugh." He stuffed the gold piece into a pocket and got down beside her. She snuggled up to him.

"I hope it stays that way."

He put an arm around her. "What's worrying you?"

She lowered her voice. "Something Old Maksis talked about after you left. He's been here longer than any of us. He was wondering where all the people who arrived with him had gone."

Orfan nibbled her ear. "His memory is hopeless."

She pushed him away. "A bad memory doesn't make people disappear. There were a dozen others picked up with him. Where are they now?"

Orfan frowned into the darkness. "Maybe they've wandered off? Bureloc picks on vagrants. They don't like relatives enquiring after transportees. That's why there are so many Tartars here—they're natural vagrants."

She silenced him with her lips. "Listen to what I'm telling you. Maksis said he came back to the yurt one day, after being out with the muskylopes, and all his old comrades had gone. He thinks the Chingiz had them put away because a new batch of slaves was due to arrive. and he believes the same thing happens every time a new batch is due."

Orfan sniffed scornfully. "Why would the Chingiz overlook Old Maksis?"

"Maybe he lets one slave live to show newcomers the ropes?"

He squeezed her tightly. "Old Maksis imagines things."

She stiffened. "This isn't imagination. How long has Bureloc been dumping homeless people here? Why are there so few Balts in the yurt and so many Tartars?"

He stroked her hair. "I don't know. For that matter, why are we slaves? I wasn't a slave on Earth."

She shivered. "We're slaves because the Tartars make us slaves. Bureloc doesn't care a damn, so long as we're relocated."

He held her tight. "What can we do about it? At least you and I don't have to work on the pipeline like the others."

She whispered in his ear. "We could escape."

Orfan almost laughed. Escape across a tundra desert stretching for kilometers in every direction? He whispered back, "Where could we go?"

She hissed fiercely. "Anywhere! I don't care. I hate this place. You know I'm no longer a virgin?"

His embrace tightened. So someone had stolen the privilege he had hoped for. He groaned. "Who did it? Tell me. I'll kill the swine!"

She shook her head. "It was a Tartar. They'd kill you first, if you tried to touch one of them."

They lay silent while Orfan pondered her news. It could happen if they remained in the yurt!

He said, "Where could we go—if we ran away?"

She tucked a face into his chest. "We could look for Old Maksis' valley."

He sighed. She was as foolish as the old man. He said, "If the valley exists—and we managed to find it—how could we live? Perhaps we might find a hotel where they'd let us wash pots for our supper?"

She thumped his ribs. "There might be someone there who would welcome us."

He listened to the other slaves snoring. It was a crazy idea! He said, "And there might possibly be someone who wouldn't. We'd do better to wait for the next lander." He fingered the coin in his pocket. "I might be able to bribe someone to let us aboard."

Voice smothered in his jacket, she mumbled, "When's the next lander due?"

He shrugged. Did she think he was in Bureloc's confidence? In any case, Old Maksis might be right. People *had* disappeared. The Chingiz might have them all executed before the next lander came.

Lisa clung to him. "Take me away, Orfan—before Liplap has us all murdered!"

He held her tight. She was asking the impossible— unless all the slaves fled together! Orfan's pulse raced. They could steal food, weapons—even muskylopes!

He nuzzled her neck. "If the others would go as well, we might make it. We could go at first dark—give ourselves two full cycles to dodge any pursuit. We could head south . . . look for somewhere warm. I'll talk to the others."

She hugged him. "Oh, yes, Orfan—yes! Please!"

He put his idea to the kitchen parliament at the end of the next indoor work cycle. He knew that most of the slaves saw him as an artful dodger who had done some sort of a deal with the Tartars to get off working on the pipeline. Besides which—there were his visits to the Chingiz!

"What does he want you for?" Rita Purins had once asked.

Orfan had shrugged. Who would care to describe the Cham's obscene appetites to a woman!

He stared around the circle of slaves and said softly, "Let's talk about escaping."

Voldemars Pics shifted sideways, so that he leaned his back against the kitchen door. He said, "Astrakhan is the nearest public spaceport we could make for."

Astrakhan! Orfan blinked his surprise. Pics was ahead of him! Spaceport "Starchief" served the Roosky half of Codo. If one could only get there—!

"I—" he began.

Eva Abolins, who had once sold fish on Leipaja dockside, interrupted him. "Did the Chingiz put you up to this?"

Orfan flushed. "If you think I'd—"

Rita Purins ignored his confusion. She addressed Pics through a screen of hair hanging over her face. "Astrakhan's not for me, Voldy. I don't want to go back to Earth. They had me in an army brothel. I won't go back to that."

Ruddy-faced Fricis Frienbergs, who had been a farm hand in Tukums before falling foul of a minor bureaucrat, nodded agreement. "A valley of our own is what we want. Somewhere in the south, where we can plough and sow, and make things grow."

Vasily Bugovics stirred impatiently. "Don't rush us, Fritz. Let's decide if we want to escape first."

"We vote?" suggested Semën Golikov. The Roosian understood Lettish well enough to follow the conversation. He spread his hands. "I *nansenist*—stateless person—on Earth. I not want go back to Earth. New home on Haven sound fine to me."

Marta Karnups, who never talked about her past, said, "I reckon I could endure living somewhere else on this world. I vote we stay on Haven—if we can find somewhere to live. Besides—Astrakhan would only mean trouble for escaped slaves."

Lisa said eagerly, "Couldn't we look for Maksis' dream valley? Orfan thinks it's silly, but—"

He glowered at her. "I didn't say it was silly. I said, if the valley really exists . . ." He smirked apologetically at Old Maksis. ". . . it doesn't lie in the direction we want to go."

The old man fingered a loose tooth absently. "The valley exists, all right, son. But I don't claim we could find a way into it. Unless you are prepared to swim several versts, probably under water and against the current, to find where the river comes from."

Anton Trofimovics wriggled out of Felix Kanders' grasp. He grinned his foolish grin. "We not swim. We be cowboys. Ride muskylopes. Maksis shows us how."

All eyes turned towards the idiot. Crazy Troffy was telling them plainly how they might escape!

Voldemars Pics said, "Maybe we ought to start making plans."

Orfan let them talk. It had been his idea, but it would be too much to expect these adults to accept him as their leader. Anyway, he had expected mistrust, and only the fishwife had shown antagonism. Let Pics do the Moses act. Orfan Judeiks would tag along.

Preparations took more than a Haven week. Each sleep period, Orfan, whose job gave him the run of the yurt, stole something to aid their survival on the steppe. Food, clothes, blankets, weapons—the Tartars were careless with possessions, and frequently drunk. So theft wasn't difficult. Weapons were the exception. But Orfan discovered a way into the yurt armory through the loose ceiling of a linen cupboard. He concealed his loot in an outside barn used only at muskylope calving time.

Early one evening, at the start of a nighttime rest cycle, Voldemars led his tribe into the desert. The night was cold and dark. Hecate showed only a thin crescent, Cat's Eye a larger one, shedding just enough light to see by. They followed Pics to the barn where he distributed Orfan's loot. Each slave got blankets, an army pup tent, a parcel of Codo rations, and a weapon.

Lisa gingerly gripped the lance that Voldemars handed to her. "Will I have to stick it into anyone?"

Orfan grinned. "I doubt it. Old Genghiz Khan't will be glad we've gone. Saves him having our throats slit."

Vasily Bugovics tucked a curved sword into his belt, then hefted a crossbow. "The Chingiz will be after us fast enough when he counts his muskylopes at daylight. Vasily patted the glass-fiber stock of his weapon. "I reckon this gadget can slow a charging Tartar."

The share-out finished, Pics led them out to the track made by the pipe gang on their work cycles. He said, "The herd crossed the pipe route today. I saw fresh droppings. Let's see if we can find them."

Michel Tasvin, shouldering an antique Lee Enfield, fell in beside Pics. "The Tartars will follow us easy on this trail," he objected.

Pics was unmoved. "We'll leave tracks whichever way we go. And the pipeline route is well trampled. Extra tracks won't show so clearly."

Rita Purins clicked the bolt of a venerable Krag Jorgensen. "If Genghiz Khan't follows me, I'll blow his ugly head off!"

Old Maksis waved the cavalry revolver he had drawn in the share-out. "Hush! Those Tartar shepherds can hear a snail fart! Pray that there are none of them around."

"I hear muskylopes," mumbled the crazy Trofimovics. The fool flourished a vintage Armalite for which Orfan had been unable to locate any ammunition, and eyed Old Maksis' revolver. "You like to swap, Max? Cowboys have handguns like that."

Old Maksis mouthed a refusal none could read in the gloom.

Then muskylope shapes loomed ahead.

Maksis halted. "They'll be hobbled," he whispered. "Go up to them quietly, slip the hobble off, and jump aboard before they wake up. Lie along the back, holding the ears. Kick with your feet to make them go. Steer by pulling one ear or the other. Stop by pulling both ears together."

They hesitated.

"It's not dangerous," he assured them. "They're all cows in milk. If you don't threaten their calves, they'll do you no harm. And, once you get them moving, they'll go forever. You can sit up and enjoy the scenery."

To the slaves' surprise, the muskylopes accepted riders placidly. Twenty-six mounted fugitives were soon plodding after Leader Voldemars.

Orfan tagged along at the tail, holding hands with Lisa, marvelling at the ease of their escape.

Voldemars called a halt at mid-cycle. Cat's Eye was a fat crescent hovering on the horizon. The air sparkled with frost. Their breath came in gusty vapors. They ate Orfan-prepared sandwiches, drank cold tea from flasks, then pressed on. By midnight they had grown weary of riding. Cat's Eye was setting, its light dim.

Voldemars signalled another halt. "No fires," he warned. "If anyone's out searching for muskylopes, we don't want to tell them where we are."

Orfan thought of the small sack of charcoal in his pack. The glow of its burning could be hidden, but there was the matter of lighting the stuff. He decided not to risk a reproof from Pics. They ate sour bread and Codo pâté, washed down with the remains of their cold tea. Fritz pushed aside the noses of questing calves to show Marta and Rita how to milk a muskylope. Orfan opened the sack of assorted ammunition he had filched. Those with firearms picked out suitable calibers for their weapons.

By dawn they were passing the first of the windmills that drove the pipeline pumps. Michel Tasvin halted his muskylope in front of it and swung the spiked mace he had chosen as a sidearm.

"*Tovarische* Liplap," he grunted. "This is in exchange for the broken foot your guard gave me."

Voldemars stayed his hand. "Whoa, there, Michel! A wrecked windmill will only tell tales on us. And a single pump out of order won't stop the Cham's hot water."

Michel stared at the whirling blades through slitted eyes.

"Don't let the Roosky toy worry you," advised Bernhards Kujucs, who could have demolished the tower single-handedly. "We'll have better targets yet."

Michel laughed, shamefaced. He lowered his mace. "Okay. I'll wait for a tartar head to bash."

Bernhards flexed mighty muscles. "I'll give you a hand, then. I owe the bastards a few knocks. And I could use the exercise—after all the piddling digging we've been doing!"

The tartars overtook them at mid-cycle. Vasily Bugovics had dropped back to ride with Orfan and Lisa. Vasily had perfected the knack of riding while facing the animal's rump. That way he could keep watch to the rear.

"Something moving back there," he murmured. He swung round on his animal. "I'd better warn Voldy."

He kicked the muskylope up to speed, riding for the head of the column.

Orfan stared over his shoulder. Six motes danced on the steppe behind. His heart thumped. Tartars?

Voldemars' voice came down the column. "We're going to turn away from the pipeline, one after the other. So follow me, and turn where I turn. Then spread out a bit. I want at least five meters between each of you."

Pics swung his mount round. Like troops on parade, each rider kept straight on, to turn where Pics had turned.

Voldemars' voice came again. "When I halt—all halt. Hobble your animals. Put your pack on the ground and get down behind it. We're going to fight tartars."

Rita Purins, next ahead of Orfan and Lisa, looked back. "Voldy is pulling rank today."

Lisa shook off Orfan's hand. "Do what he tells you," she ordered. She pushed ahead of Orfan, to take her place in the column. He watched her swing away from the pipeline, and followed her in turn. The column of fugitives now stretched three times its previous length.

Pics raised a hand. "All riders halt!"

Orfan braked his mount. He slid off and hobbled it. He threw his pack to the ground and knelt behind it. Fingers clumsy, he strung the tartar bow he had drawn in the lottery.

The six motes on the steppe had grown to charging warriors.

Orfan's heart pounded. The nomads road lean, racing muskylopes—much faster animals than the domestic cows. He saw scimitars glinting behind knobby shields. The ground drummed. His sight blurred. Off to the left, someone loosed a premature arrow. Then the tartars were on them.

The nearest warrior hurtled between Orfan and Lisa. Orfan saw the scimitar swing down. Saw Lisa roll sideways. He loosed a wild arrow. Then the tartar was through their line.

Rita Purins had followed the nomad in the sights of her museum piece. As he slowed to turn, she shot him off his mount.

Then their bit of the battle was over.

Orfan scrambled to where Lisa lay. He gazed into her eyes. "Are you all right?"

She stared back, clutching the stub of a lance. "He . . . he . . . did . . . this. . . ."

Orfan stroked her hair. "Don't fret, my love. He won't do it again."

He ran to the fallen warrior. The man wore a long-skirted jacket and fur trousers. An Armalite rifle lay beneath the body. Ammunition belts crossed his chest. Rita's bullet had taken him in the temple, just below the lip of his soup-bowl helmet.

Orfan dragged the rifle from beneath the body, then got the ammunition belts off.

Rita came to stand beside him.

Orfan said, "Good shooting, Rita. You didn't even mark his clothes."

Her teeth were chattering. "Is—is he dead? I aimed for his chest."

Orfan turned away. "Quite dead, Rita."

He left her, and walked along the firing line. Two more tartars lay on the steppe. Elmer Parn rose from a third, a reddened blade in his hand. The two surviving tartars circled in the distance, then fled northwards.

Orfan came up to hairy Karol Gegeris, who had served a spell in the Codo army. Gegeris whistled between his teeth as he polished the barrel of his Kalishnikov. From the satisfied smirk on the man's face, Orfan suspected he was responsible for the corpses on the steppe.

Further on, Voldemars Pics crouched beside a still, white-haired figure. Pics tucked a long-barreled revolver into his belt.

"Maksis won't be needing this any more," he said sadly.

Vasily Bugovics joined them. He carried the Armalite

rifle for which there had been no ammunition. He said, "Troffy won't need this either."

Pics' face grew solemn. "We beat them off, but we can't afford many victories exchanging two for four."

"If what we were playing was chess," murmured Gegeris, "I'd be castling for my next move."

Rita Purins said briskly, "Let's see how many knights we can muster before we start getting panicky. There are four remounts out there, if we can catch them."

"Leave that to me." Fritz Frienbergs approached the nearest riderless muskylope. He made soothing sounds.

It was nearing noon before the animals were rounded up. Voldemars faced his people, face troubled. "Before we move off, folks—I propose that someone else take my place. But for my bright idea of following the pipeline, Maksis and Troffy might still be—" Pics fell silent, his eyes on the ground.

"No one is plaming you," soothed Elmer Parn.

Pics shook his head. "I was wrong to keep to the pipeline trail. I thought the well-trodden ground would hide our tracks."

Fritz Frienbergs patted his shoulder. "Don't crucify yourself, man. Animals will leave a trail wherever you drive them."

Pics glared at him. "The tartars know where we are, now. They'll be back. Liplap won't forgive us for killing four of his men. We ought to get as far from the yurt as we can, but we all need rest and sleep. And I'm clean out of ideas how we can do both."

He stared hard at Vasily Bugovics.

Vasily stared back, face unreadable.

Eva Abolins shouted, "Why not let Orfan Judeiks have the job? He thought up the idea of escaping."

Orfan couldn't believe what he heard. He didn't trust the ex-fishwife. He said, "Hold it a moment, Eva—!"

She eyed him angrily. "Hold nothing. You afraid to try?"

Voldemars Pics said quickly, "I'll follow Orfan, if he agrees to lead."

Vasily's smile was bland. "Me, too. I'm sure Orfan would make a good captain."

Eva smirked. "A vote! All in favor show!"

Everyone raised a hand.

The ex-fishwife leered at Orfan. "You're elected, lad. You got us into this mess, now—you get us out of it!"

Orfan's mind raced. To be railroaded into the captaincy was a left-handed sort of compliment. And Abolins was expecting miracles. But Pics' support seemed honest enough. And Vasily Bugovics might be as good as his word. If only he could think up a plan. . . .

They stood around him, waiting.

Orfan put a hand into his pocket and drew out an object he had filched from the dead tartar.

"This is a compass. Liplap's men use it for navigating across the steppe. We can use it, too. Let's leave the pipeline and head in another direction. It might throw them off our trail." His glance fell on Pics. "And there's nothing wrong with Voldy's tactics. He obliged those tartars to split up when they attacked, so we could take them separately. That was smart. It's bad luck that two of them got away to take the news back to the yurt." Orfan hesitated. He had to find out who was boss. He said, "I'd like Voldy to be my lieutenant."

Pics' flush matched his hair. He stared about him. "I'm willing—if you'll have me after what happened."

Orfan waved authoritatively. "*I'm* captain. *I'm* choosing you."

He challenged them with his eyes. No one demurred.

He felt giddy. It was like skating faultlessly, surrounded by slipping and sliding amateurs.

"And I'd like Vasily to be my other lieutenant."

Bugovics sketched a salute. "Honored, *Mon capitan*."

Orfan let out his breath. They were accepting orders from a sixteen-year-old! He avoided Lisa's admiring gaze.

He said, "We'll travel through the rest period. We can sleep on the muskylopes. Old Maksis said they'd go forever. Let's find out if they will."

Felix Kanders, looking lost without Trofimovics beside him, shouted, "And if Liplap's gangsters find us again?"

Orfan scowled. "Felix—we fight anyone and everyone who tries to stop us finding a new home!"

They cheered. Orfan hid his embarrassment. Did this band of amateurs really hope to defeat Liplap's professionals? Their only chance lay in flight. If only they could get far enough from the yurt to put the tartars off pursuit! Orfan bit his lip. It was the muskylopes that drew the nomads. Fermented muskylope milk was a tartar tipple. They wouldn't let their booze disappear so easily.

Orfan sighed. Why had he ever let Lisa talk him into this pickle! Left alone, he might have been overseeing the Cham's kitchen before he was twenty!

They stripped the corpses of clothes, food, and weapons. They buried their dead near the pipeline and left the tartar bodies for the vulpes. They rode on, tying themselves to the backs of their animals so that they might sleep as they travelled. They halted for a snack at mid-cycle. The muskylopes showed no sign of weariness.

When they resumed the march, Orfan released his anchor line, and sat up. Trying to doze was worse than remaining awake. He yawned, brushing the icicles from the mouth-hole of his knitted helmet. Vasily Bugovics rode up from the rear to jog beside him.

"All clear astern, *Capitan*" he reported.

Bugovics' face was serious enough. Orfan hoped he didn't know that "*Capitan*" meant "swaggerer." Orfan yawned, "The Chingiz may delay pursuit while he chops off a couple of heads."

Bugovics nodded. "Those two that ran earned a flogging at least."

They jogged along in silence.

Orfan looked for his other lieutenant. He spotted Pics' shaggy mount out on the flank, coaxing a calf back to its dam.

"Perhaps they didn't go back to the yurt?" he suggested. "They would know what kind of reception Liplap would give to tartars who ran away from slaves."

Bugovics smiled. "That would suit us fine. Liplap would have to start the search for us all over again." Orfan's lieutenant slapped the rump of his mount. "You were right about these animals. They just keep on going."

Orfan nodded. He had been hoping that Bugovics would comment on the muskylopes' performance. He said. "I know how they do it."

Vasily Bugovics' eyebrows rose obligingly.

Orfan grinned. It was obvious, when you thought it over. Any steppe animal must develop some means of covering vast distances. He said, "They walk in their sleep."

Bugovics' mouth made a satisfying "O."

"And where do they get their water?" he challenged.

Orfan waved a nonchalant hand. "Frost. They lick the steppe. . . ."

Chasing a bolted calf, Pics was first to see the cloud ahead.

"It's like a fog," he reported to Orfan. "Right across our front. It could be a water vapor."

Orfan said, "We'll have to investigate."

Voldemars scratched a two-day beard. "Just say the word, Captain."

Orfan stood up on the muskylope's back, feet spread, the way he had learned in the circus. From his new elevation he could see the cloud, lying ahead of them like a white worm. He said, "Ride into it, Voldy. See if it's safe for us. I'll hold the column here 'til you give us the okay."

Pics saluted. "Give me ten minutes."

Orfan signalled a halt. No point in plunging into trouble. Let Pics find out what was causing the phenomenon, and whether the cloud hid anything dangerous. He watched his lieutenant ride into the mist. Moments Later, Pics reappeared, signalling, thumbs up.

Orfan dropped down and kicked his beast into motion. The column followed at an easy trot. The cloud came into sight, lying across the steppe in a wall high enough to conceal a mounted man, its top fraying into whispy tendrils.

As they got within hailing distance, Pics shouted, "Slow up, Captain—or you'll get wet!"

Orfan halted. From within the fog came the sound of rushing water!

He dismounted, hobbled his mount, and walked past Pics into the mist. He heard his lieutenant's breathing as Pics followed him. Hazily, he discerned rocks ahead, and foaming water.

He gripped Pics' sleeve. "What is it, Voldy?"

Voldemars knelt on a dimly seen river bank. He removed a glove to dip his hand into an eddy. He stared back at Orfan. "It's *warm*! You've found Old Maksis' *Karst Udens*!"

Orfan frowned. Old Maksis' river? Impossible. He said, "We headed south, then southwest. Maksis said it lay due west."

Pics shook droplets from his fingers. "Who cares what Maksis said! This water is warm!"

Orfan said, "So where are the mountains? And the sea?"

Bella Buksum materialized beside them. She was unbuttoning her coat. "Did someone mention *karst udens*?"

Orfan stayed her fingers. Bella was an exhibitionist, and at some future time he might enjoy viewing her charms. But at the moment there were problems to be faced.

"Hold it, Bella," he ordered. "We all need a bath. And we'll get one when we cross this river. But let Voldy go first. He can see how deep it is and find the best place to cross. We'll have to take care we don't get our clothes wet. We'll never get them dry if we do. And we'll freeze without them."

Buksum pouted. "I wasn't thinking of wetting my clothes."

Pics looked anxiously at Orfan, avoiding Buksum's eyes. He muttered, "I don't swim too well."

Orfan grinned. Being captain had advantages. He said, "Get your clothes off, Voldy! I'll send Bella away if you're bashful."

His lieutenant hesitated.

Bella Buksum said, "I'll do it, if he won't."

Voldemars began to undress.

Half an hour later Bella was wrapping him in a towel from her own pack.

Teeth chattering, Pics reported. "It's too deep to wade in the middle. And it's about a kilometer to the other bank. The water's not as warm on the far side."

Orfan uncapped a bottle of *kumiz*. He passed it to his lieutenant. "And where's the best place to cross?"

Pics tipped the bottle, gulping. "The current is not too strong. The bottom is full of rocks above and below this spot. There's a sandy spit opposite, where we could land. Elsewhere, the bank is pretty steep, and it would be difficult to land." He handed the bottle back to Orfan. "There are hills all along the other side. I think we've reached the edge of the steppe."

They crossed *Karst Udens*, naked and unashamed, their belongings tied to the horns of their animals.

Some of them crossed twice, splitting their packs, revelling in the feel of warm water on their bodies.

The far bank was clear of mist, a breeze pushing the cloud away from them, onto the water.

Vasily Bugovics led a naked troupe in calisthenics on the sandspit until they were dry enough to don their clothes.

Orfan decreed a picnic. They chewed stale crusts and Codo pâté, and talked about the hidden valley. Someone brewed tea on *kumiz*-soaked charcoal, and they drank it Latvian-style, without milk, and with a spoonful of jam stirred in.

Anna Jacobels, whose figure on the crossing had eclipsed even that of Buksum, gestured upriver. "The source of the river's heat must lie that way, Captain."

Orfan nodded, perplexed. Perhaps Old Maksis had got his bearings mixed up. He surveyed the stony uplands behind them, then addressed his lieutenants. "Perhaps we should cross back? The going will be difficult this side."

Bugovics shook his head. "If the tartars come, they won't see us through the mist. And they'd have to cross the river to attack us. We're better off on this side."

Karol Gegeris patted his Kalishnikov. "Let them come. It will be a turkey shoot!"

They loaded up their animals, brushing the icicles from the beasts' fur. The muskylopes seemed unharmed by their immersion. Indeed, one or two had to be forcibly dragged from the water.

Orfan set his mount at the slope rising from the sandspit. Someone behind started singing. The whole column took up the chorus. Orfan realized that his troops were in high spirits. Was it because they had put the river between themselves and possible pursuit? Or because no one had stuck a spade in the ground for the Cham for two days? Orfan didn't care. His people were happy.

Halfway through the second verse of "Es uzkapu kalninaji," Vasily Bugovics shouted for silence.

As the singing died, they heard voices shouting in Roosian!

Orfan shivered. Good things never lasted. Just as it seemed they might get clear away—!

He turned to stare into the mist hiding the far bank. Could he face an attack as coolly as Pics had done? He would have to try.

He shouted. "Everyone dismount! Hobble the animals. Get down behind your packs." Those orders, at least, were textbook Pics!

The ground sloped the wrong way to provide good cover. Fritz Frienbergs and Karol Gegeris stacked the packs into a barricade at the exit from the sandspit. Orfan decided not to interfere. The older men probably knew better than he how to fight tartars.

He crouched behind the barricade and slid a round into the breech of the Armalite Rita Purins had won for him. Let someone else cope with tricky tartar bows. An old peashooter was weapon enough for him!

Figures were emerging from the fog on the river below. Naked tartars astride their racing muskylopes, each man clutching a bundle of clothes piled on his head.

Orfan felt the blast of Gegeris' Kalishnikov on his cheek. A tartar toppled into the water. A yell went up from the nomads. Gegeris fired again, dropping another corpse into the stream.

Then gunfire crackled all along the barricade.

Tartars tumbled amid rocks and foam. Bundles and weapons were swept away. The muskylopes that reached the midriver channel were thrown off balance by lack of footing. Wounded were tossed into the water by plunging animals. Hardly a shot came uphill. Swimming tartars were far too busy to shoot. Gegeris stood up, picking targets.

Orfan crouched, finger frozen on the trigger of his weapon. So this was a "turkey shoot"! The once-fearsome tartars were being slaughtered.

Suddenly the battle was over. A few surviving tartars retreated into the cover of the mist. Bugovics shouted derisively, "Don't shoot if you can see the whites of their arses!"

A lone tartar, mount gone, waded through the shallows towards the sandspit.

Marksman Gegeris took careful aim.

Orfan recognized the gold belt and dangling purse. He struck up the ex-soldier's gun.

"It's Liplap!"

They permitted the Cham of Novy Tartary to reach the beach unharmed. The Chingiz stood naked but for the belt he wore. He carried a Mauser pistol in one hand, and a scimitar in the other. He shook water from his eyes.

Orfan murmured, "Put a bullet near his feet, Karol."

The Kalashnikov cracked. Sand spouted an inch from the Cham's toes.

Orfan shouted in Roosian. "You're on your own, Liplap. Your men have fled. Drop your weapons, and you might live!"

The Cham raised his eyes to the barricade. He roared, "Is that you, scullion? You will regret this!"

Orfan shouted, "Last chance, Liplap. Drop your weapons, or die!"

The Cham eyed the gun-studded barricade. He opened his hands, allowing the pistol and sword to fall to the sand. Then he clasped his arms around his belly, and began to shiver.

Orfan stood up. "Feeling the cold, Liplap? You should try your kitchen floor at midnight."

The Cham's knees began to shake.

Orfan waved a hand. "Dance for us, Chingiz! It will get you warm."

The Kalishnikov cracked without orders. Sand spouted close to the Cham's feet.

The Chingiz began to dance, capering like a clown.

Orfan called, "Let's see some life! Make it flap up and down!"

The Cham moaned, but continued to prance. He stumbled several times in the churned sand. His movements grew slower.

Vasily Bugovics stooped to whisper in Orfan's ear. "If we kill him, it could upset Codo. He's their nominee. Would you like to fight Codo marines as well?"

Orfan frowned. Bugovics was being helpful. But *he* hadn't danced for the Chingiz.

Finally, Orfan clapped his hands. "Enough!"

The Chingiz ceased hopping. He stood, panting.

Marta Karnups muttered, "Poor bastard—he'll catch pneumonia."

Orfan shouted. "Can you stand on your hands, Liplap?"

The Cham shook his head wearily, too exhausted to speak.

Orfan searched his pocket. He flung what he found

there onto the sand before the Cham. "Go back to your yurt, Liplap. We prefer freedom."

They watched the Cham wade back into the mist, shoulders slumped, clutching a coin the size of an overcoat button. No sound came through the fog to greet him.

"Maybe they've all gone back to the yurt?" suggested Marta Karnups. "I hope he finds some clothes to put on."

Orfan grinned. He had little sympathy for the Chingiz. His people had survived another crisis. There was still hope. He shouted, "Let's get moving—we've a valley to find!"

Progress was difficult. Rocky ridges and stony valleys had to be negotiated. The muskylopes found little grazing. There was less than an hour of light when Pics waved madly from the crest of a hill before the column.

Orfan kicked his mount into a trot.

From the hilltop, his lieutenant pointed into the next valley. "There's our dream valley, Captain!"

Half hidden in the fog from a cooling water discharge, Orfan saw the roofs of a power station.

Pics' face twisted wryly. "Not quite Old Maksis' valley, Captain!"

A single track railway line threaded the gorge, terminating at the power station. Pylons paralleling the track disappeared into the hills.

Orfan said, "This must be the reactor that provides Liplap with his bathwater and electricity!"

He gazed down on the fog-shrouded roofs. All along he had known that Old Maksis' valley must lie further to the west—if it lay anywhere at all on the planet!

He laughed. "It will do for us. Let's ride down, Voldy, and see what time the next train leaves for civilization!"

From *Crofton's Encyclopedia of Contemporary History and Social Issues (3RD EDITION)*

Military research and development represents what is perhaps the most perplexing problem the CoDominium authorities face. Since the ostensible purpose of the CoDominium Treaties is to create a workable system of arms control that the U.S. and U.S.S.R. can live with, there clearly must be rigid enforcement of stringent scientific research licensing regulations. At the same time, weapons must be produced, and the pressure of competition forces arms manufacturers to make small but steady improvements in weapons systems; while the CoDominium Fleet, like all military organizations, constantly seeks to upgrade its capabilities.

So long as the CoDominium held control of all military research facilities, including nations not signatory to the CoDominium Treaty, this dilemma was tolerable; but after the successful Unilateral Declaration of Independence of Danube was followed by secession of other planetary governments, the CoDominium authorities faced the challenge of unlicensed research facilities not under CD control.

This has been met in two ways. The usual practice is for CD Intelligence officers to undertake systematic infiltration and sabotage of rival laboratories. More rarely, the Grand Senate has authorized direct Fleet intervention.

There have also been persistent rumors of hidden CoDominium research stations.

THE TOYMAKER
AND THE GENERAL

Mike Resnick

The door burst open, and six armed soldiers entered the small house. Two of them trained their weapons upon the woman who remained seated placidly before her tapestry frame; the other four, each positioning himself at a window or a door, held their guns at the ready.

"Where is he?" demanded the leader.

"I don't know," replied the woman.

"You are his wife."

"Nevertheless."

"The harder we search, the harder it will go on him when we finally find him," promised the leader.

"You will not harm a hair of his head," she answered serenely, returning her attention to the tapestry. "We both know that, so why do you make meaningless threats?"

"Then let me make a *meaningful* threat," said the leader. "If you do not tell me where the Toymaker is in the next ten seconds, I will order my men to kill you."

He nodded his head, and five safety mechanisms were disengaged as five weapons were aimed at her.

She waited seven seconds, then sighed and nodded.

"Where?" demanded the leader.

"Hell's-A-Comin'," she answered.

The leader ordered his men from the house, reported what he had learned, and returned to base.

* * *

The bartender at the Devil's Lair looked up, and found himself confronting three tall, lean men with cold eyes and hard mouths.

"Where is the Toymaker?" demanded the closest of them.

The bartender shrugged. "Beats me. I haven't seen him for almost two weeks."

"Where was he going?"

"I believe he said Castell City."

The three men exchanged glances. Then the tallest leaned forward across the bar.

"If you're lying," he said, "we'll come back and kill you."

"Toymaker!" said the young lieutenant into the speaker system. "Come out! We've got you surrounded!"

The fifty marines waited for a response.

"All right, men," shouted the lieutenant after sixty seconds. "Storm the building!"

They broke down the doors and, silent as wraiths, fanned out through the building; burst into a dozen apartments, rummaged through the basement, ransacked the closets, even clambered into the hot, cramped attic.

The Toymaker was gone.

They found him, finally, hiding in the storage rooms beneath a church in Shangri-La, and they dragged him before the General.

"Very innovative," said the General pleasantly. "The atheist hiding out in a church." He chuckled appreciatively. "Not unlike the deserter hiding out in the middle of a battlefield."

The Toymaker stared at him and made no reply.

"Come, come," said the General. "There is no need to be sullen. I am not your enemy. May I offer you a drink?"

"No," said the Toymaker.

"Ah, that's right," said the General with a smile. "I

forgot. And of course you don't smoke, either. What *do* you do for amusement these days?"

"I hide from you," said the Toymaker.

"So you do," admitted the General. "But, of course, I always find you in the end."

"Next time you won't," promised the Toymaker.

"Of course I will."

"We'll see."

"Maybe you won't escape again," suggested the General.

"Maybe I won't fix your broken machines again," responded the Toymaker.

"Then perhaps I shall break some of *your* machines," said the General, unperturbed. "You have two grown sons."

"They aren't on Haven," said the Toymaker.

"That merely makes them more difficult to find," replied the General. "Not impossible." He paused thoughtfully. "I think I would find the challenge stimulating."

The Toymaker remained silent and impassive.

Suddenly the General smiled again. "But why talk of such unpleasant things? We are two old friends. Let us enjoy each other's company for a few moments before you go off to your work."

"I have no work here."

"Of course you do," said the General smoothly. "You are the Toymaker."

"I resigned."

"Your resignation was not accepted."

"That's *your* problem," said the Toymaker.

"*You* are my problem," the General corrected him. "It seems that I must continually remind you of your oath."

"I swore no allegience to the CoDominium."

"I refer to the oath you swore in the name of Hippocrates," said the General.

"I swore to heal the sick," said the Toymaker. "I have never broken that oath."

"You break it every time you hide from us, my old friend."

"No!" said the Toymaker furiously. "There is a difference between healing the sick and repairing your machines!"

"They are both living things," said the General. "Living, *suffering* things," he added.

"When you heal a sick man, he becomes well and goes on with his life," replied the toymaker. "When I mend one of your broken machines, you simply send it out to break again."

"They are not *my* machines," the General pointed out calmly. "They are *your* cyborgs."

"No longer," said the Toymaker. "Now they're your machines, and I won't keep them running so that they can continue pillaging and ransacking."

"They are human beings, and they are in agony," responded the General.

"If they were human beings, they would be dead. They are toy soldiers, nothing more, and I hope someday I can make amends for helping to create them."

"You are sworn to eradicate human suffering," said the General firmly. "They are human beings, born of human parents, and I can assure you that their suffering is genuine."

"So is the suffering they cause."

"They only carry out my orders."

"I know."

"And I only carry out the orders I am given," continued the General. "I'm a soldier, just like they are."

"Don't insult my intelligence," said the Toymaker. "*You* train them, *you* select their targets, *you* send them out on their missions of destruction."

"Only after the politicians tell me who the enemy is," the General pointed out.

"That must be a great comfort to you," said the Toymaker caustically.

"It is."

"And when the politicians get rich enough to make

peace, do all the casualties then rise from the ashes and go back to the business of living?" demanded the Toymaker.

"Not until the God that you don't believe in deigns to take a hand in the game."

"Wonderful!" smirked the Toymaker. "If you can't blame the politicians, blame God." He stared at the General. "The toy soldiers take their orders from you and you alone."

"I am starting to lose my patience with you," said the General irritably. "Calling them toy soldiers makes it sound as if this is a game. Let me assure you that it is not." He paused. "My cyborgs can stand up to punishment that no normal human could take. Each of them survives what tens, even hundreds, of normal men cannot. That means when you repair one of them, you are not only saving *his* life, but the lives of fifty or eighty men who would surely be lost if I had to send them on his mission."

"I don't even know who you're sending them off to kill!" snapped the Toymaker. "Sergei Lermontov is the Grand Admiral of the Fleet. The CoDominium reigns supreme. We are supposed to be at peace."

"And, for the most part, we are," acknowledged the General.

"Then who is the enemy?"

"It is not necessary for you to know. Your job is healing the sick; mine is making the best possible use of them once they become well."

"Are they fighting men? Aliens? Who?" persisted the Toymaker.

"They are fighting the enemy," replied the General calmly.

"Damn you!" snapped the Toymaker. "You haven't changed one iota in all these years!"

"Nor have you," said the General. "That is why you will heal them."

"I won't."

"They are in agony," continued the General. "They

scream for their mothers, they curse their God, they claw weakly at their metal and their plastic and their flesh, they beg for a surcease to their pain. You will protest, but in the end you will heal them."

"So that each of them can cause the same agony to thousands of beings who can't be put back together with transistors and computer chips and artificial skin and bone?" said the Toymaker.

"What they do when they leave here is no concern of yours," replied the General.

"I will be responsible for it."

The General shook his head. "*You* will be responsible for ending their pain. *I* will be responsible for what they do next."

"You have much to answer for," said the Toymaker.

"Perhaps," said the General. "But on the other hand, *I* didn't make them. I merely found the best way to utilize them." He lit a cigar. "And of course, they're only the first step."

"I know," said the Toymaker. "And the steps to come are worse."

"Oh?"

The Toymaker nodded his head. "I know the military. An army of virtually indestructable, superhuman warriors is merely a stepping-stone. The day will come when a handful of truly advanced cyborgs will be tied into computers and direct our fleet in battle."

"What's wrong with that?" asked the General. "The awesome logic of a computer joined in a perfect marriage to the creativity of a human brain, the pair of them housed together in an impenetrable body—the ultimate cyborg!"

"The ultimate machine of destruction."

"Think of its power!"

"I *have* thought of it," said the Toymaker. "That is why I ran away."

"It really frightens you?" asked the General, genuinely surprised. "It excites me." He signed. "I am disappointed in you; you have changed over the years."

"You haven't."

The General glanced at his timepiece. "I would have to continue speaking with you into the small hours of the morning, my old friend, but not fifty yards from here lie three young men who gave more for the CoDominium than we had any right to ask. It would be immoral to let them suffer any longer."

"Fix them yourself," said the Toymaker.

The General sighed. "I had hoped it wouldn't come to this, but I think I must remind you that we have ways of encouraging your cooperation."

"Do your worst," said the Toymaker. He shrugged, as if to display his lack of concern. "I can't repair delicate machines if I'm drugged, and my hand isn't likely to be too steady if you torture me."

"I would never harm you personally," said the General. "After all, you are the Toymaker. We need you." He paused. "But I might consider issuing an order to kill one Castell City citizen every hour until you agree to go to work."

"You'd have an open rebellion on your hands."

"I very much doubt it," replied the General confidently. "Public executions cause rebellions. Private executions tend to be overlooked . . . and these would be very private indeed, performed to impress an audience of one."

"Then issue your order," said the toymaker. "At least the blood will be on your hands and not mine."

"It will be on both our hands," said the General. "Mine for issuing the order, yours for forcing me to do so."

"No one is forcing you to do anything."

"I must have my soldiers back. You are forcing me to take steps that I would prefer to avoid."

"You can avoid them," said the Toymaker. "Just let me walk out of here. Surely you have other doctors who can put your toy soldiers back together again."

"But none with such skill as yours," answered the General.

"Then you'll have to teach them better, won't you?" said the Toymaker.

The General stared at him for a long moment. "I have no more time to waste," he said at last.

"Then let me go and stop wasting mine."

"Oh, no, my old friend. You are here and here you will stay." He pressed a button on his desk, and two uniformed men entered the room and saluted smartly. "Take the Toymaker to his quarters," said the General.

"A dank stone cell?" suggested the Toymaker sardonically.

"No," replied the General. "A warm dry room with every amenity, including a very comfortable bed." He paused. "Four beds, in fact."

"Four?" repeated the Toymaker.

The General nodded. "The occupants of the other three beds are in excruciating agony. They cry out for the help that only you can give them." He smiled. "I will make no further demands of you. You can cure them or not, as you choose,"—suddenly the General's face hardened—"but I will not let you out of that room until they are cured." The smile returned to his face. "All your equipment is there, if you choose to use it."

"This is inhuman!" raged the Toymaker, backing away as the two uniformed men approached him. "I won't be a part of it!"

The men each grabbed one of his arms and began dragging him out of the General's office.

"I'll let them die!" cried the Toymaker. "I swear that I will!"

Then he was gone, and the General leaned back on his chair, enjoying the aroma of his cigar.

"You played your role very well, my old friend," he said at last with a contented smile. "You're getting better at this all the time." He paused thoughtfully. "In fact, we both are."

A week had passed, and the General was standing outside the infirmary, peering intently through a large glass window as brand-new plastic skin was being carefully peeled back from a titanium arm.

A stocky Major, wearing a security patch on his sleeve, approached him, stood motionless for a moment, then cleared his throat and saluted when the General turned to him.

"Yes?" said the General.

"The Toymaker has escaped, sir," reported the Major.

"It took him longer than usual this time," commented the General.

"Yes, sir. We didn't want to make it too easy for him."

"And you've got a tail on him?"

The Major grinned. "*Three* tails, sir."

"Wait until he stops running, and then pull two of them back."

"Yes, sir. It looks like he'll be holing up in New Rhineland."

The General nodded thoughtfully. "All right. Once you're sure of that, start the search for him in Shangri-La, and see to it that it takes us at least four months to reach him." He smiled wryly. "One must observe appearances at all costs."

"Yes, sir." The Major shuffled his feet awkwardly. "Sir?"

"Yes?"

"I know it's none of my business, sir, but is it really all that important that we keep bringing him back here?"

"It is."

"But we've got other medics who can patch up our cyborgs at least as well as he can."

"Better," agreed the General. "He's been out of touch with the latest research."

"Then what makes him so important?"

"To answer that, you have to understand his history. His specialty was microsurgery. Cyborgs were just a sideline with him, though they were what brought him to our attention." The General paused. "To *my* attention," he amended.

"I still don't understand, sir," said the Major.

"He has three exceptional virtues," explained the General. "First, he's got an uncanny knack for miniaturization. The smaller the microchip, the tinier the connection, the better he is at handling it." The General paused. "Second, he hates the military and everything we stand for."

"That's a virtue?" asked the Major.

"In this case it is."

"Got it!" cried a triumphant voice over an intercom, and the medic that the General was watching withdrew an incredibly miniaturized device from the titanium framework of the cyborg's elbow. He held it up in a tweezers for the General to see.

The General nodded his approval, then turned back to the Major.

"And third," he concluded with a cynical smile, "he makes the best goddamned bombs you ever saw."

They stepped aside as the medic hurried out of the infirmary and carried the device down the hall, where the dentist was waiting to implant it in the mouth of a prisoner that the General would be exchanging later that day.

From Ferdinand von Habsburg, *The Imperial Marines: A Roll of Honor* (Sparta, 2657)

Seventy-seventh Division ("Land Gators"). Organized Haven, 2258, incorporating Novy Krakow Freedom Commando (First Brigade) and Battle Groups Klimov and Forester and Hamilton's Rangers (Second Brigade). First C.O., Major-General Colin R. Hamilton.

Principal duties, garrison and peacekeeping on Haven. Secondary assignment as mobile reserve for Twelfth Army. As part of Twelfth Army, participated in the Pacification of Manzikert (2290–93) and Golden Fleece War (2419). Average of 72% of personnel native Haveners of every recognized Haven ethnic stock.

In Secession Wars, off-planet service included Lavacan Campaign (Battle of Kimi), Orfanian/Tartarian Confrontation, First Battle of Tanith. . . . Withdrawn permanently from Haven 2623 and engaged in Second Battle of Tanith, Liberation of Levant, the Offensive of 2640, and the Battle of Sauron.

Since 2645, First Brigade (at cadre strength) part of Imperial Household troops, Sparta; Second Brigade engaged in pacification duties on various planets of former Secessionist Coalition. . . .

THE DESERTER

Poul Anderson

The sun was going down as I left the general's office. Clouds, tall beyond walls, hid that spark, but it kindled red and yellow in them, and the Lion Tower stood silhouetted with rays astream from its battlements. Otherwise the clouds were blue-black up to their tops, which Catseye tinged carmine. The sky was clear around it, deepening toward purple in the east, where the first stars blinked. A pair of moons stood near the planet. Their sickles looked burnished and whetted, for its own waxing crescent bore a storm that blurred it more than was common, distorted the bands across its ocherousness, and veiled the dull glow of the side still nighted. That storm could have swallowed all Haven, or any other world where men can walk. But here I felt only an evening breeze. It was cool, with smells of growth from the farmlands around Fort Kursk.

Out on the parade ground, day retreat had begun. Though I was crossing the compound some distance away, I came to attention. It was expected of any man outdoors who had no immediate business. I did, and could simply have saluted, but appearances mattered more than ever. Besides, those were men of my regiment about to lower the flag they had watched through these past fifteen changes of guard—no, these past four centuries and more. How often again would a master sergeant of Land Gators receive the Imperial standard in his hands?

It fluttered slowly down the pole. From the front of

the rank a drum thuttered and the pipes wailed. "The Marines' Farewell" sounded thin across empty paving, underneath that hugeness of sky and primary planet. I had never told anyone here that on Covenant we gave different words to the tune, words from old Earth: "The Flowers of the Forest." Already when I came to Haven, twenty-three Terrestrial years ago, there was too much mourning.

"Aloft and Away" sounded livelier, above the thud of boots, as the relieving squad arrived. I recognized its colors by a glint of light off the Phoenix image on the staff. The marching was subtly wrong, not ragged but too stiff. Pacifying the High Vales had cost the Third Regiment heavily; new recruits were few, and veterans didn't seem to take them in hand any longer. I waited till the night banner had gone aloft, then continued on my way.

Base hospital was not far off it. The visitors' ramp was out of order and I had to walk down to reception. Something always seemed to be out of order these days; what technics we had must concentrate their efforts on vital apparatus. My insignia startled the corporal at the desk. He scrambled to his feet. "Yes, sir?"

"Lieutenant-Colonel Colin Raveloe, Second Infantry Brigade," I identified myself, more to the scanner than to him. "I'd like to call on Centurion Enrico Murakawa."

His eyes widened. He didn't need to punch the register. "Sir, he . . . he's in the Plague ward."

"I know. How is he? Can he have visitors?"

"He's conscious, but— Sir, that's the *Red* Plague." The man hesitated. "I can have the duty nurse convey a message—greetings, best wishes?—but we are very shorthanded and it may take a little time."

I shook my head. "Not absolute quarantine, is it?" His face said it ought to be. "I'm going. What room?" He didn't answer at once. "I told you to give me the room number, Corporal."

He did, and stared after me when I left. Maybe I'd been a tad hard on him. Terror was natural with a new sickness that nobody understood, except that it seemed to be airborne, and that was killing its thousands in the Bolkhov and had now sought out the Marines themselves in their last stronghold on Haven. I would have been afraid too, were it not for the news General Ashcroft had given me.

I hope, though, I'd have walked those corridors and ramps, on down into whispery antiseptic-smelling depths, regardless. "Slaunch" Murakawa had been in my first platoon when I was a new-minted second lieutenant. Since, we'd campaigned together from pole to pole, jungle to desert to mountains to towns full of wreckage and snipers. He'd been involved in saving my life more than once. Maybe what counted most was his good humor that nothing could break, not hardship or boredom or the nastiness of those endless battles we fought only to see the Empire let the outposts slip one by one away from it.

Our last mission was decent. They hadn't remitted their taxes from the Bolkhov for a long time, but still they appealed to the Imperial garrison to help them restore order when the Plague raised mass panic and crime went rampant. However, soon after we returned, Murakawa and a dozen more men came down with it. I might have myself, if I'd been on patrol with them instead of in camp. Adam Soltyk might have too—no considerations of military doctrine, let alone prudence, ever kept him out of action—but he had had a different assignment and—

I dismissed memories. Enough that old Slaunch rated a word from me, and not through any third party.

The medic in charge was less shocked by my intention than the deskman. After all, he'd been living with the horror. "Avoid touching anything and you should be safe," he said. "We wear sealsuits and go through a chemical shower after every round, but we're right there in their breath." Awkwardly: "So good of you to come, sir. Not many people do, even immediate family."

Well, I thought, how many of us had families? Liaisons, yes, or course; understandings, perhaps; but few married till after their discharges, when it would be possible to stay settled. Once that had been different. The Pax prevailed, and the Marines were little more than a planetary police force. Now, why should a woman tie herself to a man who might ship out at any time, for years or forever?

No, who *would*. We were the last and were only waiting for our call. Nobody acknowledged it, everybody knew it. Leaves were for no longer than a hundred hours and the passes only for travel within a hundred kilometers of base. Just the same, more and more men never reported back; or they simply disappeared from barracks. I wondered if the Plague was stemming that leakage. Fort Kursk had the means to make death gentle. On the other hand, a deserter might hope that whatever country he sought would escape infection—not altogether an unreasonable hope, as sparse as traffic had become.

Again my mind had gone awol. The medic's voice called it back: "Morale's about all we've got to help us, you know. Otherwise supportive treatment, pain killers, and prayers. No antibiotic, no antiviral is any use. I'd think it was a native disease that's finally begun to feed on us, Haven itself getting rid of us—" He gulped. "Sorry. I realize that's impossible. Got to be some Terrestrial bug mutated, and the scientists will soon track the biochemistry down. Got to believe that, don't we? Please proceed."

The sickroom held twenty beds. Eight were occupied by those men still alive; the rest lay ready. It was dim, because normal light hurt eyes and worsened skin eruptions. I made my way through humming dusk till I found Murakawa. The mask that contained his labored, poisonous breath also hid much of the red patches and white blisters across his face. He'd shriveled. Fingers plucked the sheet. His vacant stare at a telescreen swung away and came alive when he grew aware of me.

"Colonel Raveloe," he whispered. "Judas priest! Sir, what've you come for? You shouldn't've."

"Don't give orders to your superior officer," I answered. "How goes it?"

He sighed. "It goes. I wish it'd hurry up."

"That's not the kind of talk I'd expect from you," I snapped. "Straighten out, you hear me? I want you back on duty by Landing Day."

My words had more meaning than I admitted. General Ashcroft had explained the political and military situation to me in the sort of detail the high command was not releasing publicly, so I'd understand the importance of my mission. The war was now three-cornered, a score of wildfires consuming ships and men across half the Empire. Thus far none had reached this sector, and remnant garrisons like ours stayed in reserve; but the latest dispatches told of an engagement begun at Makassar between Secessionist and Claimant armadas, while Imperial forces marshalled to go there. Best estimate was that Haven would swing less than forty more times around Catseye before the troopships arrived and bore us off to do battle for his Majesty.

Which Majesty that would be, Ashcroft confessed he didn't know.

Murakawa attempted a grin. "Yes, sir," he got out of his throat.

I bent over him. "Listen, Slaunch," I said low. "If you can hang on for another fifty hours or so, and you can goddamn well do that much, you'll win. We'll win. It took a while, because medical research hasn't been done worth mentioning when people thought they knew all about everything that can hit the human body." Not much science of any kind had been done anywhere that I knew of, but never mind. "Now the answer has been found, and I'm on my way to pick up a batch of the medicine."

Life flickered through his tone. "You, sir? Yourself? Why, that's, uh, wonderful—"

"Sh! I'm supposed to keep it confidential. If I didn't

trust you and need you, you old scoundrel, I wouldn't have stretched my orders like this."

Bewilderment: "Sir, I don't understand. The news—"

"Civilians mustn't hear yet. There could be hitches in production or distribution, or something else might go wrong." I wasn't quite lying. Word that the Marines had gotten priority could add to our problems with regions which no longer paid the Empire more than lip service, if that. The whole truth was worse, though. Something had in fact gone ghastly wrong. Adam Soltyk had never returned from Nowy Kraków.

"You're tough enough to outlive any small delays," I said.

"Yes, sir." Exhausted, Murakawa let his head sink back onto the pillow. "Okay if I act cheerful in front of the boys?"

"That's an order, Centurion."

I went on among the beds, pausing to greet whoever was conscious, let him know that the colonel remembered him. It was hasty. Nevertheless one lad mumbled, "Thank you, sir. This means so much. You're a Christian."

That took me aback. I left the Kirk before I left my birthworld. Surely no more of it remained with me than did any trace of Covenant burr on my tongue. Yet in dreams I still often heard my father speak or my mother sing. Maybe my heritage was more than a stubborn mind and a rawboned height. Maybe a spirit had quietly survived within me, and on Covenant would survive the Empire. I'd like to believe that.

Of course, I'd never know, and meanwhile there was a job to do.

Night was entire when I emerged topside. What with lamps and glowstrips on the ground, Catseye and companion moons overhead, I saw few stars. But somehow I felt them yonder, in overwhelming numbers agleam above the outback, through the thin air of Haven, stars crowding darkness itself out of heaven but filling it with their silence. How could it be that mortal men fared and warred among them?

Why, it simply didn't matter, I told myself. All our lives and histories, all our agonies and violences came to less than the infall of a single nebula or the blink of a single nova.

It was fast getting colder. My breath smoked white, my footfalls rang on pavement already hoarfrosted. Between two columns of buildings no longer used I looked down Shangri-La Valley toward the horizon sky-glow that bespoke Castell. It too had dimmed over the years. Clearer and brighter were the windows of farmsteads, but they lay widely scattered. Most were ancient grants to veterans, whose descendants had supplied the Seventy-Seventh with sons for hundreds of years. I wondered how they would do after the division, the last Imperial Marines on Haven, pulled out. Maybe for another generation or two people would pretend Double Seven must someday come back home.

Before then, how would their daughters do? We'd take no wives along to war. Whoever won, if anybody did, would probably keep us busy for the rest of our usable lives, holding down his conquests and his frontiers. I was glad—I supposed—that Lois and I decided to wait for my retirement, even though that eventually caused her to marry a civilian. Saying goodbye to Corinne and Dee would be a great deal easier.

Bachelor officers' quarters were a block of multiplexes. I'd taken mine at the far end. It insulated me from most noise and most invitations to orgies of one sort or another. A few friends in, or simply a book or a disc, was my usual preference. A slim young fellow stood at my door. Planetlight reddened his blond hair. He snapped a salute. "Private Jezierski reporting, sir." He tried for military snap but couldn't quell the purring Polski accent.

"Ah, yes," I said. "Sorry to keep you waiting. Come in. We've things to talk about, you and I."

Mainly I had to size him up. He was nephew to

Adam Soltyk; and Soltyk, whom I thought my amigo, had seemingly surprised us all.

We entered. Jezierski couldn't help himself, but stared around. The muted light made him look young indeed, almost girlish, though there were strong bones underneath. Guts, too. We didn't get many Haveners enlisting any more. They must often defy kinfolk who saw in the Empire as much of an enemy as was any outsider— even after the Lavacan raid. They must face the likelihood of exile, the chance of being killed in a strange land or beyond the sky. To be sure, the Soltyks were special. With them it was a tradition that every generation brought forth at least one Marine. And though now the White Eagle flew above Nowy Kraków in place of the Imperial standard, Cracovia was not hostile.

So I heard.

"At ease," I said. "I called from the general's office to have you meet me here because I need a trustworthy man who knows your people. Your uncle may be in trouble amongst them. For the honor of the blood, which I remember is a binding oath to him, will you stand true?"

Adam had brought the boy with him when he returned from furlough. That had been about one Earthyear ago, before leaves were restricted. He asked me to come over to his house and talk frankly. "Lech was orphaned early in his teens, by an accident," he explained. "I've become a father figure of sorts to him, in spite of us seldom seeing each other. We've kept in touch. He entered Copernican University, but wants to drop out and enlist. A good kid, though romantic. Not that that's necessarily bad." He laughed over the com. Gustiness ruffled his sweeping yellow mustache. "In fact, all proper Polaki are hopeless romantics. That's what's given us the hope to keep going, through the kind of history we've had shoved onto us. Very likely a career in the Marines will be right for him." He so-bered. "However, if he does sign on, I want him to have both eyes open."

I was always glad to visit the Soltyks. He hadn't hung back like me, but married the girl he loved. Slowly I learned, never from her, that Jadwiga longed back to her island and lived for their return visits. Nonetheless she fashioned a home for them that was like an alcove of Cracovia, and met their troubles with a steel to match his, and to his dash and impulse added a quiet common sense. I never warmed myself at more happiness than when I sat in their place, under the crucifix and the country scenes, amidst the books and other well-worn little treasures. Nor did I ever eat better. What she knew about spiced fish, soup, pork cutlets, greens—

As was their custom, we remained around the dinner table when talk got serious afterward. The two children, Piotr and Franciszka, could have excused themselves but sat in polite wonder. The vodka glowed in me. I looked across at Lech Jezierski. Above broad shoulders he bore a male version of Jadwiga's face, which meant he was handsome indeed.

"I daresay your uncle has warned you about what to expect, starting with boot camp," I said. "He's probably also given you the ancient definition of war as long periods of boredom punctuated by moments of stark terror. I might add, if you will excuse me, *Pani*—" this respectfully to Jadwiga, well though we knew each other; Cracovians had an archaic concept of manners—"that girls aren't anywhere near as easy to come by as folklore claims. Once a uniform was glamorous; but that was when people considered us their protectors."

"We *are*, sir," Lech breathed.

I shrugged. "We try. We don't do too well these days. The Lavacans were just the splashiest case of that. It'd help mightily if Haveners in general felt enough loyalty to back us with their own efforts. But most of them don't. They see the Empire as a thing that takes and never gives."

Adam frowned. "Easy," he cautioned. An excitable

boy might blurt out in public that we'd been talking subversion.

"I don't say that's right, I only say it is," I told them. "The bulk of our recruits on this planet are from territories that've gotten so miserable anything looks better. Cracovia is still fairly prosperous."

Lech flushed. "It won't be if the barbarians come!"

"And you want to help hold them off? Commendable."

"Uncle Adam—Major Soltyk knows how."

I nodded. Paradoxical it might be, but Adam Soltyk, fiery warrior, was as great a defensive leader as Fabius, Robert the Bruce, Alexander Nevsky, Washington, Sitting Bull—no, "responsive" is a better word, responsive to a superior foe, not merely huddling back in a fortress but actively exploiting every weak point. When his troops outflanked the Lavacans at Kimi, the nukes he put through may have been what turned the tide. Certainly he taught the Orfanians how to maintain themselves against the Tartarians, and so kept that small nation of friendlies alive on Haven. The jungle fighters he raised and trained would be holding Curaray for us yet if an Imperial legate hadn't come to "negotiate" with the Beneficents. The emplacements and specialist corps he advocated would make Shangri-La close to impregnable. But he'd never get them, and he might never make more than colonel. Too many feathers ruffled, too many established interests flouted.

"Well," I said, "we may not be doing that much longer. The Empire's in upheaval. Unless matters improve, we too may be called away."

"I know, sir." Lech spoke softly, but it blazed from him.

I saw his glance drawn helpless to the pictures, the keepsakes I had from worlds beyond this world. He had never so much as been in orbit, tumbled dreamlike through free fall, seen for himself the white-and-tawny glory of Haven and the undimmed majesty of Catseye. Besides, I'd had my missions elsewhere in this system, to Hecate's crags, dawn over the Rainbow Desert on Ayesha, the ice caves of Brynhild, an asteroid spinning across star-clouds, the multi-million-kilometer geyser as Comet Reyes plunged toward the sun. And earlier there had been Covenant, where villages nestle under snowpeaks aflicker with aurora; and I'd had the chance to travel as a lad, as far as the remnants and unforgotten graves on Earth; later, before assignment to the Seventy-Seventh, I'd served in the Roving Patrol, ridden with hawk and hound across a wind-rippled prairie on Tabletop, walked with a golden-skinned girl where crystal spires lifted on Xanadu, lost myself as night fell over Tanith and the jungle came to life—oh, more wonders than one room or one mind could hold memories of, and yet I had had just the barest glimpse. On some of those planets, hope itself survived.

"Yes," I said, "you'll get around in the Deep."

"Oh, sir—"

"It won't be any Grand Tour, you know. It'll be long hauls and long waits and then war. Still, you should see quite a bit, and have experiences you couldn't imagine on this back-eddy globe, and maybe, maybe end your days in a better place than here. But that's conditional. Sit down."

He hesitated. "Sit," I repeated. "I'd rather stay on my feet." He obeyed. I went to a table where I kept my pipes and started loading one. He stared. I laughed. "Don't worry, son. I've had my shots for this kind of cancer too. It's probably for the best, though, that nobody's found how to grow decent-tasting tobacco on Haven. I import mine, which costs enough to keep me moderate. The way it's going with the cost and reliability of freight, I may have to quit. The problem is incompatible biochemistries, you know. Our agriculture never has fitted comfortably into the Haven ecology."

Turning to him as I got the pipe lit, I went on: "This isn't idle chatter. I'm leading into the reason you're here. Listen.

"The Red Plague seemed like another mutation of

some bug that the ancestors carried with them from Earth. I'm not an expert, but I know how the medics deal with such things. It's practically routine. Molecular scans find the peculiarity in the DNA or RNA, a computer program prescribes a cure and tells how to manufacture the stuff. But this disease wouldn't oblige. And it's lethal, and has an unknown incubation period, and has now attacked some of our men. Do you see? It could kill off whole populations, bring down whole civilizations. The Empire's in plenty bad shape without letting something like that loose. It'd have to quarantine Haven, including its garrison. But they need us."

I passed by any questions of whether or not we'd really be doing humanity a service. We carry out our orders, that's all; semper fidelis. Anyhow, Private Lech Jezierski longed for the Deep as he had not yet longed for a women. "Fortunately," I said, "Cracovia is still . . . associated with the Empire; and Copernican University is one of the few institutions left anyplace in the galaxy where science doesn't mean a set of cookbook formulas. They've cracked the Red Plague problem there, and have the medicine."

Breath whistled between the boy's teeth.

"The announcement was confidential," I said. "Politics. Once that wouldn't've been feasible, but when the only competent scientists for x light-years around are concentrated in a single set of buildings— Well, the stuff has tested out in the hands of a relief team sent to the Bolkhov. The first actual production batches were earmarked for us. A cure and an immunizer, seems like, so after we inoculate all personnel we can safely embark for the wars. Because he's a Cracovian and has high-placed connections in the country, Major Sołtyk was dispatched to Nowy Kraków. His orders were to render official congratulations, make sure of preparations for a global eradication program, and ship us that first lot."

I planted myself before Jezierski, blew a stream of smoke at him, and finished: "The trouble is, Major

Soltyk has not appeared. They claim in Nowy Kraków they know nothing. Accident? The TrafCon satellites record no transoceanic anomaly; he must have arrived.

"Everybody knows he and I are close friends. First the general grilled me, then he told me to go find out what the hell this means. I need a guide.

"You're the obvious choice. Can the Marines count on you? Think before you answer."

Within a couple of hours, we were on a suborbital trajectory. The flyer belonged to our regiment, as did the pilot and the three enlisted men with us two. The Land Gators look after their own.

In spite of his natural distress, Jezierski gasped when he first saw the globe beneath him, edged with sunrise and roofed with stars. He pressed his nose to the window. Sergeant Reinhardt, Corporals Rostov and Li didn't quite succeed in being sophisticated about the sight themselves. But then, they hadn't been told anything except what they barely needed to know, and . . . Lech was young. For my part, I held a poker face hard-clamped over my thoughts.

We curved over and thundered back into atmosphere, across dayside. At first Cracovia was a blue-green speck afloat in a bowl of mercury. It grew fast, until it filled the forward view with mountains, valleys, plains, rivers, lakes, many-hued woods, checkerboard pasture and cropland, under wan sunlight or towers of thunderhead. It is, after all, the biggest land mass in the Occidental Ocean, a million square kilometers. Nothing near that size shares those waters before they break on the shores of Tierra de la Muerte. I suppose isolation helped the colony in early days, gave a chance to lay firm foundations without being too much disturbed. It might stand the people in good stead again.

But any flourishing ranch draws wolves, once the watchdogs have departed. (Yes, I know what wolves were, I've read my share of classic books. Did you think military men care about nothing except their guns?)

We set down bumpily on the sole spacefield. I heard our pilot wonder aloud, with profanity, when the runways were last maintained. My guess was that that had been before my own time. Like a receding tide, the withdrawal of the Empire was slow and fitful. We rolled to a precise stop nonetheless, which cheered me somewhat. I led the way out.

Here the sun stood at midmorning and Catseye had not yet risen. So the air was chill, even at this low altitude. It smelled different from the air at Fort Kursk, spicy-acrid; that was native forest crowding in reddish masses around the rim, not fields long subdued to bear Terrestrial grain. The sky was clear, pale, a frost-ring about the tiny sun-disc, but mists eddied over the ground. They didn't always hide the cracks in paving, the relentless little herbs thrusting through. Buildings and control installations looked all right from this distance. However, I saw no sign of defenses.

Though a flag above the main terminal drooped in windlessness, I knew it displayed the White Eagle. Not that Cracovia had overtly seceded. The Województwo "assumed responsibility for the province, pending resolution of the present emergency." The Imperial Governor was happy enough to have this much amicability that he didn't insist on maintaining a proconsul and collecting taxes, nor protest the raising of a purely local armed service.

Half a dozen persons moved forward to meet me. Four were in the gray uniform of that service, helmets on heads and stutterguns slung at shoulders. A man in livery was obviously attendant on the middle-aged woman in the lead. She was big, her features strong but sightly under a grizzled bob, her frame erect in an almost aggressively native blouse, embroidered vest, and wide skirt. Did she bear a resemblance to Soltyk? Yes, I decided, she did, and this was to be expected. As often elsewhere, certain families had kept leadership for centuries, and generally intermarried. In Cracovia they had special pride, special tradition, rituals and coats of arms and so forth.

I'd had trouble understanding that when I paid my first furlough visit in company with Adam. On Covenant we discourage display, for only God may judge between one soul and another. Then he pointed out that in the Marines each regimental chapel keeps the old citations and battle banners.

The woman gave me a quick, hard handshake. "Lieutenant-Colonel Raveloe, be welcome," she said in fluent if accented Anglic. "My name is Iwona Lis, associate to Wojewóde Kuzon. We wish to make everything as pleasant and expeditious for you as possible. With your permission, the squad will take baggage and we will convey you and your men to lodgings in the city."

"Thank you," I said, "but the key word is 'expeditious.' I must see his Excellency immediately, or whoever is in charge of this matter. Later we can settle in."

She stiffened. "Are you not being . . . swift?"

Anger jumped in me. "*Pani* Lis, I assume the message from Fort Kursk was clear. People are dying. We need that serum now."

The same feeling threw red across her high cheekbones. "Colonel Raveloe, the medicine is ready, together with physicians who know how to administer it. They could be en route on an aircraft of ours, or already arrived. It is your high command requires an officer of its own be the carrier. We do not think this is so unreasonable."

I curbed myself. A sigh passed voiceless through me. What answer dared I give? Well, how much did she herself know? Originally it had made sense for Major Soltyk to flit here in person, receive those precious vials, and arrange to have them sent in secrecy while he stayed behind a while to help plan the public distribution. But Soltyk had vanished and—

"*And what does it mean?*" *the general said to me.* "*No accident, that's for damn sure. Before you suggest he's taken the opportunity to desert, with friends at the* *other end to help him hide, I'll ask you not to tell your grandmother how to suck eggs."* He leaned forward over his desk. *The haggardness of him smoldered.* "But why would he? Why would they? Furthermore, this isn't another case of some wretched rat of a trooper going over the hill. That problem's worse than we've admitted. In fact, desertions are draining us; and if you speak one word about it, Colonel, you'll be up before a court-martial. But this is Major Adam Soltyk, hero, brilliant combat leader, controversial policy advocate. We can't hide his absence. We can't explain it away." The general's fist smote the desktop. "What sort of conspiracy is going? Or did Soltyk come to grief inno-cently? Maybe by violence, for whatever dark reason? We have to know. We have to have proof—and then make an example of the guilty parties. Commandant Santos told me this ranks with getting the Plague under control; and he's right. Your record indicates you are our best man to start the investigation."*

"I have my orders," I said. "They include a prompt talk with your authorities."

I made no gesture at the flyer. She saw it behind me, though, with guns and missile ports. "We were only concerned for your well-being," she said stiffly. "Since you insist— We have ground transportation to the city arranged, because we wanted to let you relax. This should give time for a meeting upon our arrival."

The upshot was that I'd be driven directly to the Palace, together with my orderly Private Jezierski, while the others were taken separately and provided for. I wondered if this was some attempt at subtle intimida-tion. Without my men at hand, would I be more pli-able? Well, I thought, if they supposed that, they were making a considerable mistake. Three infantrymen and a spaceman gave me no added strength worth noting. What backed me was Double Seven.

The cars that waited were aged but in good condi-tion. Lis and I got in back of one, her adjutant took the board and Jezierski sat in front beside him. We whirred off along a road that was also well kept up. I remarked on that.

"We take care of things we daily use," Lis answered. "You will find it true of our airports and seaports too."

I refrained from telling about neglected public facilities across most of Haven. Materials were in short and erratic supply; money to pay skilled workers was worthless; and nobody in that jumble of quarrelsome statelets looked to the future. Why should they?

"But we have no reason to spend resources on the spaceport, do we?" Lis went on. "Rather, I think, we must destroy it before the invaders come and take it."

I sat straight. "Invaders? What do you mean?"

She shrugged. "You may have a better guess than we can. The Lavacans were the first. They will not be the last, nor the worst, if rumors that seep down from the stars have truth. We have neighbors on this planet too, restless and greedy. Oh, it is a story old and frequent. We remember the Land of Fields, which had no natural frontiers. Space has none."

"The Empire—" I fell silent.

We left the woods behind and came out into the Rzeka Valley. Broad and fair it stretched, cattle at graze in meadows fenced by stones the ancestors had taken out, grainfields ripening into goldenness. Buildings clustered in villages or stood not far apart on family-owned farms. They were mostly stuccoed, with bright tile roofs. Church spires soared among them. The weathers of centuries had softened all edges while nourishing lordly groves of oak and lanes of poplar. Northward the snowpeak of Góra Róg hung like a cloud in heaven.

"I wonder how a country like this can imagine anything except peace," slipped out of me.

"What we have, our forebears spent their lives to forge and hold," Lis replied. "They came as condemned political exiles, in the days of the CoDominium. Haven was a . . . dump for unwanted peoples, because it was meager and hostile. We would be ungrateful to forget what they did. And we would be unwise. Does God give us any special right to keep what *they* earned?"

Jezierski couldn't help himself. Something agonized broke from him. Lis responded in the same language. He settled back down. "Sorry, sir," he muttered.

I guessed he'd protested that he wasn't abandoning his kindred to their fate, and she'd given him a perfunctory reassurance. It seemed well for me to remind them both: "You've kept your inheritance thus far, thanks to the Empire. You'd be ungrateful and unwise to turn your backs on it."

"We have not," she said. "Let it return as it was, and we will strew flowers in its path. Meanwhile we must be prudent."

That hurt like a nerve-whip. Dead men don't rise again reborn, nor do dead hopes.

No one spoke through the remaining fifty-odd kilometers. That suited me well, gave me a chance to ease off, gather my thoughts, eventually even smile at recollections. Sights grew familiar, places I'd visited with Adam. In this little town there had been a fair, the marketplace full of booths and music and dancing feet. In that manor we had feasted, guests at the celebration of a son's confirmation. In yonder tavern we'd japed and yarned and matched beers with local men, till Adam arm-wrestled the blacksmith and won. He was briefly solemn on Dziewica Hill, because that was where the Freedom Commando made its stand and died; soon afterward, our whole party was merry, because a caravan of Cygani came jingling raggedy-rainbow down the road. And by one lake the whole family had picnicked, and I'd met his cousin Helena and come away all awhirl, but never managed to see her again. . . .

Houses moved closer together; industrial structures loomed between them. We crossed the bridge over the Rzeka and were in Nowy Kraków proper, winding along its narrow ancient streets. More and more I remembered—the fountain on whose bronze dragon graduating students rode; a winiarnia where an artisan, a philosopher, and I argued till Catseye sank behind the Sobieski Cross and everybody else was asleep; the flower stalls in Korzybski Square, where Frasyniuk first read aloud the Proclamation of Rights; whimsical façade in Booksellers' Alley; a cubbyhole cafe where Mama made the best pierogi in the universe; the Clock Museum; Chopin Hall; the roses and bowers of Czartorny Park—from such things a country is made.

The driver stopped at Stary Rynek and we passengers got out. I looked around. What with one thing and another, it had been several Earthyears, and surely this plaza was beautiful (is, still is beautiful, I pray to a God I do not believe in). Across the way, St. Mary's Cathedral lifted stone and stained glass up to the green copper cupolas; this happened to be a moment between hours, and the broken trumpet call sounded above us as it sounded for centuries on the mother world. Lesser walls glowed rose, amber, violet beneath steep roofs. Before us the Palace presented a rank of ogival windows. Vehicles were few in this time of scarcity, but foot traffic went dense over the paving, in and out of the Guildhall at the center of things. A young couple hand in hand; tea drinkers at outdoor tables; an itinerant musician; a gang of newly discharged Home Guardsmen, wildly decorated shawls across their shoulders, whooping it up; a priest in his cassock; a venerable man throwing bread to the pigeons; a painter at her easel, trying to capture the scene; homebound school children, books under their arms; ordinary folk on ordinary business—from such things a country is made.

"Follow me, please," said Iwona Lis, and led Jezierski and me up the stairs of the Palace.

The rotunda bustled and echoed with people, underneath its dark dome where the translucent image of our galaxy spiraled. The halls beyond were likewise busy, the rooms opening onto them crowded with desks and workers. I'd remarked on that, the last time Adam and I had dropped in: "You seem to have bred your share of bureaucrats."

He had answered wryly, "This is the only place we can house our public affairs, records, law courts, administrations, and the rest. Originally it was for ceremonies and cultural events, you know. But that was when computers and communications made most offices unnecessary. As they break down and can't always be fixed, while the Empire has stopped handling things for us, we need more and more government of our own." He paused. "We need it if Cracovia is to hang together. Farms are going under for lack of markets, fertilizers, biocontrols. Desperate men are taking to banditry. The big landholders are starting, each of them, to become a law unto himself." He rattled a laugh. "Why do I give you a sociology lecture? You've seen the same everywhere on Haven. You've heard it from everywhere in the Empire. Come, let us look at something more attractive."

That had been the reception chamber into which I was now ushered. My group and the two men who waited for us were lost in its wainscotted stateliness. I glanced up at the ceiling, where crossbars made a set of niches for holding coats of arms, those of the aristocratic families surrounding those of the Imperium. No, they had not replaced the latter with the White Eagle . . . yet. And, yes, in the courtesy space left vacant for distinguished visitors, there were the twin lightning-bolt sevens.

It similarly boded well, or less than ill, that two important individuals greeted me in the flesh—unless they wanted to gauge me better than you can in a com screen. True, neither of them was the Wojewóde; but I got a polite if unapologetic explanation that he was chronically overbusied and that Lis' call from the car had given very short notice.

Brigadier Jacek Skarga was stocky, bald, iron-faced, a Marine called out of retirement to lead the lately formed Home Guard. His years had only toughened the leather of him. He showed tact, saluting simultaneously with me before shaking hands in spite of the gap between our ranks. (Abruptly I wondered whether he was telling me I represented a foreign power.) "Since you are largely concerned with Major Soltyk, I hear, it seemed best I discuss this with you myself," he rumbled. "First things first, however. The Plague." He nodded at his companion.

Professor Zygmunt Geremek was dean of the school of medicine at Copernican University: a lean man with a gray beard and relaxed manner, except for his eyes. "Welcome, Colonel Raveloe," he drawled. "Shall we sit down?"

Before the great fireplace and its flanking statues of the Angels of Victory and Mercy stood a table of heartfruit wood, flame-grained, gloriously carved, inset with tamerlane bone. We took seats; after I gave him a sign, Jezierski settled at my far side. A couple of servants padded in with cakes and authentic coffee.

Professor Geremek smiled, while never letting his blue gaze waver off me. "The delay in conveying the antiviral to your division has been unfortunate," he said. "But we have at least put the time to good use. Such chemosynthesizing units as we possess and can spare have been producing Agent Beta at full capacity. That is the cure, you understand." He smiled again, still more carefully. "We had to give it some name, no? A substantial quantity is ready for Fort Kursk—more than enough, I am sure, to deal with all cases there and in the environs. Needless to say, we will transmit the production program and other relevant information. In fact, we plan to distribute printed copies to regions which do not possess reliable electronic communications but may still have synthesizers in working order."

Recalling Slaunch, I could not but ask, "What does this stuff do?"

Geremek raised his brows. "You do not know?"

"I was brought in on the business just hours ago, sir. It's been under wraps."

"Ah, yes. The Imperial mind . . . Well, then, as for application, the agent is a liquid to be injected intravaneously.

Depending on how advanced the case is, from one to six shots are required. The kit includes a blood test to make certain the virus has been wholly destroyed. Thereafter the patient gets nursing care while he recovers from the damage done his system. Of course, he must be protected against reinfection."

The implications of that slipped past me at the moment, like a night wind I barely felt. My interest was too aroused. "You realize, this is a remarkable phenomenon," Gerek was continuing. "I believe something analogous occurred long ago on St. Ekaterina, but I have found no technical account here on Haven, and in any event that was merely a plant disease."

"What do you mean?" I asked.

"You were not informed?" His tone expressed mild surprise, which was a way of putting me in my place. I wasn't dealing with any unworldly academician. "The Red Plague is an attack by native life."

"What?" Briefly, ridiculously, I had before me images of a cliff lion, a land gator, a swordfin—sure, the big carnivores of Haven sometimes killed and ate people, while people ate muskylope, humphrodite, clownfruit, the sweet gel we misnamed "honey"— "But that's impossible."

"Why?"

I must needs rise to his challenge, prove that I did know elementary biology. "Incompatible chemistries. Haven proteins have some of the same amino acids as ours, but not all; similarly for lipids, sugars, the whole range of nutrients, vitamins, trace elements in compounds our bodies can break down. If we tried to live off native plants and animals exclusively, we'd soon be dead of a score of deficiency diseases. Neither can Haven microbes live any length of time off us."

"What of viruses?"

"Still more impossible. The genetic material here resembles DNA and operates like it, but is not identical. The nucleotides—" I broke off. "Evidently something weird has happened."

"Good, Colonel," Geremek murmured. "Excellent." Did I see wariness strengthen in Lis and Skarga? "Yes, it was doubtless inevitable sooner or later, as nature played her eternal game of changes and permutations. A Haven virus has linked with one of Earth origin—an ordinary influenza virus, which has the means of invading human cells. The Haven component is a simple thing which requires only those amino acids common to both ecologies. It coils around its carrier so as to block the action of our immune system and of every antiviral we have hitherto known, since none of those 'recognize' molecules so alien. The result bears superficial resemblances to porphyria. However, it progresses too fast for conventional treatment to be of significant help. Without Agent Beta, it must be one hundred percent fatal."

Sweat prickled under my arms and down my backbone. "But this drug will cure it?"

Geremek nodded. "Oh, yes. Once we had the idea of what was happening, we knew what to look for and how. The molecular structure was soon analyzed. Thereafter we could design a suitable reactant." He repeated his sharp smile. "If you are interested, it is a perfusive enzyme. It breaks the chemical bonds between the two viruses. Both become impotent and quickly perish. Then the body is free to flush out the toxins and set about repairing itself."

Jezierski stirred in his chair. He uttered a few words. The others stared at him. Recognizing his faux pas, he looked down at the table, where his fists lay knotted. His cheeks blazed. "I'm sorry, sir," he mumbled. "Got too excited."

"What did you say?" I inquired.

"Why, uh, well, I asked . . . whether a man, a recovered person . . . can catch the sickness all over again."

The tension which had been gathering in me uncoiled itself in action. "You're quick, son," I said, and flung at Geremek: "That's true, isn't it? You don't have a vaccine."

"Not yet," the scientist answered blandly. "A more difficult problem. We are working on it."

"When do you expect to have an answer?"

"If we knew that much, there would scarcely be a problem, would there?"

"In frankness," Lis added, "work will go faster if outsiders leave us alone. Take the cure and go."

I shook my head. "No." Caution intervened. "I'm grateful for what you've done. The whole planet soon will be. But you realize it isn't enough. The disease is highly contagious—also during an incubation period which may be several hundred hours—right?"

Geremek nodded as before. "Then without a vaccine, we can't conquer it, we can just contain it," I went on, my voice harsh in my ears. "We dare not risk letting it into space. It could outrun any health care, overrun the Empire."

"We intend to point this out to the Governor," Lis said.

"But they need us—the Marines—" I collected words. "Restoring the Imperial peace may well require every military resource we have."

Skarga stopped bothering to veil his scorn. "Fighting the civil war will require it," he rasped. "That is what you mean. You withdraw and leave worlds like this defenseless. The Imperial peace!"

"We follow our orders," I cast back. "I thought a *former* officer would understand that."

"Gentlemen, please," Geremek broke in, soft-toned. "Let us avoid pointless quarrels. We have a cure for the Plague. Any recurrences can be quickly, almost routinely treated. The Marines alone have the organization and resources to get established a global system of production, delivery, and application. I would guess this as requiring two thousand hours of intensive effort. That is your first duty, Colonel."

My mind automatically translated his precision into round figures. Twenty-five or thirty days— The division wouldn't likely be called that soon, and meanwhile doing something real would boost morale no end. "Very good," I replied, and refrained from adding, "As far as it goes." Instead: "Let's get cracking. You don't have a suborbital vehicle of your own, do you? No? Well, please bring everything necessary to the one I came in, at once, including experienced personnel to demonstrate for our medics. My pilot will take off for Fort Kursk the minute it's aboard."

"What of yourself?" Lis demanded.

"And the enlisted men with you," Skarga said.

"We stay a while," I told them. "The reason you weren't simply requested to send the shipment by your fastest conveyance is that our man who came to take possession of those first few grams you informed us you'd have ready, he's gone."

Skarga drew his brows together. "So I have gathered, from *Pani* Lis' call. Why do you make so important a business of it?"

"My commandant does. Your good faith is not necessarily denied, but you can see why we had to make as sure as we reasonably could that nobody was planning some lethal trick. Besides, Major Soltyk is our service brother. We are not about to write him off. Sir, in the name of the Emperor, I require the facts of the case."

Skarga sighed. "They are few. The advance information was that he would land at the municipal airport but did not know the precise time. He did not explain why, but said he would call the Palace when he arrived. A four-seater stratojet with Marine insignia did put down. It is in charge of the Guard and you are welcome to inspect it and take it back. Airport personnel paid little attention. From casual witnesses we have learned that a single man was inside. He wore civilian clothes. After the vehicle was in garage, he took the slideway up to the terminal. That is the last anybody knows." His grin was cold. "The city police are not accustomed to tracing missing persons. Nor is the Guard, which has much else to keep it busy. Besides, by the time Fort Kursk inquired of us, hours had passed."

"What do you think, sir?"

"I have not had an opportunity to think about it until now. Do you realize that airborne pirates have been raiding northern Cracovia? Hit-and-run attacks from Gletscherheim. The king claims he is powerless to stop them. We do not believe him, but it does not matter. We are preparing for hot pursuit of the next squadron, and will clean its home base out. Further incidents will bring punitive action more widespread." His eyes reminded me that this was the proper work of the Marines. Mine replied that we were spread too thin.

"Soltyk could have met with foul play," I insinuated. "For instance, your pirates may be shrewd and well-informed. Delaying a campaign against the Plague would mean more chaos for them to operate in."

"Far-fetched," Lis scoffed; but I knew how the specter of terrorist tactics must stand before her.

"Or it's possible Soltyk made . . . a mistake," I said. "If so, I must speak with him. He's too valuable an officer to let go. My lady and gentlemen, I have a printout from the Governor directing your cooperation."

"Its legal force is questionable," Lis answered stonily. After a silence which brimmed in that cavern of a chamber: "Be that as it may, we have nothing to spare for you. You must work by yourself."

"I shall so report," I said. "You will not obstruct an agent of the Imperium."

"No, no," she promised. I thought how empty that was.

We were quartered at the Hotel Wasa. It was a dignified old place, four stories of mullioned windows and pastel walls overlooking the shops along its street. The wares were as sparse as its guests. We four were alone in the dining room, except for a waiter who probably had his job in lieu of a pension. Most items on the menu were unavailable. We ate adequately, though, with scarcely a word between us. Afterward I told Jezierski to accompany me back to my room. The corridors were empty and still. Portraits of forgotten magnates stared at us.

When my door had closed, I said, "At ease. Sit down. Would you like a drink or something?"

"The colonel is too kind," he almost whispered. "No, thank you, please." He settled on the edge of a chair.

I took my seat opposite him, leaned back, crossed shank over knee, bridged my fingers, and peered across them in the most fatherly way I knew. "You're my consultant, remember," I said. "My guide, assistant, and bodyguard if needful—comrade in arms." Despite the trouble in him, he dropped his glance and blushed like a girl. "I want you to speak frankly. You can't offend me with the truth."

"I will . . . do my best, sir."

"I'm sure you'll continue to be a credit to the service. Now, what do you make of that scene at the Palace? Of this whole situation?"

"I don't know, sir. What can I?"

"You mean you're just a country boy? Come, come, Private. For openers, all your life you've known your uncle, his family, the entire society that made him what he is. He had clear orders. Does it ring true he'd be vague about his time of arrival? That he wouldn't promptly report in, but disappear?"

Jezierski ran tongue over lips. His eyes lifted, and I saw abrupt desperation. "Sir, he cannot be a traitor. He cannot. It's impossible."

"That's my impression too," I reassured him. "Naturally, Intelligence has questioned his wife and children. They seem as honestly bewildered as you. Jadwiga— *Pani* Soltyk wants to come here with the youngsters and, m-m, wait things out in familiar surroundings. Would it be wise to allow that?"

"Oh, please, sir—"

"It's up to the commandant, of course. I daresay he'll let them. For instance, they could ride with the returning Cracovian doctors. After all, when the division leaves there'll be nothing to prevent them going wherever they like, if they can get passage and if the crossing can be made safely. But first we need to know what's afoot. Suppose Major Soltyk has been—lured astray and kidnapped. Better not expose innocents to the same danger."

"How could he have been, sir?"

"Well, someone may have contacted him clandestinely. That would be easy. But who? And what's he—they—up to?"

The pain sharpened in Jezierski. His face had gone chalky. I could practically see the turmoil behind it. If Uncle Adam was loyal, a faction among his people must be enemy.

I doubted matters were that straightforward. If Jezierski reflected on the nuances of the conversation I'd been in, he'd likely feel the same doubt. For the present, it seemed desirable to steer him off that with hints of melodrama.

"Another strange thing," I said. "We had the distinct idea originally, back at base, that not just a medicine but a vaccine was ready."

"Surely a m-m-misunderstanding, sir. Technicalities—and Anglic is not our, not the Cracovian language."

"Well, it still looks odd to me. I'm a layman, but I do know some molecular biology. Cadet officers in my day got the kind of education they don't any longer. Assuming development of the vaccine has lagged, what's the reason? Or has it?"

"The professor told us, sir. A harder problem."

"Really? Once the chemistry of the Plague was understood well enough to tailor an enzyme that stops it, I should think it would be a fairly standard matter of genetic engineering to make an immunizing agent. How about a modified strain of human intestinal flora to manufacture the enzyme and release it into the bloodstream? That sort of thing's been done for centuries, against everything from diabetes to Greenstein's Syndrome. Inject everybody on Haven—or, I suppose, just everybody who may have been exposed—and you eradicate the Plague entirely. Agent Beta is a mere stop-gap." I paused. "Or else it's an unnecessary detour."

"But, but why would—anyone—falsify the work?"

"To keep the Seventy-Seventh on this planet?"

"Cracovia doesn't have the only experts." A touch of pride: "The best, but not the only ones."

I nodded. "Given the information that Geremek's team is providing, we can find people to go on from there. They'd be slower, but in due course—an Earthyear or two?—they'd have the vaccine. Then the division can ship out." Again I gave him a moment to think. "That may be too late for a certain party in the war."

Jezierski gaped.

"Do you begin to see why this is a mystery we *must* crack?" I pursued. "Geremek and company may have been truthful. Or they may not have been. Our mission begins with finding out which."

After a long career, I could put on an excellent show of decisiveness. The fact was that I had only the vaguest notion of what to do. A few fragmentary ideas had come to me in the past couple of hours, but I depended on Jezierski's leadership, and on making him believe it was mine. "Before enlisting, you studied at the university, didn't you?" I asked rhetorically.

"Yes, sir. Physics. I didn't finish."

"Why not?"

"Oh, it got to feel so . . . futile. Nothing but memorizing texts and repeating experiments. Who's made any real discoveries these past two or three hundred years? Better to enter the priesthood. That would mean something."

"But you chose the Marines. With us, you could hope to get into the Deep."

He swallowed hard.

"Well," I said, "you did acquire learning we need. You know your way around that place."

Cracovia used the regular Haven calendar; but unlike people in Castell, here they didn't ordinarily stagger their schedules. They preferred working and playing together as much as possible. I suppose somehow this arose from a unity that most civilizations within the Empire have lost. The sun was approaching noon when Jezierski and I went forth into an empty and utterly quiet street. We'd planned for that.

I'm not in Intelligence, but in the course of pacifications I've necessarily picked up techniques. A detector from my baggage indicated we were free of electronic surveillance. Once outdoors, my eyes soon verified we weren't being followed. I had decided we should keep our uniforms, because they lent some show of authority and a change to civilian garb might excite suspicion if reported. Let any stakeout assume we were just taking a stroll, working off restlessness brought on by the day zone shift.

Though we walked along in the most ordinary fashion we could manage, our boots racketed loud in our ears. I caught echoes off high walls and out of twisting alleys. Among the parked vehicles I saw as many unpowered as not. With scarcity upon them and worse to come, folk were breeding horses. Nevertheless the city remained clean. So did fronts and windows.

Catseye had risen, close to half phase, dayside luminous with stormswirls, darkside showing ember glows even through a sunlit sky. The spire of St. Jan Pawel's pierced it like a spear. Three companion moons were wanly visible. A few clouds drifted on a cold breeze, tinged coppery toward the planet, silvery toward the star. Beneath them on the ground, the mingled lesser shadows came and went.

Copernican University was in the middle of town. It didn't have a campus like American (where native weeds were crowding in around mostly abandoned halls). A number of buildings stood near each other. The four oldest defined a paved quad. A guard—Home Guardsman, uniformed and armed—stood at its gateway. Jezierski and I halted. We exchanged looks. His said he hadn't expected this either.

After a second he trod close and spoke in Polski. The sentry, a young fellow like him, answered with a smile. Jezierski turned to me. "This is a friend of mine from student days," he said. "They have begun keeping watch during sleeptime because there has been crime, theft, wanton destruction." His mouth writhed. "In Nowy Kraków, sir! . . . What shall I tell Sergeant Michnik?"

If yonder boy had already made sergeant, and nevertheless drew sentry-go, it said much about Skarga's command, and little of that was favorable. Not that I blamed the brigadier. He was able and conscientious —no genius, but Alexander or Napoleon couldn't have created an army all by himself. How many good officers did Skarga have? They were few enough in the Seventy-Seventh.

I thought fast. "Explain I have a mission, which you needn't describe," I directed. "Say this is a free spell, and I'd like to see your famous institution."

Jezierski winced. He must hate lying to his compatriot. He did, though, and Michnik gestured us through, without a salute for me. He seemed amiable, so perhaps it hadn't occurred to him—nobody had ever told him—I was his superior in the Imperial service.

Cloisters surrounded the quad. I imagined students colorful and cheerful, professors serene and honored, in waketime; and I wondered how much longer they would be. "Hurry up before somebody else notices us," I muttered.

We passed by the stargazing statue, through a bronze door where the Great Equations stood in relief, down a row of time-dimmed murals to another door, and on through. Jezierski had told me it was traditional to leave this holy place unlocked. Evidently a youngster with a rifle was still believed to suffice. Beyond lay a dim chamber lined with books, codices as well as micro. Atop one shelf, I recognized a bust of Alderson. My attention flew to the desks and office equipment, yes, *that* computer terminal.

I sat down before it. Jezierski and I had already

discussed procedure. The board was standard, but he
didn't know every trick you could play with it, whereas
I didn't know the language in which Geremek doubtless
kept his records.

Jezierski leaned over my shoulder. "First we must
obtain the file code, sir," he said needlessly. "Touch
KOD—*kodeks*. Now spell out G, E, N, E, T, Y, K, A."
In a couple of minutes the display was giving us the
data on Red Plague research.

Time dragged then, scraping my nerves, for he must
pick his way through unfamiliar technicalities. I could
only help by telling him when a report was obviously
irrelevant and by gradually deducing the form of logic
tree used.

In the end we had a name. Agent Alpha. The
immunizer.

That was what we had. Nothing else. We went back
over the ground twice to make sure.

I swiveled my chair around and looked up into
Jezierski's eyes. Light from the screen and a narrow
window picked them wide out of dusk. "We-ell," I
breathed through the silence. "Most interesting. Not a
word about it in the whole damned database."

"Sir, there is—I saw implications mentioned—"

"Sure, that was inevitable. The professor hasn't had
time to censor everything out."

"Maybe they have n-n-not begun this next stage of
the work."

"Impossible. I told you, the cure and the preventive
have got to be two parts of the same thing. You can no
more learn about one without making progress on the
other than you can design a new missile without regard
to the propellant. No, somebody's wiped the file on
Agent Alpha."

He lifted his hands like a man fending off a blow.
"Destroyed it, sir? *Nie! Nigdy!* I will not believe!"

I rose and laid a hand of my own on his shoulder.
"Easy, son," I said in my gentlest tone. "The informa-

tion would've been copied off first. The disc is hidden somewhere, likeliest in somebody's possession."

"In God's name, why?"

"I'd guess because the research is in fact complete. A program for making Agent Alpha exists. Come on, let's get the hell out of here. We've been lucky so far, sort of, but it can't last."

Jezierski was stunned. After I'd removed the traces of our visit as best I could, he shambled along beside me, staring ahead. I tried to cover by staying between him and Sergeant Michnik as we went out. But that gaze followed us. Soon after the guard went off duty, word would be going around about this curious visit.

I wasn't sure how long it would be before Skarga heard—Lis, Geremek, the whole gang. The chances were we were dealing with a handful of amateurs. Still, they were tough, smart, determined. If I didn't act fast, I might well find myself blocked off from acting at all.

What were they after?

My thoughts rattled in the hollow streets, between the blank walls. To Jezierski I'd suggested that a faction in Cracovia favored a faction in the war for the Empire. Maybe one contestant had promised special treatment if Double Seven was kept off his neck. Then doubtless the promise was to the nation, not to individuals, considering what a fierce sense of community most Cracovians had. Lis and her associates weren't monsters. They were releasing Agent Beta, lest millions die. But they were withholding Alpha until the military situation had changed beyond retrieval.

None of that conjecture felt right. Space traffic was thin these days; the Marines monitored it without difficulty. You'd need a considerable volume of clandestine messages to and fro to work up a plot like this. Moreover, it would have had to have reached its decision point very recently. Though Geremek denied it now, the original word to Fort Kursk, that brought Adam Soltyk here, indicated that both Alpha and Beta were on hand. The leaders in Nowy Kraków had changed their minds almighty quickly, and tried to cover their tracks.

They'd tried too thoroughly. That blank file gave them away. If Geremek planned to insert a convincing fake, I'd anticipated him.

His group was bound to find out soon. I had to keep ahead of them.

But how? Going where?

I looked around. Nobody was in sight. Just the same, I drew Jezierski into a lane. A cat lying on a window ledge watched us, idly curious. The breeze had sharpened to a wind. It whined and bit.

I shook Jezierski out of his daze. He looked at me the way a trapped animal might. "Listen," I said. "We've come upon treason. Without that vaccine, our division is stranded on Haven, effectively crippled. We can't serve." I didn't add that we were unsure of whom we would be serving. "We can't get into the Deep.

"Now I don't for a minute imagine that more than a few individuals are involved. We've got to let the high command know what we've discovered. However, I think we—you and I, Lech—are in a position to discover more. A unique position. Let's take advantage of it.

"Think what'll happen if the Marines come to search for the traitors and Agent Alpha. They'll ransack the island. The innocent will suffer along with the guilty—or much more, because the guilty won't wait to be arrested, they'll disappear. Cracovia considers itself a nation. People will furiously resent troops coming in to occupy it. Incidents will lead to bloodshed, maybe to a little war, the kind this world has already seen too many of. Do you agree?"

He nodded mutely.

"Adam Soltyk's vanishment can't be a coincidence," I went on. "I am not, repeat not accusing my old friend of anything. I'm certain he's incapable of treachery." That was an altogether honest statement. "He may have been fooled, himself betrayed. In that case, I'll do what

I can to smooth things over." I hoped Jezierski didn't notice my voice stumble there. "Or he could be a prisoner, or— Well, we need to find out, don't we?

"Have you any idea where he might be?"

Jezierski must try three times before he croaked, "Sir, this is a big island. Farmhouses, villages, wilderness—"

"I know. Or he could be dead." That battered at the boy's resistance. "However, the indications are he moved about on his own. Suppose he felt, for whatever reason, wise or unwise—suppose he felt he'd better lie low a while. Can you guess where that might be? Someplace out of the way but familiar to him, with emergency exits or hidey-holes. Sure, it's a long shot, but give me your best guess."

I waited a moment before finishing, "On your honor, Private Jezierski."

Reinhardt, Rostov, and Li were playing cards in the sergeant's room. The air was blue and bitter with smoke. They sprang to their feet when I entered. "At ease," I told them. "You'll have a spell more to cool your heels."

"No action, sir?" Li was obviously disappointed.

"Not expected," I answered. "Stand by." I handed Reinhardt a sealed envelope. "If it happens you return to base without me, this must go to the high command. Under all circumstances. Understood?"

They stared. "Sir," ventured Reinhardt, "you aren't headed into danger alone, are you?"

I suspected he was as much shocked by the irregularity as by anything else. A commissioned officer puts his life on the line where necessary, yes, but otherwise he issues orders to his juniors. I forced a grin. "No reflection on you three. This is a delicate matter. Private Jezierski will be my interpreter and backup. I rely on my experienced men to convey my message in the unlikely event of trouble. There's a Marine flyer available for our use." I briefed them, having earlier obtained the information at the Palace. "Or if you must, commandeer whatever else you see fit. But that's strictly contingency. Give me thirty hours to contact you before you start worrying."

They had already begun. I felt it as I left.

Jezierski was in my room, crouched before the com. Forgetting to rise, he turned a stiffened face toward me. "They w-w-will not release a military vehicle, sir," he reported. "You must call yourself." He pointed to a display cell. His finger shook.

"Oh, I expected that," I said. "I had you try making the requisition for me just to expedite matters." He left the chair and lurched aside. I sat down and punched. It was scant surprise when Lis' countenance appeared. Her or Skarga, I'd thought; the circle of conspirators must be small.

I went straightway on the offensive. "Greeting, *Pani*. You pledged full cooperation with his Majesty's investigators. But your depot refuses us transportation, apart from the inadequate vessel Major Soltyk arrived in. Why?"

"It is . . . most unusual, Colonel Raveloe," she replied. "In the middle of sleeptime—"

"Not unexpected, though, since you left standing orders you be called. What other possibilities have you covered?"

"Furthermore," she continued as if she hadn't heard, "you demand a fighter craft. What do you intend, that an ordinary transport will not serve?" With a slight sneer: "You could send for a taxi. I am sure you have a generous expense account."

"Converting Imperial credits to gold isn't simple, *Pani*, especially at this hour. As for the haste and the type of flyer, let me remind you that my duty is to learn what's become of one of our most valuable officers. Suppose he's been captured by those pirates I heard mentioned. Far-fetched, maybe, but— My duty is also to return alive, in order that I may serve the Empire further. It's basic to provide myself with means of protection." I put a knife edge on my tone. "Do you deny me this? Please think. His Majesty's Governor has been patient with Cracovia, but he cannot overlook outright rebellion."

"You exaggerate, Colonel. This is a difference of judgments." She bit her lip. "May I ask what you plan to do?"

I was prepared. "A reasonable question. Look, I don't know why you're so antagonistic, but I'm willing to be frank. The odds are all against my success in this assignment, and the time I can devote to it is limited. But I must make my best effort. It seems to me that that should start with an aerial survey. Maybe I can turn up a clue. For instance, in spite of having bandits to combat, your people might not recognize a guerilla encampment for what it is, whereas I might well. Then I'll make inquiries in Major Soltyk's home area, around Wielki Lato. You remember I have a kinsman of his with me. If we get a lead, we'll try to follow it. If not, which I admit is much more likely, we'll return here, consult with you and headquarters both, and probably go home."

Relief struggled with vigilance. "I see. Thank you. How long do you propose to search, and in what pattern?"

"Unless I do discover something, I have about two hundred hours. Private Jezierski suggests a preliminary zigzag flight path, southeast to, uh, Cape Wrak, then to-and-fro northward."

"Yes, that will be best," Lis said hastily. "Very well, I will give an authorization. It will take perhaps an hour to clear channels. Do you wish to be at Gwiazda Field at that time?"

We went through brief courtesies. I switched off and turned to my companion. "All right," I said. "Go rouse 'em in the kitchen and get us a well-loaded food basket." Squinting: "What's wrong?"

He shivered where he stood. "Sir, you—you lied to Pańi Lis."

"Well, I was diplomatic." Sharply: "No more haggling, you hear?"

"Yes, sir. I, I did not mean to be—insubordinate—"

No, I reflected, not exactly. He had only, wildly, insisted, there in the alley, that action was futile if I didn't follow his advice. *"Sir, I do know where he may have gone. But we must not take the others. The colonel understands? Private talk."* Tears came forth. He wiped them with his wrist. *"Y-you wanted me along because I know the country and my people."*

I had refrained from requiring him to tell me what he meant, regardless. He might have refused, and tried in some incoherent fashion to justify himself at the court-martial.

"Go fetch that chow," I said. "Include plenty of coffee."

Alone, I got out my sidearm and secured it to my belt. That would be our single weapon. Guns and missiles were not what I wanted a pursuit craft for.

I went to the window and stood, not really seeing the gracious roofs and the spires above them. My thoughts were colder than the wind that whistled down the street.

The flyer was a Lance-15 two-seater, part of the equipment the Cracovians had "inherited" when the Forty-Fifth left Haven. It wasn't the best they had, I knew, but it was well maintained and the gauge showed fusion potential sufficient to circle the globe three times. I took it straight up and lined out southeast at its top stratospheric cruising speed.

From the fire control seat at my back, Jezierski's awed whisper cut through the murmur within the cabin. "How beautiful our world is, sir. We must keep it."

The sky engulfed us in purple. Away from the mighty shield of Catseye and the diamond glare of the sun, stars glittered. Haven curved underneath, silver-swirled with clouds above wrinkled land and gleaming sea. "But it is not like the Deep," he added.

That gave me hope he was strengthened for what lay ahead.

Which might be nothing, of course. He hadn't claimed certainty.

From afar I spied a squall. They're common west of the Catseye dawn line in the lower latitudes, where air masses of different temperatures collide. My instruments declared this was a big one. Good. "Hang on," I warned, and dived for its darkness.

We pierced chaos. Wind roared, yelled, dashed rain over the canopy till all I could see was lightning. The craft bucked, dropped, yawed. Twice we nearly went into the drink. But I had full control throughout. After ramping about in the storm for minutes, I broke free and streaked low above the water. Grayback waves snatched hungrily after us, then damped out until we jetted over blue-green brilliance adance with whitecaps.

"That was, uh, uh, that was amazing, sir," Jezierski stammered. "I expected m-my jaw would pop out the top of my head."

I laughed, mainly to encourage his show of spirit. "Well, maybe it was a bit much, but it seems to've worked." I'd taken for granted that the Cracovian air corps had us under surveillance both by ground-based radars and by at least one craft with more legs than this. Why else had Lis kept us waiting before we could board? Now, according to my instruments and intuition, we'd shaken any watchers. Given their limited capabilities, they might take several hours to reacquire us.

I didn't think Lis or Skarga would question me very closely about my maneuver if I returned to Nowy Kraków. They didn't want an open break with the Imperium.

"No time to waste," I said, skimming along, and displayed a map of the west coast. "Here, lean over and point. I'll switch to progressively larger scales till you've zeroed the destination."

"Reda Bay, I told you, sir. South shore, about seventy-five klicks from Port Morski, which is the nearest town."

The ultimate detail was a satellite picture of a small house on the edge of a cliff. Behind it and on either side was wilderness, native forest. "A *domek*, sir, a holiday home that belonged to my parents. Uncle Adam—Major Soltyk often joined us there. It's my other uncle's now, but he and his wife don't like the location. The last I heard, they had not sold it. Who has money any more?"

"Vacant and isolated. Uh-huh."

The voice at my back, which had been intent, cracked across. "But why would he hide, sir? He can't be—a deserter—before God, he can't be!"

I thought that the prospect of leaving Jadwiga and the kids for years, possibly forever, could give motive. Not enough, though. They had faced the possibility when they married, and he had not resigned, because he believed that guarding civilization mattered too much. Today no resignation would be accepted—not till after the war—but eventually he might hope for discharge and some way of getting home, if any Imperial ship dared by then to cross this part of space. And if he remained alive. Would they? Civilians went in terror of being left to defend themselves. That was why we downplayed the likelihood.

"No, he's not a quitter, absolutely not a coward," I agreed. "But something strange is afoot. Shut up and let me pilot." Let me think. Let me grope in winter blindness.

At our speed, we approached the goal within half an hour, rounding the southern end of the island, swinging north, veering east. Land fairly leaped over the horizon. Here it was rugged, standing a hundred meters above a white fury of breakers. Reefs and shoals must make the tides higher and rougher than elsewhere, and they are more so on Haven than on most habitable planets. Above the tawny limestone, russet treetops billowed before the wind. The far shore of the bay was invisible from this height; the one sign of man was the cottage. Low and sturdy, with vines blossoming scarlet over whitewashed walls, it belonged to this landscape in which it had stood for centuries.

A landing strip lay vacant at the rear. I set down vertically, threw off my harness, flung the door open and sprang forth. My hand was on my sidearm. Wind soughed, full of salt and chill; the sea-thunder came over the cliff edge like an endless drumbeat; wings soared lonely overhead. Already wireweed and prickle bush were reclaiming what had been a garden. They surrounded the strip. Our jets had scorched them a trifle. Nothing stirred within the house, nobody stepped out.

I beckoned Jezierski to follow me and walked to it. The door was unlocked, as was customary almost everywhere in Cracovia. (How much longer would it be?) We entered. Light slanted through windows, over a snugness of generations-old furniture, books, discs, heirlooms, antiquated but serviceable electronics. When Jezierski shut the door, thick walls enclosed us in silence.

We looked through the four rooms and came back to the first. "It seems I was wrong." Jezierski sounded glad. "Nobody here. I'm sorry, sir. But it was only a guess."

I shook my head. "Somebody's been around till, I'd say, an hour ago or less. Food in the pantry, well, that's stuff that would keep. The beds are stripped, but used linen could easily be squirreled away in the woods. What I notice is that there's no dust, and that the heat's turned off but the interior's warm."

"Somebody else—maybe gone for a walk—"

"Without a made-up bed to welcome him home? No, Adam Soltyk got out. He hoped we wouldn't show, at least not immediately."

A noise like a sob, then: "Do you mean . . . somebody called and warned him? How could they know?"

"They didn't, for sure. They must have contacted

him on general principles, told him he'd better hide himself more thoroughly till they gave him the all-clear. It could have worked, if we'd arrived much later."

"They took him away?" Jezierski asked eagerly.

"I think not. No char marks on the brush, except ours and some so faint they're many hours older. Fetching him would be kind of chancy. An aircraft descending to this empty spot could well be noticed in Port Morski or aboard a ship at sea. Investigators could pick up the gossip. That would be a clear sign he had help, which could bring on disastrous consequences. No, I think a strong reason he went to earth here is that the location has more than one covert." I turned to confront him. "You'll know where."

He backed away a step before he caught himself. "No, sir. We have a whole forest around us."

I caught his gaze and hung on. "You've got a better idea than that, son. You're not a skilled liar."

He broke. Again I saw tears. "Please, sir!"

"Has the situation changed? Has our duty? Doesn't the fact that Soltyk scuttled from us make it the more urgent to track him down?"

Anger brought blood to cheeks. "He didn't scuttle!"

A gulp, a shudder. Flatly: "Very well, sir. For the honor of my kindred." The phrase did not sound pretentious. Jezierski looked beyond me. His fists clenched, unclenched, clenched. "There is a cave at the foot of the cliff. Pieczara Syreny, we children always called it. Uh, M-mermaid Grotto. One must be careful, because the water is crazy. But places inside are above high tide. Sometimes for an adventure a grown-up took us down. We played pirates or—"

"Well, let us go!" he screamed.

"Good for you, Marine," I said softly.

Flashlights were in a cabinet from which other items of camping gear seemed to have been removed. We helped ourselves and departed.

Brush screened the head of a trail down the heights. Without my guide I'd never have found it, for it was little better than a set of precarious footholds, snaking along natural projections and cracks. My muscles strained to hold me. I kept having to clutch rock or gaunt bushes lest I go over. Wind hooted and slashed. As we neared the sea, spindrift blew blinding in our eyes, bitter onto our lips. Surf crashed and spouted. I felt its impact tremble through the stone. Jezierski led the way, agile, joyless.

The tide was flowing, but had not yet covered a strip of beach at the bottom. I slipped on wet cobbles, skinned a knee, regained my feet and slogged on. Chill smote me. My clothes were drenched. But my sidearm didn't suffer from it.

I'd never have seen the grotto from the bay, either. A holm, on which the waves burst in white curtains, blocked that view. Through the scud I descried a blackness which was the mouth. Military reflex made me scan the terrain past it. There also, the cliff didn't rise quite sheer. Crags, ledges, erosion holes would enable an active man to climb. If he went up, he'd emerge, breathless, in the woods. Desolation like this was right for what we had to do. A sunlit meadow or a Catseye-lit lakeshore would have been mockery.

We halted before the entrance. "What now, sir?" I could just hear Jezierski's hoarseness through the racket. He'd lost his cap; the blond hair clung to his skull.

"Does the cave have any traps for the unwary?" I asked.

"No, sir, if you are careful."

"Then I'd better lead." Else he would be my shield; and I was his commanding officer.

At first light from outside touched the vaulting of the roof, the water that churned and snarled over the floor. A ledge on the right led into flickery shadows. They deepened as we went inward, until I thumbed my flash against them. That left me alone in a shifting puddle of paleness. The currents and rips filled it with their echoes.

Ahead of me, the passage bent around a corner. "Douse your glim," I ordered Jezierski, softly under the noise, and did likewise. We stood for what felt like a long time. My eyes adapted. I picked out a dim glow seeping around the edge. Crouched, I slipped forward for a peek.

The cave ended several meters beyond. Most of the space was occupied by a shelf whose roughness loomed above high-water mark. The glow was from a portable heater-cookstove on top. Adam's sleeping bag and food supplies must be there too. Himself? I moved ahead, onto a wide space below the shelf, keeping rock always next to me.

Brilliance struck. I stood dazzled. "Hold!" rang a remembered voice. "Not a move. Either of you." A shot cracked. I heard the bullet whang off the wall behind us. "You are covered."

He'd outwitted me, I realized with my guts. Probably he'd kept watch near the cave mouth, seen us approach, retreated to ready his ambush. He had the drop on us. I couldn't even have seen where to aim.

"Hands on heads," he commanded. I let my flashlight fall and set the example for Jezierski. Should I force my friend to kill us?

Through the wet surge at my heels, I heard his footfalls approach. They stopped. The beam wavered. "Colin," he choked. "Lech. Not you."

"Nobody else," I retorted. "Can you fire on men of Double Seven?"

"I will . . . do what I must," Soltyk answered. "Have care. Why did you betray me, Lech?"

His nephew cried aloud.

"Don't blame him," I said, for that pain was hurtful to hear. "The top brass sent me after you. I co-opted Jezierski; he had small choice about that. True, he could have played dumb and left me without any realistic hope of finding you. I'm not saying he would have, but he could have. What made him help, made him suggest we look here, was the absence of any data on Agent Alpha, the Plague vaccine. It had to have been concealed. That was too much. Who is the betrayer, Adam?"

"Sir," Jezierski pleaded, "Major Soltyk can explain. He is honest, he has good reasons for everything, I know he does."

"You have the program with you, don't you?" I hammered.

"What makes you imagine that?" Soltyk growled.

I sighed. "Adam, after these many years I can tell when you're bluffing. But in this case, it's only logical. The higher-ups in Nowy Kraków had pretty clearly connived with you. They had also, pretty clearly, abstracted the Alpha file. That was scarcely a coincidence. If they were helping you hide, the chances were they'd leave the disc in your care."

"You're a quick one, Colin. Nobody expected you'd search the medical database right away, as it appears you have. I won't waste time denying the program exists. It's lying up there with my duffel. Can you guess why?"

"Kuron's people—I suppose the Wojewóde is party to this—they made it plain in retrospect. Their intent is that we shall think Alpha is still under development. That'll give them leverage against us. We could complete the project ourselves, but much slower and at high cost to our limited technical resources. For a start, they can insist we drop our hunt for you, because on the scale necessary, it would be too bothersome; their scientists would go on strike. You're a mighty important man in Cracovia, aren't you, Adam?"

"Yes," said the voice from behind the mask of light. Slowly: "The question is what to do about you two. You must have left a record of what you know and what you were about to try. This won't be a safe place for me any more. But I have an entire island full of refuges, and Alpha for my hostage."

"*Nie*," said Jezierski. Sweat sheened on the highlights of his face. He breathed like a runner at the end of a marathon.

"Be reasonable," Soltyk urged. "Let me see. . . . Yes, I'll go up the trail first. Don't follow in my sight. You'll have ample time to get on top before the tide. I'll have taken your flyer, but somebody will be along in due course, or it's not too long a hike to Port Morski. Then for God's sake—for everybody's sake, Colin—see if you can't keep matters from reaching a crisis."

"*Nie,*" Jezierski said again. "You must not. For our honor."

He sprang. Soltyk shouted. Jezierski paid no heed. He landed between me and yonder firearm.

"Sir," he called, "please do not kill him if you can avoid it. Let him explain."

He held his right hand out. Though he spoke in Polski, I knew what it meant. "Give me your weapon, Uncle." Behind him, I drew my own. He would not die unavenged.

Soltyk cursed, once. His pistol clattered across the rock. I retrieved my flashlight and pinned him in its beam. The old half-grin of battle lifted his mustache. "You called my bluff," he said almost merrily.

"Well done, Private Jezierski!" I exclaimed in my poverty of words.

"Tell the colonel why," the boy coughed forth. "Tell us, tell us."

Soltyk shrugged. "Shall we make ourselves more comfortable?" he asked.

"Sure." We took our various flashlights and aimed them aside. Diffused, the beams brought us halfway out of darkness.

"You are not a traitor, not a deserter," Jezierski said, barely hearable in the hollow noise around us.

"Not the usual sort, anyhow," I declared. "Those top-flight people wouldn't have taken the risks they did if you were simply quitting, Adam. There must have been some contact before you flew to Cracovia; I imagine you pulled a few wires to get the assignment. How long did you intend to withhold Agent Alpha?"

"Only till the division is sent for." Soltyk's tone stayed

level. "We could have delayed that embarkation, but not by much, and it might have caused the worst of the war lords to win, when we hope that the least bad will. No, the Wojewóde means—meant to announce at the proper time that the research was completed. In fact, a supply of the immunizer would have been secretly produced, sufficient for the Marines. In exchange, in the hurry of departure, we'd try for certain concessions, certain amnesties, a transfer of weapons and other equipment to us."

"Try," I said. "You couldn't be sure. But if everything had gone fairly well, the scheme would have protected Adam Soltyk. That's what it was mainly about."

He nodded. "Correct. Not because I'm so great, but— The last Marines are leaving. The wars, the reavers, the barbarians are coming. We must prepare ourselves, and our defense force is desperately short of everything."

"Especially good officers," I said. "And you were always among the best. Yes. As soon as you could appear in the open, I suppose, you'd become Skarga's second in command. Shortly you'd succeed him; he's elderly, and the time ahead is terrible."

He reached out as if to take both my hands. "Right, Colin, right. I came to understand— What's one man more or less, in that dance of death among the stars? This is my country, these are my people, I could not forsake them."

Never had I seen such joy as burst from Jezierski. "You hear, sir! No traitor! Patriot! I knew it!" He cast himself into his uncle's arms.

Above his shoulder, Adam Soltyk sought my gaze. "What will you do about this?" he murmured.

"Stand aside, Private Jezierski," I directed. Shakily, he obeyed. I gestured at the floor. "Take the prisoner's weapon." He hesitated. "Take it, God damn you!" I yelled.

When he had, I stood before them and said: "Private Jezierski wanted us two to come by ourselves. That was

rotten military practice, but I agreed, because otherwise—
Well, he realized that in the presence of witnesses,
plain talk and quiet compromise would be impossible.
You're a bright lad, Private. May you go as far as your
talents deserve."

"You don't intend to bargain, then?" Adam asked, as
calmly as before.

"How could I? I have my orders, and . . . the Imperium has my oath. I must bring you to Fort Kursk,
Major Soltyk."

He nodded.

The pistol shuddered in Jezierski's hand. "What will
they do with him, sir?"

"He'll be court-martialed," I answered. "Probably
he'll be shot."

Jezierski moaned.

"We're having too many desertions," I said. "We
need to make a conspicuous example." The waves clashed
and hissed. "But I wouldn't expect any attempt to pros-
ecute the rest of the conspirators. That part is best
hushed up."

"I hope so," Soltyk put in. "We shouldn't undermine
what's left of civilization on Haven."

"We're supposed to defend it."

"I know."

"Sir, please, please," Jezierski begged.

"Shape up, Private!" I rapped. "Stand clear. Don't
give the prisoner a chance to jump you. If he tries
anything funny, shoot. That's an order.

"Major Soltyk, you told me the Alpha disc is on the
shelf. Very well, I'll fetch it."

When I climbed back down, neither man had moved.
The murky light showed both their faces congealed,
like metal that has set.

"Now," I told them, "the craft we came in won't hold
three. I'll go topside and call our men in Nowy Kraków.
They'll claim the vehicle you brought, Major Soltyk,
and we'll fly home in tandem. For the time being,
though, you two stay in this cave. Then if a Cracovian

party lands, I can try to explain things away, stall them till Reinhardt's squad arrives. How long before high tide closes off the mouth?"

"Perhaps two hours," Soltyk replied.

"Time enough. Private Jezierski, I leave you with your responsibility. Carry it out as honor requires. Major Soltyk, whatever happens, I will convince my superiors your wife is blameless."

"Thank you, my friend," I heard him say. He saluted.

I returned the gesture and left them.

The sea licked at me as I made my way out. On the beach and the lower trail, it whipped me with a salt storm. The rising violence of it rang in my head. The climb was stiff.

When finally I reached the jet and got in, I was so cold, wet, and tired that I must sit with my hands to the heater duct till the numbness left them and I could code transmission for Reinhardt. "All right," I instructed, "get that vehicle and come join me." I gave him the coordinates.

"Is there a big rush, sir?" he asked. "Unless we bull through, it may take an hour or two, the way people seem to drag their feet around here."

"No, take it easy, don't give offense, things are under control. But destroy those sealed orders I gave you. They're obsolete."

I stayed put as long as seemed wise, against that possibility of Skarga's men appearing. At last the waters had risen so far that I'd better go lead the others up.

Hip-deep, I fumbled and stumbled into the Mermaid Grotto. The currents hauled at me. Their chill bit my bones. I waved my flashbeam and shouted. Surf and echoes gave answer. Darkness thickened.

If I didn't leave at once, the sea would eat me.

Back in the jet, I raised Reinhardt. He, Li, and Rostov were on their way. "Change of plan," I said. "Proceed straight to Fort Kursk."

"Yes, sir," he acknowledged. "Who shall we report to?"

"Me. I should reach it first."

His silence pressed inward. I drew breath. "You may as well hear the news at once," I proceeded. "I have what we came for, not just a cure for the Plague but an immunizer against it. A deserter—his name will be spat on—he'd stolen the program, meaning to use it for a bargaining chip. The Cracovian authorities were dismayed but incompetent. With Private Jezierski's help, I tracked him down and retrieved the disc. Unfortunately, it now appears he made a break for it while I was calling you earlier. Private Jezierski seems to have died gallantly in an effort to prevent that. At least the deserter died also. Keep this confidential for the present, Sergeant. I must inform the high command in more detail."

"Oh, sir! That poor kid."

"A pity, yes. He realy longed to go with us. Well, we can't make a big thing of an incident. Carry on."

I secured my harness and took off.

The sun ahead is only the brightest among a thousand thousand stars. It waxes ever faster, though, as our troopship accelerates inward from the last Alderson point to the next battle.

We can still take some ease. Yesterday evenwatch, Ashcroft and I got a little drunk together in his cabin, after we'd finished discussing problems of morale and discipline. My promotion has been quick, same as in the lower ranks, given the casualties we've taken. "I do sympathize with the men," he said, somewhat blurrily. "The girls we left behind us— We won't see them again. That's become unmistakable. Forget them. Except we can't, can we?"

"Not easy," I admitted. "But you're coping."

"And you're lucky, you're free of ghosts." He ran fingers through his gray hair. "Or are you, Raveloe? I don't want to pry, but—Soltyk's widow— She is a remarkable woman, and you did help her a lot. I thought for a while— But, sorry, I don't want to pry."

I shrugged. "Nothing to pry into. She accepted my protection and my making arrangements, for the sake of her children. She never pretended any different. When I saw them off on the flight to Cracovia, all she said was, 'Perhaps when we meet on the Judgment Day, perhaps then I can forgive you.' "

Catseye had been alone in heaven. Its light made coral of those high cheekbones and big eyes. There was frost in her breath and her hair.

"I wonder how they're doing," Ashcroft mused.

"We'll never know," I said, and drank.

Our ship drives on through the Deep.

From the Castell *Times,* May 7, 2627

THE EMPEROR HAS NO CLOTHES

Gregory Nicholls

It's painfully clear to this columinst what no-body says in public—that the Empire has left Haven lock-stock-and-battlecruiser.

Yes, it's time to say it out loud, even shout it. The Empire has left this refrigerated mudball for good! It's been a fact for more than four standard years, ever since the last Imperial Governor and the last Imperial Marines departed.

But does our worthy Governor-Elect (who's still waiting for an Imperial Writ) and the rest of the Government House gang recognize what any six-year-old can see? Of course not. Hush, hush, Daddy will be back.

Sure he will.

We could probably live without Big Daddy, if those incompetent nabobs in Government House knew anything about governing, let alone protecting the citizens. Witness last year's attack by three pirate ships who called themselves "the Black Hand." They should have been turned to orbiting junk, instead of bringing an end to interstellar travel in the Byers System. They might have wrecked Haven, too, if General Cummings and his Militia hadn't known their business well enough to take out two ships. Now even Cummings doesn't have the men or firepower to face another major raid.

The economy is in even worse shape. Last week the government had to conscript workers to keep the power plants operating. Three workers were killed "resisting arrest for disciplinary offenses" —which means sneaking out the back door. Inflation is up to one hundred percent in a good week. Even the police need two jobs just to keep the soy goo on the table.

What we have here is government by absentee landlord. There are worse things, but now nobody seems to be able to reach the landlords. It doesn't help that some of the tenants are trying to form a cooperative and beating up anybody who won't join. Down the hall, another group is treatening to burn the whole place down roasting muskylope steaks!

Meanwhile, the superintendant is arguing with his wife over whether they need a sprinkler system. She says, "Get it." He says, "Let's wait until we hear from the landlord."

Sorry, folks, but somebody's got to say it. The landlord's closed his office and left town. It doesn't look as if he's coming back—not in our lifetime anyway.

It's time for the Super to get off his arse and start regulating the rent—currency reform, martial law, curfew, or whatever else it takes. We don't have much time. No one's heard from South Continent for two years. What authority the government has stops these days two hundred kilometers outside Shangri-La. Without the Militia, there wouldn't even be that much government.

It's time we all took a good look at the Emperor and what he's not wearing these days.

*   *   *

Note: Two days after this column was published, the *Times* announced the "resignation" of Gregory Nicholls for "personal reasons." Since May 11, he has been officially listed by the Castell Police Department as a "missing person."

RATE OF EXCHANGE

Roland J. Green
AND
John F. Carr

Charity Boulevard was as crowded as any street in Hindutown. Homemade booths of every size, shape, and color jammed the sidewalks, a few military-surplus tents joining them in pushing the pedestrians and street hawkers into the gutters or out into the street itself. John Hamilton, younger grandson of the Baron of Greensward, slowed the fans of his car as he reached the corner of Charity and Hope.

He thought wryly that this was only too appropriate a place for the busiest black market money exchange on Haven. If there was any charity or hope left on Haven, the transactions here would have a good deal to do with it.

In the five years since Government House shut its doors, inflation had pruned the Haven mark until an old copper pfennig was worth a thousand paper marks. Imperial currency, what there was of it, went a hundred thousand marks to the crown. The official rate of exchange was five thousand to one, but all that official edicts had done was to create a thriving black market where prices changed by the hour.

John's grandfather, the Baron, preferred to do things by the book, on the Imperial Exchange. Or at least he had, until John showed him that he was being cheated by a factor of twenty to one. Then he'd let John do things his way. Hundreds of dependents at Whitehall and elsewhere owed their hopes for survival to the financial stability of the Hamiltons. Duty to their people was something both the Baron and his grandson understood very well, even if they might disagree about methods.

Besides, being turned loose on the black market money exchange was finally letting John render a service to his family. It was about the only one he could render now, apart from whatever his gambling winnings might add to the family exchequer.

Hamilton lowered the passenger window; half a dozen heads promptly thrust themselves forward. "One hundred sixteen thousand marks for each crown, yer lordship," cried a brown face with a dirty black eyepatch.

"A hundred seventeen-five," cried a boy who looked barely into his teens.

"One hundred twenty and not a pfennig less," replied Hamilton blandly. If he'd had either the time or the disposition to haggle, he was sure he could get one twenty-five, but he didn't want to stay here among the garbage reek and the bright-eyed black marketeers any longer than he had to. Neither were improving the hangover that was shortening both his vision and his temper.

A large man in a faded red satin shirt with a yellow stain across the front cried, "I'll take it, yer lordship. Now, how many crowns would ye be wishin' to exchange . . . ?"

"Twenty."

"That will be two and four," said the man, removing two wrist-thick bundles of currency from one pocket and counting out the change from his other hand.

Hamilton took the money and, without counting it, put it quickly into one of his pockets while he handed his Imperial crowns to the man in the red shirt. Once, just to make sure he wasn't being cheated, he'd spent twenty minutes counting every bill only to discover that he'd been overpaid by twenty thousand marks—at that time, about enough to buy a small bottle of fig brandy. There was too much competition in the currency market for anyone to risk cheating someone who might spread the word, or take even more drastic action.

It was too early to hit the markets for this week's supplies, so Hamilton headed for Dupars. It was the last functioning gentlemen's club in Castell City, which probably meant the last one on Haven itself. Most of the people with either money or the wits to see the trouble ahead had left with the last Imperial Governor. Those who'd stayed were the aristocrats with neither family nor wealth, a handful of the rich who'd rather die as big fish in this little pond than live at the price of starting all over again, ne'er-do-wells like John Hamilton, and a few people who loved Haven as their homeworld, warts and all. John's grandfather was one of the latter sort.

Dupars was surprisingly crowded for two in the afternoon. Or maybe it wasn't so surprising. Haverstill never turned away one of his former patrons who needed a drink or a meal, no matter what his circumstances. Half a dozen gentlemen would have eaten their last meal weeks ago without Haverstill's generosity.

The Hamiltons themselves might have been as badly off, if John's sister Matilda hadn't discovered great-grandfather's long-lost chest of silver Imperial crowns and gold ingots while planting mushrooms in the cellar. Mattie had shared her secret only with the Baron, John, and the family banker. Everyone had thought the Old Baron eccentric, to say the least; some had even doubted his hoard existed. Now, silver went for thirty thousand crowns per hectogram, or close to three *billion* marks, and great-grandfather Edward was beginning to look like a genius whose foresight had so far saved his family.

Haverstill came over to greet Hamilton in person, as usual. "How's his lordship, sir?"

"Well enough, Haverstill. He has a new project this month."

"What is it this time?"

"Rebuilding the main gate. He thinks the old one might be too flimsy, if the mobs from Castell ever break out into the countryside." Personally, Hamilton thought fifty centimeters of durasteel was overkill. It would stop

anything short of a tank (an endangered if not extinct
species on Haven), but it would do nothing for the
habitability of Whitehall, which didn't have much to
spare in that respect anyway.

But Haverstill was nodding in cautious approval.
"Whitehall would be just the place to weather a siege."

"You think that's really likely?" If he did, it was
information worth having. Haverstill had contacts at all
levels of Haven society, from the upper echelons of the
Provisionalists to day-laborers and beggars.

"Times are hard, sir. Without the bioplast there'd be
little peace in Shangri-La, I fear. Then there's the
Provos, who'd like us all to eat bioplast and soy steak.
There could be riots and worse if the Emperor can't
spare us a regiment of Marines and that quickly!"

This was surprisingly unguarded talk for Haverstill,
and on politics! Things must be getting worse faster
than anybody else knew—or at least was willing to
admit. Hamilton walked over to his usual table, his
thoughts so thoroughly elsewhere that he nearly col-
lided with the club's last working robot.

His usual companions were in their seats, but their
brittle cheerfulness was missing. Even Morgan, a local
furniture manufacturer, failed to greet Hamilton with
his usual raised eyebrows.

"Sit down, John," said David Steele. He was a wealthy
planter who hadn't harvested anything except dividends
since Hamilton had known him. Lord Whakely, the
remaining member of the card games, sat with an untouched drink beside him, staring at the center of the
table as if he expected a hangman bush to sprout there
at any moment.

Hamilton took his seat and said, "What is this? A
wake? I came here for amusement, gambling, and the
pernicious influence of bad companions. Now here you
all sit, sober as a bench of deacons or Imperial Magistrates. Have I missed something?"

Steele silenced him with a sharp look. "Whakely here
has suffered a bit of a reverse."

"What do you mean, a bit? And what would you know about it anyway?" said Whakely. Obviously some previous drinks hadn't gone untouched. "You sit there clipping coupons the banks have to redeem in Imperial crowns. You're a wealthier man every time you take a sip of your drink! Well, the bastards are forcing *me* right out of business!"

"Your bearing factory?" asked Hamilton. "But—everything needs bearings, or at least every piece of machinery. Now that there's no off-world competition, your business should be booming." Hamilton decided that he *had* missed something, but this time he didn't feel like making a joke about it.

"Oh, business is fine," said Whakely, waving a finger under Hamilton's nose. "So damned fine that the Government bowed to Provo pressure and decided that bearings are Essential Materials."

"Damn!" said Hamilton. It wasn't a very sympathetic remark, but at least the pieces were falling into place now.

"You understand. I can't raise prices now without Government sanction. That could take weeks. Meanwhile, I'm ruined. I was surviving by overbuying steel, warehousing the surplus, and selling it later when it had doubled in value. By winter there won't be a non-essential factory operating in the whole Shangri-La Valley. That means there won't be any factories at all by spring!"

"It can't be that bad, can it? Don't you get a price break on Essential Raw Materials, as well as reduced taxes?"

"Taxes!" The word came out like an obscenity. "The miscarrying Parliament can't raise taxes fast enough to keep up with inflation! Any tax breaks'll be too little and too late. The state-subsidized mines have already cut their production in half during the past year. The workers make more by stealing the ore and selling it on the black market. Where do you think I've been getting my cobalt and tungsten?"

"Sell the factory, then," said Steele, with a chill in his voice.

"To whom? For what? The only thing left that has any real value is land. Who's crazy enough to sell that to buy a factory guaranteed by Government decree to lose money? The Government's already taken over half the factories in Castell. The only ones that are still running are those they've staffed with conscripts guarded by troops."

"I'll buy the factory," said Steele.

Hamilton saw Whakely go bright red and his hands turn into fists as he tried to rise. Morgan's arm held him in his chair.

"Hear him out," said Morgan. Whakely subsided. Steele smiled.

"I mean it. I can use my losses as a tax write-off."

Lately Steele had taken to buying bankrupt plantations for just that reason. Behind his back they called him, "Loot, Pillage, and Steele," or things even less polite. Hamilton wondered if this would go on until they were calling him King Steele. That sobering thought turned his attention back to the man himself.

"—all things considered, five billion marks seems a reasonable price for the plant, including buildings, land, inventory, and all the records including the software."

"Five billion! It's worth ten times that right now and probably twenty times by tomorrow morning. John, you were out changing currency. What's the mark going for today?"

"A hundred and twenty thousand to one. Or at least it was an hour ago."

"You see?" stormed Whakely. "You're trying to ruin me!"

Steele laughed. The harshness of that laugh told Hamilton he'd played his last "friendly game of cards" with the man. Maybe he should never have played the first one.

"You're already ruined, Whakely. I'm just offering you a raft to get off your sinking ship. Whether you take it or not is up to you. I'm sure the new owners will be more amenable to reason."

This time Whakely's struggles to rise almost knocked his chair over, until Morgan whispered in his ear. He turned white and slumped down.

Morgan turned to Steele. "If you make that offer in Imperial crowns, you might have yourself a factory."

Hamilton wondered what had caused Whakely to turn into putty, then realized that he didn't want to know. A man with a wife and four children, one of whom needed constant medical attention, had too many things to fear at a time like this.

Steele scratched his chin. "Fifty thousand crowns, and that's my final offer."

The thought of Whakely's factory being sold was suddenly more than Hamilton could bear. Howard Whakely had inherited a sizeable fortune along with his title, then spent most of it starting the factory—"in order to do something that's worth a damn!" Over the years it had grown into a major concern, employing over two hundred men.

Hamilton looked at the dejected Whakely. "Don't sell, Howard. I'll loan you the fifty thousand crowns. Use it to play the currency market, keep the factory afloat, and pay me back when everything's back to normal."

Whakely sat up, staring like a man who thinks he's just heard his death sentence commuted. "Do you mean that, John?"

"I certainly do."

"You'd better think it over, Hamilton," said Steele. "You and the Baron aren't that far from Whakely's porch, if you take my meaning. Unless you've got a license to print the stuff?"

John felt his blood chill. The last thing they needed was hostile eyes turned toward the state of the Hamilton finances. And Steele's would be hostile. The man was obviously much more ambitious, not to say ruthless, than Hamilton had been prepared to believe. The

Baron had said as much, last year, but he hadn't listened. Too late for regrets now; the damage was done.

Morgan was smiling, but Whakely still hadn't recovered. His voice shook as he said, "Thank you, John. Thank you from the bottom of my heart. Cecilia's back in the hospital again, and you'll never know how much this means."

"I think ye may be makin' a great big mistake, m'lord," said Steele, deliberately shifting into Lowtown patois to remind everyone of how he'd clawed his way up from poverty. Hamilton wanted to kick himself. Had he been playing cards and drinking—yes, and probably letting secrets slip!—for two years with a man who secretly hated and despised him?

Morgan pushed his chair back and rose, to stand with his feet wide apart and his hands at waist level. "Steele, get the hell out of here before I turn you inside out and hang you out to dry! And don't ever come within five meters of this table again. You're no friend of mine, or anybody else here," he added, as Hamilton and Whakely nodded.

"You're all making a mistake," said Steele. "You'll all find out, too, and sooner than you'll like." He turned and strode out, arms pumping back and forth.

Morgan sighed and shook his head. "And to think I was sure I knew better than all the people who warned me about him. Sometimes it's a wonder that I can find the bathroom when I need to go!"

"Where Steele's concerned, you're in good company," said Hamilton.

They all laughed. Morgan ordered another bottle of Tabletop bourbon and proposed a toast to friendship and good companions. The whiskey was warm going down, but it couldn't take the chill out of John Hamilton's blood, nor make him forget Steele's parting look. He opened his belt pouch, took out five hundred crowns, and handed them to Whakely. "I'll have the rest for you Friday."

"Christ, John . . . I don't know how to thank you. I really don't . . ."

"Then don't try. I know how much that factory means to you. I'm just glad I could help. Now I have to go and tell the Baron."

"You don't think he'll mind—?"

"No." Hamilton knew he'd made the right decision, and that his grandfather would back him all the way.

Morgan held the bottle over Hamilton's glass. "Another drink?"

"No thanks. I want to get to the market while there's still anything left to buy. See you both Friday."

"Thank you, Shaw."

The butler bowed himself out. Albert, Baron Hamilton of Greensward, turned and offered a seat to General Gary Cummings.

The two aging men might have been cast in the same mold, then customized by hand. The Baron carried just over ten kilos of fat over solid muscle, and his complexion was ruddy from an open-air life. Cummings carried no spare weight, but his dark face was furrowed with worry lines and his eyes were red from too many sleepless nights.

"Since you're in uniform, I have the feeling this isn't a social visit."

"Quite right, Baron."

"Christ, Gary. We've known each other long enough to drop that kind of court nonsense. You know my name."

"All right, Albert."

"Al to my friends."

Cummings' sternness broke into a grin. "You win. Al, we've got problems."

"Personal, or does 'we' include the Militia and the Shangri-La Valley?"

"Everything. We had to decommission another regiment last week. That leaves us with exactly two understrength regiments for the whole valley."

"That's ridiculous! Those—raiders, pirates, whatever you want to call them—hit us hard enough. You'd think after that the politicians would be looking to our defenses. We take another raid like that and civilization on Haven will be on its way downhill with no stopping short of the bottom. Is this the Provos again?"

"For once, no. The Government's doing their work for them. The damned inflation is what's killing us, Al. We can barely keep the troops fed, never mind trained, armed, and equipped!"

"Why doesn't the Government just print more money?" asked the Baron. "They've done that for a lot of less deserving causes!"

"Oh, they've tried. But the value of the paper goes down even before my men are off base. They're lucky to be able to buy anything at all. Before much longer the legal markets will be completely bare. Who wants to produce anything when they get less for their finished product than they paid for the raw materials?

"The Government steps in, of course. We escort the workers to the shops—and 'escort' is putting it politely. But what do we do when there's nothing for them to work with or on? Two weeks ago they had to start running the iron ore down in convoys because bandits were running off with the ore trucks and selling them and their contents!

"Al, everything is going to the black market. I could do a better job with the Army if I declared myself Warlord and started looting for my supplies!"

"Why don't you? The way things are going, it will come to that. Either that, or turn your command over to some Provo hack. We both know what that will mean."

The General grimaced. "Another socialist-workers' hell, like Stalin. Ever seen it?"

"No, but I've been on Diego."

"Hereditary serfdom isn't as bad as what they have on Stalin. I don't know why the Empire didn't clean them out centuries ago, unless they were being kept around as a horrible example. Now the barbarians are inside the gates, and it's too late for housecleaning.

"But I'll be damned if I join the barbarians. I gave

my oath to this so-called Government, even if they don't know a horse's ass from its ear!"

That was a door closed politely but firmly in the Baron's face, very much as he'd expected. To change the subject, he shrugged and said, "I suppose the Government really couldn't do much now if they wanted to. They'd have had to start even before the Imperial Marines left. For us, that was like the Roman legions leaving Britain. Then it was uncertainty, pirate raids, civil war, and invasion. We've got as far as the pirates, and my money is on civil war being next."

"Literally, I notice. That's a new gate on the—on your castle, if you don't mind my being frank?"

"Why not? I don't mind admitting I'm lucky to have it. When Edwin Hamilton built Whitehall there were convicts running around in packs in this area. Nobody thought he was paranoid then. This wasn't the only fortified manor out here, either. Most of them are gone now, and none of them were Whitehall even at their strongest.

"Old Edwin must have been about the last man on Terra to make a fortune raising sheep. He emigrated because CoDominium Terra didn't have much of a place for self-made men. He collected plans of all the old Scottish castles and took the best features from each one. He was no architect, but that didn't hurt. Instead of doing a stress analysis, he just piled on another truckload of stone anywhere things didn't feel right. By the time he was through, this place was proof against anything short of nukes."

"You owe him one. Now, how are your herds and flocks doing? One thing I can do is buy our meat, wool, and leather on the hoof and cut out all the middlemen. I've got enough butchers, weavers, and tanners in the Militia to do the rest. I also came to deliver this."

The Baron looked at the sealed packet with the Imperial Seal on it, addressed to him. He sucked in his breath.

"Where did you get that?"

"From Fort Fornova. A ship on its way to somewhere else dropped off a drone courier and programmed the autopilot to land the message pod near Fornova."

"How close was 'near'?" asked the Baron. His own naval experience was far enough in the past that, when he wore Imperial uniform, most Imperial equipment still worked most of the time. Things had changed, and not for the better.

"About twenty kilometers up into the hills. Much farther and we'd have had to leave it. As it was, we lost fourteen men to bandits getting in and out."

"I'm sorry, Gary. You shouldn't have—"

"Don't start feeling guilty, for God's sake! We took out four or five times as many of the bastards. A lot more are going to be looking over their shoulders instead of raiding the valleys, at least for a while."

"I suppose you've read it?"

"We had to. This was the first Imperial communication in two bloody years! But I won't keep you in suspense. It's from Raymond."

"Raymond!" The Baron hastily broke the seal, went to the phone, and inserted the wafer into the message slot. His elder grandson Raymond appeared on the screen, wearing Imperial Navy dress blues.

"Granddad. Sorry it took so long getting this out, but we've been on the move for almost a year and a half now." Raymond's brown hair was thinner and there were lines on his face that hadn't been there when he left Haven just six years ago. "Be sure to give my love to Matty and John."

"They won't let me say too much, but I'm sure you'll soon be hearing about the big victory off Tanith." For the first time Raymond smiled. "We whipped their asses, Gramps! I wish you could have been there." He grew sober. "But it cost us—" The words blurred into static and the image into swirling colors, where the Imperial censors had wiped the message. "I'm lucky to be here at all, and no matter what happens when we hit Sauron it will be a while before they release anybody from active duty.

"A lot of remote planets have used the war to—" More static and colors, lasting much longer than before. "They say my time's just about up. I love you all and I'll be home as soon as I can. I've seen Aphrodite, Friedland, Levant, and even Sparta, but it's really true—there's no place like home. Goodbye."

The Baron stood rigid, staring at the blank screen until he knew his face would be expressionless. Then he turned to Cummings. "They're winning the war, but it's killing them."

"That's what my security people guessed. Did you see the Imperial Cluster on his shoulder?"

"No, I didn't. I'm afraid all my attention was on his face. I'll play it back later for the family."

"The other three people who sent messages also had the Imperial Cluster, although one of the awards was posthumous. We're pretty sure that's why they were able to find a captain willing to 'lose' a courier drone as he passed through the Haven system. Consider what it used to take to earn the Imperial Cluster. Either the Board of Awards has gone 'round the bend, or—things are the way you put it."

"I'd have liked to hear about those 'remote planets.' I wonder—are we going to have an outie problem again?"

Both remembered the history of the early Empire, and the knockdown, dragout fights against those planets that refused to make their peace with the Empire, even on the most generous terms. The "outies" had made a fair amount of trouble even when the Empire was young and strong, and then they hadn't had an organized alliance or the Saurons behind them. What widespread rebellions could do now, if they outlasted the Saurons . . .

"The war could go on for years, decades even," said the Baron. "That means we really are going to be on our own. We'll be lucky to see so much as a merchant ship."

"What do you want the Empire to do?" said Cummings irritably. "The Saurons have an old and ugly dream—a super-race ruling the rest of us as slaves. They aren't the first, either. But we have learned something from Hitler and the others like him. We can't leave a single Sauron alive, even if it takes half a century and means bombing a dozen planets to radioactive ashes!"

"You don't think I disagree, do you, Gary? It's just that knowing we're on our own means that we have to start planning for the worst that much sooner. We certainly can't rely on the Government to be any more help than they've been already.

"The Provos are living in cloud-cuckoo land and they'll never leave it. The Governor-Elect and Parliament will need more than a few family letters to convince them. They'll want a proclamation from an Imperial Envoy before they'll appropriate two marks!

"And the Empire will never admit that it can't hold territory, let alone tell us about it! Some third assistant sub-undersecretary will punch a button, another light on the wall map will go out, and another planet will be listed FILE CLOSED. The Baron sighed. "If only we'd had a seat in the Imperial Senate, just maybe . . ."

"Maybe our children's grandchildren will see the Imperial Eagle on Government House again," said the General. "But for now, I think you're right. We have to make the best of a bad job, and for starters I suggest not worrying about the rest of Haven. Let's concentrate on the Shangri-La Valley."

"Fine. How are you equipped, after the raid?"

"It could be worse. We have two shuttles left. That's enough to service the satellite network, or what's left of it. What else could we use them for? There's no need for interplanetary craft if there's no place else to go in the whole Byers System!"

The Baron knew where the bitterness in Cummings' voice came from. He'd talked himself blue in the face for fifteen years since the Marines started leaving, trying to get the spaceports fortified, then seen most of them wrecked in a few hours.

"Manpower isn't good. As I said, we only have two regiments, each at something like three-quarters strength. The raid cost us, although I don't think that particular crew will be coming back again. The rest of it is inflation. I can't really crack down on people who desert to take care of their families when I can't even feed and clothe them properly! But, Al, you may be able to do something about that, apart from your flocks and herds. I understand you've got quite a cache of silver and gold bullion here at—"

"Where the hell did you learn that? It couldn't have been the servants. Only Mattie and John knew about it, and I can't imagine they'd talk. John—no, I won't believe it. He wouldn't."

"As a matter of fact, he didn't. It was George Morris, at the First Imperial Bank."

"That bastard—!"

"Security had somebody at the bank who noticed the silver coming in, and did some homework. What could George say, when I laid the cards down on the table? He knew you'd be mad as hell, but he stands to lose a lot too if the army can't meet its payroll."

The Baron shook his head in weary disgust. "So what do you have in mind?"

"I'm not here to rob you. I'm desperate, not stupid. I do want to propose a deal that should keep us both reasonably happy. Al, you did your twelve years in the Navy. You can count fingers held up in front of your face. If we have to pull all the troops out of the Shangri-La Valley to someplace where we can feed them, what would you give for the Valley's chances by next summer?"

"About one Haven mark."

"I'd count it in pfennigs, myself. The bandits have been snapping up isolated farms and travelers for months. Now we're getting reports of them raiding whole towns. The most I can hope to protect is the Valley and Castell City, and maybe help Graytown, Falkenberg, Hell's-a-comin', and the small towns train their own defensive forces. I won't even be able to do that much, unless I can hold on to the men I already have.

"Al, I want some of that gold and silver, to pay and supply my men. In return, I'll give you an armored car or two, and a full company of Militia assigned to White-hall." Cummings sat down in his old pose, straddling the chair, with his chin resting on the back. It didn't hide his exhaustion.

The Baron gripped him by both shoulders. "Piss on the rest of Haven, and I hope those idiots who call themselves a Government drown in it. I'll help an old friend any time. In fact, I may be able to make a better deal than you think. How many tanks do you have left?"

"Three. The techs think they can cannibalize two more. The armored cars are in pretty good shape, though. They're smaller targets, faster, and use less fuel."

"That means you've got plenty of durasteel to spare, I suppose?"

"Yes." Cummings had the look of a man who's already waded halfway across a swamp and knows he won't get any muckier if he goes the rest of the way.

"The machine shop and its software survived the raid, or so I've heard."

"You heard correctly. We can make almost anything you might want. So—what do you want?"

The Baron told him. For a moment Cummings looked as if the swamp had suddenly turned to quicksand. Then he laughed. "I'd say you were crazy, but I'm not that sure. Okay, I'll deal. Shall we talk prices and delivery dates?"

It took less than fifteen minutes before the Baron was able to lean back and pour out two large glasses of Covenant malt scotch. Cummings sipped his apprecia-tively.

"How's John?"

"Shaping up quite well. It was hard for him, being the youngest and always second best to Raymond in everything. Not that Edward was the greatest father, either. Then after Raymond left, and the accident . . ."

He paused. The car crash that had killed his wife and his son was a memory that still hurt if he didn't keep it at arm's length, even after five years. "John was always wild, but never vicious. These last few months, he's helped us a great deal with his black market currency dealings. It's not a skill I'd ever expected my heir would need, but in these times . . ."

Now I've said it. I've called him "my heir."

What else was John? Win or lose, Raymond wouldn't be coming home. The Empire had too much work to do and too few good men to do it. And Raymond was a combat officer. He'd be trying to live up to that Imperial Cluster the way he always had to any honor or praise. His luck would run out long before the Empire ran out of work for him.

The Baron felt his eyes fill, and this time didn't try to stop it or hide it.

When he knew that his voice would be steady, he added, "John's growing up, too. He helped keep a friend out of Steele's grasp the other day. I was damned proud of him!"

"Steele? He went up against David Steele?"

"Of course. Did you expect him to join with that contemptible opportunist who's been making a fortune off of everybody else's misfortunes?"

"Of course not. But Steele's dangerous."

"Tell me something I don't know!"

"Do you know he has ambitions for the Governorship?"

"You're joking!"

"I wish I was. Steele's got more connections than the Provos and more money than the First Imperial Bank. He owns a piece of about half of Parliament. He also has a short temper and a long memory for insults, and I'm beginning to think his ambitions go even beyond the Governorship."

"You're—no, it sounds like you aren't joking."

"Bad times can be good ones, for people with lots of ambition and no scruples. I'd suggest you don't let John go to town again without a couple of the toughest bodyguards you can find. If you can, keep him at Whitehall."

"Maybe my plan isn't so crazy after all."

"Crazy? It may just turn out to be the best idea I've heard since the Marines left. If I didn't have to try to keep the Militia together for a couple of years, I'd throw in with you."

"You'll be welcome any time."

"Thanks." Cummings stood up, drained the last of his Scotch, and shook hands with the Baron. "I'd better be going, if I want to be back to Fornova in time for the evening briefing. I'll put the technicians on our project right away. Expect the first shipment in about two weeks.

It was the first time they'd dined in the Great Hall since Raymond's farewell at the end of his last leave, six years ago. It seemed even emptier than it had then. The walls were hung with tapestries and family banners, with the Imperial flag at one end. The six-meter slab table (brought from Earth by old Edwin, or so the legend said) seemed lost in the middle of the wide stone floor. The three Hamiltons sat at one end, the Baron at the head.

"I'd like to propose a toast," said the Baron, raising a cut-crystal glass of Dayan Chardonnay. "To Castle Whitehall. Send her victorious, happy, and glorious, long may she reign."

Today they'd finished the east wall, making the outer perimeter entirely secure. A month ago, John Hamilton would have thought this was nothing to boast about, but that was before his last visit to Castell and a narrow escape from the food riots.

He'd begun to take the idea of self-defense a great deal more seriously since then. He still doubted that the mobs would ever get far enough to test the gates of Whitehall, but life on Haven was clearly getting meaner and coarser and would get a lot worse before it got any better—which it probably wouldn't in his lifetime. Empires didn't concern themselves with backward frontier outposts when the barbarians were fighting their way into the palace.

"Sitting in this hall by ourselves is depressing," said Matilda. "Couldn't we have some friends over the next time?"

"Not a bad idea," said the Baron. "It's just that the timing is wrong. Most of our neighbors are either following our lead and fortifying their manors, or they've left the area. The Chandlers have moved to their estate in the Shannon Valley. It's supposed to be quieter there. The Klimovs tried their hand at farming, gave up, and moved back to the city."

"I suspect we'll see them back before long, if they're lucky," said Hamilton. "The authorities are right on the edge of losing control of Castell. Half the police have resigned because they can't feed their families on their pay. The other half barter their off-duty hours for food and goods, or rob the shops they're supposed to protect."

"When is this all going to end?" asked Matilda.

Hamilton and his grandfather exchanged looks. Mattie had a lot of her mother in her and not much of her grandmother; there was always a question as to how many unpleasant truths she could face.

"I expect we haven't seen the worst of it," began the Baron, as the butler walked in.

"My lord, we have a visitor. A Captain Mazurin of the Colonial Militia."

"Send him in."

The Captain wore a travel-stained field-gray uniform. He bowed to the Baron, then took the offered chair. "We have your first shipment, sir."

"Very good. Shall I give you the first chest now or later?"

"After we've unloaded will be fine, sir."

"Excellent. If you and your men would like to spend the night, I'll have the steward prepare some rooms."

"Thank you, sir. We could use the rest. We had to fight off a bandit attack today."

Matilda gasped. The Captain grew more animated as he realized that an attractive woman about his own age was present. He told of an early-morning ambush that ended badly for the bandits when they discovered that this isolated military convoy had an escort of three platoons of Militia.

"Hunting rifles and pistols aren't much good against assault rifles and rocket launchers. I might have even felt sorry for the—for the bandits, if we hadn't found forty-odd women in their camp. They'd been kidnapping the wives and daughters of the small farmers they killed. Excuse me, ma'am."

"What did you do with the women?" asked the Baron.

"Some of them wanted to go back to whatever was left of their homes. Most of them we brought with us. I'd very much appreciate it if you'd let us leave them here."

From the look on his face, Hamilton suspected that the Captain was at his wit's end over the women. It was certainly a situation that would have tried a considerably older and more experienced officer.

The Baron smiled. "We'll be happy to take them in. They can stay, or we'll arrange transportation to any surviving relatives. Since we have quite a few single men, I suspect the ones who stay will find themselves welcome."

"Thank you, sir. I feel—responsible—for them, but I wasn't sure I could answer for my men's behavior all the way back to Fort Fornova—excuse me again, ma'am."

Hamilton followed the Captain and his grandfather out to the courtyard—what the Baron called the bailey. He wanted badly to know what the Militia was delivering to Whitehall. He also wasn't going to waste his breath asking before his grandfather was ready to answer.

The courtyard spotlights showed a convoy of twenty trucks, some of them still disgorging Militiamen, and three armored cars. Hamilton saw bullet holes in the covers of the trucks and a few in the flared skirts of the armored cars, as well as half a dozen men being carried on stretchers toward the dispensary. Captain Mazurin, he suspected, had played down the seriousness of the fight with the bandits.

Warden Dunn was directing a dozen servants loading sacks of grain into one of the trucks. Hamilton wondered if Mazurin was supposed to leave a platoon or so of Militiamen in exchange. The castle garrison—it was so easy now to think in terms like that—had over a hundred able-bodied men, most of them familiar with hunting weapons. Maybe the Militiamen were to train them in infantry tactics—but then, some of the bodyguards were ex-Imperial Marines and the Warden himself was a former Battalion Sergeant Major.

Then the Militiamen started wrestling heavy crates out of the back of another truck, and John had his question answered. Captain Mazurin cut the crate open and pulled out a medieval-style steel helmet. John recognized the style as a sallet, a late style of helmet introduced when gunpowder was already changing the face of the battlefield.

When Mazurin finished unloading the crate, a dozen of the gleaming steel helmets stood in a neat row on the stones. Now Hamilton had another question. Had his grandfather lost his mind? What good would these helmets be, except for a costume ball? He could think of a lot of things worth more as the price for their precious grain stocks!

"Stand back," shouted Mazurin, drawing his sidearm. He fired point-blank at the nearest helmet.

Sprooonnnngggg! The helmet jumped and tottered. Hamilton didn't see where the ricocheting bullet went. He was too busy staring at a helmet totally unmarked except for a tiny nick and a gray smear of lead.

"That's our best durasteel alloy," said Mazurin proudly. "It will stop anything short of a spent-uranium slug. Of course a man can still be knocked down, or even break something if he's hit in a limb. If he's hit in the head, he still has to worry about concussion, whiplash, and crashing great headaches. But any brains he has will still be in his head where God put them, instead of scattered all over the landscape."

The Baron looked like a proud father.

Someone else opened another crate and started laying out breastplates. A third crate held steel shoulder pieces—Hamilton couldn't remember what they were called. He did remember that you usually wore some sort of padded garment under armor—an "arming doublet" was the name he recalled.

"We have to build a little heavier than they did in the Middle Ages," Mazurin went on. "You're not going to be turning any cartwheels in these, but a fit man should still be able to run. We made them in six different sizes, so they'll fit any average or large man less than ten kilos overweight."

He picked up a durasteel gauntlet, put it on, and wiggled his fingers. "We're also working to much closer tolerances, with computerized machine tools. We can do things the old Milanese and Nuremburg smiths never dreamed of. Here, try this."

He handed Hamilton the gauntlet and a pen. Once he got used to the weight, Hamilton found that he could actually write with his armored hand. He scribbled "Long Live the Empire" on three of the breastplates, then took off the gauntlet and handed it to his grandfather.

The Baron held it as if it was a newborn hound puppy. "Tell General Cummings that he has my undying thanks. He's done far more than I expected. Anything I can do to repay him . . ."

"You've already repaid us more than enough, sir. The specie and food will keep the Militia going, and if we can do that we can do a lot of other things. We're not as vulnerable to the troubles and to Castell, now that we've evacuated Fort Kursk and consolidated at Fornova and El Alamein. It would have all been wasted effort, though, if we couldn't meet the payroll or keep the rations coming in."

The Baron looked at the grim walls around them as if

they showed him some other time or place. "I wish I could do more, Captain. Your Militia may be the last hope for civilization on Haven. This," pointing to the armor, "is my insurance. Or the insurance for my grandchildren and their grandchildren and all the grandchildren to come for God knows how long. If I'm wrong, they'll pack it all away and laugh at me as I laughed at old Edwin the hoarder when I was young. But if I'm right, this may be all that lets my grandchildren *have* grandchildren."

The Baron shook his head, then spoke briskly, as if his mind had returned from wherever he'd been letting it wander. "How much did you bring?"

Mazurin clearly wasn't the sort of officer to leave details to his NCO's. He started reciting figures without even referring to his belt computer. "A hundred fifty durasteel sets of armor and five hundred cold-rolled steel ones. The cold-rolled steel won't stop more than pistol slugs and shell or grenade fragments, but I suspect there will be enough of those flying around to make it useful."

The next shipment would include a hundred durasteel helmets and a thousand cold-rolled ones, as well as fifty durasteel back-and-breastplate combinations. The last shipment of the order was expected within twenty-five days—fifty more complete durasteel armors and eight hundred back-and-breasts, three hundred of them durasteel.

"Now, sir, may I ask a question?"

"Go ahead."

"Why so many?" Mazurin lowered his voice. "I thought you didn't have more than a hundred men of fighting age . . ."

"We'll have a good many more before long, Captain. Once they're all trained, I intend to build an outer wall with towers around Whitehall. I suspect we won't have any shortage of recruits, either.

"Those suits we can't use ourselves, I'll give to my neighbors. Or at least those neighbors who think they're worth an alliance with the Hamiltons. If we all stand armored shoulder to armored shoulder, we should be able to keep at least this part of the Valley peaceful."

Mazurin shook his head. "I wish I could say that won't be necessary. But you wouldn't believe me if I did." He frowned. "Come to think of it, I wouldn't believe myself."

The knock on the door echoed through his bedroom like a gunshot. John Hamilton twisted out of his bedcovers, wondering for a moment if Whitehall was under attack. The knocking began again; this time a voice accompanied it.

"Master John! Wake up! There's someone here to see you."

As his heart slowed, Hamilton began to pull his clothes on over his thermal underwear. Outside the big cities where they had energy to burn (and for how much longer?), nobody on Haven ever went to bed in anything less. Even now, late in an equatorial summer, it was cold enough in the room to set his teeth chattering.

"Just a minute."

He opened the door to face Richard Dunn, the castle Warden—and that was another term that no longer felt strange or archaic on his tongue. "What is it, Richard?"

"There's a Lord Whakely here to see you, sir."

"A who—Whakely! It's late. What's he doing here?"

"He just arrived from the city in a hovercar with his wife and children. I believe he's asking for sanctuary."

Hamilton found Howard Whakely and the Baron hovering over the kitchen fire. "Good to see you," he said, shaking hands. "But—what are you doing here at this hour?"

Whakely gave him a what-a-stupid-question look. For the first time Hamilton noticed the man's tight-drawn face and eyes bloodshot with fatigue.

"Escaped from Hell! Castell's gone mad. The police went on strike and the streets really did run with blood. The Provos attacked Government House. Murdered the Governor-Elect and everybody they could catch who wasn't a sympathizer. Then they took over the media and declared martial law.

"The miners, some of the businessmen, and Big Al's Syndicate didn't like that idea. They fought back. It took the Provos about three days to put them down. The Provos pretty well wrecked themselves in the process, though."

"Thank God for small favors," said Hamilton.

"Very small," said Whakely bitterly. "While everybody who wasn't in that fight was watching it and hoping to stay out of it, David Steel proclaimed himself King of Haven."

Hamilton's laughter was a bark. "King! The man really has gone mad. Only the Emperor has that right."

"He's thought of a way 'round that. Says we're no longer part of the Empire, but something he calls an Independent Monarchy."

"I'm sure the Empire will have something else to call it when they return," said Hamilton. "Like 'treason' and 'rebellion.' " It was something he knew had to be said. He also knew that it was a question of "if" rather than "when,' and so did everyone else in the room. "Why haven't we heard anything about this over the Tri-V or the radio?"

"Steele's got control of the stations that weren't wrecked in the fighting. He's censoring everything that goes out. I suppose he knows that the rest of Haven might have their own opinions about what he's done. I know he's trying to get an army together before anybody can scrape up the firepower to oppose it. He thinks he's a general as well as a king—a regular Napoleon."

The Baron made a noise indicating disgust too great to put into words. "All he's going to do is start civil war in the Valley, when the rest of Haven's already on the brink. Cummings told me he was dangerous, but this . . . By the way, what's the Militia been doing while Steele was running amuck?"

Hamilton and the Baron exchanged glances. They

knew pretty much the answer to that question, thanks to General Cummings. What they wanted to find out was how much the general public—which now included David Steele—might know.

"Nothing, so far, Baron. They evacuated Fort Kursk about a month ago—stripped it of everything moveable. Nobody I've talked to knows where their main base is now. I suspect they've been lying low since the strike began."

Hamilton and his grandfather didn't suspect that, they were quite sure. They were also relieved to hear that nobody knew where Cummings had concentrated his forces, which included most of the heavy weapons and armored vehicles left on Haven. The Militia's arsenal could make a large difference in how long David Steele's cardboard "monarchy" lasted and how much damage it did.

"The Provos revoked Cummings' commission," Whakely went on. "They also proclaimed the Militia disbanded and did a lot of other equally stupid things, none of which stuck. They couldn't raise troops of their own when they didn't have any way of paying them or any idea of what to do about the money situation besides printing more fancy toilet paper.

"Steele, on the other hand—that's the main reason I'm here. He found out about the Whitehall hoard. The first objective for his army—"

"What!" roared the Baron. "How did he find out?"

"Morris talked. They threatened to torture his son and he told them everything. Killed himself afterward, the poor bastard. Couldn't live with what he'd done. But he left word with his cousin—Steele wants the gold and silver, wants Whitehall, and wants John dead."

"How long do we have?" Both Hamiltons spoke at once.

Whakely shrugged. "Ten days at the outside."

The Baron gripped Whakely's hand so hard Hamilton saw the man wince. "I don't know what brought you to travel all this way to warn us, but I thank you and I thank God that you did."

Whakely tried to look at Hamilton but succeeded only in looking at the floor. "It was the least I could do to repay your son for helping me keep a little of my self-respect. It is I who owe your House, Baron."

"Nonsense." Hamilton recognized the slightly pontifical tone his grandfather used in announcing major decisions. "It is we who are in your debt for this warning. Should you wish, I would like to offer you a place in our House. Later, when this plague from Castell has been dealt with, we shall find you new accommodations of your own."

"So be it." Whakely knelt and held out his right hand. "You have our Oath."

As the Baron grasped Whakely's hand in both of his, a chill crawled up and down John Hamilton's spine. His grandfather had turned the clock back twelve hundred years. Or had he? Perhaps history had just turned back all by itself, and his grandfather was only the first man wise enough to recognize the fact.

Hamilton wasn't sure he was going to like this new era on Haven, which Howard Whakely had begun with his oath of feudal allegiance to the Baron. He was sure that his early life was doomed whatever happened—and more than likely, his grandfather had thought out the best way of ensuring that there *was* a later life.

John Hamilton raised the visor on his sallet and looked out across the jutting hillocks, to where a plume of smoke rose into the sky like a finger raised in warning. It was one of the hovercars they'd sent out on reconnaissance early this morning. The car's destruction was the first tangible sign of an enemy they'd been following for five days through radio intercepts.

Hamilton still wasn't used to the weight of his armor, but now that weight felt more comforting than confining. So did the massive Gauss gun on his shoulder, ready to throw its slug soundlessly more than a kilometer from the walls.

General Cummings had been able to spare only half a

dozen of the magneto-dynamic weapons, which some-one had once described as "the ultimate sniper's rifle." Even with computerized, laser-assisted telescopic sights, they needed a marksman to get the best use out of them. Hamilton was proud that it was his scores on the rifle range and not his rank that had given him one of the Gausses.

What seemed like an hour but was only about five minutes later, the first enemy armored car topped the hill on Whitehall Road. Five others followed, at inter-vals even Hamilton knew were much too short. Follow-ing them came a positive circus of hovercars, wheeled cars and trucks, busses, a few heavy load carriers, and even half a dozen alcohol tankers. The heaviest weap-ons seemed to be light cannon on three of the armored cars, but the sheer numbers were still awe-inspiring. One estimate they'd heard was fifteen hundred vehi-cles; that was beginning to look conservative.

Right now, though, it was a case of, "The more enemies, the bigger the target." Cummings' last ship-ment had included thirty medium anti-tank missiles, able to use wire-guidance, beam-riding, or fire-and-forget modes equally well. With a target this big and no electronic countermeasures to worry about, the Baron elected to use fire-and-forget.

The first flight of missiles screamed over the walls, locked on to their targets, and raced to meet them. In flames and thunderclaps, four armored cars, several busses, and three of the alcohol carriers went up. So did what must have been a truckload of ammunition. It left a gaping crater in the road, as well as so much smoke Hamilton saw cars colliding in the low visibility. More cars bunched up or drove off the road—to en-counter the pits, deadfalls, and caltrops with hundred-millimeter spikes distributed generously over the ground.

The second flight of missiles had some trouble find-ing targets in the smoke, and Hamilton had more trou-ble seeing how much damage it did. He was sure that the remaining armored cars were gone, though, and the total confusion in the rest of the convoy suggested more damage back there. Still more smoke was rising from either side of the road, as the skirmishers started picking off immobilized armored vehicles and any crews stupid enough to bail out.

By the time a messenger reported that the skirmishers were retiring, about a third of the convoy was destroyed or immobilized. How many men that took out, Hamilton didn't know, but anybody on foot was going to be meat for the skirmishers as they retired, and would be too late for the main party if they arrived at all.

Hamilton realized that he'd been clenching his teeth so hard his jaws ached, and forced himself to relax. They'd been luckier than anyone had dared hope, starting with knocking out all the armored cars in the first exchange of fire. Bunching them up like that had been just plain stupid tactics, the kind you prayed that your enemy would use.

Was Steele really that stupid, or was he short of competent officers—or officers he could trust, (which was probably more important to him than competence)? It would be useful—hell, it might be vital!—to know which. That would mean interrogating prisoners—a job Hamilton would be quite happy to leave to Warden Dunn . . .

When the convoy started moving again, it moved slowly, as if expecting another missile attack. When they realized it wasn't coming, they speeded up, but except for a few all-terrain models, they stayed on the two-lane road.

At half a kilometer the Gauss-gun snipers opened up. At that range a depleted-uranium slug with a steel jacket would go right through most unarmored vehicles.

One car swerved off the road, a mass of flames. Several others rammed their neighbors. The entire convoy ground to a halt again. The Gauss gunners banged away industriously until somebody had the wits to rally the heavier trucks and use them as bulldozers to clear the road. That took care of another fifty-odd vehicles, as well as a host of Hamilton's armor-piercing rounds.

Now the road ran straight toward the castle gate across level ground, free of obstacles. The convoy spread out, some vehicles heading straight toward the walls, others stopping to unload their men. From both vehicles and dismounted men came vigorous, though ragged, small-arms fire. The walls of Whitehall began to be an unhealthy place—or they would have been—for unarmored men.

The dismounted men seemed to be keeping their distance from the walls. A moment later Hamilton realized why, as one of the trucks rammed the gate. The explosion that followed rocked the walls to their foundations and hurled a couple of men down into the courtyard, to lie still. Hamilton picked himself up from the wooden platform and peered through the smoke toward the gate. It looked a little warped, but it was still in place.

Hamilton thanked God and a number of other factors, starting with his grandfather's foresight and a hundred millimeters of durasteel. Then he inserted a magazine of anti-personnel rounds in his rifle and searched the smoke-shrouded ground for lucrative targets.

What turned out to be half an hour went by in a series of enemy feints and charges. Some of the attackers had looted police or Militia body armor. Nemourlon wouldn't stop a Gauss-gun slug, though, and some of the men on the wall had hunted muskylopes or tamerlanes. They could hit a standing man in the head at a hundred meters.

Most of the attackers seemed to know little more than which end of their weapons to hold and which to point at the enemy. Hamilton was hit twice, both times by glancing bullets that only made his armor ring, jarring him. After that, he discovered that his own aim improved, with the knowledge that, if necessary, he could stay in the open and take his time without getting hurt.

Finally the enemy pulled back out of small-arms range, to the cover of the rough ground on either side of the road and the abandoned or wrecked vehicles there. One ragged company went to ground in the old Hamilton fig orchard; that meant no more brandy from those ancient trees. They'd never find out, either, if one of those trees really was the original one where Sergeant Mike Finnegan of Falkenberg's Forty-Second had given them the name of Finnegan's Fig.

Well, you had to be alive to drink brandy or take an interest in history. Hamilton slung his rifle and descended the stairs into the courtyard, looking for his grandfather.

The Baron wore a suit of armor custom-made to accommodate his extra girth. He stood helmetless in the middle of about a dozen men, all arguing vigorously.

"We only get one strike," he said as Hamilton came up. "So we have to make it count. What do you think, John?"

"About what, Grandfather?"

"Cummings promised us one missile strike. I've been holding off on requesting it until the enemy's morale was down."

"It's down about as far as it will go now, I think. Not breeching the gate really shook them. We're lucky they didn't ram the wall. If we give them enough time, somebody will think of doing that."

"Then let's not give them the time." He turned to the communications officer. "Get the coordinates of their main body and put it on the air to Fornova."

The man disappeared at a run. Most of the other officers also left, to organize the counterattack that would follow a successful missile strike. Hamilton didn't want to think about the aftermath of an unsuccessful one.

The communications officer came back. "They're firing two salvos, both time-on-target for extra effect."

"Gary Cummings always did like those little frills and flourishes," muttered the Baron. But he was moving toward the gate as he muttered.

Hamilton followed his grandfather toward the hundred armored men now assembled by the gate. One unsuspected virtue of the armor was that it discouraged his knees from knocking together. There had to be more than three thousand armed men waiting out there; even if the missiles took out half of them that meant the short end of fifteen-to-one odds . . .

One of the sergeants came up to Hamilton and pointed at his Gauss gun. "Better leave that behind, sir. No damned good in a close-range firefight. They'll be all over ya faster'n shit before you can aim."

He handed Hamilton an Ekaterinagrad Arsenal 7-mm assault rifle, or at least a clone of one, with a fifty-round magazine. " 'Fraid there's no bayonet with it, sir."

"I thought bayonets were strictly for ceremony."

"They're real good for riot work, too. That's what we're going to be facing out there, 'long as those friggin' rockets land on their heads and not ours."

Hamilton raised the rifle and shook his head. He should have thought of most of this himself. It still hadn't sunk in that this was a real battle with real people killing and dying, not a Tri-V show he could turn off when he got bored.

It had damned well better sink in fast, he told himself, or he'd be lucky to survive the rest of this battle, never mind the next one. And there would be a next one . . .

Light brighter than any sunlight Haven ever saw flooded the courtyard. Hamilton closed his eyes and opened his mouth, but the blast wave still made his ears ache. He opened his eyes to see dust and small pebbles flying over the walls. The banner on the tower stood out stiff from its pole, until the pole itself snapped off. The ground quivered like a drumhead, and Hamilton needed the sergeant's grip on his arm to stay on his feet.

Before the first blast had died away, the whole sequence came again. This time part of the wooden firesteps on the east wall collapsed. Nobody was on them, though, and only one man was close enough to be hit by falling timber.

As the blast of the second salvo died away, the man lurched to his feet. Hamilton heard the whine of the electric winch opening the gate. The gate crept open halfway, then jammed.

That was enough to show Hamilton a scene from Dante's *Inferno*. Walls and columns of greasy black smoke, patches of red-orange flame, dead men and even worse, the ones running around like human torches . . .

Before Hamilton could be sick, he was swept forward through the gate. After that he was too busy keeping up to think of much else. He was an officer, after all, and not just any officer but the Baron's grandson and heir. If he just behaved like a feudal warrior often enough, maybe everyone would believe he *was* one.

He nearly lost both his nerve and his lunch as they began to squish across bodies and pieces of bodies, not to mention a few that *moved* when you stepped on them. Before Hamilton could react, though, he found himself facing a living man, on his feet and running at him with a pistol. The assault rifle rose almost as if it had a will of its own and the man went down.

A wall of smoke loomed ahead; Hamilton held his breath and charged through, hoping he wasn't walking into a fire left by one of the incendiary warheads. He burst out on the other side, to see a solid mass of shaken and trembling men raising their hands. Twenty armored figures faced them, weapons leveled. One began firing into the crowd; he got off three rounds before Hamilton ran up and knocked him down with the butt of his rifle. Something had to be done fast, or there would be a massacre that would taint everyone here today . . .

"Surround the prisoners. Disarm them, and shoot anyone who tries to escape." His voice seemed to carry the conviction that he knew what he was doing; the Whitehall men started herding the prisoners into a circle. Another fifteen armored men tramped out of the smoke; Hamilton sent them off to secure any useable vehicles.

By the time he heard engines coming to life, he'd made a rough count of the prisoners. Between those in sight and those reported by messengers, they ran well over two thousand. That was a problem he hadn't expected. What in God's name were they going to do with a mob like this? They didn't have any way of feeding or housing them . . .

Five more defenders tramped up; to Hamilton's relief one of them was Warden Dunn. Now he understood one of the reasons for sergeants: to keep the officers from having to stand around, too obviously not knowing what to do next. He gave Dunn orders for getting the prisoners to whatever safety this battlefield offered, then went to look for his grandfather.

The Baron was standing in the middle of the courtyard when Hamilton came through the gate. The next moment he was at his grandson's side.

"Are you all right, John?"

"I'm fine, Grandfather. But I've got some bad news."

"Were our casualties heavy?"

"Just a handful, and only two dead that I've heard of. The missiles took most of the fight out of them. But we've got *two thousand prisoners* out there!"

The Baron rubbed his hands together. "Good, good. That's even better than I'd hoped for."

"What do you mean, better? Where are we going to keep them? How are we going to feed them? If we can't—"

"Slow down, John. We need those men as badly as they need us, only they don't know it yet."

"What?"

"John, how many men do we have at Whitehall?"

"Three hundred, minus the casualties." On one side of the courtyard he saw his sister bandaging some of the men-at-arms.

"Right. Most of them are soldiers; they will be the knights. Where do you think we'll get the peasants?

Remember, a lord has to be self-sufficient. That means a labor force to turn this place back into a working farm. The estates of our friends and allies, too."

Hamilton laughed. "I should have known you'd have it all figured out, Grandfather. But there's going to be more fighting before we can start putting crops in the ground."

"I know. I'm going to offer the prisoners the opportunity to take an oath, after putting in a few weeks building the new outer wall. I don't think many will turn us down. Those who do won't get to go along on the raid. They'll miss the chance for women and booty—"

"Raid? Women? Where?"

"The cars and trucks that still run are going right back to Castell, carrying our soldiers. I think those clowns in the city need a few lessons on how to conduct a raid."

It made sense, once Hamilton thought it over. A few raids on Castell, and David Steele would be too busy defending his capital city to think of stealing anybody's gold and silver. Either that or he'd be booted off his gimcrack "throne" for failing to defend his people. And since he'd probably lost a good percentage of his trustworthy officers in the attempt on Whitehall . . .

"Grandfather, I could almost feel sorry for David Steele. He should have remembered something when he decided to fight you."

"What, John?"

" 'Don't start anything you can't finish.' "

From *ACTION REPORT, ADMIRAL COM-MANDING TASK FORCE 46.2*

At 1423, Red Flight of Fighter Squadron 97 (Carrier CENTURION) engaged a Sauron heavy cruiser, scoring an estimated seven hits. Two fighters (Lt. DeTar and Ensign Hassan) were lost in the engagement, which was broken off due to fuel and ammunition depletion and the evasive action of the Sauron vessel.

The ship was last seen accelerating at 103% of normal maximum, on a course for the Alderson Point. Fragmentary emmission data suggest the intention was to make a Random Jump. It is estimated that the chances of the ship surviving such a Jump in spaceworthy condition are less than 12%. It is also estimated that the ship has less than .004% chance of surviving in condition for further interstellar flight.

THE COMING OF THE EYE

Don Hawthorne

At the point in the Byers Star system where the physics of the Ancient Einstein ended and the Revisionist Alderson began, a tramline existed, along which ships with the Alderson Drive could leap with very little effort from star to star.

That point now shifted, its substance altered slightly, and the near emptiness of space was abruptly filled with several hundred thousand cubic tons displacement of starship.

Strapped into an acceleration couch on the bridge was Vessel Commander First Rank Galen Diettinger, of the Sauron Fleet Heavy Cruiser *Fomoria*. He stirred slightly in the command seat, waiting for the lag effect of jump to wear off. As his vision cleared, Diettinger realized he could make out more details of the bridge surrounding him than he might have liked. Fire had blackened a third of the room, while smoke still drifted lazily in the red glow of the combat lights.

Somehow, they had made it. In Diettinger's mind was an image of the Homeworld as they had jumped. Firestorms and mushroom clouds pockmarked the land. Even the seas roiled as the Imperial ships sought out the undersea cities. A great red wound ran along the main continent of Lebensraum as the Imperial assaults split the planet's crust, while in the space above, the bright lights of the homeland's hopelessly outnumbered Fleet pulsed as each ship died. All but one.

Diettinger stood, stretched, and stepped down on wobbling legs to stand behind Second Rank.

"Summon Weapons and Engineering to the bridge; wardroom meeting of all command ranks in ten minutes." Second Rank began calling the various personnel at their jump stations.

"Positional fix," he said to the Navigations officer beyond Second Rank's duty station. Navigation shook his head.

"Nothing yet, sir. Very low energy emission signals from the system overall. Looks like a real backwater."

Diettinger frowned. Good, and not good. A place to repair and refit the *Fomoria* would have been ideal, but would likely be heavily defended, as well. And they had no strength to secure as such. Next best would have been an area in which they could hide, and this system seemed to fit the bill nicely. But after their escape from three squadrons of Imperial heavy fighters, that would mean two pieces of extreme good fortune in as many hours.

Saurons were trained to think in terms of probabilities, rather than superstition, but the result was essentially the same; Diettinger did not trust that much luck at one time.

The hatch behind him opened, and Engineering stepped through. The Weapons officer accompanying him was bleeding from an arm wound; not serious. Few injuries that did not kill a Sauron outright were.

"Status." Diettinger said to the Weapons officer.

"Point defense systems at thirty percent. Main armament intact, servo-mechanisms down. Repair estimate of thirty hours with materials and crew on-hand."

Diettinger almost smiled. He did not expect fighter craft in this place, wherever it was; their ninety-five percent consumption of Jump-Core power was the maximum possible without guaranteed engine meltdown. It would certainly have carried them far away from the front lines. So point defense didn't really matter. But the main armament could shoot, if not yet aim. He had expected the news to be far more depressing. On that account, Engineering did not disappoint him.

"Jump-Core failure. Total. Manuevering fuel down to twenty percent from a hull breach, four maneuvering engines down, one beyond repair." Formoria only had six. "Internal systems now running on cells. Cells damaged. Forty percent destroyed, twenty percent damaged, forty percent operative."

"You have discretion on manpower and materials necessary for repairs," Diettinger told Engineering. He turned to Weapons. "Dismantle point defense systems and pack them for transport. All repair is to go into returning the main armament to ready. Rig all ordnance for planetary bombardment. Calibrate beam stations for precision surface interaction ops."

Weapons barely raised an eyebrow as he saluted and turned to follow Engineering out the hatch.

Diettinger turned back to Second Rank. She was frowning in obvious puzzlement.

"Wide scan status, Second."

"No interplanetary traffic or communications, First Rank. An automated refueling station in orbit around the inner gas giant. All non-automated signals and emission come from one of the same gas giant's moons."

"Position, sir." Navigation announced.

"Speak."

"Byers Star system. The moon referred to by Second Rank is the only settled body. Local name: 'Haven.' An old CoDo relocation colony, Imperial since the Terran Exodus. We're really on the fringes, sir. Files show no Imperial presence in this entire sector for almost a decade."

Diettinger scowled. That made three pieces of luck, he thought. Well, perhaps he was garnering some of the lost good fortune of all the billions of Soldiers left behind on and above Sauron. The scowl became a smile. Now he really was becoming superstitious.

He consulted the chronometer implanted in his skull: two minutes to the wardroom meeting. Diettinger turned back to Second Rank.

"When Engineering has maneuver up to nominal, make for that automated refueling station. Approach from Haven's blind side. Avoid all detection or other satellites, at all costs. Inform me when on final approach to the station."

Diettinger hurried through the hatch and down the hall. He was experiencing emotions rare among Saurons. Excitement. Anticipation. Out of sight of his fellow Soldiers, he actually grinned.

He was starting to feel lucky.

There were no distinctions of services among Soldiers, only of caste and rank, so the Deathmasters and Breedmasters were directly subservient to him, as a First Ranker. The tone of the conference, Diettinger knew, would have to be maintained along those lines. The Survey officer was presenting as much information as she had on the system they had reached.

"The world is called 'Cat's Eye'; the single habitable moon is Haven. Rotational period for the moon is 87 hours standard, with a longer relative 'day' owing to the considerable illumination provided by the gas giant. Drier than we might like, at only a sixty-percent hydrographic index . . ." The voice of the Survey officer droned on through the communications panel in the wardroom, but the impassive faces for the listeners belied their keen interest.

They were learning about their next conquest, after all, and as soldiers, and especially as Soldiers, they would need every bit of information available to them.

What they had not yet realized, Diettinger thought, was that Haven was to be far more than just another conquest. But that would come soon enough.

Survey ended her report, and Diettinger threw the switch that secured the wardroom from further communications.

"Breedmaster Caius," Diettinger addressed the Soldier charged with the standards of racial and genetic purity among the detachment under Diettinger's command. "How many female Soldiers aboard, including those in the EVA Commandoes we took on back at Sauron?"

"Seventy-three." Diettinger considered the answer a moment, then continued.

"All such personnel are to be removed from active combat and other responsibilities as of the end of this meeting. Also to be removed from the duty roster are those Soldiers aboard, now serving in any capacity, with a Genetic Preference Rating of A-5 and above, as well as any personnel with Ferility Ratings of three or higher."

The physical qualities of the elite EVA Commandoes aboard would make that order cut sharply into available forces, but if Breedmaster had an opinion, he kept it to himself. Diettinger's order was acknowledged with a brief nod.

"Deathmaster Quilland." Diettinger looked farther down the wardroom table, but not to the other end, not quite yet. He wanted the figure seated there to hear all the groundwork before the full plan was revealed. "As senior Staff Rank aboard, you, the Ground Force commanders, and the other Deathmaster Ranks are to review all planetary data as Survey Ranks acquire it. In forty hours, present me with your recommendation of areas planetside that our available forces can secure and hold against counterattacks from such opposition as we might expect to encounter from the locals."

If Breedmaster had reserved his opinion, the Deathmaster did not. Fond of nurturing his caste's reputation for ruthlessness, he broke into a wintry smile at the thought of local resistance having any effect whatsoever against a force of Sauron Supply Clerk Rank cadets. But elite Commandoes? The concept hardly warranted consideration.

"Acknowledged, First Rank."

Despite Imperial propaganda to the contrary, Saurons were not automata, and Diettinger was pleased to see his orders puzzling some of his officers. But now, the hard part. Diettinger looked to the end of the table.

Seated and at ease, the Soldier there yet looked tense as spring steel. Since a portion of his anatomy was not dissimilar to that material, that was hardly surprising.

"Cyborg Rank Koln." Diettinger addressed the figure, deliberately adding the obsolete distinction of "rank." To be a Cyborg was by definition to be a superior being, and many in Sauron society had allowed this attitude to subvert the military chain of command. If his scheme was to have any hope of success, Diettinger would have to overturn that subversion.

"Acknowledged." The voice that answered was rich, warm and deep, resonant with humanity—and identical to that of every other Cyborg Super Soldier. It never failed to awe Diettinger at the power that was—had been—Sauron's, the power to shape the very stuff of life itself.

"You and the other Cyborg Ranks will aid the Deathmasters in the details of said planning. You will not participate in combat operations."

Cyborg Koln's shoulder shifted as he sighed briefly. It made a faint ringing sound as sections of augments met within the genetically-toughened flesh. "May I ask why?" Of all the castes in Sauron society, only the Cyborgs were permitted the luxury of such a question. The very capacity to ask had been trained out of most others.

"You and the other twenty-seven Cyborg Ranks are to present yourselves to Breedmaster Caius for propagation research."

There was a sharp intake of breath on Diettinger's right as Caius realized both the extent of this task and its implications.

"Acknowledged," Cyborg Koln said after a brief pause. Diettinger sensed that he had not resolved the issue but had at least bought himself some time. He nodded once, then addressed the table again.

"There is no Sauron Unified State any longer. No Sauron Trade Bloc, no Sauron-dominated Coalition of Secession." He activated the display screen, and the image of the sundered homeworld glared darkly from it.

"There is, in fact, no Sauron."

The recording played out. The silence was absolute.

"What is left of the homeworld is by now occupied by the forces of the Empire. No matter. The surface of Sauron will be unlivable for a hundred years or more. The war is lost. But the race must not die."

Diettinger's emphasis on the last words would have been expressive among other human species; among Saurons it was almost melodramatic. But it had the desired effect on those listening. They could guess what was coming, and they wanted to hear more.

"This system is isolated. Trade charts of the area have not been updated in over seventy-five years. Records indicate that not so much as a regiment of Imperial Marines has been in this sector in ten years. Fate," he smiled; none of them believed in fate any more than did he, "has brought us here to stay. This must now be home."

He began to outline his plan.

On the main continent of Haven, along the densely populated equatorial region of the Shangri-La Valley, the last operational orbital surveillance station remaining was entering its Trueday duty shift. Warren Delancey arrived at work with the pastry and hot morning tea typical of clerks throughout the universe.

An offworlder might have noticed the starchiness of the pastry and the poor flavor of the tea, but Delancey had grown up in the years of Haven's decline, even before the Empire finally left for good. Good tea was for him but a dim memory. And Haven had not seen offworlders for a long time.

Delancey's duties now consisted mostly of simple study. The last trader ship to come through had been an independent bearing a paltry few hundred tons of marginally useful items, whose captain and crew had admitted to finding Haven only by accident. At that, they had been looking for some place else. Delancey sighed.

No point dwelling on the past, he thought. And nothing to be gained. Today's task at hand greeted him in the form of a hundred pages of manuscript.

"What's this?" His assistant, a young student named Alec Farmen, idly (and rather rudely, Delancey thought) picked up the manuscript and began flipping through it.

"Orbital data program from the University. They want data on the degree of oscillation—"

"—oscillation in the storm 'pupil' of Cat's Eye, right?" Alec finished Delancey's sentence, dropped the manuscript in disgust and collapsed sprawling into a chair. "God, how can you stand it, Warren?"

Delancey scowled. He did not much care being called by his first name by a fellow ten years his junior, but what could you expect from young people these days? Rude, undisciplined, sullen. Most of them went straight from their farms or the cities into one bully-boy private army or another.

As for Alec: well, his usefulness was unquestioned. He could tinker about and fix nearly any piece of equipment they had here at the station, but God, he could be irritating. He stayed on at University only because he couldn't abide even the poor discipline a para-military life might force on him.

The University, Delancey thought. A center of learning. He almost snorted. Everyone knew the University had become a joke. Enoch Steele Redfield and his Redfield Satrapy only kept it open because it was a source of technology. And technology meant weapons.

In the thirteen years since the final collapse of the central government, two things had been happening on Haven. Rival city states tried to absorb or kill each other off, and Haven itself tried to kill everybody. The planet had never been hospitable, only tolerable. Now, with the high technology and industrial strength of the Empire rapidly fading from memory . . .

". . . going on, I mean, how would we know?" Alec was speaking to him. Or, more accurately, at him.

"Eh? What did you say?"

The young man heaved the great, expansive sigh of all youth at the stupidity of the universe. "I said, if the war had ended or was still going on, how would we know about it? I read the newspaper every day. I see the same pointless muskylope dung—" Delancey started at the vulgarity "—in the 'News of the Empire' section year after year. There's nothing 'new' about any of it; it's all recycled filler material, The Emperor's third cousin's seventh niece has married the same minor lord about fifteen times, now, by my count."

Alec leaned toward Delancey. "I mean, when was the last time you actually read or even heard of a message packet from Coreward, eh, Warren?"

Delancey shook his head, more in exasperation than agreement. Of course Haven had been abandoned by the Empire, but her people hadn't yet given up hope that it was only a retreat, not a withdrawal. Alec's generation was growing up with the stigma of that abandonment, knowing it for what it was.

"Alec, just do your job, all right? Just get to work, and . . ." at a loss for words, he finally just grabbed the manuscript and thrust it at the younger man. "And do your job, yes?" he repeated.

Alec rose and stalked off, the pages of the manuscript fluttering in the speed of his departure. Delancey turned back to his terminal. The equipment had been old twenty years ago, and now the data line at the bottom of the screen had actually burned into the panel.

Delancey shrugged. People got set in their ways. Why shouldn't their machines? He suspected the data line had stopped working right years ago. Not that it mattered. Nothing ever happened in the Haven system, anyway.

The screen showed no activity within range of Haven's remaining surveillance satellites. If there had been any, a section of the data line would have flashed amber, and Delancey could have called up enhancement of the detection.

Delancey might then have known that his life, and indeed life as he and everyone else on Haven knew it, could now be measured in hours.

"Until off-world communication from Haven is neutralized, nothing is to connect us in any way with either the operations at the homeworld or even as Saurons." Diettinger was addressing the Survey Ranks in the wardroom.

"Our physiognomy is unmistakably Sauron; there is little we can do about that, except for our troops to avoid being seen until the landing is secured. By then, it won't matter. Should any of the cattle"—he used the Sauron term for any noncombatant—"or their soldiers manage to send off a message announcing their plight, they must think they are being attacked by pirates or raiders." Diettinger added: "These days, with the Empire collapsing as fast as it is, no one will bother to do anything about that."

Diettinger took a sip of water. There were only two thousand gallons left aboard, and it was strictly rationed until more could be brought up from the surface of Haven. "You have the data I asked for, Second?"

Second Rank's face showed frank disapproval. She was a Soldier, and while her training taught the wisdom of covert actions, this latest wrinkle did not sit well with her.

"Yes, First Rank. Pirates in these outlying sectors name their ships and outfit their ground forces after myths: an expression of the swaggering attitude prevalent among the criminal element in cattle. Of such fictions extant throughout this arm of the Empire, those of Terran origin are still the most widely known. There is an ironic appeal to the one I've chosen. It fits both our needs and character, and even contains a reference to our racial name; an interesting note, as the origins of the word 'Sauron' are largely unknown."

Now it was Diettinger's turn to raise an eyebrow. "I just said there was to be no connection, Second Rank. Is this an act of rebellion against your new status as a noncombatant?"

The wardroom went still as Second Rank's temper flared silently in her eyes. As she spoke, she calmed sufficiently to remove the edge from her voice.

"Respectfully, First Rank, it is not. The myth at issue is an obscure piece of adventure fiction. It possesses several almost complete artificial languages, one of which has many tonal qualities and guttural expressives designed to evoke specific racial responses in readers of standard Anglic. The language there is useful even as a code, since my records indicate that the work of fiction from which the whole myth derives has sunk into oblivion."

Diettinger listened to Second Rank's defense with some enjoyment. Verbose for a Sauron, he thought her. Second Rank's need to justify her actions was, he suspected, what had kept her from First Rank status.

"Using the myth," Second Rank continued more calmly, "requires the alteration of our uniforms to a small degree, as well as the outlines of our ground-attack fighters and the transponders on the *Fomoria* herself."

"Acceptable. See that it's done. First modify the fighter craft; I want very large markings of whatever style you've chosen. Use them in several low-level attacks to announce our presence to the locals. The temporary billets in the docking bay will have to be moved; Supply Ranks are to be responsible for that." The Survey Ranks acknowledged the orders and left to carry them out.

Diettinger considered a moment. "You have a tape of this obscure work of fiction, Second Rank?" he asked.

"Fragments only, First Rank."

"Let me see it."

Second Rank produced the tape. It was labelled on one side: DOMINANCE MYTHS/HUMAN NORMS/TERRENE.

Most likely from one of the old Breedmaster's political research tracts, but possibly from Second Rank's private collection; she was rumored to be something of an anthropologist and historian.

The other side of the tape bore its title. Diettinger read it aloud.

"*The Lord of the Rings* . . ." he said. Perhaps Second Rank was right, he thought. There was a sort of power in those words, at that.

Captain Marinus Leino of the Novy Finlandia Air Force had just taxied his small biplane onto the runway for takeoff. Behind him, the four other planes of his squadron waited their turn, their bright metal skins gleaming in the early morning Trueday sun. As he looked back towards the hangar for clearance, he spotted the mechanic, Flynn, running towards him, a communiqué flimsy in his hand. The biplane's engine was designed for virtual silence, but Leino still had to shout; Flynn's hearing wasn't what it used to be.

"What's the matter?" Leino's voice held some concern; his wife was expecting, and in Haven's thin atmosphere, there was no such thing as an easy birth.

Flynn staggered against the thin metal frame of the ship, gasping for breath. He handed the note up to Leino in the cockpit.

"Just came in," the older man gasped. "They said you had—to check—it out; goddammit!" Flynn caught some breath and spat, cursing his age and infirmity. And to think he had once taken the Emperor's shilling as an Imperial Marine. He cursed again.

Leino smiled down at him, setting the throttle to idle as he read the note.

TO: MARINUS LEINO, CAPTAIN, NOVY FINLANDIA AIRDEFCOM
RE: COASTAL PATROL, 1TD, SABBAD

YOU ARE INSTRUCTED TO PROCEED POSTHASTE WITH

FULL SQUADRON TO CENTRAL BORDER DISTRICT,
COASTAL, THERE TO RNDZVS W/AIR UNITS OF REDFIELD
SATRAPY. DO NOT—REPEAT—DO NOT FIRE ON REDFIELD
UNITS; THEY ARE UNDER YOUR COMMAND FOR JOINT
OPS, INVESTIGATION OF CONFIRMED—REPEAT—CON-
FIRMED SIGHTINGS OF SUPRAORBITAL SCOUT CRAFT.
ASCERTAIN ID SAID S/O CRAFT AND RETURN. DO NOT
ATTEMPT TO ENGAGE SAME.

N/F AIRDEFCOM

END.

Leino laughed outright at the last order. Engage an
orbital fighter with a biplane? Good thing they ex-
pressly forbade it, he thought sarcastically. Idiots.

"Is this some sort of joke?" he asked Flynn. The old
mechanic waved his hands in exasperation. The propwash
whipped his clothes and thin hair.

"How in the hell do I know? You think I run like this
for the jollies? You're the flyboy, you find out!" Flynn
stalked off, cursing anew.

Leino grinned. Might as well get to it, he thought.
He would hardly have believed the report himself, but
for the rendezvous with the Redfielders; to get the
Novy Finlandia government and the Redfielders to cooperate on anything would take nothing less than off-
planet contact.

He sincerely hoped there was no mistake; putting his
boys in close formation with those Redfield thugs was
not his happiest duty. But he didn't worry—much.

His squadron's guns were loaded. He was confident
they could handle anything fate might throw their way.

Orbital fighters, he thought again, and laughed, shaking his head. Almost anything.

The *Fomoria* refueled without incident at the automated station orbiting Cat's Eye. Meanwhile, her four
surviving fighters were making low level runs to the

surface of Haven, then back out to a close orbit. Their occasional strafing attacks on communications centers were accompanied by false signals to the "pirate fleet" standing off from Haven, supposedly in orbit around Cat's Eye.

Diettinger was conferring with Weapons on the bridge as the Fomoria cleared the station on five maneuver engines; Engineering had done his best, but the sixth engine had, indeed, been beyond repair.

"Charges status." Diettinger said quietly.

"Telemetry indicates full functions, all, First Rank."

The station dwindled rapidly as the Fomoria pulled away at increasing speed. Finally, it was lost from sight against the immensity of Cat's Eye's dark spot, the 'pupil' of the gas giant.

Diettinger waited a moment longer. With his next order, their fate would be sealed, for the Fomoria had taken on only half-tanks for her final operation. With the station gone, their bridges would be burned behind them. Steeped as Diettinger was in martial history, the parallels to the Sauron role model of the Ancient, Julius, were not lost on him.

"Activate."

Weapons did not hesitate. With the press of a key, Cat's Eye's pupil developed a brilliant white cataract, fading in an instant as the station was consumed.

"Very good." Diettinger said simply, turned and went back to the Chair. In him now was the excitement he felt before any battle. They were only human normals on Haven, to be sure; not even Imperial Marines. Not much, really, as opponents went. But Survey had told him that the planet was so inhospitable that, with the loss of what little technological base existed there, it would prove as worthy an adversary as any Soldier could hope for.

"On to Haven, Second Rank." Diettinger spoke matter-of-factly, subduing the fact that maneuvering the *Fomoria* into position for the strike would be Second Rank's last official duty as a Soldier. Diettinger had already extended the deadline for her relief, but soon it would be unavoidable. She was far too valuable as breeding stock to risk in ground ops. She had to accept it, but she didn't have to like it, nor did he. Although he wasn't quite positive why.

Warren Delancey leaned forward and tapped his screen. His data line was flickering again. That was twice in the past hour. Not that it mattered; he was due to be relieved in another three hours. But it was annoying. Enoch Redfield took a dim view of technicians who were on duty when equipment failed, for whatever reason.

There it was again. The band flickered amber, green, red, and then back to its usual blue. Quite distracting. Delancey supposed he had better do something about it, after all. The old computers weren't much, but they were a damn sight better than almost anything else on Haven.

Delancey thought he had just about traced the problem to its source when Alec breezed into the room behind him.

"How's it working?"

Delancey looked up, distracted. "Hmm? How's what?"

Alec pointed to the terminal, grinning.

"I found a couple of bad boards in the system a few hours ago. I've been setting new ones from the stores. Is your screen any better?"

For a moment, Delancey was almost touched by the younger man's solicitude; it was evident by his tone and manner that Alec was attempting an act of rapprochement, something he had formerly seemed incapable of. But on returning his gaze to the screen, Delancey's low opinion of the youth returned.

"Evidently not. Look at that." Delancey jabbed an accusing finger at the screen. The data line was bright orange. The words flashing on it in brighter yellow read:

UNIDENTIFIED WARSHIP IN SYSTEM. ENHANCEMENT? Y/N

Alec frowned. He was obviously torn between wanting to believe the detection and admitting he had erred in his tests on the new boards he had installed. "Well, couldn't it really be . . . ?"

Delancey's smirk of disapproval killed the question on the young man's lips.

"At least with the bad boards, something worked. Now I can't even recall the storm oscillation data. You must have lost the fix on the transceiver at the refueling station." Delancey's voice had taken on a patronizing, accusing tone. If Alec had lost the transceiver, that would likely be the end of the boy. Only one vessel was left that was able to reach the station. It was kept in neutral territory and was commonly owned by all the fractured power groups on Haven. That meant no one used it much. No one, especially, was going to be happy about using it to fix some University student's blunder.

"You'll be lucky if they don't just launch *you* into orbit." Delancey muttered as Alec left the room. Or both of us, for that matter. He decided to call his relief and tell him not to bother coming in; the fewer people who knew about this, the better. Maybe Alec could get things back to normal before anybody found out about it.

"The designation of the *Fomoria* now reads as the '*Dol Guldur*,' First Rank. Markings match those applied to the outer skin of the suborbital fighters and Full Battlesuits. All uniforms now bear the patch with the insignia and trappings described in my report."

Second Rank showed Diettinger photos of the units mentioned. In particular, the flarings added to the battlesuits rendered them unrecognizable as Sauron in make. The plain grey uniform tunics of the command Ranks and those of the troopers now carried extraneous decoration to aid in the deception. And all bore the insignia Second Rank had provided: a lidless eye, wreathed in flames. Diettinger smiled thinly at the patch he wore over his own left breast pocket.

"Suitably sinister," he said. "Very good work, Second." Second inclined her head at the compliment. Such praise was rare in Sauron society, and Diettinger's carried more warmth than he had intended.

"I read those fragments, by the way, Second." Diettinger changed the subject. "I fail to appreciate the irony in some mythical dark god of terror and oppression bearing the same name as our people."

Second Rank frowned.

"That was not the irony I referred to, First Rank."

"Indeed? Clarify."

"It isn't that the myth matches us; it's the other way around. The *Fomoria* was named for a race of mythical demonic conquerors from the seas of Old Earth, who engaged in a war of extermination against the land peoples of an island kingdom. Like the myth in those fragments, their leader was . . ." Second Rank stopped, swallowed.

"Go on."

"Was represented by the symbolism of an eye. In the fragments, it is a single, flaming red orb. In the myth of the Fomorians . . ." Second Rank seemed to be gathering her will for the next part of her explanation.

"In the myth of the Fomorians, their leader was a fearsome, brilliant giant: Balor of the One Eye. His eye was pried open by soldiers on the battlefield, and its power was such as to destroy all who came under its gaze."

Diettinger was openly grinning, now. "What a delightful fairy-story, Second," he said. "And did they win?"

Second Rank shook her head. "No sir. They did not."

Diettinger's grin went to a half-smile, the lines in his cheek deepening under the patch that covered his empty left eye-socket.

"That's because it was only a story, Second."

Leino's squadron had formed up in minutes, and rapidly climbed to a cruising altitude of two kilometers.

Their operational ceiling was much higher, but Leino wanted to save oxygen for high altitude reconnaissance at the rendezvous point. Haven's air was thin enough as it was; at altitude it was almost non-existent; the oxygen would be a precious commodity throughout the mission.

Engines hardly louder than the hum of the guy wires in the slipstream, the five biplanes were at the sea in minutes, then turned north to follow the coastline up to the Coastal Border District, the newest demilitarized zone between the Redfield Satrapy and Novy Finlandia.

Leino considered the approach to the border with a grim shake of his head. Every year his equipment and recruits got better, but there were fewer of both. Every year, the Redfield Satrapy seemed to double its available forces and their inferior equipment.

Inferior, but far more easily maintained. And there were many more of them. Leino wondered how many times in human history the best had been overwhelmed by the numerically superior mediocre. Best not to think about it, he decided. His ship's chronometer told him they should be within radio range of the Redfield squadron by now.

"Signal, signal," he spoke, holding his throat microphone. "This is Novy Finlandia Recon Number Seven, Leino commanding." It was also Novy Finalandia Everything Else, Number Seven; he didn't think the Redfielders were fooled into believing Novy Finlandia had ships to spare for specialized duty. But he repeated the identification and proceeded to hail the as yet unseen Redfield squadron. "Approaching rendezvous point for joint operations. Redfield Satrapy aircraft squadrons, do you read?"

The answer came back after a few seconds. "Affirmative, Finlandia Recon, this is Redfield Interceptor Squadron Viggen, Viggen commanding." For a moment, Leino was impressed; only the very best pilots had their squadrons named after them. This Viggen fellow must be quite the golden boy of the Redfield Satrapy Air Force.

"You are twelve degrees south-southwest of our position, time-to-contact, seven minutes, over."

Leino grinned. They would have to let him know that they were aware of his aircraft's speed and range capabilities. Still, for Redfielders, they were being positively civil.

"Confirmed, Viggen," he answered. "Seen any spooks today?"

Leino's attempt to lighten the mood was apparently unappreciated.

"We will hold at thirty-five hundred meters until we have you in visual, Recon. Viggen out."

Leino passed the information on to his squadron, closed the circuit, and sighed. The damn Redfielders had no sense of humor.

"To maximize the speed of the initial attack . . ." Weapons was presenting his bombardment operation plan to Diettinger and Second Rank in the wardroom. ". . . I have posted the '*Dol Guldur*' on a contra-orbital run along the equator. Thus even Haven's minor rotational speed is added to our orbital velocity. We can make a complete circumnavigation well within time constraints, even allowing margins necessary to acquire and fire upon the target positions indicated as they come over the horizon."

Diettinger was concerned at the ease with which the crew accepted the *Fomoria*'s new name, not to mention the open delight they had for the new uniforms. As Soldiers, they were expected to follow orders unquestioningly, and Diettinger had, indeed, ordered them to refer to the ship as the *Dol Guldur* and themselves as pirates, to get into the feel of the deception. Still, he sometimes felt that the appeal of the whole thing was getting out of hand.

He returned his attention to the holographic projection of Haven, on which Weapons was indicating various target zones.

"Haven's cold climate and thin atmosphere have concentrated virtually all of her population in the equatorial region. Within that region, only the lowest altitude zones—valleys and coastal areas—have enough air for comfort." Contempt crept into Weapons' voice as he spoke. "The typical cattle aversion to hardship has lined them up in perfect targetting position, sir."

Diettinger nodded. He studied the holographic display. Across its surface were scattered points of light in white, yellow, red. Concentrations of industry, energy generation, and communications, in relative order, as determined by the Survey Ranks. There were pitifully few of any of them. Diettinger indicated one particularly large cluster on the major land mass.

"Survey is confident that this concentration in—what is this valley called?"

"Shangri-La, First Rank." Second Rank provided the name with a hint of irony.

"Shangri-La. This concentration poses no real threat? No planetary defense positions of any sort, nothing they might have kept secret all these years?" Diettinger felt he might be unduly concerned about such matters. But he had only to consider the consequences of failure to realize that the phrase "unduly concerned" was meaningless.

"Highly unlikely, sir," Weapons said. "The Haveners don't seem to know the meaning of security; their comm broadcasts tell us the disposition of their fractured governmental militaries down to the ammunition allocation in their local militia." Weapons was obviously scornful of the attitude these cattle applied to their own security, but still pleased at how easy it made his job.

"Good. Then the target priorities remain the same." Diettinger held his right hand an inch off the table, placing a finger against the metal surface as he enumerated each item: "We eliminate all satellites of out-system communications capability. Anything we might find useful, such as weather or surveillance satellites, are to be left alone. Planetary emplacements capable of off-world or out-system communications—evidently they relied very heavily for such things on the transceiver equipment we saw at that automated refueling station. We won't depend on it, however. These ground targets are to be nuked."

Diettinger paused a moment. "Will doubling up on these targets leave us any nuclear weapons in stores?"

Weapons nodded. "Plenty, First Rank. We had little chance to use our stocks against the Imperials."

"Good. Then also modify some for enhanced electromagnetic pulse. Use your own judgment for how many, but guarantee me no coordinated broadcast communications on Haven for at least one hundred hours. And none whatsoever to be beamed off-planet."

Weapons acknowledged the order as Diettinger finished the target list; energy generation centers were next, industrial centers last. Without power, the industrial targets would be useless anyway, until the Saurons appropriated them. The soldiers would be bringing their own energy generation equipment to Haven.

Cutting off all communication from Haven was critical to Diettinger's long-range plans. Any signal leaving the target world would crawl along at the speed of light and take decades to reach Imperial ears. But the Empire might take centuries to collapse to the point where it no longer posed a threat to Diettinger's people. And he had no doubt that the discovery of a remnant of Sauron, however pitiful, would bring as many Imperial ships as could still jump, for a last battle of extermination. And this time, there would be no escape.

He turned to Second Rank. "You established the flight plan for this orbital run, Second?"

She paused, watching him with a level gaze. "Yes, First Rank. All the information and target dispositions have been entered into the flight program. Navigation can activate it from his station. I have constructed the program with enough detail to let even a cadet use it." Her bitterness was unmistakable, inexcusable, and, Diettinger realized, impossible to alleviate. If they were to survive as a race, as an ideal, it would depend on the success of his plans from this day on.

And the greatest part of those plans lay in breeding.

"Thank you, Second Rank. Well done." Again Diettinger could not hold back the warmth in his praise of Second Rank. He knew how she felt at relief from her duties, and he honestly regretted losing her. He marvelled that he had kept an officer of her qualifications at all, in those last dark days of the war.

Sadly, though, he realized his sympathy was not enough. Nothing ever could be. Diettinger thought it ironic that, as Soldiers, the living embodiment of the term, Saurons had always been taught to willingly make any sacrifice required of them. But how did you ask them to sacrifice being Soldiers?

Diettinger answered his own question. You didn't ask, he knew. Soldiers never asked, never were asked, anything. Soldiers gave and took orders.

"Report to Breedmaster Caius in Bay Seven." Diettinger made the order brief. Second Rank saluted and left the wardroom without a word.

The silence had returned, Diettinger noticed. Saurons were not a gregarious race, but the tension over the operations of the next few hours had brought them all to even deeper levels of concentration on the tasks at hand. Diettinger went to the bridge, where Navigation told him the desired trajectory had been achieved.

"Status on scout fighters?"

"Reconnaissance shows no concerted military effort planetside. Individual city-states seem to be alerted to the fighters, but no sign that they know about our position, or even that we're here."

Diettinger shook his head. The *Fomoria*—that is, the *Dol Guldur*—must be visible to anybody with a decent telescope by now. He sighed. This really was going to be depressingly easy, he thought.

"Give the fighters another fifteen minutes, then re-call them. Secure for planetary assault."

"Acknowledged, First Rank."

*   *   *

Leino saw the Redfielders first, six ugly wood and low-reflection canvas triplanes in formation above his own ships.

"Leino here. Redfielders, please acknowledge."

"We have you, Novy Finlandia. No contacts, here. Base informs us our ground observers spotted two, repeat, two Extra-Atmospheric fighter craft this vicinity. Reports Ex-At fighters did some damage to ground targets, not serious. Any luck with your group?"

"Negative, Redfielders. No contacts our altitude. You have oxygen aboard?"

"Of course."

Leino shook his head. Just trying to be polite, he thought. "Let's split up into two-plane groups. One of yours, one of mine; our craft have a slightly higher ceiling than yours. My man goes top cover over your man, both get as high as possible. We can rotate the pairs as their O_2 gets low."

The Redfielder did not answer immediately. Perhaps he was offended by Leino's reference to the superior ceiling of his own ships; with fighter craft, altitude was everything. Touchy people.

"Good show, Leino," the Redfielder came back coolly. Leino was mildly surprised at the compliment. "But our craft use less fuel than yours, and have much greater range. Your man should take a quick jump to altitude, straight up to maximum, straight down; ours can circle below him."

Leino caught the humor in the Redfielder's voice and barely suppressed an outright laugh of his own. Despite the obvious merits of the Redfielder's modification to his own plan, the temptation between two fighter pilots to out-boast one another was irresistible.

"Acknowledged, Viggen. This round to you."

"Thank you, Leino. Standing by for your orders."

Leino did laugh, then. Orders said there would be no dogfighting between their forces, but that didn't mean they wouldn't still find some way to duel.

Delancey's relief had been only too glad to accept a day off from orbital surveillance. Delancey hoped that Alec could fix whatever he had done wrong before anybody in the Redfield forces called them on it. Some officer, Kettler, of the Redfielder Air Force had tried calling him three times already, and Delancey felt his story of 'sunspot interference' was wearing a little thin on the man's nerves.

The data line stubbornly resisted every effort to change it from amber to anything else.

Worse still, it was now flashing a secondary red line on the left and another on the right.

ALERT: SUBORBITALS DETECTED IN ATMOSPHERE	ALERT: UNIDENTIFIED WARSHIP HAS ENTERED CLOSE ORBIT
ENHANCE? Y1/N1	ENHANCE? Y2/N2

UNIDENTIFIED WARSHIP IN SYSTEM. ENHANCEMENT? Y/N

Delancey hissed in irritation and began pounding keys. What had that fool been doing, playing war games with the master program again? He spun hard about in his chair, his elbows hitting a forgotten tea cup and spilling the icy brew across his lap and the floor.

"Alec!" he shouted down the hall. "Dammit to hell, boy! Do you want to get us both shot? What the devil are you doing back there?"

There was no answer. In a moment, Delancey heard Alec's footsteps as he raced up the corridor toward him. The boy burst into the room, grabbing the doorframe to stop himself. The look on his face sent Delancey cold. Alec seemed to be terrified and elated at the same time. Was he using drugs? the older man thought; is that why he had fouled things up so badly?

"Warren . . ." Alec was at a loss for words. "It's real."

"What?" Delancey asked in a small voice. He knew very well what, but he couldn't believe it.

"The ship. It's out there, whatever it is. I've checked and re-checked everything a dozen times over. I did everything right. It's the old boards that were bad. There really is a ship out there. A warship, Delancey! An Imperial warship!"

He ran past Delancey to the screen and began hamming at keys with trembling hands.

"Enhancement, hell yes, I want enhancement!" Alec muttered. Delancey, overwhelmed by the younger man's energy, began to get excited, too. But he was older than Alec; in the excitement was also fear. Warship, the computer said.

They tensely watched the screen as the computer began accessing its outdated files for something which looked like the vessel the satellite had spotted. In a few nanoseconds, it had acquired enough of a suitable list of comparative data to be reasonably sure of its assessment.

ENHANCEMENT COMPLETE:
WARSHIP IS SAURON HEAVY CRUISER, 'TALON' CLASS NOW ORBITING IN CONTRA-ROTATIONAL BOMBARDMENT PATH

DEFAULTING TO EMERGENCY NAVAL ALERT CHANNEL VIA 'CAT'S EYE' REFUELING STATION RELAY DISH

EMERGENCY NAVAL ALERT CHANNEL INOPERATIVE. RE-LAY STATION NOT RESPONDING. PRESUMED DESTROYED.

Delancey's first thought was incongruous relief that it had not been his and Alec's fault that the station transceiver signal had been lost. In a moment, he forced the words out.

"We've got to tell someone, Alec."

Alec stepped slowly back from the terminal, sat down in the chair beside Delancey. "Who?" he asked finally.

"Who do we tell? Against Saurons?" He ended in a ragged shout.

Delancey looked around him at the large, empty room, most of its computers long gone. Gone too were the Imperial orbital defense techs who had once watched over Haven. All that was left was dust, neglect, and the ghosts of machines long since cannibalized for the very metal of their bones. A great, hollow, drafty place with a puddle of cold tea on the floor. Abandoned. Forgotten.

Thrown to the wolves, he thought in sudden bitterness.

"Who could do anything about it?" Alec whispered.

After another moment of stunned inactivity, Delancey realized he was shaking. But not in fear, not anymore. In anger. He yanked the telephone from its cradle and began pushing buttons with a grim rhythm.

"Hello, Defense Operations? I want to speak with the Redfield Air Command, Colonel Kettler, please."

The second pair of Redfield/Finlandia planes was maneuvering to relieve the first as Leino watched from a circling pattern due west. A boring and silly exercise, he had decided, but it did give him and his men the chance to study the Redfield ships and pilots at close quarters.

The last skirmish with the Redfield Satrapy had brought a few of their planes down in Novy Finlandia territory, and the technicians were both delighted and astonished to find that the enemy aircraft had wooden frames with canvas skins; except for the engine, almost no structural metal at all. This made them more fragile than the Finlandia aircraft, but lighter and more agile as well, much less prone to stall or lose control in the thin atmosphere of Haven.

It was Leino and the fighter pilots like him who had to learn that the Redfielder ships were also practically invisible to Finlandia's powerful radars, modified from designs for detecting metal-skinned jets. They learned that the Redfield planes didn't appear on their screens until very close, indeed. And they learned it the hard way.

It made an interesting match, Leino thought. He himself had brought down three of the Redfielder's ships in that last flare-up, but the enemy had given a good accounting of themselves, as well.

Something gleamed along the coast, two thousand meters below. Two somethings, Leino corrected himself.

"Viggen, this is Leino, do you read?"

"Leino, this is Viggen, I see them. Do you have a signature?"

The Redfielder's voice had gone tense. Leino's radar had not sounded its detection tone. He increased the gain, aligning his aircraft towards the two glittering streaks below, already very much closer than any conventional aircraft could have gotten so quickly, and climbing. There was still no image on his screen. And they were obviously metal jets.

"Negative, Viggen. Either they're jamming us or using—"

Leino's voice choked on the word "deflectors;" the level of technology required to render jet aircraft invisible to radar was so far beyond his experience as to be practically mythological.

Another voice came on over the channel, one of Viggen's squadron.

"They're splitting up, sir, one making for—Krysta!"

The spook passed so close that Leino could clearly see the great, flaming eye insignia on the fuselage, could even make out the pilot in fully secure extra-orbital flight gear.

Pirates, he realized, and in the next instant a thunderous shock wave of displaced air battered Leino's aircraft straight up and back. Leino's face struck the instrument panel, shattering glass, and blood filled his eyes. The shock wave must have deafened him, too, because he couldn't hear his engine. He hoped it was his ears, anyway, as he wiped the blood from his face. He would need the engine to recover, now; his airplane had gone into a flat spin.

*　　*　　*

Fighter Rank Vil smiled at the fragility of the cattle's craft. Museum pieces, he thought in wonder. He hadn't actually meant to destroy them, only shake them up a bit, but at least two of the triple-winged high ones, the ones that didn't register on his radar, had simply disintegrated as he passed. Fascinating, really. He looked down at the remaining cattle ships, most out of control, one or two fighting to recover from his pass. He saw no parachutes.

Interesting, he thought.

Still, any survivors would have the word out that the "pirates" were here, in force. He and his wingman, Stahler, had been waiting all morning to show off their newly painted fighter craft.

Fighter Rank Stahler hailed him on the combat frequency. "Amazingly fragile ships."

"Affirm. What do you think of my introduction to the cattle of the *Dol Guldur*'s air superiority?"

"Effective, but a bit overpowering, don't you think?"

Vil checked his screen and visuals. He shrugged unconsciously.

"Evidently not. A couple of the kites are reforming. We should have time to scrap another pair before returning. Let's go subsonic; be sure to give them a good look. I'll show them some vertical thrust maneuvers."

"Have fun," Stahler said without emotion. He had not embraced the pirate role as wholeheartedly as Vil, and he had never believed in arrogance toward an outclassed opponent. Desperate foes did desperate things, and could very easily surprise you.

The flat spin was often fatal, Leino recalled from his flight school classes. None of the aircraft's control surfaces interacted with the surrounding airstream the way they had been designed to. Novy Finlandia craft used to have tail 'chutes or canard airfoils to help in such situations, but that was a long time ago.

Leino began going over every technique he knew to recover from the spin. Every aircraft type recovered in a different way, and you couldn't really be sure how a particular ship would do it, if at all, until the time arrived. By then there was often no time to learn.

But he was lucky; he had altitude, his engine was still running, even his hearing had come back; in one ear, anyway. The airframe was making a high-pitched rattling sound, like a snare drum.

Leino dropped the flap opposite to the direction of the spin and kicked the rudder likewise as far as it would go. The airframe groaned impressively, but there seemed to be little effect otherwise. The ground was a good deal closer, now. Leino repeated his last maneuver and added a hard push on the stick, then yanked the throttle.

The biplane shuddered as its engine roared, the tachometer needle snapping past the red-line. The ship stood on one wing, turned onto its nose, and dropped like a stone into a power dive. Wonderful, Leino thought. At least before I was going to die sitting down, not face first.

But he could recover from a dive. He pulled out with a scarce hundred meters of daylight beneath him. He didn't black out, and that was a blessing, too. Recovering with a roll, Leino regained his former altitude to see the formation utterly shattered. Three aircraft were missing from the Redfielders, and one of his own as well.

The spooks were nowhere to be seen, but at the speeds they were obviously capable of, they could be back at any moment.

"Viggen, this is Leino, do you read?" His voice sounded funny to him; he ran his tongue over his gums, finding very little left of his front teeth. I must look wonderful, he thought; blood running down my face and no teeth. The wife'll love this.

"Leino, this is Viggen, I read you; thought we'd lost you for a few seconds there. Nice flying."

"Thanks. What the devil were those things?"

"Looked like supra-orbitals. Insignia make them pirates, by my guess. And pirates would make that sort of pass on ships like ours; arrogant bastards. Shock wave took our four of our boys. Sorry, still no pickup on radar."

The radios squawked with another signal.

"Break, break, break. This is Viggen Four." It was the Redfielder pilot who had been at high altitude with one of Leino's men.

"Go ahead, V-Four." Viggen said. The Redfielder squadron was indeed well trained; despite the obvious superiority of their opposition, they had all reformed into flying formation, and Leino's boys were right with them. Leino felt a little better. He was airborne among some of the best Haven had to offer.

Not that it had saved four of them when the supersonic skytrain had gone by.

"I have visual on the spooks, bearing 227 degrees, very far below your position, closing fast. Doesn't look like they're making the same speed as before, sir."

"Leino, I am to defer to you in this mission," Viggen's voice came through with a hard edge of desire. "What are your orders, engage or disperse?"

"My orders for my group were specific that Finlandia ships were not to fire on your ships, nor to engage these things, Viggen."

"You are breaking up, Leino, say again." Viggen's signal was crystal clear.

"Leino out."

Good luck, Viggen, he thought. I would very much like to have met you. He banked his craft and watched the Redfielders position themselves for the interception courses that would perhaps allow them a firing pass at the spooks.

"Time to recovery of fighters?" Diettinger asked.

"Seven minutes, sir. Attack run to commence in twenty-seven minutes, by Second Rank's program."

Diettinger noted the tone in the mention of Second Rank, a respected officer, as dynamic as she was competent, and blooded as a Soldier; the bridge crew resented her re-assignment. Saurons, they felt, were Soldiers to fight, not livestock to breed.

Diettinger knew they were only half right. Saurons were warrior stock, bred to fight.

He kept silent, however. Against his will, he realized he missed Second Rank, too.

"Vil, this is Stahler. Do you see what I see?"

The rhetorical question brought a grin from Fighter Rank Vil. The cattle were actually turning to attack them. Bright flashes of light along the cowls of the antique enemy aircraft revealed the firing of their archaic slug-throwers.

Vil held a straight and steady course, compensating for the loss of lift with the vertical thrusters, cutting his speed back as much as possible to give the cattle an unmissable target. The high velocity slugs flattened themselves against the Sauron fighter craft's skin and canopy, to no effect.

"My turn," Vil said aloud. He acquired four of the read aircraft with his weapons radar; for some reason the attackers actually bearing down on him still did not register on his sensors. No matter. Four light missiles lurched away from the underbelly of his ship, lancing up to the rear aircraft in seconds.

Leino saw the missiles. Instinctively, he allowed the one bearing down on him to come as close as he dared before pulling the stick back and dropping into a hammerhead stall. There was a sound like a pickaxe piercing a steel drum, and Leino actually saw the missile pass through the thin metal of his upper right wing and fly on, the fire from its rocket motor melting a hole around the puncture point and setting his sleeve and headgear aflame.

Either the wing hadn't offered enough resistance to detonate the warhead, Leino thought in numb disbelief, or the proximity fuse had failed. Either way, he was still alive.

The same could not be said for the remainder of his squadron. Clouds of blast-dispersed smoke hung over columns of flaming debris tumbling groundward, glittering in the bright, late-morning sun.

Leino slapped out the fire on his arm and headgear before it could spread to the oxygen supply in his mask; if that happened, he knew, he was gone. Not that he held much hope for himself, now. The vibration in the airframe was rattling his teeth, and he could barely hold the stick on a steady course.

He looked over the side to see that the pirates were actually hanging in midair. Resting, he supposed, on vertical thrusters, as the Redfielders circled and fired on them, to no apparent effect. One of the pirates began to ease forward, apparently readying to make another pass.

Leino made a decision and thought of his wife and unborn child. He hoped it lived. He hoped it was a boy. Haven was a bad place for a girl without a father.

"I confess I'm beginning to enjoy this, Stahler," Vil signalled. "One more pass?"

"We have to leave some of them alive to spread the news of the *Dol Guldur* pirates; recall time coming up, anyway. Leave that biplane alone and take out as many of the triplane stringbags you can as we leave." He had decided Vil could have all the fun if he wished. Stahler had little stomach for slaughter. It was inefficient.

"Good enough," Vil readily agreed. Despite all his training as a Sauron Soldier, there was something of the freebooter in every fighter pilot who ever lived, and Vil was no exception. But if all fighter pilots are rogues, then all are heroes to some degree as well, and of that, Marinus Leino was a prime example.

The Redfielder craft, Leino knew, were even more fragile than his own. If his ship was rattling fit to shake apart, theirs could not survive another close pass by the pirates, and it was obvious to him that another such flyby was about to occur.

From above and to one side, he could see the pirates begin their vectors. Leisurely, almost insultingly slow. They were giving him a wide berth. Letting him have plenty of room to run home and spread the word of the godlike, star-spanning pirates who had come to call; look on our works, Haveners, and despair, Leino thought with a grim smile.

The taste of blood from his face and gums was salty and warm in his mouth. He spat. Perhaps he could send these fellows back home with a message of his own.

"Surprise," Leino whispered, and pushed the shuddering stick forward. The biplane quivered, humming like a guitar string, as it nosed over into a dive.

Fighter Rank Vil saw the kite above and to his right begin a dive, and promptly dismissed it from his thoughts. Its pilot had obviously decided to take the moment to make his run to safety. The recall signal sounded, and at the same moment, another tone went off in the cabin; this one strident, warning. His radar's proximity alarm was activated. And Fighter Rank Vil's Sauron reflexes did something they had never done in all his thirty-two standard years. They failed him. Shock had numbed them.

Stahler watched incredulously as the cattle's obsolete kite slammed into Vil's right front quarter. The fighter craft's atmospheric intakes were wide open, supercharging air through the engines for the vertical thrusters. Great chunks of the ramming ship were gobbled up by the turbines, which proceeded to shred themselves to bits on the invading materials.

Fuel feed lines ruptured, spraying aviation fuel into the empty maw of the gutted turbine housing; most of its insides had been spewed out the rear and bottom fans, along with the remnants of Leino and his plane. The fuel ignited in the superheated environment, in tenths of a second spread to the fuel tanks, and Fighter Rank Vil and his ship vanished in a colossal fireball.

Stahler saw the other kites beating away, almost at ground level by now. He was intensely impressed. Vil had been a Sauron and a comrade Soldier, but even cattle deserved praise for such an act. Ignoring his own recall signal, Stahler executed a slow circle, standard tribute among fighter pilots to a downed enemy since man first took his wars to the skies. Then he nosed the fighter up and took her out of the atmosphere.

Diettinger was mildly surprised at losing one of the fighters in combat. When he found out how, he too was impressed. Haven bred warriors. So much the better. He would need such people.

The moment the docking bay notified him that Stahler's ship was secured, Diettinger turned to Weapons.

"Weapons, stand by."

"Acknowledged, First Rank."

On the screen before him, Haven turned, filling the view with its blue-green immensity. The new homeworld, Diettinger thought. The Breedmasters were optimistic that the planet's history and its rugged environment would have produced a hardy strain of humanity, many of whom would be acceptable for interbreeding with the Saurons settling there.

But before they could settle, they would have to be sure they would not be discovered. The race must survive, at all costs, Diettinger knew. And that meant Haven must not ever be found. Not until its new masters were ready.

"Status."

"Primary communications centers coming into range of beam weapons now, First Rank. Low-orbit EMP satellite warheads armed, ready for detonation." Weapons turned. "This is the main concentration in the lowland valley."

Diettinger rubbed his good eye. His last one, he thought. The old myths spoke of the god Odin, who had traded an eye for wisdom. *I should certainly hope it made him wiser to lose an eye,* Diettinger thought.

In Second Rank's legend, the warrior Balor used his one great eye as a weapon. The system itself bore a gas giant with an eyelike storm cloud. Now their disguise was as servants of a great, flaming orb. Diettinger wondered why, with all these eyes in his thoughts, he couldn't discern the future of his people more clearly. He shook his head. Too tired, he thought; I'm beginning to ramble.

He had no real doubts about the course he had set for his people, and certainly no compunctions regarding the effects it would have on the teetering civilization of the world below him. Still, he had been at war for twenty years, and the thought of it all ending with a final, eternal run-to-ground depressed him. He shook his head again, sighing at his fatigue. There were few things sadder, he thought, than an old soldier.

"Begin." Vessel First Rank Galen Diettinger gave the order that ended the world.

The first visible action was the detonation of the enchanced EMP devices in Haven's upper atmosphere. Even as squabbling city-states on the surface finally began negotiating on how best to deal with the "pirates," their communications ended in mid-word. Weapons' timing and deployment was precisely accurate.

The *Dol Guldur* was large and low enough to cast her shadow on the clouds, the lands, and the seas of Haven as she passed over them. As that shadow passed, it left a swath of destruction in its wake beyond the experience of any living Havener.

The orbital surveillance station where Delancey and Alec waited for the end went in a massive nuclear fireball, along with the University nearby; both had been on the prime communications centers list.

At the Novy Finlandia airfield where Flynn was listening to hysterical radio reports before the EMP, no nuclear weapons were employed. Here the Dol Guldur's beams sufficed. The hangars were neatly, almost comically sliced into collapsing segments, their dusty, oil-soaked interiors quickly catching fire, consuming themselves.

Men ran to and fro, no real sense of direction in their movements, only a frantic, desperate need to put distance between themselves and the scene of destruction.

But the destruction was all around them, and running from one ignited hangar only brought them face to face with another.

Flynn alone retained some measure of calm as he trotted into the field office and spun the big telescope there over to the skylight. The day had been one of Haven's razor-edged, clear winter ones, visibility unlimited. Flynn was sure he could get at least a glimpse of the attackers' ships.

The sounds of explosions outside affected him little; he was, after all, nearly deaf. Looking back along the angle of the steepening beams, he found their source, the great tapered cruciform shape of a starship, long end forward. It was gliding almost directly overhead now, seeming to be moored to the surface of Haven by the dozens of threads of destructive energy connecting it to the carnage there.

Flynn could just make out the huge device of the flaming eye on its underbelly, but he recognized the general construction style and displacement of weapons. He was not fooled.

"Saurons," he whispered, more in wonder than fear or loathing. "I'll be a son of a—"

The last particle weapon discharge from the *Dol Guldur* was a direct hit on the field office. Master Mechanic Flynn died in despair, sure the Saurons must have won the war if they were down to annexing places like Haven.

The *Dol Guldur* maintained its orbital strike on the surface of Haven for three days, at intervals. During that time, it began sending Commandoes down to the surface to secure and inspect the areas Survey had reported as suitable for long-term occupation. When fires below burned out, Diettinger ordered the area to be given another pass. If an area tried so much as a transmitted appeal for mercy, he ordered it atomized. Tight-beam communications were the only form of contact between the ship and the groundside Saurons. Not so much as a radio wave was to leave Haven's surface.

Diettinger held no animosity for the Haveners; one did not hate cattle, after all. Nor was he by nature a cruel man. He had fought in many battles, and had always shown courtesy to his foes whenever possible. One such act had cost him his eye. But before you could show courtesy, both sides had to understand the rules of the game; and the only rule the Haveners needed to know right now was: Don't Talk.

As of now, courtesy did not enter into his equations, nor mercy. This battle was far more important than even the defense of the homeworld had been. For this battle could be won.

By the end of the first day of the bombardment, Colonel Edon Kettler, late of the Redfield Satrapy Air Force, had used up every bit of pilot's luck he felt he had. No matter. The airstrip maintained by the Cummings Satrapy at Fort Fornova was lined up neatly below him, and his landing was perfect. On solid ground again, he eagerly accepted the bolt of brandy offered him by one of the Fort's watch commanders, a husky sergeant-major in a gleaming breastplate.

When the Empire and its technology had been in evidence on Haven, people would have laughed at the notion of such archaic-designed armor. The Redfield Satrapy and the Cummings Brigade at Fort Fornova had had their disagreements in the past, however. Kettler did not laugh.

"Right this way, colonel," the sergeant-major said, gesturing towards a small jeep idling at the side of the runway. "The General's expecting you."

The driver threw the car in gear the moment Kettler hit the seat. He had thought flying through turbulence and updrafts inspired by the strike were bad, but God, this road!

The jeep bounded through the gates of Fort Fornova and skidded to a halt in the middle of the courtyard. Kettler was out of the jeep and running for the main doors before it had stopped. He was immediately ushered into the great room.

At the end of the long walk was the table where Cummings' aides received envoys. Kettler was suddenly all too aware of the rumpled uniform he wore; there had been no time to take a flight suit. Here all the uniforms were old, but they were well-used, not worn. As he walked forward to meet the General, Kettler thought about his own troops. He feared the worst for them.

When that technician Delancey had told him what was going on, Kettler had simply commandeered an aircraft and left. But he had not deserted his nation.

Enoch Redfield himself had spoken to him on the aircraft radio, personally thanked him for realizing what had to be done, and then had proceeded to contact General Cummings at Fornova. He had received permission for Kettler to try. Then the EMP hit, and Kettler lost contact.

General Cummings looked at him impassively for a long moment before he spoke. "Colonel Kettler," the General said simply.

Kettler saluted. "At your service, General Cummings."

"You have a personal request for me, I believe?"

"In a manner of speaking, sir. Bluntly, it concerns Fort Fornova Garrison's 'secret' stock of nuclear weapons."

The General laughed, grinning broadly. But it was a rueful smile.

"I think I'd trade fifty Gauss riflemen for one of Enoch Redfield's spies," the older man said. He gestured for Kettler to sit and pulled out a rolled map of the Shangri-La valley. An aide spread it out on the table before them.

"Now," said General Cummings, "Let's see what we can do."

*   *   *

Water had been brought aboard the *Dol Guldur*, and Diettinger was sure he had never tasted any so sweet. It was twenty days since the bombardment of Haven had ended, and the groundside forces had firmly established their bridgehead. Diettinger was speaking with Deathmaster Quilland planetside. Quilland's forces had consolidated in a small mountain pass in the northeast corner of the Shangri-La Valley.

"By your leave, First Rank." Quilland looked fit and well, if a little flushed; Haven's thin air took its toll, he reported, until one got used to it. That he and his men were "getting used to" air pressures that rendered human norms delirious was immaterial; they were Saurons, after all.

"Speak, Deathmaster. You seem pleased."

"I am, First Rank. I have the final report on this settlement area; the hard data is being beamed up now, but you asked for a brief verbal when available."

"Proceed."

"The valley below us, in addition to being almost completely protected by the surrounding mountain ranges, also enjoys higher atmospheric density than most other areas on Haven. Evidently the locals found this valuable; most of their females fail to carry children to term in the thin atmosphere elsewhere, and these valley cattle had established a taxation system for entry and egress when the outlying districts needed areas for birthing purposes."

Diettinger found the information encouraging. Sauron genetic engineering did not extend to secure birthing capabilities among their females; in fact, quite the opposite. With high standards and constant experimentation in gene-crossing, Sauron women also had great difficulty in carrying fetuses to term. The advanced technology of the Sauron state had dealt with the problem through massive artificial reproduction and gestation programs. That option was no longer available to Diettinger's people, and anything to make the transition easier was wonderful. He felt he knew what Quilland was getting at.

"I take it you and your men are now occupying one of the major way-stations built by the locals to regulate such entry and egress?" he asked. He gestured to a towering structure of natural stone and heavy timbers looming behind Quilland, a stronghold if ever he had seen one.

"Better than that, First Rank—the only way-station. The air in the upper reaches of these mountains is too thin for most of the cattle to tolerate, save for a handful of passes such as this one. Of these passes, only a few are open during the summer thaw, and of those, only this one is wide enough to allow mass transportation of personnel and trade goods.

"I recommend establishing a citadel here, with material from the *Dol Guldur* and most of our troops. This valley has few concentrations of heavy elements, and every scrap of steel we can salvage from the ship will be of extreme value. The citadel I suggest will regulate the flow of the cattle to and from the valley and its critical safe-birth zones, letting us exact whatever tribute we require and cull the indigenous population as we see fit."

Diettinger nodded. "It also guarantees us access to those safe zones." He did not add that his first concern in the matter of tribute would be acceptable female breeding stock from among Haven's populace; with only seventy-three Sauron females available, he did not have to. "Proceed, Deathmaster Quilland. We have only one Combat Engineer in the complement, but he shouldn't have any trouble generating building plans with the help of the fortification programs in the ship's computer."

Quilland saluted, and Diettinger broke the connection.

Before the image faded, Diettinger noticed the flaming eye insignia on Quilland's raised arm. The need for secrecy was past. Indeed, what cattle had been captured and interrogated seemed only too aware of the true identity of their invaders, though not their reason for taking so worthless a place as Haven. They all thought the Saurons had defeated the Empire and were claiming Haven as spoils of war.

And yet none of the troops wanted to relinquish their insignia. The "pirate" designation they had abandoned immediately, with noticeable relief. But something was in their character that had not been there before, Diettinger thought, something the insignia and more rakishly cut tunics was fostering. A swagger, he decided.

He wasn't terribly happy about it, but it did tend to subdue the appeal of the Cyborgs among the ranks, and that he was happy about.

Time to consult with Breedmaster Caius.

The Breedmaster looked up from his data terminal as Diettinger entered. He almost seemed to be smiling. Diettinger was sure it was a trick of the light; Caius was virtually humorless.

"First Rank," Caius acknowledged. "I was about to contact you myself. Cross-fertilization tests on the cattle gave the expected results: full compatability."

Diettinger grunted in relief. "Progress on the Cyborg issue?" he asked. Despite the difficulties they posed to his continued leadership, the survival of the Super Soldiers was crucial to his long-range plans for his people. The Empire that had destroyed Sauron was dying, he knew. The first race to emerge from the Interregnum with a techno-military lead would dominate human space for the next thousand years. The Cyborgs could be that edge.

But Caius shook his head. "Very bad, I'm afraid. Cyborgs were typically altered within their gestation capsules, all through their development, with the chemical, physical and biological augments that make them what they are. That technology is of course lost to us now. But there is some hope."

Caius called up a list of information on his screen.

"That hope arises from the fact that the word 'cyborg' is almost a misnomer. The Cyborg's abilities, unlike those of the failed experiments conducted by the Imperials, come not from artificial constructs implanted within their bodies, but from synthesized, purpose-built genetic material, which the fetus assimilates as it develops. Much like the 'royal jelly' process that creates fertile queens out of sterile workers."

Diettinger looked blank.

"Terran bees," Caius explained. Diettinger understood the reference, if not the fact.

"This synthesized DNA was fashioned in toto by our scientists, but its necessary similarity to normal Sauron genetic structure allows for the occasional ability of Cyborgs to breed true, even down to the concentration of metals in their bones." Caius turned to Diettinger. "End of genetic biology lesson, but for one thing. For at least the first few generations, the female mates for the Cyborgs must be of the highest physical and genetic qualifications, to allow any chance of survival for the offspring of such unions, to say nothing of the mothers."

"Then,' Diettinger said slowly, "every attempt will have to be made to protect the Cyborgs and afford their assigned mates the utmost care. They will be mated only with Sauron females, I presume?"

"That would allow the greatest chance for success."

"Make the necessary arrangements." Removing the Cyborgs from combat duty would go a long way towards finishing them off as competitors for social dominance in the new order. But the loss of Sauron females as mates for the crew was a problem. Quite a few had already established liaisons with one another.

No matter. The race came first. Diettinger really had no choice. He took a stimulant and hurried down the corridor for his meeting with Engineering.

The engine bay was a cacophony of noise that set his teeth on edge as Ranks worked at gutting the *Dol Guldur* for her precious high technology. Around him, the walls were bare metal in most places; the jump engines had already been disassembled and removed, as had the non-functioning maneuver engine. Soon the walls themselves would be attacked by the engineering crew, hacking away at the *Fomoria*—the *Dol Guldur*, Diettinger corrected himself—like leafcutter ants. Someone was speaking to him, and he started.

"What is it, Engineering?" he almost shouted.

"First Rank."

"Status."

Engineering seemed to study him closely before he began. "Of the three remaining fighter craft, one has been disassembled planetside and is en route to the Citadel. The remaining two have been converted to shuttles. Thus far, seven hundred seventy tons of metal have been downshipped to the landing zone on Haven."

"Time frame?"

"A two-and-one-half-hour round trip, First Rank, allowing for loading, off-loading, and refueling."

That was too much time. Diettinger had miscalculated the load-bearing capacities of the converted fighters.

"My apologies, Engineering, but I will have to redirect your crews. Begin loading personnel and technical equipment immediately. High grade metals will be moved to the center of the ship; we'll have to risk them making it intact through the drop."

Engineering did not look too hopeful, but acknowledged the order. Then he added, "Permission to speak, First Rank."

"Granted."

"You require rest, sir. The sooner the better. The fate of the remainder of the Sauron race is in your hands. We depend on your judgment and acuity for our survival." Engineering's voice dropped slightly. "Also, the Cyborg Ranks are still a threat to your authority. They will not hesitate to exploit any sign of weakness on your part."

There was little warmth in the admonition and much truth. Still, the concern in his fellow Soldier's voice was not lost on Diettinger.

"At once, Engineering. And thank you." Although

how he was going to get any rest after just having taken a stimulant was beyond him.

Engineering nodded. "These new orders will keep the engineering section occupied for another seven hours, and if I may extend my conscription privileges, I can keep the rest of the on-board crew busy for at least twice that long. Rest easy." He left to reassign the crew and Diettinger headed for his own cabin.

Once there, he removed his uniform and showered, his first in Haven water. Hygiene was important to the Soldiers, and the water brought up from the planet had boosted morale considerably. Overcrowding was gone, too; much of the crew and all of the Commandoes were planetside.

And the innards were being ripped out of the *Fomoria*, Diettinger thought. He could not go on referring to his ship as the *Dol Guldur*. That was a game for the younger men in the crew. For him, the ship was becoming a hollow place. The soul was going out of her.

And, he thought, her commander's fatigue had him lapsing into maudlin images. He pulled off his eyepatch and massaged the smooth, numb flesh beneath it. Sauron geneticists would normally have replaced the organ, but he had only lost it in the past year. Regrowth would have required his removal from active duty for at least a month, and there had simply been no time. Sauron's war had come home too soon.

Diettinger stretched himself out on his bed and tried to use his training to counteract the effect of the stimulant he had taken. Saurons slept in three levels of increasing rejuvenative power and correspondingly reduced outside awareness. He was determined to get to the third level. He knew he needed it.

He also knew the crew needed him, and as a result, he only got as far as second.

Deathmaster Quilland was pleased. The fortifications were proceeding well.

Best of all, though, were these cattle. They had already mounted several effective, if limited, assaults on his outlying positions. Two Soldiers had been lost, and several weapons, in exchange for only twenty-eight enemy. Quilland had decided that such a ratio meant these cattle showed promise. Haven indeed bred well.

Quilland favored the cattle with a thin smile. Perhaps his favorite example of their character had come only an hour ago. Assault Rank Bekker's squad had almost been wiped out by his own men; the cattle had taken a Sauron radio from Dyksos' unit and called in mortar fire from the Sauron RAM positions on the heights, into the Sauron team that was assaulting their position!

When the deception had been realized, only barely in time, all the cattle had escaped. One of his Rankers had asked Quilland if the cattle here could possibly be that good.

It would appear so, Quilland thought.

Diettinger finally shrugged off enough of the effects of the stimulant to reach full recuperative sleep. The state left a Soldier completely defenseless, and was only used when in a secure area. Thus Diettinger had no way of knowing when Second Rank entered his cabin.

Second stood in the doorway a moment, then closed and locked it behind her. She could see that Diettinger's defensive senses had not awakened him at her entry. Third-level sleep, she decided. Good.

She sat down at the desk in a corner of the room and waited.

"*Fomoria*, this is Groundmaster Helm. Shuttle now departing." As in any such operation, in any military, his actual rank was immaterial; while he was the designated Groundmaster, he exercised the power of life and death over anything that moved within his domain, from the lowest ranker to Diettinger himself.

The landing zone was at the northeastern limit of the Valley, directly at the base of the mountain pass in whose upper reaches sat the Citadel. An early attack

against the landing zone had been mounted by the
cattle and suffered disastrous losses. They had scattered
and fled, and had not made the same mistake again.

Sauron patrols had collected local beasts of burden,
and these were used to immediately begin the trans-
shipment of materials up into the pass. All technical
gear had particular priority: eugenics equipment first,
data processing gear second, energy supply gear third,
and so on.

Groundmaster Helm felt the most crucial machinery
was being neglected and assigned extra men to its security. Fifty Soldiers stood guard over the vast array of
heavy machining and engineering equipment. Helm
knew the Saurons were here to stay, and even the
best-cared-for weapon broke down eventually. With this
gear they could manufacture spare parts for all but the
most advanced energy weapons in their arsenal. Helm
was not about to let anything happen to it.

Unlike virtually every other Sauron in the force,
Helm had not embraced the myth they had used to
invade Haven; when Diettinger canceled the order to
use the code name *Dol Guldur*, Helm had gratefully
reverted to calling the ship by her true name. He didn't
care for myths. And he cared even less for the way most
of the younger Soldiers had taken to swaggering in a
manner worthy of the pirates a few cattle still believed
them to be. Helm thought it bad discipline to allow
such behavior in time of war.

The last lights of the shuttle disappeared, and Helm
immediately dispatched the last team of bearers to begin driving the load animals—muskylopes, the locals
called them—up the pass to the Citadel.

The wind came up as Haven's Truenight drew close,
and even Sauron ears began stinging in the biting chill.

Helm consulted his implanted chronometer, now modified to the Haven time cycles for this time of year and
area.

"In five hours the sun comes back up," he told his
relief. "*Fomoria* will be brought down within an hour

after that. This whole zone is to be cleared and all equipment and personnel secured in the Citadel before drop time."

"Acknowledged." The relief Groundmaster glanced over the area, took in the sprawling vista of men, women, and machines, draft animals, electric carts, troopers' kits, crates, and weapons. A non-Sauron would yet have remarked at how orderly everything was; not a scrap of paper anywhere, not a single piece of gear out of place. The relief was confident the time limit would be easily met.

So was Groundmaster Helm. He handed his terminal pad over to the other Soldier. "Ranker Bohren, you are Groundmaster in Command. See you in two." Helm saluted and left for the command tent at the edge of the landing zone. It was a measure of his concern that the tent was next to the manufacturing equipment cache.

Stepping through the seal, Helm went over the records of the last shuttle lift, confirmed his notations, and opened the beam to the *Fomoria* above.

"*Dol Guldur* here, Deathmaster." It amused Communications to bait the officer with the now widely used name of the ship. "One moment, please; First Rank is in his cabin. I'll wake him."

Diettinger came on line a moment later. He appeared displeased with something, but nothing in the First Rank's tone indicated problems for Helm.

"The staging area is being cleared of the last of the cargo, First Rank. The landing zone will be ready for *Fomoria* on schedule."

"Acknowledged, Groundmaster. Check back with me for final clearances. Diettinger out."

Helm sat at the darkened screen for a moment; he was sure he had glimpsed Second Rank seated at the table in First Rank's cabin. Helm shrugged. Not his problem, he decided.

"I think it not only impolitic for you to be here, Second Rank, but positively rude. And possibly insubordinate."

Diettinger had been awakened by Helm's call, but

his first sight had been of Second Rank seated at his desk in the darkened room.

"Permission to speak, First Rank."

Diettinger waited a long time before he gave it.

"There is a power struggle going on behind the scenes, of which you are only partly aware." Second Rank said.

"I will deal with the Cyborgs in my own manner, Second."

"No doubt, sir. But I do not refer to the Cyborgs. I refer to Haven."

If Diettinger had been a cat, his ears would have swiveled forward on his head. "Clarify."

Second Rank gathered her thoughts. She had been organizing this argument in her mind for the past hour; she had better get it right the first time.

"Saurons are soldiers, not pioneers. We are the development of thousands of years of refinement in the martial arts and sciences. Thus, we could only come about within the framework of an ordered civilization, such as the Empire."

Diettinger almost groaned. Second Rank was a historian, after all.

"Now we have come here; a battle of conquest, but with no further battles to follow. Every trooper here has grown up under the auspices of a starfaring military society. Conquer and move on to the next battle." She shook her head. "Such a lifestyle is gone forever, now. We are here to stay, and as our survival instincts, both natural and engineered, begin to activate, we will adapt our character to the environment far faster than we will our genetic structure."

"And what do you think will be the result of this adaptation?" Diettinger asked. Despite himself, he was fascinated by Second's line of reasoning.

She gestured with one hand. "You see it all around you. The dominance myth I used has backfired. The Soldiers have embraced it wholly. Faced with an inferior opponent, Saurons previously conquered and left it at that. The possibility always existed that the next one might be better. But now there is no longer a greater Sauron social order outside to judge our actions; our troops begin to act, to think of themselves as pirates. They swagger, they boast, they are full of their own superiority. Before, only enemy noncombatants were referred to as 'cattle'; the term is now applied to all non-Saurons on Haven. In time, patrols will not return. They will simply establish their own minor fiefs among the weaker Haveners. Military discipline will dissipate. What structure we have will collapse as we are assimilated by the vacuum of authority on Haven.

"In three generations, at the outside, the Sauron race will degenerate into barbaric warlords,, our martial heritage a thing of dim myth. And at that moment, the race will die."

Diettinger could feel the tension in her, and in himself. The only hope for his people was their adaptation to Haven. But at what price?

"Do you have a recommendation for avoiding this situation?"

"Of course, First Rank. I would not be here otherwise."

"Speak."

"You are the First Rank. You must become the First Soldier."

"Martial virtues are not social virtues, Second."

She shook her head. "Nor can they ever be. But with you as political and military figurehead, the Sauron system can start anew here, on Haven, as it was on Sauron hundreds of years ago. A society of militarists; soldier-citizens, bound by codes of military behavior, dedicated to the propagation of the warrior race as an ideal."

Diettinger and Second Rank looked at each other in silence for a long time. Finally he spoke.

"You are suggesting, then, that I re-establish the dynasty, here on Haven, with myself as patriarch."

"Such an act would legitimize your status as First Soldier to the Cyborg Ranks, as well as to the troops.

They all support you, First Rank, but a world of sheep can be very seductive to young wolves."

"The establishment of such a dynasty requires issue with Sauron parentage on both sides. All such Sauron females are already assigned to Cyborgs."

"Come, now, sir," Second Rank's voice dropped. "Surely by now you've arrived at the most obvious reason for my being here?"

Diettinger nodded, sighed. He wasn't going to get back to sleep, after all.

Lieutenant John Vohlt lay flat against the cold stones of the cliffs that shielded him from the Saurons along the floor and opposite rock walls of the Valley. His chest ached from contact with the chilling rock through his parka, but the pain was bearable—and it helped keep him awake. The long range scanner he held to his eyes was the last one in his unit, probably the last from the entire force General Cummings had sent up here to the northern Shangri-La.

By the time Vohlt and his team had arrived, Colonel Harrigan's forces were ready for their planned maneuver. What little organized resistance there had been to the Saurons was over. There remained only the deceptive attack before they pulled out of the Valley. Colonel Harrigan had not come to get his force butchered in a last desperate act of defiance.

Well, not the entire force, anyway, Vohlt thought with a humorless grin. That would be his team's job.

"You'll take your men up through here." Harrigan had indicated Vohlt's route on a map of the Valley passes, pointing out a small depression in the rocks. "There's a small—as in hand-sized—plateau here, and you can make camp in the overhang just back from it; it should keep you out of sight of the Sauron opticals and any air reconnaissance they might have."

Harrigan had taken a bottle of domestic rum and poured a healthy amount into his tea. The command tent was bloody cold.

"You'll have to pull this up by hand, of course. We can't risk anything as big as a muskylope being seen."

Vohlt had nodded. "Can we have the rum, too, sir?" he had asked, grinning.

Harrigan had smiled back, sadly. "Why not?"

Vohlt and the five other men had left an hour into Harrigan's attack. When the "rout" came, they had split off and quickly hid in the passes. Vohlt lifted a metal capful of rum to his lips and sipped it carefully. He hoped the Colonel and his men had made it.

Behind him, the four surviving members of the team were sleeping.

Beyond the bedrolled men squatted the object they had laboriously manhandled up into these rocks. Harrigan had admitted that it would not defeat the Saurons; it wasn't powerful enough to take out their staging area, and had arrived too late to use there anyway. The Soldiers were on Haven to stay.

But General Cummings felt it would go a long way towards keeping the Saurons cautious for some time to come. Haven was no major world; it couldn't stand against even one shipload of Saurons. But it could still bite.

The image in Vohlt's opticals was fading; he shook the device and looked through again. A little better. The charge was going, he decided. He switched it off to save the little cell's energy and considered the item in his hands; light intensifying binoculars with range-finding capability and up to 10×120 power magnification, more than you could ever possibly need. But when the last of the charge was gone, it would be half a kilo of junk, he thought. He set it for simple lense magnification, no power, and put it back in its case until it would be needed. Maybe he could rig up something out of the basic lenses after the charge was gone.

He laughed at his trivial plan for the future. He had almost forgotten why he was here.

Groundmaster Bohren checked his chronometer and reviewed his accomplishment: an hour yet to Trueday, and the landing zone was as bare of people and equipment as if it had never been occupied. He turned and followed the last group of load animals and personnel, wending their way up into the pass towards the Citadel. Towards home.

Diettinger found himself looking again at the face of Second Rank, sleeping on the cot next to him. Even more than most Saurons, he was a realist; a moment's consideration would have told him that it would come to this, but he had simply not taken the time. Or perhaps he was determined to avoid the truth of the matter.

As it happened, he seemed the only one in the crew surprised at this turn of events. When, after the long and fruitless argument with Second Rank over her decision, he had admitted the wisdom of it, he had called Breedmaster Caius.

"Second Rank is to be removed from the roster of Cyborg mating personnel, Breedmaster Caius. You may list her as officially mated to me hereafter."

"I have already taken that liberty, First Rank," Caius had matter-of-factly informed him. Diettinger raised an eyebrow.

"Indeed? And would you care to share your justification for such an act with me?"

Caius was utterly blasé. "Your Genetic Preference Rating is A-3, Fertility Rating two, well within the parameters you established for breedworthy personnel. Second Rank's qualifications and genetic code complement your own almost perfectly. Better, in fact, than those of any Cyborg in the pool." Caius paused a moment. "I had merely prepared the matchup as a hypothetical one. Purely as a guideline."

"You would agree, then," Diettinger said drily, "that the mating of myself and Second Rank, and any issue resulting therefrom, would help in establishing ourselves here on Haven?"

Caius nodded. "It would have the added virtue of

offsetting the considerable influence the Cyborgs have among the troops, as well, First Rank."

Diettinger nodded, smiling thinly. "Yes, Second Rank herself pointed out something like that to me. Thank you, Breedmaster. Diettinger out."

And now he watched as Second Rank—Althene, he reminded himself; her name is Althene—turned in her sleep, moving towards his warmth. With an awkwardness he sensed he was rapidly losing, Diettinger gathered her into his arms, pulled her close, and closed his eyes.

Better late, he thought, than never.

He woke at the bridge summons to find himself alone in the bed. The sounds of a woman in his bath were unfamiliar and yet utterly unmistakable. Diettinger keyed the intercom.

"Diettinger."

"Groundside secured, sir; Citadel signals ready to receive the Dol Guldur whenever we are ready to send her."

Diettinger scowled. As always when he had slept too long, he awoke irritable.

"Communications, we are about to end the life of what is probably the last ship of the Sauron Home Fleet; pass the word to all ranks that henceforth she will be given the courtesy of being referred to her by her true name."

"Acknowledged, First Rank." Communications' tone reflected his humility. "Engineering reports the Fomoria ready for drop."

"Very good. Muster all remaining shipboard personnel in the shuttle bay in half an hour."

"Acknowledged, First Rank."

Diettinger cut the bridge link for what he suddenly realized was the last time. He looked at the communications console in reflection for a moment, then turned to see Althene standing in the doorway to the bath. Silhouetted in the dimness of the room by the bright light behind her, she was an image as old as humankind.

Diettinger thought of the jokes cattle made about Sauron matings; none bore repeating. Cattle would never appreciate that the Saurons were just as emotional as any other race of men; more so, since they were trained not to deny the basic nature of the species. Non-Saurons saw Diettinger and his people as sexless automata. The prejudice had not spared many a captured Sauron female from rape at the hands of enemy soldiers.

"Althene," Diettinger said her name aloud.

He could only sit and look at her for the moment. The price of four decades and more of solitary living, he thought; the speaking of emotions was a skill that required practice, and he was sorely lacking that.

"Yes, Galen," she said quietly, her tone one of affirmation. Cattle would have said it sounded like "Acknowledged, First Rank," but Diettinger knew the difference.

"It's time to go."

She nodded, went to the desk where she had left her kit bag. Diettinger watched her every move. How had he lasted this long, he thought? Relations among crew members on Sauron ships were inevitable, and if the genetic potential was promising, encouraged. Yet in the three years he had served, not once had he considered his former Second Rank in anything more than a professional light. Perhaps there had not been time. Or perhaps he had known that the first step toward intimacy with this particular woman would be a very, very steep one. And the last.

Now, he thought, there would indeed be time. Time for himself, and for Althene. There still was much to do before the subjugation of the world below them was complete, and more beyond that before the Sauron race was safe and could begin to rebuild. But that would be resolved by his heirs.

No matter. He had done the hardest part, he felt; he had given his people a chance, if a slim one. Time now to keep some small part of his life separate from his duty as a Sauron and a Soldier. And Althene would be that part.

"Ready?" he asked. Althene nodded.

Smiling, he slid the door open and held it for her as she passed through.

The corridors of the ship resonated with the sound of their passage; all material that could be stripped from her was long gone, particularly anything flammable, and their boots rang on the naked durasteel decks. Power was at minimum, so they took the access ladder to the shuttle bay.

Waiting were Engineering, two of his assistants, Communications, Navigation, and the shuttle pilot, a Fighter Rank whose name patch identified him as Stahler. Diettinger thought the name was familiar.

"Stahler." He read it aloud.

The Fighter Rank cracked to attention. "Yes, First."

"You were on the mission that lost one of our craft to the locals. I understand the cattle pilot rammed your wingman?"

"Yes, First. Brilliant compensatory maneuvering by the enemy pilot flying an utterly obsolete ship."

Diettinger had been impressed by the news when he first heard it; Stahler's personal rendition did nothing to dampen that earlier respect. Haven evidently bred hardy sons and daughters. All to the good for breeding purposes, but such resolve to fight would bear close scrutiny of the "subjugated" peoples waiting below on the surface of the new homeworld.

"Everyone accounted for, then?" Diettinger asked Engineering when he had dismissed the Fighter Rank. Engineering nodded, held up a portable computer.

"This is our remote piloting device. Fomoria has sufficient fuel left to maneuver and brake for the worst of her descent; after that, the engines will have drained the fuel tanks dry to avoid igniting residual hydrogen in the heat of entry into Haven's atmosphere."

"Excellent, Engineering. you will allow Second Rank—" Diettinger caught himself at the physical and facial reactions to his form of address. "I beg pardon.

You will allow the Lady Althene the honor of guiding the Fomoria to her last berth."

Engineering bowed and presented the portable to his former superior officer. Althene accepted it with a murmur of thanks and a look of pure gratitude at Diettinger.

"Make your goodbyes, then," Diettinger said, scanning the naked, featureless bay surrounding them. Every piece of equipment and metal removable had been shipped down to the surface; now even the air was getting stale, life support equipment having left two hours ago on the shuttle's last cargo run. Caius had insisted it would be necessary for decent hospital facilities and breedchambers.

Outwardly an unemotional people, the Saurons were no less prone to pathos than anyone else; they simply resolved such emotions more quickly. Single file, they followed Fighter Rank Stahler up the ramp into the cramped shuttle, found seats and strapped themselves in.

Althene activated the terminal immediately upon securing herself into the acceleration couch. Diettinger, seated beside her, watched as the screen resolved itself into a miniature duplicate of the Second Rank station on the bridge.

In minutes, the Fomoria was "dry," internal atmosphere vented into space. With internal power down, Engineering threw the switch that blew off the shuttle bay hangar doors. As the great triangular slabs drifted away, Haven was directly visible for the first time. Beyond the horizon of the new homeworld hung the colossal mass of the parent planet.

"Cat's Eye," Diettinger said aloud. The gas giant's storm center was aligned almost perfectly with Haven's horizon and the Fomoria's orbital path. The Cat's Eye was looming over the equatorial horizon of Haven, an aroused god peering over an azure fence, directly into the hangar bay of the Fomoria.

" '. . . and the warriors of the Tuatha Da Danaan halted their charge, for there before them the Fomorians had brought forth onto the field of battle their mightiest

Champion, who was Balor of the One Eye.' " Althene was looking out at the spectacle, quoting from the myth she had drawn from the history of old Terra.

" 'And lo, the warriors of the Fomorian host brought forth great bars of bronze, for the touch of iron was anathema to them; and with these bars they prized open the orb of Balor, and from it issued forth the Death, and the army of the Tuatha Da Danaan withered as autumn leaves cast into a forge . . .' "

For a moment, Diettinger wondered idly what 'autumn leaves' were. No matter, he decided. He had the feeling he would soon know both the meaning of the phrase and the reality for which it served as metaphor. In many ways, he thought, the battle has only just begun.

The shuttle exited the Fomoria's hold and took up chase position three kilometers from the great, gutted starship. Studying the data on her screen intently, Althene seemed to see something she had been waiting for. "Drop window approaching, First Rank," she said.

Diettinger smiled. Once a Soldier, always a Soldier, he thought. "Take her in, Second Rank," he said. This time no one reacted to his use of his new mate's former active duty rank; Diettinger's consort was being given the honor of piloting the Fomoria on her last flight, the only time a Sauron starship had ever intentionally entered a planetary atmosphere, for of course such ships were never designed to make planetfall; it was fitting Althene should fly it with her full rank restored.

From their position to the right and rear of the Fomoria, the passengers of the shuttle watched as the great ship's maneuvering engines glowed feebly.

"The Fomoria will drop aft foremost." Althene reviewed the drop plans to Diettinger, more in affirmation of her upcoming duties than in any need to instruct the First Rank. "That lets the mass in the engine section absorb most of the punishment and heat from the atmospheric entry, as well as deflecting the ionization effect away from the bulk of the vessel trailing. The denser materials of the engines will also burn away more slowly, prolonging the protection of the forward sections."

Diettinger nodded, his mind already elsewhere. The Fomoria would create a huge ionization field as it entered Haven's atmosphere, he realized, and he turned to Engineering.

"How much difficulty will we have contacting the surface after Fomoria begins entry?"

Engineering considered a moment, frowning.

"We'll be effectively cut off, First Rank. If you've anything you want to tell the ground forces, you'd best do it now."

Anticipating this need, Communications had kept a tight beam link with the communications station at the Citadel. Wordlessly, he passed Diettinger a handset.

"Diettinger here."

"Ground Force Commander Quilland standing by, First Rank."

"Drop is initiated, Deathmaster Quilland. Status?"

"Ground Forces are stationed in the foothills and along the valley floor on the drop zone perimeter. No cattle activity for the past three days. There was a skirmish two days ago with forces from some central valley fiefdom, very good, very well-led, but they evidently realized the futility of a protracted conflict with our forces." Despite its wording, Quilland's voice carried no tone of arrogance; and in fact, his assessment of Colonel Harrigan's decision to break off the engagement was entirely accurate, if not complete.

Diettinger was still uneasy. He felt he had prepared for every eventuality, but his training reminded him that the commander who could do that had yet to be born.

"Double the watchfulness of the perimeter troops, Deathmaster. The cattle didn't have much to resist with, but they gave all they had. Such people do not accept defeat readily."

"Acknowledged, First Rank. Permission to speak."

"Granted."

"The entire Ground Force wishes you and the Lady Althene good health and a Long Line."

Sentimentality like this was inevitable from a swashbuckler like Quilland, but Diettinger was pleased, nevertheless. It let him know the troops were firmly behind him, despite the sometimes overawing influence of the Cyborgs planetside.

"We thank you, Deathmaster Quilland." Althene smiled briefly, her attention still riveted to the control terminal balanced in her lap.

"We'll see you at the Citadel, then, Commander."

"Until then. Diettinger out."

"Fomoria entering atmosphere, First Rank," Althene spoke without looking up. "Three minutes to first braking fire."

Diettinger looked out the port beside him for a glimpse at the Fomoria. The ship was falling towards Haven like a short sword dropped pommel-first. The aft engine section and the extended drives and launch bays, the 'hilt,' were blackening with the gathering heat; seconds later, the anti-corrosive coating vaporized, and the metal beneath began to glow red.

Fighter Rank Stahler paced the big ship down, keeping the shuttle at a safe distance yet easily in range of Althene's remote control terminal.

"First braking fire."

The glow from the heating tail of the Fomoria was dimmed by the glare of her engines firing. With no oxygen stores aboard her, tons of her remaining fuel wee consumed inefficiently as the intakes gathered meager quantities of oxygen from Haven's thin upper atmosphere.

"Slowing appreciably, First Rank. Fomoria now entering stratosphere." Althene looked up from her terminal to Engineering. "I had some trouble with my signals for a moment."

"It's partly range, partly the ionization effect; communications to and from Fomoria will be increasingly difficult, then impossible. All the braking will have to be done before that happens."

"Boosting the signal won't help?"

Engineering shook his head. "Like trying to shine a dim light through a steel wall, Second Rank. Sorry."

Althene shrugged, returned to there terminal with a frown, and began calling up more data. In a moment she looked up again at Engineering. "Can we risk leaving fuel in the Fomoria's tanks until after the ionization effect has dissipated?"

Engineering looked at Diettinger, then back to Althene. "I would estimate a sixty percent chance such fuel would be ignited by the heat. The Fomoria would likely disintegrate."

Althene looked at Diettinger. "Too high a risk."

He nodded. "Survey tells us Haven is drastically poor in metals in this area. The hulk of the Fomoria will be our single greatest asset in the years to come. We can't be roaming this continent picking up the pieces. Do your best, Second Rank."

Althene nodded.

"Signals very erratic. I'm initiating full and final braking fire, then."

As the atmosphere of Haven began surrounding them, the world outside the shuttle ports was lightening. Away and below them, the Fomoria was fast disappearing in a colossal cone of orange-white flame, superheated gases of the ship being consumed in entry into atmosphere.

Althene pressed a switch, and the cone erupted downwards as the last of Fomoria's fuel went, along with much of her maneuver engines. For a moment, the great hulk became visible amid the flames as its descent slowed almost to a stop. Then it began to fall again into its own mass of smoke and debris. Seconds later, it left the cloud and began falling Havenward once more.

There was enough atmosphere around the shuttle now that they could hear the roar and feel the shock waves of the Fomoria's drop, and Fighter Rank Stahler pulled away slightly, expertly compensating for the buffeting.

For a moment, Diettinger wanted to ask if the Fomoria might hit the Citadel itself, but there was really no point in worrying about that. If that happened, they might just as well spiral the shuttle into the ground after it. If that happened, it truly would be the end. Diettinger turned back to the window, but the Fomoria was fading from view in the high cloud cover over Haven's Shangri-La Valley. Stahler was diving the shuttle to catch up with it.

Soon, now, Diettinger thought.

Vohlt jerked awake at the touch on his shoulder. Only his training had kept him from crying out in his sleep; gods, what a dream, he thought.

Behind him, Pederson hobbled over from the small stove. His toes had gone black with frostbite in the last two days of waiting, and all their food was gone. If the Saurons didn't make their move soon, Vohlt and his men would die in vain. Bleary-eyed, he looked up at the man who had awakened him: Turlock, older than Vohlt by a season, younger by two wars.

"There's something coming, sir. I think the pirates are making their drop."

"They're not pirates," Vohlt grumbled as he rose on ominously numb feet. "They're Saur—"

His sight of the sky over the northern valley shocked him silent. The high clouds were roiling back in the turbulence of the fireball dropping through them. It seemed to be directly overhead, and primal instinct churned Vohlt's insides as he watched what was beginning to look like a burning city falling directly at him.

He needed something to do, he realized, before he panicked. He knew, logically, that the ship was not targeted to hit anywhere near him.

He also knew, logically, that there had been no reason for the Saurons to come to Haven in the first place.

"Is the launcher ready?" Vohlt asked, forcing his gaze downward and reaching for the image intensifier gear.

"Yes, sir. Powering up now. Be ready in another minute; didn't want to chance the Saurons detecting emissions from the generator."

Vohlt switched the power back on to the opticals and looked back up at the descending starship. The date line at the base of the viewfield faded in and out as he put the added strain on its charge of a time-to-impact equation. Three minutes, sixteen seconds flashed along the data line, then the entire image went black.

"Well, that's it for these," Vohlt said in resignation, handing the glasses over to Turlock, who put them to his eyes in a perfunctory gesture, scanning the valley from his standing view.

Vohlt walked stiffly to the launcher crew, glad that the weapon they were giving their lives to use was not prone to human weakness.

"What was that?" Deathmaster Quilland had been looking off to the sides of the Valley at the steep foot-hills surrounding, when something glimmered in the morning sun. Just a brief flash, indistinguishable to lesser than Sauron vision.

'I didn't see it, sir," his aide replied.

"Looked like a reflection; metal, or perhaps optics. Scan that zone" —he indicated the relative position on the map before him— "for any emissions; electrical, nuclear, infrared." Something was very wrong, Quilland felt. "And hurry."

Pederson's feet were beyond hope, but his hands and brain worked well enough. He adjusted the targeting equipment and nodded to Vohlt.

"Acquisition?" Vohlt asked, tension winning over fatigue in his tone. Pederson nodded.

"Heat signature alone from that sum'bitch is enough to go by; but I've got it just about locked."

Vohlt checked his watch. He could hear the distant roar

of the falling Sauron spacecraft in the not-distant-enough distance. Two minutes, twenty-three seconds to go.

"Get your final lock on. Paint it with everything you need."

"I have an odd reading, Engineering," Althene spoke aloud. Fighter Rank Stahler was working to keep control of the shuttle against the air turbulence caused by the Fomoria; Diettinger's eyes were locked on the craft itself. Engineering leaned over to check Althene's terminal.

"Looks like a radar emission. Too regular to be entry phenomena, too weak to be anything but a reflection." Engineering looked up; Diettinger had turned at the word "radar," and their eyes met.

"The cattle are targeting the Fomoria with something." Engineering said. Althene's head went up in shock, but the look on Diettinger's face was unfathomable. The First Rank nodded and turned back to the window.

"Enemy targeting sensors, Deathmaster, emissions at level nine and locking on target." The astonishment was impossible for the Ranker to keep from his voice. Quilland's jaws clamped as he grabbed the communications microphone.

"Suppressive fire, immediate, these coordinates," Quilland spoke rapidly in the monosyllabic combat tongue of the Saurons; simultaneously, he pressed the switch that fed the coordinates of the emissions trace to the launcher crews waiting along the rim of the Valley wall.

In seconds, targeting lasers converged on the small space in the rocks Quilland had spotted only by blind luck earlier.

Vohlt saw the small pinpoints of reflected green light on the stones around him and instantly recognized them for what they were.

"Got it, Pederson?"

Pederson nodded. Vohlt looked over the rim of their

rock shield and saw tiny white puffs of smoke all along the Valley walls. The Saurons were launching their suppressive strikes on his position. He and his men had seconds to live.

"Okay, men, this is it. Drop the other shoe, Pederson."

Vohlt took the small canteen with the last of Harrigan's rum from its resting place on the rocks and drank it down.

"Guess wrong, you bastards," he said aloud, as the roar of the missile engine behind him drowned out the high-pitched whine of the approaching Sauron tacticals.

The air superheated with the passage of the missile they had laboriously dragged up into position; seconds later, the Sauron birds detonated, on target.

"Direct hit, Deathmaster." The ranker's voice was quiet, still tense; a great cloud of dust hung over the position the cattle had launched from. A moment later the ranker added, "Sir, too late; sensors show the enemy missile still targeting."

But Quilland did not need sensors to see the bright needle of light exiting the cloud: a silvery arc rising smoothly upwards towards the Fomoria and the shuttle, chasing them down.

His gaze shot to the readout. Saurons depended little on computers for rapid calculations, and his own mind extrapolated the data it presented. He swore aloud.

The Saurons, he felt, were doomed.

"The cattle have charged, First Rank." Stahler spoke over the cabin intercom to Diettinger in the control compartment.

"Interdict their missile."

The shuttle gave a sickening lurch as Stahler maneuvered to interpose it between the hulk of the Fomoria and the approaching missile. Engineering's lap terminal and various other items flew against the wall as the small craft fought the G-forces of the violent maneuver. Diettinger looked away from the view of Haven and at Althene.

"I anticipated this, I'm afraid. We cannot allow the cattle to destroy the Fomoria," he told her. "Nor to irradiate it with a high-yield weapon, preventing our people's use of it." He turned to his mate; all too briefly that, he thought.

Second Rank was doing something else with her terminal; the image of the Fomoria control station on its screen was replaced by one unfamiliar to Diettinger, then she turned it away from his view. He smiled at her sadly.

"Second Rank, you are relieved from duty." She smiled back at him, shrugged: a gesture that understood all the things that now would never be. "I am sorry, Althene," Diettinger said.

Althene nodded. Engineering sat back. Too bad, he thought; he would have enjoyed the challenge of life on Haven, he had decided. But duty to the race came first.

Stahler fought the controls to move the shuttle as quickly as possible; the former fighter was ungainly now and badly out of position. Diettinger had guessed the cattle might take such an action, but of course he could not know which direction they would launch from, and the shuttle was on the wrong side of the hulk.

Fomoria had perhaps forty-five seconds left to impact; the missile would hit it in thirty. If it had any decent yield at all, the remains of Fomoria would be scattered over the entire Shangri-La and worse, likely irradiated. The Valley was so metal-poor that control of the Fomoria would have made the Saurons absolute rulers of the Valley and, eventually, the planet. Diettinger had no choice but to sacrifice their lives for it.

Fighter Rank Stahler's concentration was locked on the view ahead of him; the approaching missile, the falling, precious Fomoria, his own craft's relative position to both. He did not see the blinking red warning light on the control panel.

EVADE EVADE EVADE ENEMY LOCK-ON
EVADE EVADE EVADE

The Fomoria was not the missile's target.

Diettinger reached out for Althene's hand; she had retained her portable computer and picked it up to place it aside. She looked at Diettinger for a moment and smiled.

"I'm sorry, too, Galen." She threw a single switch on the terminal. The shuttle lurched yet again. The control stick wrenched itself from Stahler's hands and the small craft dropped into a vertical power dive. The Havener missile lost its target and activated its optional acquisition mechanism. The missile flew on, detonating within the mass of the immolated Sauron starship, hundreds of feet above the valley floor.

"What happened? What in hell happened?" Quilland had lost all composure at the sight on his crew's screens. One moment the enemy missile was heading for the shuttle. The shuttle, Quilland thought in rage at these hideously crafty cattle. The next instant, the shuttle was gone, and the missile continued on to detonate within the flaming mass of the Fomoria.

The ranker shook his head in confusion. "Hopeless, sir. It looks like something happened aboard the shuttle; she dove off the sensor screens like a falcon. I had to replay the data to tell even that much; I can't find her on sensors, now, but how could her pilot pull out of a dive like that?"

Over the northernmost expanse of the Shangri-La, the Trueday morning sun was dimmed by the huge pall of the Fomoria's destruction. What meager segments of the ship remained fell in blazing fragments to the ground with thunderous impacts. Quilland could see the shock waves rippling out from the impact points, feel the vibration through the granite beneath his boots.

He gave up trying to see where they all hit. It was hopeless. Nothing remained larger than a boxcar. Quilland sighed. Now his troops would be required to make recovery sojourns into the flatlands of the hostile Valley, exposed to the Haveners far more than he cared to think about. Dangerous, Quilland thought, but not impossible. He grunted. Be good for them, no doubt, in the long run. Give them more chance to learn about these cattle than all their previous pacification raids had allowed.

Deathmaster Quilland gave a short, grim laugh. "Pacification," he said out loud. The Sensor Ranker beside him looked up curiously.

"We haven't even come close to 'pacifying' these cattle," the Deathmaster told the lower Ranker. His short laugh of a moment before became an open smile. "I doubt that we ever will."

Stahler recovered the shuttle with room to spare; the resulting sonic boom over the Citadel brought several messages of congratulations from the Soldiers stationed at the communications outpost there, once they were sure it was not an impact explosion.

Diettinger was looking at Althene closely. She returned his stare. Engineering was repositioning himself in his acceleration couch after tending to the body of Communications; unprepared, the young Sauron had snapped his neck during the violent maneuver, dying instantly.

"Thank you for relieving me of command, First Rank," Althene was saying. Diettinger turned to her. "On active duty I would have been guilty of disobedience in using my terminal to override Stahler's controls."

Diettinger stared. She had kept the lapboard terminal long after control of Fomoria had been lost; now Diettinger knew why. She had been infiltrating the control panel of the shuttle, anticipating his plan to sacrifice the craft. The strange control panel he had seen on the readout had been that of Stahler's station forward.

"You knew," he said.

Althene shrugged. "I guessed." Their voices dropped as the speed of the shuttle decreased; Stahler was making his final approach for landing.

"The cattle's choice of our shuttle for a target over that of the Fomoria makes little sense to me," Diettinger said. "The military value of the hulk is unmistakable."

"They weren't thinking in military terms, Galen," Althene spoke quietly, firmly. "They were making a statement, one with little strategic value, but of high importance in terms of morale."

"Clarify, O Muse," Diettinger said, laughing in relief. Althene laughed back.

"They must have guessed our commander would be aboard. They can't eavesdrop on tight beam communications, but they'd be aware of them."

Diettinger laughed again. "You flatter me, Lady. I cannot believe the cattle would waste a nuclear weapon on me."

Althene smiled sadly. "I am a historian, First Rank," she said formally. "And history shows that humanity will not always make the best choice in a seemingly hopeless situation. As often as not, they will make the most satisfying one. This time, they were the same. The cattle wanted to hurt us, even if they couldn't beat us. The elimination of our entire command structure would have little impact on us under battlefield conditions; underofficers would advance to fill the void." She shook her head again.

"But this is not a 'command structure.'" She took his hand. "It is a dynasty, now. And Haven cannot be a battlefield any longer. It must be our home."

Diettinger nodded. "Our strength was always our discipline," he said quietly. "But it made us predictable." He rubbed his eyepatch as he spoke, suddenly weary. There was time, at last, to be tired. "No doubt it was why we lost the war."

Althene lowered her head in silence. There was nothing to say.

"It may be the single distinction of our existence on this world," Diettinger spoke again after a moment, "that we are never to really understand our enemies here; nor they us." He turned back to the window.

Outside and below the shuttle, Sauron troopers advanced in march order to meet their commander, a ritual considered meaningless in a society based on duty and efficiency. But the bright flags and patches of a flaming eye fluttered and gleamed in the sun, and there were other priorities on the troops' minds, now.

Their king was safe, Diettinger realized with an ironic smile. Haven was already changing his people, as it had its own. But perhaps for the better, despite Althene's warnings. Closely watched, firmly guided, the children of the Sauron race might yet spring forth from this place and set the universe to right.

The cattle had acted in a way unanticipated by almost all the soldiers. But his dream for the Sauron race would go on, if with greater difficulty at the loss of Fomoria, because one of his soldiers had thought like the cattle.

Cattle? he thought, as the shuttle bumped lightly on the cleared space in the courtyard of the Citadel. The tower loomed high overhead. From its roof fluttered the red, white, and black banner of the lidless, flaming eye.

No, not really. Some, but by far, not all. Haven had been at war for a very long time, longer even than Sauron and the Empire. Haven's people had fought first their world, then each other, with little experience wasted. There would be few but the best left among them by now.

"We may make Soldiers of these Haveners yet," he told Althene with a sudden grin.

They stood in the hatch, to the cheers of the assembled ranks below and around them, then they stepped down the ramp onto the surface of the new homeworld.

"Perhaps they will even make Haveners of us."

From GGHQ FILES, MACH (Top Secret)

—alarming rise in disciplinary offenses among the Soldiers. Theft has risen 78%, substance abuse 41%, assault on comrades or superiors 81%, and neglect of weapons/equipment 4%.

I would further call the First Rank's attention to the 113% rise in medical treatments for psychological dysfunction resulting from combat stress. Approximately one-half the disciplinary offenses have been committed either by persons previous treated for P.D. or else in my judgment very close to such a condition.

While I will not presume to advise the First Rank on tactical or strategic matters, I must call his attention to the fact that the current offensive is creating certain conditions that may have contributed to the rise in disciplinary offenses and P.D.

(1) The dispersal of our advanced units, making resupply of non-essential supplies difficult.

(2) The comparative safety and abundant supplies of the command echelons, who are emerging as a distinct group within the ranks of the Soldiers.

(3) The shortage of transport.

I am aware that for some time it will continue to be essential to remain on the offensive, penetrating enemy territory with mobile columns to destroy any troop concentrations or dumps of modern weapons. I am also aware that the command echelons need a higher degree of security from enemy guerrilla operations, to carry out their function of coordinating the operations of the mobile columns.

Yet I cannot remain silent in the face of such circumstances as ordinary liquor being only marginally available to Soldiers in the mobile columns. I must therefore recommend:

(1) That the mobile columns be allowed longer periods of relief between operations.

(2) That during these periods, every effort be made to supply the Soldiers with adequate recreational facilities and materials. (I do not accept the rumors that the command echelon personnel have been illegally appropriating such materials for their own use, but the widespread belief in these rumors is certainly becoming a significant morale factor.)

(3) That transport be allocated for (1) and (2), even at some cost in offensive capabilities.

We are far from a home that no longer exists. We are surrounded by enemies who outnumber us hundreds to one and do not lack courage. We must not only be invincible, we must *appear* invincible. To let our mask crumble from small causes is other than wise.

Very respectfully submitted,

Caius, Breedmaster, MACH

THE GREAT BEER SHORTAGE

Janet Morris and David Drake

"Sauron fucking *super* soldier!" the young group leader was yelling at the closing door of the officer's bar from which he'd just been thrown. "I didn't *ask* for this—not to be born like this, not this duty, not any goddamn bit of it!"

It was night, Catseye long set up there somewhere beyond massed clouds that hid all starlight. The troop leader didn't mind that at all—he saw best in the dark. He liked it black. And black as a Haven woman's heart it was out here in the boonies at Firebase Three—black as Troop Leader Merari's mood.

No goddamn beer for his troops, though they'd been out on long recon for ten days, fighting the Haven resistance, the pirates, whatever the hell moved on this hostile planet.

Back at the Citadel they'd have beer, you bet, like the Assault Leaders and the cyborgs had it here.

Not that the desk jockeys outside Shangri-La'd share it with the guys out here who weren't brass, guys who got their butts shot up following orders. *And it ain't just the orders that're pisspoor either, it's the damned planet and the "plan" that got us here.*

Trash the local government, vaporize Haven's industry, that was the plan. *Take 'em out from orbit, hose 'em down from aircraft and hovers, and when you're done with that, Field Marshal Lidless Eye and all your mechanized Division Leaders, some guys got to go bleed*

216

*all over the damned jungle to clean out the scattered
pockets of resistance you cyborgs created.*

The troop leader had just brought his boys in, what
was left of them. Didn't matter to anybody but the
body-counters that you took a tenth of the casualties
you inflicted. Didn't matter to his wounded or his dead.

They deserved the best Firebase Three had to offer—
they deserved some goddamned beer, if anybody did.

Troop Leader Merari put his hands on his hips and
hollered at the closed bar door: "You wouldn't treat me
this way if I had my Gatling. I'm goddamn coming back
with my Gatling and then we'll see you throw me out."

Backing away as the door opened and a three-star
Assault Leader glowered at him, Merari might have left
it at that.

But the three-star said, looking huge in that doorway
spilling light like the blackout-curtained bar windows
couldn't, "Come on, son, take it easy. There's booze in
your own bar. RHIP, Soldier."

"RHIP?" Merari shouted hoarsely, pumped up on
the rotgut he'd found in Artillery's own bar, where
there was nary a drop of beer for a chaser. "I got all the
RHIP I can eat, *Sir!* I got blood that clots so quick it'll
probably give me apoplexy or an aneurism by the time
I'm forty. I got great night vision, so great I'm near
dayblind here. I got reflexes so enhanced I might just
spasm to death for the hell of it. So you don't want to
get me excited, *Sir.* No, you don't. And you want to let
me and my boys in there, or you want to give us a few
barrels of beer—we bled for it, we deserve it."

Goddamn, but that didn't go down well. Back into
the blindingly bright bar went the three-star and out
came MPs even bigger than Merari himself—older,
meaner, and wiser, with Haven AKs pointing right at
his gut while they waltzed him back to his troop's
barracks—a flimsy bunch of decidedly unkevlared tents
out at the firebase's perimeter.

When they left him there, telling him he was lucky
he hadn't gotten himself manacled and tossed into the

stockade, Merari glared away everybody who came near him.

Fuck 'em all. No women was bad enough, but no woman and no beer. . . .

He *was* going to go get his Gatling, or some shit. He was going to stick the muzzle right up that Assault Leader's ass and see how good *his* breeding was.

The indigs called the soldiers "Saurons." Maybe they deserved the name, but not the sneer. And some of the genetically-engineered soldiers were better engineered than others. Luck of the draw, quality of the mother. It all varied. Some Saurons were more equal than others. Merari was one hell of a night-fighting machine, enough of one to know he wasn't going to live to sit in the officer's bar. His kind didn't. He was too fast, too strong, too damned enhanced to survive to an old age or a high grade—and too smart not to know it.

You didn't volunteer for this outfit, you were born into it, like some family curse. And now what was left of that family was going to make or break it on Haven, a miserable loo of a planet full of hostiles. It wasn't quite running with your tail between your legs. But it was hiding, and hiding wasn't what Merari was bred to do.

You weren't supposed to know so much about the hows and whys of this fucked-up LZ, and why it was permanent—not down in the ranks, you weren't.

But Merari was too smart for his own good, and he had friends up at Intelligence, back where the *Dol Guldur* was being salvaged into bits and pieces.

A long stay. A new home. And the Lidless Eyes hadn't given a damn what kind of welcome the troops were going to get. They just blew the hell out of Haven's planetary defenses like that was going to solve the problem.

Now there was a fucking insurgency to deal with, if you wanted to dignify it with a name like that. And Merari's boys were on the front lines.

He didn't even know where the hell he was, in relation to Shangri-La. He knew his quadrant, and every damned hill's number, so maybe he could get his boys in and out of strike zones, but that was it.

You could find Firebase Three, no sweat—it was where the brass was. The fucking enemy could find it, too. Military Assistance Command Haven—MACH—squatted out here and thumbed its nose at these locals, hosing down surrounding territory, and then was surprised that the indigs didn't bring their women in voluntarily so the brass could lay 'em flat.

Goddamn crazy way to run an occupation, if you asked Merari. But nobody did, not even his own troop when he started trashing his tent and then, in the following silence, slipped out the back.

Gatling ought to set those fuckers straight.

He went charging through the undergrowth, short cutting to the motorpool, sure that blackness all around would conceal him, in just his grays and a flak vest. Full kevlar was too hot, too constraining, and Merari was feeling like the superman he'd been bred to be, jacked up enough to start a war of his own.

He heard a noise when he'd nearly reached the motorpool and reflexes overrode his rational mind the way they were supposed to: he was hitting the dirt, rolling for cover, and drawing his issue side arm before he could blink and try to focus on the motion in the dark.

He ought to be able to see it. His nightsight was the best in his outfit.

But he couldn't. He couldn't see a damned thing.

He stopped stock still on his belly in the dirt, propped up on his elbows. Rolling in this damned brush was noisy. He went to listening, holding his breath. He could hear insects screwing, his boys said.

But when the unmistakable pressure of a gun's barrel conjoined the base of his skull, it caught him totally by surprise.

"Freeze, Sauron," came the voice from behind.

Picked up the few words they needed to know of a civilized language, these indigs did.

Every muscle strained and still, Merari said, "I'm frozen." He wanted to hear that voice again. There'd been something funny about it, funnier than just the accent. He was pretty good at accents. He wanted to know who and what had caught him with his pants down, and he wanted to know why.

"Good. Drop the hand weapon; drop your belt; drop your pants and don't ask questions."

"What the *fuck?*" Now he knew what had been odd about the voice he'd heard—it was husky, deep, but it was a woman's voice, almost certainly.

"Now you're getting the idea."

"Wait a minute, lady," Merari objected.

The muzzle of something slapped stars into his medulla oblongata. "Drop 'em, in that order. Then roll over, slow."

Balls, he hoped nobody came upon him while this was happening. The only plus he could figure was that, once he rolled over, he'd have lots more options. And when he did, he could see his attacker.

But it was goddamn degrading while he was still on his belly, especially once he'd dropped the gun in the leaves and seen a blackened hand, shadowy in the black night, reach out to take it and realized how small and frail that hand was. His quick-release webbing buckle came off easy, and with that went the rest of his weapons, beyond what breeding had given him.

Roll over and you've got weapons at hand, boy, he told himself, but the sting of being captured by a female wasn't helped much by that advice.

When he did roll over—slowly, because she knew just how to make sure he couldn't scissor her down and she kept the muzzle of her expropriated Sauron gun against his skull, and then his forehead, the entire time—she straddled him, sliding the gun down his face, until its muzzle was pressed against the soft skin under his chin.

"Okay, Soldier, I bet you can guess what happens now." And she reached down for him, one knee firmly planted on the tangle of pants confining his thighs. "Just lie still, fella. If you're a good boy, it won't hurt at all."

It didn't, though at first he wasn't sure she was going to get what she came for.

She kept the gun under his chin and it's hard to keep up your end of a conversation that way. So he didn't make a sound until she got what she wanted.

Finally, she sat up on him: "Set a land speed record that time . . . corporal, isn't it?"

The pressure under his chin eased and he knew he was supposed to answer. Hell, so far, not too bad. If nobody heard about it, not bad at all. But she wanted ID, he knew: "Troop Leader Merari, at your service—in another half hour or so, if you care to wait."

She said. "Don't get cute, superboy," but he heard her chuckle, "Damn, why couldn't he see her? Was she black skinned? Or just covered with blacking? He could see eye-whites and teeth, like she was some Cheshire cat, but that was all.

Or almost all. When she raised herself, he saw a flash of white upper thigh, a slash of white lower belly and pale pubic hair. Camouflaged, then.

"Up, come on, Soldier. Sit up and put your pants on, nice and slow."

The gun came away from his flesh and he could see her shadow move as she pulled up her own pants.

Now! Take her while she's distracted.

But it was only an instant and somehow he didn't want to wrestle her to the ground and take her in for interrogation—where everybody'd know what she'd done to him. And he definitely didn't want to kill her, which was probably because she'd taken some of the fight out of him the best way that can happen.

"How come you did this? How come you picked me?"

"Did this?" came the woman's voice as she backed a few, slow steps away, soundless as a cat. "Well, there's an old saying . . . if you can't beat 'em, join 'em. As for picking you, you just happened to be in the right place at the right time."

"Shit, and I thought you'd been stalking me for months, crazy in love."

"Right," she said. "I'll be back to try you again next month, Troop Leader Merari, if this doesn't do the job. That's the best I can do."

What was he supposed to say? Thanks? But while he was thinking it over, she slipped a few paces farther into the bush and the last thing he heard before she broke for parts unknown was: "Count to a thousand before you pick up a weapon, or you're dead meat, meat."

Nasty bitch, but he stayed there. He really didn't want any commotion about this. Never live down being raped by an indig who weighed maybe a third what he did.

Sauron fucking superman, he was.

There was only one thing to do for his wounded ego and his soldierly pride.

He retrieved his belongings, buckled on his weapons belt, and resumed sneaking up on the motorpool. When he got back to the officer's bar with his gun-jeep, they were going to give him all the beer he wanted.

You bet.

The stockade at Firebase Three was reasonably comfy, considering what the Senior Assault Group Leader, MACH, was trying to keep inside.

They had an exercise area fenced with electro-wire—pointing in at the top, of course. They had a nice dark hole for the real bad boys—it would have been for solitary except there were too many bad boys in the stockade for private rooms—and that was where Merari ended up.

There were two other guys in there, and he could see 'em clear as day at night, though they turned to gray shadows whenever anybody opened the slot for the breakfast feeding.

One of them never said anything, he just glowered at the far wall, night and day. Once in a while he'd get up and run headfirst into the far wall repeatedly, until he knocked himself unconscious, but that was all. He didn't bother Merari, and he didn't bother the other soldier in the hole, the guy with a fifteen millimeter cartridge around his neck on a chain like some sort of jewelry.

Two weeks after Merari had been thrown in here for shooting up the officer's bar at point-blank range from his gun-jeep, the guy with the chain around his neck said something to Merari for the first time:

"Hey, I'm Section Leader Coleman," he said very quietly. "Call me Coley." He held out a huge, scarred hand.

Merari hesitated before he took it. He'd thought none of these guys ever talked. They weren't supposed to—you were supposed to maintain silence, because this was solitary confinement, no matter how many of you there were. He looked at the Runner, as he'd nicknamed the guy who bashed himself into walls. The Runner was staring at his booted feet. They all observed basic discipline: guards came by to check that you were dressed for daytime, stripped for night, like it mattered.

Grasping Coleman's hand at last, Merari said, "TL Merari—or used to be. Whatcha in for?"

"I'm a sniper."

Did he mean his section was the sniper unit? Merari shivered: you didn't see those guys, but you heard about them. Or did he mean he'd shot somebody, or lots of somebodies, probably at regiment level or above where you wouldn't hear about it in the ranks? "Oh yeah?" said Merari aloud. "That's nice, Coley. That's real nice."

"Nah." The sniper reached in his blouse pocket and pulled out a smoke. Merari had seen Coleman smoke before, and couldn't figure out which guard was slipping the stuff in to him.

"Want?" The sniper held the pack out.

Merari took one. He'd have firebombed an enemy village for one of these, when he'd been with his troop. Now, he'd steeled himself against the vice, ignoring Coley whenever the other prisoner smoked his hoarded butts. He'd had dreams about Coley offering him one. When the match came, his hands were shaking.

"Thanks, man. I trashed the officer's bar, but it was their fault. They had beer and they wouldn't give us any . . ."

"I heard," said the sniper. Then he came up on one knee and his neck bulged as, smoke loose between his lips, he stuck his head close to Merari's.

The coal of the smoke, so close, was nearly blinding. But Merari's ears worked fine:

Coleman said, "I've got 117 notches on my AK's stock—personal kills at close range."

"Great. Nice shooting." What did you say, closed up with a fuse like this guy?

"Doc says I'm going back to the Citadel soon, for observation. Funny, that was what they called what we were doing—Observations."

Merari laughed nervously in the pause he was supposed to fill.

Over in the opposite corner, the Runner looked at them both, hissed like a snake, covered his ears with his arms, and turned his face to the wall.

The cartridge on its chain around Coleman's neck swung freely, back and forth, as the sniper leaned even closer. "Know what this is, Merari?"

"Bullet."

"Bullet that's going to kill me. That's what they don't know at Regiment—they can't kill me, long as they don't have this.

"But you're going back there—to the Citadel." Wearing it, asshole.

"Yeah, that's what I'm sayin'. Tomorrow." The sniper sat back and with a fluid motion looped the chain over his head and held it out. "Keep it, buddy? Wear it for me? Till I get back."

"Sure thing." I'll take the damn thing, anything you want, you crazy bastard. If I had a gun, I'd solve your problem and all that would be left is spent brass.

But they didn't give you guns in the stockade hole.

Coleman watched carefully, pupils dilated, as Merari looped the cartridge's chain over his own neck and tucked it inside his blouse. Then the sniper leaned back against the wall, finished his smoke and went to sleep. Coleman's snoring could have waked the dead.

Merari didn't sleep at all that night, just sat and watched the bigger man, feeling the cartridge burn against his bare chest.

Crazy. Sniper outfits weren't on anybody's duty rosters. This guy had a whole *section* like him, back where he came from? Spooked the hell out of Merari, just thinking about it.

The next morning the door opened and Merari was blind in the sun.

When it closed again, Coleman was gone.

The Runner started to jog in place. Merari ignored it. Next to the sniper, the Runner wasn't any sort of trouble.

A week after the sniper had gone, the Runner spoke to him for the first time: "That guy, Coleman?"

"Yeah?" Merari was happier without chat; he didn't want to know anything about this wingnut; he was out of here in a week's time.

"He won't get back to the Citadel, you know—not alive."

"I figured something like that," Merari said wearily, and turned his own face to the wall.

The next night, all hell broke loose outside: the *swup* of shells; the crack and whistle of hypersonics; the blinding glare of flames.

Merari was up and beating on the door in seconds, yelling his heart out. He had a real aversion to being oven-baked.

There was a lot of shooting. It must be an indig attack. They won one every once in a while, and that meant expropriated weapons.

Expropriated weapons made him think about the girl who'd got his pants down last month.

And, as if he'd dreamed it, there she was beyond the cell door jerked suddenly open.

With her was Coleman, covered with black grease and smoke and blood, big as an APC. "C'mon, buddy," Coleman ordered.

And to the woman (—the tiny, black-on-black woman with the golden hair between her thighs that he could see as clearly as if she were naked—) holding a shotgun on him, Coleman said, "See? My friend. Got my luckpiece. Told you he'd still be here."

"Out of there, Merari!" The woman's voice was husky. "Move, Soldier. You don't want to get dead fighting for the privilege of staying in jail."

"It's awright, kid, trust Coley," said the big sniper. "None of these'll be around to tell on either of us. We'll just roll on back to the Citadel and give 'em whatever story we want—the sole survivors. They'll believe us." Coleman raised his automatic rifle, pointing it past the troop leader.

Merari glanced back at the Runner, curled in his customary corner. "Hey, *no*, man," he said hastily to the sniper. "He won't talk."

"Well," said Coleman. "Yeah . . ." But he fired anyway, a short burst thunderous with its echoes. He reached out his hand.

Merari stepped from the hole, slipping off the cartridge's chain and giving it to Coley. "Yeah, all right. Maybe it'll work."

Maybe saying so would keep him alive a little longer.

But as things worked out, he did get back to the Citadel, and so did the sniper named Coleman.

It took a while. They had to get the little woman pregnant first, before she'd let them go.

From *McGraw's Encyclopedia of Military Science,* 82nd Edition (New Aberdeen, 2628)

Jarnsveld's Jaegers

Frystaat military unit, usually in service with the Empire.

History:
As the name "Jaeger" (hunter) implies, this regiment was originally raised (c. 2043) during the early settlement of Frystaat, to protect work crews and settlers from the local predators. Later it also came to fill a garrison/police role in suppressing trouble among the convicts and political deportees shipped to Frystaat by the CoDominium.

After the breakup of the CoDominium and the virtual depopulation of Earth, Jarnsveld's Jaegers (JJ) found its original functions more and more redundant as the local militias and national conscript army grew in size and effectiveness. Gradually it assumed a new role as an elite, all-volunteer cadre and rapid-deployment "fire-brigade" unit. During the era of interstellar anarchy immediately after the Great Patriotic War, it was used with decisive effect in several stellar systems in Frystaat's immediate neighborhood.

The Republic of Frystaat initially followed a policy of limited trade and alliance against any power strong enough to rebuild interstellar unity. With the rise of the Spartan hegemony, the Landholders decided that a change of tactics was in order. No possible combination of independent systems could face the former CoDominium fleet, which had transferred its base and allegiance to Sparta. Instead, the Republic voluntarily offered allegiance and actively assisted Sparta in extending the dominion that eventually became the Empire of Man, in return for a high degree of internal autonomy.

The most potent instrument of that assistance was JJ. Small, but highly trained and well-equipped, JJ was used not in conventional main force operations but as an instrument of irregular warfare. Missions ranged from subversion and assassination through counterinsurgency and anti-terrorist work. The unique characteristics of the settlers of Frystaat made them even more formidable than their high degree of training and esprit de corps warranted, particularly in the small-unit infantry operations in which they specialized.

In the present era, JJ has been actively engaged in attempts to suppress secessionist movements. They have also acquired the distinction of being the only unit ever to fight a successful ground action against genetically engineered Sauron troops without superiority of numbers or firepower. . . .

Recruitment:
Recruitment to JJ is by voluntary enlistment, or lateral transfer from the regular service of the Republic. Enlistments are four standard years for other ranks and six for officers. A term in the Jaegers is considered to discharge all military obligations.

Most of the Jaegers are "younger son" types. Service tends to be traditional in certain families, and is also attractive to the restless (travel offplanet, otherwise rare for Frystaaters), the eccentric (the regiment is very much a world to itself, and is tolerant of anything that does not interfere with the mission), and the ambitious (those who survive two terms are eligible for land grants and interest-free loans).

Organization:
Total strength usually ranges from 2,500 to 3,500 men, with the following table of organization:
  Regimental HQ (administrative) company
  Three rifle battalions (two in peacetime)
  Logistics company
  Engineering/special weapons company
  Support company (medical, etc.)
The basic tactical unit is the five-trooper "stick." Above this level all groups are expected to have "plug-in" capacity, able to combine and shift as need and opportunity dictate.

Training, Tactics, and Philosophy:
A few typical sayings:
"The guns are clean; the troops are ready to fight; everything else is bullshit."
"Winning battles by attrition is to the art of war as a paint-by-numbers kit is to the Mona Lisa."
"You don't win by killing the enemy, but by breaking their hearts and making them *run*."
"We are not a numerous people. Our casualties are expenditures from capital, not income."
"Quality defeats quantity; maneuver defeats mass."
"Outsmart them. There's *always* a way."
"Win. If you can't win, *cheat*. There are no rules."

Frystaat military thought holds that the one basic problem of war is *uncertainty*. A commander cannot really be certain of anything, from the behavior of his own troops to the accuracy of his

maps. You can *never* tell what the opposition is
going to do. Furthermore, once engaged no amount
of real-time communication equipment will save
you from the "fog of war." Even if the machinery
works with unjammed perfection, it still tempts
superiors to risk information overload, which par-
alyzes decision making.

Historically there have been two approaches to
this problem. One (exemplified by pre-Napoleonic
Prussia, the 20th-century Soviet Union . . .) attempts to reduce the uncertainty by simplifica-
tion. Training and discipline are repetitive and
rigid; a tactical manual lays down all the acceptable answers; initiative is forbidden; battle plans
are rigidly adhered to regardless of circumstances.
"Nobody thinks, everybody executes" (Frederick
the Great). This system is characteristic of states
with small, paranoid elites and large, expendable,
but untrustworthy masses of subject cannon fod-
der. A typical feature of such systems was the
KGB automatic-weapons units that followed Soviet troops into battle, machine-gunning stragglers. Soldiers, divisions, and even entire armies
are treated as fungible goods, like ammunition.

The other approach accepts, embraces, and attempts to *use* the "fog of war." This involves a
radical decentralization of command authority,
trusting those closest to the information to use it
properly. Plans are treated as a basis for creative
improvisation. Flexibility is cultivated, the capacity to "roll with the punch," winning by shock
and psychological dislocation rather than simply
chewing up the enemy's men, machinery, and
units.

Certain qualities are implicit in this method:
really good staff work, not mere formula-following;
high unit and individual morale; meticulous training in tactics; training that is intelligently *understood*, rather than followed by Pavlovian rote.

Rarest and most precious of all, the *combination* of discipline and individual initiative. Historical examples would include such units as Rogers' Rangers, the S.A.S., and the Long Range Desert Reconnaissance Group. In terms of armies, the post-Von Seekt German Army and the Israel/ Dayan Zahal. In terms of philosophy, Liddell Hart's/Gerasimov's "indirect approach."

Forces of this type require a different ethos, a "band of brothers," rather than "Fear your officer more than the enemy (Frederick the Great). It also requires a different type of recruit, people who already have well-integrated personalities and the capacity to work intelligently in groups. They still require hard training and respond to the traditional motivators (primary-group identification, unit esprit), but not to the hammer-them-flat approach necessary to turn "the scum of the earth, enlisted for drink" (the duke of Wellington) into reliable soldiers.

This conflict of styles has always existed. However, post-gunpowder technological and tactical developments have generally favored the second type. First, increased firepower forces tactical dispersion. Until the middle of the nineteenth century, armies could literally march into battle shoulder to shoulder. This kept every soldier under the eyes of his officers, his NCO's, and (just as important) his comrades. Napoleon's armies were larger than Frederick the Great's, but he could still oversee the entire course of a battle from a hilltop, and battles lasted no more than three days.

Industrial-era productivity permitted armies too large to oversee in the old sense, but the generals were still unwilling to admit the need for dispersal on a battlefield dominated by firepower. This was not merely conservatism. They knew that the training system was designed for the traditional battlefield, and there was no way of telling what would happen if the men were turned loose. Furthermore, they knew that dispersed operations required more and better training.

The turning point was the First World War. In 1916, the British sent their troops forward at the Somme in long rows, walking upright. This produced 60,000 casualties and no gains in a single day. The soldiers were short-term volunteers, and their commanders had no faith in their ability to perform any but the simplest military tasks. Ironically, these enthusiastic, comparatively well-educated volunteers were better suited to flexible tactics than the slum dwellers and dispossessed Irish peasants of the British regular army!

Later in the same war, the German Army (usually less conservative than its opponents) organized many of its best divisions into "Storm Troops" (a title later made odious by the Third Reich). These were trained to operate in small, self-suifficient groups, infiltrating the enemy lines instead of battering at them, attacking weakness rather than strength. Pockets of resistance were isolated and left for the follow-up elements; the aim was to pierce rather than push back the enemy front and reach the "soft underbelly" of administrative and logistics units. It was an infantry version of what, when mechanized, became known as "blitzkrieg."

Needless to say, Frystaat has always favored the second type of army, with the Jaegers the distilled essence of the whole philosophy. An army of aristocrats, self-motivated, they are the product of an environment that has been culling weakness out of its human inhabitants for more than five centuries. They are also an army of supreme pragmatists, fighting with a cold, intelligent ferocity, uninterested in fripperies or "gallant last stands."

Weapons and Equipment: DZ-7: Light assault rifle. Manufactured Armscore works, Martizburg, Frystaat.

Weight: Three kilograms, loaded.

Length: One meter.

Method of operation: Delayed blowback, selective fire.

Ammunition: 7mm X 20mm caseless. Crystal monofilament core, treated glass sabot.

Muzzle velocity: 2,800 meters per second.

Range: 1,000 meters maximum; 800 meters soft targets; 300 meters hard targets.

Penetration: In soft targets the sabot undergoes explosive decomposition, producing massive wound trauma, while the penetrator tumbles. In hard targets at close range the sabot vaporizes, acting as a lubricant, while the penetrator rod will pierce up to 10mm of homogeneous steel armor or 90mm of concrete.

Sights: Electro-optical; passive light-enhancement, random-variable laser designator, infra-red (with computer display analysis of subsurface structures). May be programmed for burst selection or slaved to master computer. See *Bonephone.*

Construction: Boron fiber in synthetic resin matrix.

Status: In service with armed forces of Frystaat Planetary Republic and some Imperial special-forces units. Also widely used on Frystaat as a small-game rifle.

NA Milrf: Semi-automatic military/sporting weapon. Manufactured Angus-na-Og. Small Arms Works, Dunedin, New Aberdeen.

Weight: 4.2 kilograms, loaded.

Length: 1.3 meters (with bayonet attached).

Method of operation: Gas, semi-automatic. May

be operated as straight bolt-action if gas ports blocked.

Feed: Detachable box magazine, 20-round capacity.

Ammunition: 7mm X 55mm metallic case. Jacketed lead alloy, hardpoint, optional tracer.

Muzzle velocity: 875 meters per second.

Range: 2,000 meters maximum, 1,000 effective.

Penetration: Soft targets to maximum, light body armor/helmets to 600 meters.

Sights: Adjustable post-and-aperture iron sights. Others may be fitted.

Construction: Stainless steel, aluminum. Stock wood or fiberglass; parts exposed to gas chrome-washed.

Status: In service with police, paramilitary, and militia units throughout the Empire of Man. Also used for hunting. A sound though traditional design, cheap, easy to maintain, and "idiot-proof," if not particularly capable. A heavy-barrel version with a bipod is available as a Squad Automatic Weapon. Used as an introductory training weapon by some regular military forces.

Chameleon Suit: Protective/camouflage garment. Manufactured Veldpoed Works, Maritzburg, Frystaat.

Weight: 5 kilograms.

Description: Loose-fitting one-piece suit with wraparound helmet/visor.

Functions:

(a) Protection. Multiple layers of nemourlon with boron fiber/ceramic inserts at strategic points. Full NBW protection with filters and overpressure. Will stop all shell/grenade/mortar fragments, conventional small-arms ammunition, and hypervelocity assault-rifle rounds at more than point-blank range. Filters effective against spores, etc.

(b) Sensor. Helmet contains microcomputer, 100mb RAM, AI software, option for direct neural input. Heads-up display for maps, schematics, weapon aiming points, etc. Microphone pickup for sounds, directional taps into electromagnetic communications, cryptographic and encoding capacity. Satellite links. Millimetric-wave and laser tracing, counterbattery ballistic calculations. Passive and active nightsight devices.

(c) Concealment. Fiber-optic surface and computer-scan duplicate background, incl. thermal output. Absolute match while still, high degree in motion.

(d) Life support. Water recycling. Solid wastes dessicated. Automatic medication against shock, infection, etc. Controls circulation in damaged areas. Diagnostic software. Stimulants available.

Power: Integral biological-waste fuel cell, molecular-distortion batteries.

Status: In service with armed forces of Frystaat Republic, some Imperial special-forces units. Modified version common Citizen outdoor wear on Frystaat, especially in unsecured zones. Exports limited due to policy and cost (2,300 Frystaat *kryrand*, equivalent to 3,000 Imperial crowns.

Bonephone: Computing-communications device. Manufactured Atlas Bioelectronics Works, Nieu Nylstroom, Frystaat.

Weight: .1 gram.

Description: Featureless ovoid. Implanted, usually behind mastoid process. Microfiber link to central nervous system. Protein circuits.

Functions:

(a) Communications. Acts as medium-range radio link—"artificial telepathy." Multi-channel with data-linkage capability.

(b) Information processing. Limited read-write storage capacity (maps, etc.); can also interface with machinery, mainframes, etc., which have data linkage capacity. "Picklock" tapeworm program for breaking into other systems. Can be networked to provide intelligence-enhancement programs.

Power: Oxidant from bloodstream.

Status: Implanted in all JJ recruits after completion of Basic Training. Export banned.

Bows: Three kinds used by JJ, for hunting, training, and covert operations.

(1) Self-bow. Classic homogeneous wooden stave. Fully-trained JJ troopers are expected to be capable of making it in the field.

(2) Reflex bow. Classic built-up bow, using horn, wood, and sinew. Also known to have been produced in the field during both training and combat operations.

(3) Compound bow. Double-stave design. Extensive use of fiberglass and synthetic resins in Frystaat-manufactured bows. Large-scale exports for match archery, hunting, and special-forces units prior to the Secession Wars.

NECESSITY

S. M. Stirling

Byers' Sun had set behind the peaks called Shield-Of-God, when the elders of Eden came to put Ruth on the cross. Each of the thousand souls of Strong-In-The-Lord was there to witness, as were chosen men from the other valley hamlets.

Sheep, Ruth Boazsdaughter thought, standing beside the metal X. Unbound, seal-brown hair floated about her delicately triangular face; a knee-length wool shift provided scant protection from the chill wind. Even in high summer, even here in the deep valley between sheltering cliffs, Haven's nights were cold.

She raised her eyes, ignoring the guards whose hands gripped her slight shoulders. Above, the great banded disk of Cat's Eye glowed in white and crimson. Shadows walked over rolling bunchgrass-covered hills, down to the Malachi River and the adobe houses of Strong, huddled behind the rampart amid stubblefields that smoked dust.

A stir and mutter ran through the crowd; they drew back parting, men doffing their sheepskin caps and bowing, women making awkward curtseys in their long skirts. A dozen men marched stolidly through the opened laneway, middle-aged and bearded, uneasy in their new ceremonial robes. Her gaze locked on the one who led them, meeting eyes that were the same blue-green as her own. Boaz, Prophet of the Lord God, ruler of Eden Valley. Father and executioner.

She forced her teeth together, fighting against the

237

chattering that might be mistaken for fear; the milk-white skin of her arms was roughened to a texture that reminded her of a goose she had plucked last week. Had she ever sat warm beside a fire, smelling coal-smoke, hot iron, baking bread? The wind flicked grit from between the red coils of screwgrass, into her face; it tasted of salt and ash. Her father halted and opened the heavy volume in his hands. He was a small man, slight with the wiry strength that ran in his line, hands roughened and face weathered by a life of labor on a planet not kind to Earth's children.

"I sorrow to see you thus, daughter," he said levelly. The voice was beautiful, mellow and resonant, carrying absolute conviction. And the eyes were not ordinary at all, at this distance. She fought against the familiar calling of them, against the desire to throw her arms around him and ask Da to make it better.

I am sixteen Terran years, she thought. *I am not a child.* "Evening, Joachim," she said, addressing a man beside her father. "Aunt Mary will be worrying that you'll catch your death."

Boaz sighed. "These are the elders of the Church," he said. "Speak with respect."

"These are farmers I've known all my life, dressed up in fancy nightshirts and about to commit murder because you've convinced them you're the voice of the Almighty, Father."

She had expected anger. Instead, astonishingly, he stepped closer with a whisper that pleaded. "Ruthi, don't make me do this . . . for your mother's sake."

Ruth answered in a clear, carrying tone. "You killed Ma; you can kill me; you can't make lies truth, or the planet outside this valley go away by wishing it." She paused, and added with slow deliberation: "I hope Mother looks down and spits on you in hell."

For a moment Boaz' face twisted out of humanness. "*Shut your mouth or I'll have it gagged*," he hissed, and she felt a drop of spittle warm on her cheek. And smelled the grain-spirit on his breath.

He never touches it, she thought. A grudging honesty made her add to herself: *He's doing what he thinks is necessary, whatever the cost. That's something he's given me.*

Boaz turned to face the crowd. "The Lord be with you," he called. Most of those in the crowd had known that voice from earliest childhood.

"And with thy spirit," they replied.

"We are here," he continued, "not in anger, but in sorrow. This strayed lamb . . ."

Her thoughts ran ironic counterpoint: *But that pomposity you can keep. You taught me to read, Father; that was your first mistake.*

". . . refused to bear meekly the tribulations sent to test the Lord's people . . ."

. . . Refused to accept that being fusion-bombed by a shipload of Sauron renegades was an act of God . . .

". . . would not put aside the vanities that brought the Lord's wrath on this world . . ." The voice rolled on.

. . . said we could cobble together a hydro generator, why should we have to live like Dark Age peasants, God gave us minds, Father . . .

". . . lead others astray, even seeking speech with those who follow not the Way of the Lord . . ."

. . . tried to get Joshua to use the radio; the Saurons landed, if we could get a message off-planet the Empire might send help . . .

". . . forsaking womanly silence, spoke out against measures needed for the common welfare in these troublous times . . ."

. . . you burned the books! My father taught me to love those books, you're not my father, you're something that's taken body and face and voice . . .

She remembered clutching the worn copy of *Alice*, fighting and clawing as strong hands tore it away; the memory brought her closer to tears than had the knowledge of death.

He was finishing: ". . . yet even now, if the Lord

does not take her in this night of suffering, she may
return to us chastened . . ."

"Hypocrite," she muttered. Even with warm clothing
and food, a night in the open was no easy matter; she
had not eaten for days, draining the reserves of a body
naturally slender, and there was nothing between her
and the wind . . . Hypothermia would kill her in hours.
She closed her eyes and ignored the hands that lifted
and bound her to the icy metal, biting her lip as the
cross was lifted and the post slipped into its hole,
jarring. Her weight fell against her bound wrists, cramp-
ing her chest; she pulled for the first straining breath.

There was a sharp cry. She opened her eyes to see a
struggle in the front rank of the spectators; a burly
young man with tow-colored hair was lunging and
heaving beneath a pile of bodies. Another man gripped
a red-stained arm, swearing, dancing around the pile of
bodies looking for an opportunity to kick; a hunting
knife lay glinting in the Cat's Eye's light.

"Joshua!" she called. It was faint, hoarse, but the
struggle ceased. She waited until the honey-colored
eyes won back a measure of control. "It's . . . useless,"
she croaked, straining her body upward for breath to
speak. "Go . . . live . . . remember."

The crowd melted away. The last thing she remembered was a sudden stab of fear: Boaz was gone, and
she could not defy this shape of iron, or fight the night
wind.

"Sixteen . . ." she murmured. Blackness.

The wind was stronger towards midnight, here where
the high steppe met the Shield-Of-God range. Thin,
cold enough to leave a rime of hoarfrost, it spilled up
the scree and gullies of the Bashan Pass and over the
saddle into Eden.

Piet van Reenan worked his fingers silently in the
thick gloves; it was important to keep them supple, and
the wind sucked heat. He had been a hunter for many
years, of animals and of men. The discomfort was not

ignored, it was accepted; he would kill when the time came with the same dispassionate recognition of necessity. In the meantime he waited, eyes barely above the level of the gully, sweeping methodically upslope towards the wavering yellow light that marked the blockhouse. There was no true night under Cat's Eye, only a twilight form the gas giant Haven circled. The scientists called it a brown dwarf and Haven its moon; to the human eye it was a bright circlet of color, mantling the land with a deceptive gloaming.

He felt a sudden dangerous nostalgia. There had been many nights like this, in his years with *Jarnsveld's Jaegers*. Special op, clandestine insertions on hostile ground, the clammy weight of a chameleon suit and a tension as familiar as the beat of your pulse. . . . He pushed it away; there was no regiment now, no backup or pullout, no authority higher than his naked will, and that was lonelier than he had awaited.

Enough, he told himself. *You hated soldiering anyway, Piet: it was the least bad form of exile. You'll be homesick for Frystaat next, just because you were born there.*

And he would leave his bones here on Haven, soon or late. There had been no reliable news for nearly a decade, but even then the Imperium had been tearing out chunks of its own flesh like a brain-shot landgator. The Sauron attack had been the final spasm; the single fleeing shipload of Sauron *soldati* who had blasted Haven's meager civilization to radioactive ash obviously expected leisure to digest their refuge. He would accept their Intelligence; no spaceships would leave the Haven system in his lifetime.

coming in, captain. The bonephone relay was like thought. *prisoner. no pursuit*.

"Prepare for covering fire," Piet whispered. There was a brief, faint rattle as the ten bows and five rifles of the support-squad readied. Jan was reliable, but every good man found somebody better somewhere, and they never advertised.

The scouts came gliding from cover to cover; even
with the microcomputer implanted behind his mastoid
feeding data into his cortex, Piet almost missed them.
Missions like this rated the last, precious pair of chameleon suits. They slid over the lip, boots crunching in
the loose gravel; one carried a limp form in a fireman's
hoist, zipped into a foil nightbag. She grunted as she
laid it down.

"So?" Piet said. "And the clippie won't be missed?"

Jan Marais flipped up the visor of his suit. "Cake-
walk, sor," he said. "Could've driven a bliddy hover-
craft past that blockhouse." He jerked a finger at the
form in the bag; the other scout peeled back a flap to
reveal the face of a girl, absurdly young. "Ag, *cis*,
man."

"Had her on a *varken* iron *cross*, captain," he continued. "No guards, so they'll think her friends lifted her.
She might be in a mood to talk, hey?"

Piet shrugged. "*Ja*," he said, and paused. "Atrocities
are common enough, but this was waste," he continued.

"My sentiments exactly *chaver*," Ilona ben Zvi said
with a smile, and resealed the bag. Bending, she lifted
the long bundle easily and slid down the slope toward
the ponies.

"*Bitch*," Jan muttered in the *taal* of Frystaat.

"She didn't do her job?" Piet said, surprised.

"Nie, Captain: she learns quick, natural talent; fast
and mean enough to make up for less bulk." He grinned.
"I just don't *like* her, sor."

The leader shrugged. "With 'like' and a tickey you
can buy a postcard." Dropping back into Anglic:
"Mazyidis, ha-On, you keep the watch. Everyone else,
mount . . . and *trek*."

Ruth awoke to the sound of voices overhead, incredi-
ble warmth, a maddening itch in hands and feet.

". . . *nie berhoots ans my nie*," a deep voice rumbled, in a language she could not place. "*Ein mooie
meisie . . . Skiet hulle dood, Kapetein*."

There was a shrug in the answering voice. *"Maaks nie, kerel . . ."* It switched to Anglic. "Ah, the young lady is with us."

That startled her eyes open. A face swam into view, haloed against a lamp. A man's face, not old or young. Square, straight-nosed, pale green eyes, clipped butter-yellow hair and mustache, shaven chin. The skin was mahogany-brown, then paler below the throat. A disjointed thought ran through her: *Hot-sun tan. Permanent.*

"Permit self-introduction, *g'spaza*," he continued. "Piet van Reenan. Late Landholder of Theiuniskraal on Frystaat; late Captain in Jarnsveld's Jaegers, late political exile here on Haven. Now leader of this band of refugees."

She blinked, moving cracked lips and following the words with difficulty. He was not a native Anglic speaker, the clipped accent told that. But his Anglic was the pure court speech of the inner worlds, not the archaic provincial dialect of Haven.

"Oh, shut up, Piet." A new voice, a woman's. A new accent, liquid guttural. A hand slipped gently under her head and another brought a bowl to her lips. This face was a natural olive, blade-nosed and regular, bowl-cut hair and snapping eyes black. It would have been comely, save for the burn-scars on one cheek. "Can't you see she's barely conscious?"

The warm milk soothed a pain she had not realized she had until that moment. She drank eagerly, and fell asleep in mid-swallow.

The next sight she remembered was the blond man, sitting across from her in a bell tent, reading. He was dressed in a green tunic and trousers with many pockets, boots, a pistol belt; a tall man, block-shouldered. When he saw her eyes on him he came to his feet, seeming to float erect.

"How do you feel?" he asked.

"All right," she replied. She looked down at her hands; they were lying outside the wool coverlet of her cushion-bed, heavily bandaged. They itched; everything seemed very distant, and none of it important.

"You told me your name," she continued calmly. "The other time. You talked like the Emperor, on the Foundation Day tapes, when I was a little girl."

Piet laughed, teeth white against the dark-brown of his face. "Bravo, *g'spaza*; I had a Spartan nurse, as a child."

"But you're not from Sparta. You're from a hot-sun world. A heavy world, too."

He nodded, raising an eyebrow in respectful surprise. "Frystaat: F5 star, 1.21 standard gees," he said. "You've traveled?"

"No, but I read a lot. Before they burned my books."

"They?"

"The people who put me on the cross," she said. "The Elders, and my father, Boaz. He's the prophet, now. Or so he says." She sighed. "You must have taken me down. Thank you very much."

Piet smiled again, more warmly, at the tone: a well-brought-up young lady, minding her manners in the cannon's mouth. *Like little Eva*, he thought. There had been a few letters from his younger sister, before the mails broke down. His father had not even sent notice of Mother's death.

Then it rammed into him. Her *father* the prophet?

Smoothly, he covered the instant's shock. "It was the least we could do. If you want to thank anyone for your life, Ilona ben Zvi carried you back and Allon here healed you."

She rolled her head on the pillow, blinking in surprise. The small grizzled man had been so quiet. . . . He reached out, touched her forehead and felt one wrist.

"Thank whoever gave you a sound constitution and a strong will to live, young woman. Hypothermia, frostbite of the extremities, malnutrition, dehydration, repeated floggings by a maniac . . . With a good hospital, I could have had you on your feet in three days. As it was—" he threw his hands up, indicating the interior of the tent: brazier and smokehood, a few wooden boxes, a lamp, cushions and rugs. "A saline drip, warmth, rest, chicken soup, and native hardihood."

Ruth half-listened, catching the "frostbite." "My hands?" she said, stirring the bandaged lumps she had no strength to raise. Any Havener knew about that.

The little doctor patted her shoulder. "I'll be honest; you may loose a few fingernails on the left. It's not so bad. . . ." Her eyes traveled down to his own hand, saw the torn fingertips.

"Cold?" she murmured, feeling warm darkness stealing up her spine.

"Pliers," he answered.

Suddenly, for no reason, she felt tears trickling down her cheeks and knew she should have been mortified. *I'm so weak*, Ruth thought.

"Good as new in another few days . . ." she heard. And she slept.

". . . disorder," Piet finished. "A dirty soldier is careless; a careless soldier gets dead. Remember that, Zadek, and see that your people do."

The ten group-leaders leaned back against saddles or cushions and relaxed. As usual, the command-council was being held in the Captain's tent, with the flaps up on all sides on this summer's day. Land rolled away, flattening to the south; northward the huge barrier of the Afritberg ran from horizon to horizon, snowpeaks glistening in the morning sun. Part of that whiteness was dry ice; the higher peaks were at altitudes that would freeze carbon dioxide. And it was those mountains that sheltered this stretch of steppe from arctic winds and brought enough rain to let saltbush and bunchgrass flourish.

Camp had been pitched about a spring, on the southern slopes of a low hill. Dull-green egg trees speckled the slope, rushes and sword ferns waved vivid in the little slough at slopefoot; the wind smelled green, faintly spicy with the almost cinnamon scent of the trees. Tents spread down the slope in orderly rows, by combat-group, synthetic fabric on light-metal frames mingling with the newer wood and felt and leather. Most of the ten-score adults were out with the herds that clumped across the plain to the south, sheep and yak, orange Scots cattle and awkward-looking muskylopes native to Haven; the horse-herd was picketed closer to camp, a mass of shaggy little mongol ponies, barrel-bodied and hammer-headed.

Not arabians, Piet thought. He snapped his fingers and the Turk servant-girl scuttled to pour another glass of honey-sweetened tea from the samovar in the center of the circle. *But gods, they can survive.*

"Now, Gimbutas," he continued, sipping.

Ilona laughed, lying back against her saddle on the patterned wool of the carpet. "A secret weapon to make the haBandari master of Haven?" At Piet's frown, she shrugged. "Apologies, O Khan."

She glanced across at Kosti Gimbutas. *Not a bad sort for a Litvak*, she thought. *And a good engineer, but Hertzl's ghost, he's dull.* Unconsciously, she moved her head so that the braid fell across the burn-scars on its left side, and settled herself to listen. The Band oper-ated by Frystaat military custom, although scarcely a dozen were of that breed. That meant a tradition of small-unit work, without an elaborate administrative structure: Initiative was not encouraged, it was de-manded, and that meant information had to be widely shared. *We were lucky*, her mind japed. *An Imperial Marine officer from Sparta, say, we could have got. What did that Boer bastard Jan say was their motto? "March into the cannon's mouth, eyes closed and a ramrod up your ass?"*

The man from the wrecked town of New Vilnus held out his hands a moment, pitted with cinder-burns, be-fore rummaging through the bundles piled around his feet. "Turns out a jacklet engineer can make a pretty good blacksmith," he said. "By *Perkunaz*, it's tricky, though, even with those pointers you gave me."

Piet waved a hand. "Book-knowledge; you have the skill."

"Now I do. . . . Well, the lance- and arrow-heads were easy enough. Here's the first saber; that *was* difficult."

The captain gripped the rawhide binding of the hilt and slowly drew the meter length of steel, a smooth gentle curve with an edge that sparkled, sharp enough to cut the light. A thick wrist turned, and the sword spun in a circle, swift enough to propeller-blur. There was a sound like parting silk.

"*Very* good," he said. "We can start classes as soon as there's enough." For a moment he sat, staring at the metal. *Six hundred years of starflight*, he thought. *And it comes to this. We never learn.*

"The compound bows are even trickier," the techmaster continued. "I mean, you *have* to have a bearing race for the little wheels at the ends of the staves, or you lose mechanical advantage to friction. Ever tried to hand-file roller bearings that small? But we'll do it. Easier if I had a fixed workshop, a waterwheel, maybe some coal . . .?"

"Patience, techmaster," the commander said. "I'm coming to that. Dr. Allon?"

The grizzled man shuffled a folder of papers in his mutilated hands. "General health is good. Surprisingly so." He passed a hand over his cropped scalp. "So, maybe I was too used to panspecific antibios. Turns out, even with the shortage of water for washing, the UV keeps the bacteria down. Make sure everyone gets plenty of exposure, it's one of the few good things about this thin atmosphere of ours. The herbal remedies are going well, and that contraceptive seems to work."

There were exclamations of delight at that. A third of the Band was female, and they were too shorthanded for unscheduled lay-ups.

The doctor sighed. "Which brings me to the perennial problem. Without a pressure chamber—which we cannot build—the chances of a successful pregnancy for anyone who isn't Tibetan or Quechua descended are about . . . 3%." He paused. "We need an area at least a thousand meters lower, or we'll be extinct in a generation. Old and alone before that."

Their eyes turned to Piet. He sat impassive, crosslegged on a nest of cushions, and sipped the tea. The taste was bitter and comforting, the sun pleasant on his bare torso. He was cold, of course; it must be about twenty degrees Celsius, like a winter's night at one of Frystaat's poles. The Imperium had given him an estate here on Haven; cheaper than killing him, with the van Reenan's influence; he had called it New Theiuniskraal. There had been a solarium courtyard; he and Sarie had lain there in the sun, sometimes, watching the twins play among the spiny wax-leafed plants of their new homeworld.

A 20mm cannon shell had taken her in the back when the Saurons strafed them.

"Jan," he said, without taking his gaze off the distant mountains. "Tactical report."

The ex-NCO spread a map on the carpet with thick, spatulate brown fingers. There was a rustling as the staff and group-leaders crowded about. Few of them had been professional soldiers before the breakup, but the past four years had altered the perspective of the survivors.

"Valley runs northwest to southeast," he said, tracing the slant-sided rectangle. "These mountains on the south, high but thin: four passes, but only one that'll take wheeled traffic. There's a river running near the Shield range, twenty kilometers, whole length, to a small swamp in the south, then out under the cliffs. Four settlements, one abandoned; main one in the southern part of the Valley, just below a dam where the river crosses a rocksill. Lots of irrigated land. Earthworks around all the hamlets, brick watchtowers, all pretty new. From the looks, I'd say they ran it all up in the last couple of years. Blockhouse in the main pass. Used to be about . . ." His face grew abstracted as he consulted the bonephone reference file mentally. ". . . three thousand people. Probably a little less now, eh, man?"

"Appraisal," Piet ordered. Jan spread his hands.

"Ag, Kapetein, a dozen dopped-up *hotenots* with sheep-shears could take it."

Ilona nodded. "That blockhouse, it's a joke. Boulders and cement, but the idiots put it right by the trail; the field of fire's pathetic, lousy observation. Infiltrate around it, satchel charges. Hit the villages before they can concentrate, so maybe we'd have to use the mortar . . . Day and a half, all told."

"Then what?" Piet said.

She blinked, surprised. One of the group-leaders drew a palm across his throat. "What else is there?"

The Frystaater sighed. "Look, you people. We've decided it's no good trying to settle down. New Vilnus was a special case; the Saurons bombed you, but it was stragglers and Turki raiders that finished you off. Ilona, Allon, you *Ivrit* found out the hard way how vulnerable farmers are on Haven, now that there's no law. Herdsmen can move; they're hard to pinpoint for an attack. They can keep all their adults organized and under arms without neglecting survival tasks, which farmers can't. You had about as good a defensive setup as your numbers allowed, but still . . ."

The dark-haired woman had flushed, then gone white about the mouth. Allon looked down at his hands, thoughtfully.

"We haven't forgotten," she said, hand tight on her knife-hilt. "I still think we might have gotten rid of Kemal's scum, but it would have cost . . ." She shook her head. "All right, Captain. As I hear you, you say we need the Valley intact, but we don't want to settle there?"

He nodded and stood, with one hand gripping the frame of the tent. "*Ja*," he said softly. The skin of his torso was light brown; muscle rippled under it as he moved, without the slight padding of subcutaneous fat that most men have. "This is the best grazing we've

come across, and it's empty. . . . Chukdun and his
Uighurs further south, but that's dry and they'll have to
spread out thinner than we do. With the Valley . . . we
could use the things they grow and make; the winter
grazing would mean we could increase the herds to the
summer grazing limits. . . . Most of all, we could have
children. And anybody who wanted to live around here
would have to pay toll for passage into our little pocket
lowland. Unless they'd rather go south to Shangri-La
and ask the Saurons."

The officers considered. "Hmmmm," one of them said
at last. "But Captain, these are Harmonies, and a pretty
eccentric bunch at that. We could conquer them, but to
hold . . ." He shook his head. "Not without a bigger
detachment than we could afford. It's one thing to keep
a few Turki prisoners around the camp, but there are
more of them than us. Guerillas, assassination."

Piet made a gesture of assent. "*Gut*, as I thought,
too. Oh, maybe we could wear them down; as I said,
farmers are more vulnerable to that. And there *are*
things we could offer in exchange for tribute: protection, for example; surplus livestock; maybe trade, later,
when the steppes settle down. But it would be unsta-
ble, and we aren't numerous enough to take chances. I
feared we'd have to exterminate them; that's a bad
second-best; the Valley would be too tempting empty,
and we have to move with the seasons. But there's the
girl, Ruth."

"Ahh," Ilona sighed. "She told you something."

He turned to face them, mouth set in a line. "No,
what she *is*. She's the daughter of their Prophet, in
there."

Jan snorted. "Not his favorite, man, or he's got a
bliddy strange way of showing affection."

Piet leaned forward, hanging his weight on the bar
above him. "*Nie*, but . . . from what she's said so far,
Boaz, this prophet, put her on the cross because she
was spreading dissent among the younger people. Must
have done it well, too, to warrant execution."

The bar creaked as his hands closed on it, crushing. "She probably doesn't have a real party or followers; *magtig*, she's only sixteen Terran, hey? But smart, she spotted right away I was from a high-g world just by the way I moved. She gives us a lever, a carrot as well as a stick—a way of aligning ourselves with one of their factions and using their own symbols. People will submit to a symbol when they wouldn't to a naked sword. Especially if the alternatives are bad enough, and they must be at each other's throats in there."

"How can you tell?" Allon said shrewdly.

For the first time that morning, the captain smiled. "Look, I'm a hard man, *nie*?"

They nodded, and his smile grew into a grin. "And when was the last time you saw me crucify a teenage girl?"

He saw comprehension dawn; it was difficult, after thinking of themselves as bandits for so long. "It'll be tricky," he warned. "We'll have to find out more, get the girl on our side. Ilona, I'll want your help on that. First, we'll take the blockhouse, so we can isolate the situation, but then . . . how does it feel to be an army of liberation?

His grin grew sharklike. A chuckle started, spread; in a moment they were howling with a savage merriment. "And the best of it is, it's *true*," one wheezed.

Piet was the first to grow silent again, staring out at the peaks of the Afritburg. "*Home*," he murmured softly.

The blockhouse was boring, Righteous Geraldson knew. But that was no excuse for the sinful waste of the Lord's precious time implied in the playing of card games.

Besides that, Scripture plainly stated that the casting of lots was used in ancient times to determine the Lord's will; hence gambling was sinful. Granted that the prophet Boaz had not yet pronounced on this, but . . .

"You two," he said, clearing his throat. The young men looked up, resignation on their sparsely bearded faces. "If you cannot sleep, clean your weapons or read the Bible."

Both sighed; one gathered up the tattered, dog-eared cards; the other resignedly began to field-strip his rifle, a New Aberdeen 7mm semi-automatic. Five of the twelve men in the tiny fortress guarding the Bashan Pass had rifles, and the leader carried the Valley's single captured machine-pistol. This was, after all, the most important post.

"Yes, Elder," they muttered.

Set into the slope of the pass a hundred meters above the roadway, the inside of the structure was a plain D shape of mortared rock; the curved outer surface was pierced by loopholes and a door of welded steel beams. The inner wall held the chemical toilet, bunks, fuel cell, and ventilators. Building it and the village walls had taken much labor, and much of the remaining material and fuel in Eden. But none had grudged it, not after the Uighur attack that had destroyed Matherville and almost overrun the Valley; they had gone hungry that year, but Boaz had carried a hod and broken rocks with his own hand.

The Prophet saved us, Righteous Geraldson thought with admiration. A holy man, yes, but truly a *man* as well.

That brought his eyes uneasily to the figure of young Joshua Tomsson crouched in a corner. It had taken six men to beat him into unconsciousness when Ruth Boazdaughter was put on the cross; only the fact that he had lain confined had saved him from more than a scourging when she disappeared. The thought brought a flush of anger, but there was still a trace of queasiness at the way the young man stared, the sledgehammer that was his personal weapon across his lap. A sour smell told Righteous that he had not bathed since then either; the big-boned form was slumped, the strong lines of his face stubbled. It was a pity there was no father in Joshua's household to rebuke his weakness;

even if the girl was his betrothed, she had been too unbiddable to make a good wife, and too narrow-hipped.

It had been hard for the Prophet. Yet . . . *if thy right eye offend thee, pluck it out*. These were no times for weakness.

Recalled to duty, Righteous, too, began to strip and clean his submachinegun. He had just disassembled the bolt when a knock came at the door.

For a moment he accepted that. Then he sprinted to the lookout, shoved him aside roughly, peered out into the faint light of the Cat's Eye. There was no one in front of the heavy door, nothing in the smooth clean firezone that stretched down to the roadway.

"Alert!" he called. "Everyone up, put out the lights!"

Men scrambled from their bunks; the cardplayer cursed, fumbling in the dark for the parts of his weapon. For a moment the cramped space echoed with clatter and the sound of colliding bodies. Then there was silence, broken by panting and the heavy *click* of the Edenites' leaf-spring crossbows. The smell of acrid tention-sweat filled the air.

Battle-readiness swelled, then diminished. Half an hour passed, and Righteous began to doubt his memory. *Perhaps it was a falling rock?* Echoes were tricksome in the heights.

At that moment, the ring of *plastique* on the rooftop trapdoor detonated. It was not a very large explosion; much of the force and most of the noise followed the line of least resistance upward into the night. Quite enough remained to cut the mild steel door clear of its collar and send it straight down with a muffled *thump* and monstrous echoing *clang!*

"*Back—get back!*" Righteous began to scream. He was the first to turn, and saw the grenade fall through the light-flooded hole in the ceiling, saw it bounce off the fallen trapdoor with a hollow sound that told of a plastic casing. He watched it roll, and knew for a single frozen moment that he was dead; he gathered his resolve to throw himself on it.

Then it burst with a soft, muffled *pop* that filled the interior of the bunker with thick, impenetrable black smoke.

For a precious second the Edenite commander stood gaping, as the conviction of death fought with the whirling confusion of stimulus-overload. With an enormous effort he drew his mind together and forced it to function. A thought possessed him; the image of bullets slashing back and forth between the narrow stone walls of the blockhouse.

"*Don't shoot!*" he called. It was the last command he gave.

Outside, Jan Marais had waited patiently in a jumble of rocks a hundred meters from the door of the fortress. The chameleon suit made a motionless man virtually invisible; even a slow walk was enough time for it to adjust. It was pleasant to have an assault rifle in his hands again, too, worth the cold and the rocks digging into his belly. On Frystaat an assault rifle was a small-game gun, youngsters trained on them. For the more dangerous fauna, you needed something with a shaped-charge explosive head. But the DZ-7 was a fine weapon for this work, the standard tool of the *Jaegers* in the old days. Hypervelocity bullets, a glass sabot wrapped around a monofilament crystal penetrator rod; the rod would blast through light armor or thick concrete, with the glass vaporizing as a lubricant. In a soft target, the glass shattered explosively and tumbled the monofilament into a small, infinitely sharp circular saw.

Smuggling the carbon-fiber stock to his cheek, he squinted through the sight. Instantly the crude hand-welds of the door sprang into view, mottlings of color indicating the underlying structure. Panning across, he found the hinges.

Good, he thought. *Only two, and narrow*. Amateurs tended to do things like that. . . .

Humming silently, he adjusted the rifle to six-round burst with a mental command through his bonephone, regretting that there were only a dozen of the 150-round drums left. Full auto lasted only a second and a half, but you could saw through boulders with that.

ready, he commanded the weapon. A red laser spot appeared in the sight; random-phased frequency shift would make the dot invisible to anyone not looking through this instrument. And the rounds would strike *exactly* where the spot lay; it even allowed for the spread on auto-fire.

He saw figures stirring on the slope above the farmers' pillbox. The flash from the explosion was a faint brightening through the gunsight as it adjusted. The rough-clad figures above the blockhouse swarmed down onto its roof. The smoke grenade would be going off about . . .

jan. now. His finger stroked the trigger once, twice. Light erupted from the hinge-areas, incandescent fragments of crystal and steel, too small to do damage. A third burst cut the bar.

And a dozen Band warriors rose from the rocks, running for the blockhouse as smoke poured from the gunslits. They ran with trained speed, but the block-built figure in the lead drew away from them as if they were standing in place. He struck the door, running through as it collapsed with scarcely a pause.

Tot siens, Kapetein, he thought resignedly. He was expendable, but the chameleon suit he wore was not to be risked in close combat. *I promised the Ou Baas I'd look out for you, but it's never been easy.*

Righteous Geraldson felt the destruction of the block-house door only as a smell of scorched metal and shower of sparks on his back. Neither halted his lunge for the fan-switch; his palm slapped down and the high-capacity system coughed into operation, assisted by the gaping hole in the roof. More smoke billowed out as the armored door crashed inwards; thus there was just enough space cleared for the Edenite to see the first figure drop through the blasted trapdoor, hit the floor rolling and bounce erect. Another followed, and another, as he pulled the hatchet from his belt and plunged forward.

He checked a half-step as the scarred face before him became that of a woman, dark hair bound back to expose a terrible burn-scar. She seemed to be unarmed, save for a half-meter hardwood stick in each hand.

"*Whore of Satan!*" he howled, spittle flying. His axe cut for her neck.

Somehow the blow did not land. Instead, he found himself drawn around by the weight of his strike; There was the sudden, agonizing pain of a blow on the nerve-point of his elbow.

He was almost face-to-face with the woman now. "*Daver Ivrit?*" she enquired politely. The other stick's tip rammed into his crotch, and he doubled over convulsively.

"You could at least insult me in my own language," she continued, rapping him sharply behind the ear with the first *yawara*-stick. He folded bonelessly to the floor.

Piet struck the door running, just as it was beginning to topple; even in Haven's .86 gee his heavy muscle and dense bone had considerable mass, and he was travelling as fast as a galloping horse. The door crashed inward; Piet landed on his feet, came erect in a chest-high puddle of black that thinned rapidly. The taste of it was like oil as his lungs pumped; his pupils dilated until they swallowed the iris, almost as efficient as a starlight scope.

Most of the Edenites were down. One was within arms length, a tow-haired youth with a sledge raised.

Joshua had crouched through the attack in the same red-shot grey haze that had gripped him for the last four days. But the sight of Righteous Geraldson falling under the stranger's sticks had roused him; not to rationality, but to the killing rage that despair had denied him. He crouched, whirled aloft a hammer that suddenly seemed weightless.

A face appeared before him, out of the billowing cloud. An alien face, green eyes and bright hair shocking against dark skin. A man shorter than he by a head, with empty hands; not that a weapon would have deterred the sledgewielder. He swung with blurring speed.

A hand slapped down on the hammerhead before its stroke was a quarter done. He could see no movement: The man's hand simply appeared to cross the meter of space without motion. Even so, the force of the blow should have broken bone, caused pain at least. Instead, the brown fingers closed around the massive steel, and the shaft was whipped out of his hands without visible effort, fast enough to burn his palms with the friction. Then the stranger held the hammer out at arm's length, hands at opposite ends of the shaft. His hands flexed; the shaft snapped across. And he grinned; he grinned at Joshua.

"*No!*" the young Edenite bellowed. His fist lashed out, heavy and knobby, with all his weight behind it. He gave an involuntary yelp of pain as it struck the dark-skinned man's stomach; the other grunted slightly.

"That . . . *hurt*," he said mildly. The hand moved again, seeming to stretch impossibly. It closed on the thick leather of the farmer's jacket, lifted his 100 kilograms into the air, and shook him methodically, shook him until the world blurred and his body went limp. The floor came up to strike him.

"No casualties, Captain," Ilona said, as the Bandari warriors shoved and kicked and lifted their prisoners out into the cool twilit night of Haven. "Barring a few bruises, and one of ours with a cut arm." She twirled the dense-grained sticks and thrust them through the belt of her glazed-sheepskin jacket.

"*Up against the wall. Spread 'em! Move, move!*" Dazed, those of the prisoners still walking submitted to a rough search and binding. All except one; Joshua plunged forward with a cry as righteous Geraldson was carried out and laid down.

"*You killed her!*" he shouted, throwing himself onto the prone form and locking his hands about its throat.

Jan Marais was standing nearby. Sighing, not bothering to remove the assault rifle from the crook of his left arm, he stepped forward and slapped the young Havener across the side of the head with an open palm. Joshua dropped bonelessly.

"You Frystaaters are show-offs, you know that?" Ilona said, shaking her head.

"Why not?" Piet asked, stretching and inhaling deeply. This had gone exactly according to plan, which was a minor miracle by military standards. All the enjoyment of combat, without the blood.

"Right," he continued. "I'll leave you Firstgroup as a blocking force; take the local's guns to back up your bows, hmmm, the MG and the mortar as well. This spot's a deathtrap; go over the saddle and downslope, dig in—heavy weapons well back. When the relief comes in, see them off; no killing unless they try a real push. Tell them we've got their people and we'll parley later. You come back around dawn; Jan can handle it from there."

She nodded. "A good night's work."

Piet looked at the unconscious body of the young giant who had tried to strangle his leader. "*Die Boer mek sy plan*," he murmured. "You, my impetuous friend, are going to be *useful*."

Ruth awoke to bright sunlight, filtered green through synthevcanvas. She knew this was true waking, not the dreamlike drifting of deep illness. Curled on her side she saw a hand before her eyes, now lightly bandaged in gauze; she could smell an unfamiliar sharp medicine on it. Somewhere there was the thud of hooves, a rhythmic wooden squealing, the pungent scent of dung fires and cooking.

Her eyes focused on the carpet beside her head. There was a book there . . .

"*Alice!*" she squealed. "And *Through the Looking Glass!*"

The bed creaked. She started in alarm, then relaxed as she saw it was the woman with the burn-scar.

"Ilona ben Zvi," the woman said. Nodding to the book: "You talk in your sleep, the Captain's chased the White Rabbit, too." She lifted a tray. "Yigal, Dr. Allon, says you can go back on solids. But slowly; then get dressed, Piet wants to talk to you."

The odor of porridge and cream and egg tree tea made her mouth water; she forced herself to spoon carefully, and was full before she had expected. The clothes proved to be a problem; trousers, which she had not worn since she became a woman, four years before.

These people aren't of the Lord's Chosen, she told herself firmly. *And it's just custom, not law.*

And the look and feel of synthetic underwear, just out of the wrapper, was a pleasure long forgotten. Eden had been making do with half-cured hides and cut-up blankets since the trucks stopped coming; the jacket and boots were soft well-tanned leather, the breeches plain coarse wool, both new.

She finished the laces and looked up. "Mrs. ben Zvi—"

"Ilona."

"Ilona, I'm grateful, but . . . I've got so many questions I don't know enough to know what to ask."

The scarred woman shrugged. "You're just outside the Bashan Pass into Eden, with van Reenan's Band— the haBandari, we've taken to calling ourselves. Piet pulled us together, these last few years. He's from Frystaat, used to be a soldier before he was exiled here. The Saurons bombed him out; the rest of us . . . well, we *Ivrit* come from a village called Degania, we were overrun by Turkmen bandits. Then there's the people from New Vilnus . . . about two hundred of us in all. Adults, that is."

She paused, fingers playing with two steel-tipped

sticks thrust through her belt. "You've only been attacked once in there, not so? You've been lucky; half the people on Haven have died since the Saurons came." She laughed bitterly. "We always thought of ourselves as a primitive backwater, farmers and ranchers . . . Farmers with tractors and gene-tailored seeds, ranchers with satellite commo links and airjeeps! That's all gone, and nobody knows how to live without it. They're killing each other out there, Ruth: for a can of food, a box of ammunition, for the fun of it."

The scar tissue stood white against her skin, and Ruth was suddenly, shockingly aware that there was a pattern to it. Ilona nodded. "Knifeblade."

They stood, without thought, Ruth clutched the book to her. Ilona continued: "Piet's . . . a hard man, but fair, when he feels he can be." They walked into the sunlight.

The Bandari camp was more orderly than Ruth would have expected for wanderers, cleaner than Strong-In-The-Lord, crowded behind its wall. She watched quietly as her escorts guided her; the rows of dormitory tents, the weaving area with its knock-down looms, a small portable smithy. The folk were well-dressed, well-fed; they greeted the two leaders with smiles, waves, an occasional salute. And they were all armed.

"There doesn't seem to be as much . . . stiffness as I'd expect," she said, looking up at Piet. Close up, he was shorter than she had thought: square face, neck a wedge into broad shoulders, torso slab-sided; face and arms had a gaunt look that puzzled her, until she realized they had none of the underskin fat a normal man had.

"I was a history student, originally," he said. "And we Frystaaters don't have much use for that 'tin soldier' shi . . . er, foolishness."

Ilona chuckled. "Frystaat's an . . . odd place, from what I've heard. Aristocratic republic, but the underclass aren't allowed arms at all. Combat units are all gentry and their retainers, so officers aren't social superiors, just . . . how did you say it, Piet?"

" 'Functional specialists.' Expected to lead by example and force of personality. Still, people need some ritual, a sense of belonging. . . . I'm familiar with the way my homeworld's military build loyalty and solidarity, and it works, so . . ." he shrugged.

"What's Frystaat like?" Ruth asked.

He stroked a finger along his jaw. "Bad." He considered. "We were settled about the same time as Haven, around 2040. Fifty years later, there were only a hundred thousand people."

"Oh?" she said.

"After five million immigrants."

"*Oh.*"

She realizes what that means, he thought. *A little.* And remembered.

"Heavy gravity," he said softly. "Birth problems, heart problems, bone problems . . . If you fall, you break. Three month storms, with dust like industrial abrasive, winds 140 kph, over forty Celsius half the year. Weather's a solar-powered machine, after all. So is life. There were oceans on the equator once; now it's a death zone, over the boiling point all year 'round. Life . . . adapted, and it was more energetic than Terran to begin with. Things with armor, with tentacles, with stings . . . At least you can use antitank weapons on the bigger ones; there's a midge, about the size of your thumbnail, that burrows in shady patches of sand. Stings you, lays eggs, and then the eggs hatch and eat . . . *fast.*"

"Why did anyone go there?" Ruth asked, shuddering.

"They wanted to be . . . by themselves," he said. "They weren't popular, my ancestors. Their enemies joked that they'd exited themselves to Hell." He touched his mahogany-dark skin. "And they picked a planet where nordic caucasoids develop skin cancer unless they darken; there's an irony there, I'll tell you about it someday." With a bitter laugh: "For a *real* irony, just when they were beginning to find their feet, the

CoDominium Bureau of Relocation started dumping deportees on them. They couldn't afford machinery, so BuReloc gave them slaves. . . . Ore and minerals out, convicts and welfare clients in; Frystaat was the perfect prison-planet, it killed them as fast as the transports could land them. Their descendants are slaves still, and the Landholders've never allowed enough technology to tame the planet, because then we'd have to teach the bonds to read . . . Frystaat, garden-planet of the Imperium."

"But you still love it, don't you?" Ruth said, earning a hard stare.

"You *are* a perceptive young lady, aren't you?" Then: "Ah, here's our school; I thought you might be interested."

School was an awning stretched out from one of the vehicles in the circular wagon-laager. Two-score children sat reading or drawing on wooden boards with charcoal-sticks. Inside the wagon itself she could see stacked cartons of books, real books with leather covers. She hugged *Alice* closer and suppressed an urge to burrow.

"That's the bookwagon," Ilona said. "Piet's, most of them: weigh kilotonnes, but he *will* drag them around."

"Civilization is portable, Ilona," he said. To Ruth: "We're going back to a subsistence economy, here on Haven. And that's *complicated*, takes hundreds of skills nobody knows. But the books have them, and we can relearn them. Not just the children, either: everybody learns, and everybody with something to teach imparts it. Ilona's our livestock expert, for example; Kosti Gimbutas teaches metalwork; I do unarmed combat and historical ecology . . . survival skills."

In the open plain beyond the wagons, riders were galloping. She could see their bows; arrows flickered out to targets bound to hay-bags, flechings and heads flickering in the bright sunlight. Shouts and laughter came on the wind, with the summery ozone-smell of warm grass. Then shouts from closer by; the class was breaking up, and half of it boiled around the three.

"Is this the girl from the Valley? Will she stay with us? What Group's she going to be in, Oom Piet?" The questions rattled on.

"When're we going to start practice with swords, Tantie Ilona?"

"She's pretty!"

One of the older boys was shoved foreward by his companions. Grinning and blushing, he produced a bar of iron forge-stock from behind his back. Piet groaned, and Ilona shook her head.

"Come on, Oom Piet," he said. "Just *once* more?" The others chorused agreement.

"Bloody cheek," he muttered. "Oh, all right." He gripped the bar by the ends, took a deep breath, closed his eyes. They flared open, and the air came hissing out of his lungs.

"*Disssssaaa!*" For a moment the iron trembled, then metal as thick as paired thumbs began to bend smoothly. He twisted it into a perfect circle and tossed it to the ground. "Careful, torsion heat . . . and you young *sklems* have work to do, or shall I ask your groupleaders?" They scattered.

"What does 'Oom' mean?" Ruth asked.

" 'Uncle,' " Ilona replied, grinning. Piet scowled.

"Back to the command-tent," he said, glancing down at Ruth. "No sense in straining you too soon, and now there are some questions for *you* to answer."

She stiffened. "I'm grateful to you for saving my life, and for your kindness, but . . . they're still my people."

"Ah, good," Piet said, nodding. "No leader can expect loyalty without feeling it."

Ruth almost stumbled in surprise. "*Leader?*" she squeaked. Then more normally: "Captain Piet, I'm just a girl."

"Just one who merited execution for subversion," he said. "Which means you must have had some effect. Your father—"

"*I have no father!*" Startled at her own venom, she halted.

"Boaz, then," Piet continued, urging her with a placatory gesture. "Boaz must have thought you a danger. These are hard times, and in hard times people fall back on old myths; you have the blood, the *mana*. Also personal force."

They reached the commander's tent, at the apex of a pyramid from which the others radiated. A hawk groomed on a perch by the door, and two brindled cats drowsed in the sun. Ducking under the flap, she glanced curiously around the interior; it held a folding cot and desk, chests for clothes, racks for weapons. A meal of stew, flat tough bread, soft cheese, milk, and tea was laid out; her stomach growled, the overstressed body demanding to renew its reserves. They settled crosslegged about the food, the two Bandari waiting with amused patience while Ruth said a brief grace.

Tearing a round of the bread gingerly between sore fingers, she nodded at a picture by the cot, a simple hologram of a woman smiling with two children in her arms. "Who's that?" she enquired.

"My wife," Piet said quietly, glancing out the open sides of the tent. "And our daughters. The Saurons killed her, when they strafed New Theiuniskraal."

Ruth looked at her hands. Piet continued, in a voice as emotionless as glass:

"Do you think your fa—Boaz—is a good ruler?" At her obvious relief, he smiled. "I've got . . . other sources of tactical intelligence. What I want is your opinion."

She sprinkled salt on her stew; they had been very short of it in Eden, and her mouth craved the taste.

"No," she said, after a considered interval. "Not just what . . . he did to me."

"You see," she went on slowly, "he was a good man once. I was . . . very young then, but I remember. He was always strict in the Faith, the men wouldn't have elected him Bishop otherwise, but he was a fair man. He even let me read in his library, said that hearing of other ways would make me stronger in the Way."

"But then . . . when the garrison withdrew, things

started to become worse for us; people shot at the supply trucks, and we had to call out our militia more often. Fath . . . Boaz was Mayor, too, and he got to be tired all the time. He had to deal with the government in Shangri-La all the time, too, and he started making speeches, how they were idolators and trying to oppress the Lord's people."

She gripped a cup of tea between her hands, her face turned inwards to old pain. "Then . . . the Saurons came. We heard the broadcast from the south, from Shangri-La, and then it cut off right in the middle." She raised her head. "Why did they do it? We'd never harmed them!"

Piet sipped. "The *soldati* never let that bother them . . . one of the reasons they lost, besides striking too soon, overconfidence. I had a good monitor at New Theiuniskraal and listened in. The *Dol Guldur* was running from defeat, but they seemed to think that there wouldn't be any pursuit for a long time, generations. They've taken over Shangri-La." His lips skinned back from his teeth. "They owe me a debt; someday. . . . Go on."

"Then they bombed us, not a fusion bomb, but it destroyed the power-receptor at Matherville and killed a lot of people. And then things got really bad: The clinic was in Matherville, and it was summer, so all our stored food went bad. Then . . . those ranchhands, the Uighurs, they'd killed their bosses and they drove right into Eden and started doing . . . awful things . . . they were drunk and . . ." She paused, fought for control. Ilona nodded grimly and looked away. "The men fought them, and they went away."

"Fa—Boaz, he just became sort of . . . strange, after that. Ma was . . . hurt, and there wasn't any doctor, so she died. Boaz had all the medicines smashed up, and said the Lord would provide. But there's been a lot of sickness, and . . . I knew a little, about cuts and midwifing, but Boaz said it was devil's knowledge; he had the books burned, all of them."

She was silent for a moment. "Then . . . the Uighurs, the prisoners, he had them—what they did to me. And left them up there . . . the smell, the smell!" More calmly: "Then he said he was the Prophet, not Bishop, that God was telling him what to do. He told the people to build the walls, and that was right, but then he had them build a new Temple, even when the crops were waiting. The crops have been bad, too; we can't get seed from the breeding-farm anymore."

"Hybrids," Ilona said, and subsided at Piet's glare. "Go on."

"And . . . the machinery's all gone, and we work and work, but we're always falling a little further behind somehow. Boaz won't let us try to open the coal mine up at Northvalley, or make a new power-station at the falls, or use the radio, or . . . anything." She looked up and whispered. "And I'm so afraid they're all going to die, all my friends and Auntie Susan and . . ." She stopped, blinking.

Piet leaned forward, hands on his knees. "This is good grazing, hereabouts. The ranch houses have all been burned out; did Boaz take them in?"

"No," Ruth whispered.

"So they died. The Band is thinking of settling down in this area, moving south in the winter and then back in spring, but we'd need access to the Valley; you know why." She nodded; any Havener was conscious of that. "If we approached Boaz and his Elders peacefully, would he let us, for fair payment?" She bit her lip, shaking her head.

"Ruth, Haven is going to be a bad place for farmers now. On Terra, very long ago, nomads—wandering herders—split off from the early farmers. They could use areas that were too dry or cold for cropping, but nomadism was a more ecologically marginal—that means—"

"I know."

"Ag. Well, it means herding is less stable than farming. And herders need farmers more than the reverse;

need grain, and things that can't be made on the move. But nomads are *stronger* than farmers, without machine technology; they can move faster, strike harder. They don't have crops that can be burnt, and they can use a larger proportion of their adults as fighters without starving. And Haven has more desert and steppe than Terra, Ruth."

He chopped the air with a hand. "The Band *must* have access to a valley. If we have to take it, we will. But Ruth, there aren't enough of us to *control* your people against their united will; enough to *destroy* them all, yes."

"You'd . . . kill them all? Even the children?" Ruth asked. Her shock went beyond emotion, and she felt a hollow calm.

"We could adopt . . ." He paused, rubbing a hand across his face. "In order to live, it is sometimes necessary for a man to kill." His eyes locked with hers. "But he should not kill more than he must; he loses something, a respect for life. And there are certain things a man should not have to see; either to suffer them, or to do them." His voice grew soft. "They are too hard for him to forget."

He clenched a fist for emphasis. "Ruth, what I ask—what I *demand*—is that you help me find a way that will give both our peoples a chance. A way that both can live with. And Ruth, your people *need* us."

"Oh?" she asked, clenching her fists and swallowing.

He smiled at the defiance. "We, ah, Bandari, have taken what we needed, fought for it when we had to. We've lived as we must, not as we would. But that valley is an invitation to any of a thousand maggots and jackals out there, infesting a dead planet."

"We have our defenses," she said. Almost physically, she set herself against that force that flowed out from the strong square face. *I have to have time to think*, went through her. There had been too much conflicting data; she felt confused, whirled away.

"That blockhouse in the pass? Why, I could take that

without losing a warrior. Or even having to kill the men holding it."

It was the first weakness he had shown, an empty boast. "We may not go around killing people for a living," she said, raising her chin. "But that blockhouse has walls of stone, and our men can fight."

"But not very well," Piet said with a smile. He whistled sharply. "I think you may know this young man."

Slowly, she turned. For a moment, she did not recognize Joshua for the huge purpling bruise on the side of his face, as if he had been slapped with a board. He smiled, painfully; she felt herself frozen, her chest gripped with an iron vise.

Piet rolled to his feet, went to one knee and gripped her chin between thumb and forefinger, turning her head to meet his eyes. The touch was gentle but as irresistible as a machine.

"*G'spaza*," he said softly. "A man's words may not mean much, and his true intent is known only to God. The only thing you have to judge by is his actions, in the light of his capabilities. Consider what I've done, and what I *could* have done had I wished. Consider, but not for too long." The Bandari leaders rose and left them.

Ruth waited until they were alone.

"Joshua, Joshua," she said in a voice that shook. "Are you all right, did they hurt you to make you talk, are the others alive, what . . . ?" She touched the bruised flesh of his face.

The young man looked at her for a moment before speaking. "Alive," he croaked. For a moment, despite herself she recoiled. Then she forced her hands back to his shoulders; it was not Joshua's fault that Eden had so little soap.

"Have they . . . hurt you?" he asked suddenly.

"No," she said. "Oh, no: They have a doctor, and everything. They . . . look, Captain Piet even gave me a new *Alice*!" There was a pause, and the sheer absurdity of it struck them; they laughed, and Joshua tossed back his tow-colored hair with a gesture she remembered.

"They didn't hurt any of us, either," he said, shaking his head ruefully. "It wasn't much of a fight, that fool Geraldson . . ." His mouth thinned to a line, and he touched the bruise on the side of his face. "This wasn't from the fight, this was afterwards, Ruthi. I tried to strangle him afterwards, and one of the Band hit me to make me stop." He laughed again, harshly. "They didn't have to torture me—they would have had to gag me to stop me telling them everything!" He slapped a fist into a palm. "Boaz is going to regret trying to kill you, little Ruthi. And *not* killing me."

She stared at him, appalled. "Joshua, how could you? You don't know *anything* about them, they could be bandits, they could want to kill us all or make slaves of us . . . This isn't *personal*."

"*Boaz tried to kill you!*" Joshua shouted. Then, calming himself: "You're going to be my wife, Ruthi. I'd be no man if I didn't defend you, would I? Besides, we have to get rid of Boaz, and this is the only chance. I realize that it's hard for you, but this is men's work."

Stricken, she closed her eyes. *I think my decisions have been taken away from me*, she thought.

"Oh, Joshua," she whispered, touching the tips of her fingers to his lips. "What have you *done*?"

"Prophet," the young man said.

Kneeling, the slight figure of Eden's ruler glanced up from his steepled hands. He looked at the one who had interrupted him, and that one flinched before his eyes.

"The . . ." He swallowed. "The bandits, they want to parley, they've sent forward a white flag."

"Have them shot down where they stand," one of the Elders growled. "Like any vermin in our fields."

"Sir!" the younger man said. "They're under a flag of truce!"

Boaz rose to his feet. "*Are they of the Chosen?*" he said. His voice was sibilant, but the young militiaman was chiefly conscious of the eyes. They seemed to glow,

filling the field of his vision; the cool wind vanished, the
view of the Valley dun and gold with harvesttime, the
smells of horse and gunoil.

"*Are they?*" the voice whipcracked.

"Nnn . . ." He cleared his throat and tried again.
"No, Prophet."

The leader nodded. "Still, there is no harm in listening. We are bidden to be 'As gentle as doves, as wise as
serpents.' "

The Eden militia had dug in, in a loose semicircle of
rifle-pits about the upper mouth of the pass, loose
because they had neither the men nor weapons to
invest it closely. And the demonstration of mortar and
machinegun fire a week ago had impressed them deeply.
Motionless, they crouched in their holes, or behind
crude *sangars* of piled rock, uneasily conscious of the
tumbled heights above them. The road to the pass
switched and curved before them, burrowing among
boulders; the afternoon wind had set in, blowing down
from the steppes, flicking grit into their faces.

Boaz stopped behind a chest-high barricade. There
was a clatter of hooves from above, and six horsemen
trotted their mounts down the rutted track. One carried a lance, with a white pennant; others were variously
armed, rifles and curious wheel-tipped bows. All wore
bowl-shaped helmets with a cutout over the face, and
all had leather breastplates emblazoned with a leaping
antelope.

"Close enough!" Boaz called, when he could see faces.
Human beings were his art, and he did not like to talk
to a man whose eyes he could not hold. Or a woman; he
saw with an angry flush that the rider with the lance
was female, brazen and scar-faced in gear of war.

"Say what you would," he called.

The leader of the raiders removed his helmet, reveal-
ing a startling contrast of dark skin, blond hair, level
green eyes. He held a rifle, butt casually propped on
one hip.

"I am Captain Piet van Reenan," he said, in a voice pitched to carry. Under his breath he added: "And thank you for the audience, Prophet."

"We are the Band. We've no desire to harm any man in Eden, nor rob you, nor interfere with your religion. All we wish is access to the Valley for our women; you're Haven-born, you know our need. In return, we can offer protection for your passes, which we've show *you* need. We have a doctor, and medicines; we have cloth, and salt, and metal." He wrinkled his nose slightly. "And soap."

"*Silence!*" Boaz thundered, feeling a rustle along the line. "We of the Chosen can defend our own," he went on. "Let you into our home? We're not so foolish as that! Rage if you will, idolator; you'll break your teeth on our defense."

The stranger chieftain laughed, an incongruously merry sound as men gripped their weapons with the sweat of tension on their faces.

"Your crops are ripe, farmer," he said, pointing with the muzzle of his rifle. "How long can your men remain here, before the wind and the birds harvest the grain for you?"

The sound that ran through the Edenites was almost a moan. Last year children had died so that they might keep the seed corn; this was the first good harvest God had given since the Saurons came. To lose it . . .

He continued, remorseless: "As for this joke of a trenchline, look south!" He chopped the butt to his right; even then, several pairs of eyes recognized the weapon. It was a New Aberdeen 7mm, the Eden militia issue. Then they followed the direction.

Two columns of smoke rose from the Shield-Of-God range. Signal fires.

"This is the only pass that will carry trucks," he continued. "But not the only one that warriors can ride over." He stroked his pony's neck.

Boaz felt the blood drain from his face. His men might just be able to gain the shelter of Strong-In-The-

Lord's walls, before a mounted force from the southern passes surrounded them. Just barely . . . if they were not pursued with vigor.

"That you're alive this moment is proof of my mercy," the stranger finished.

"Mercy? Where was mercy for our brothers in the blockhouse, fallen defending their people?"

Piet leaned forward with a hand on the cantle of his saddle. "I was hoping you'd say that," he said more conversationally. "You should guard your infallability, Prophet."

The woman waved her lance. From behind a turn in the road came twelve figures, several walking with support from their comrades. A silence thickened until they were close enough to be recognized.

"There are your men, safe and sound!" Piet shouted. "Nothing worse than sore heads and bruises. I make you a gift of them." He tossed the rifle into the air and caught it; the other riders turned and trotted up the pass. He remained, his horse half reined about. "I may even give you their weapons back, and teach you how to use them, if you see reason. I've killed none of your people—" he thrust a hand out, pointing at the erect, silent figure of Boaz, "—which is more than can be said for *him*, who hung his own blood up to die because she told the truth!"

He turned, and called over his shoulder: "I give you an hour's grace to get behind your walls," before heeling his horse into a gallop. Its hooves struck sparks as it climbed.

Boaz screamed and grabbed for the rifle of the man beside him. He resisted, as much from unconscious horror of what he saw on his prophet's face as from thought. A single shot rang out, less loud than the echo-rattle of hoofbeats on stony ground. By main force, Boaz pulled sanity back upon himself.

"Back," he said hoarsely. "Back to the town. *Now*. *Move*."

* * *

The nights were cooling toward winter in the second week of the siege of Strong-In-The-Lord. The citizens had watched the nomads camp in their fields; watched them drill, hawk, and hunt antelope along the mountain foothills; watched them reap Eden's harvest and pile the stooked grain in ricks. Even without the menace of the mortar set up beyond the reach of their best weapon, they would not have fired on the causal figures below the walls. That grain held all their families hostage to slow death, and even the prophet did not order an attack that would end with torches in the straw. No messages came from the other hamlets. The people waited, counted the food-stocks in their late-season barns . . . and listened to the young men who had been prisoners.

Two thousand meters from the wall, Piet crouched in a gully and waited for such night as Haven had. The command-staff were about him, and Ruth's face floated white against the shadowed earth. Even at this range, the rest of her was near-invisible in the ill-fitting chameleon suit. She clutched the machine-pistol to her nervously, trying to remember her brief familiarization with it, and all the details of the message from within the walls.

"Ruth," Piet said softly. His hand brushed her cheek. "I've come to . . . like you, in this little time. I'd rather not send you into this danger."

"It . . . isn't a matter of what we want, is it?" she said, equally low.

"No. Not for us, who have responsibilities. We do what is necessary, because we must." He paused. "I'm sending you because it *is* necessary, whatever young Joshua says. Also, because I *respect* you." He chucked her under the chin. "Remember, move slowly and you're invisible. We'll signal for them to drop the line."

She nodded, flipped the visor down, touched hands with Jan and Ilona. A meter form the lip of the gully, her crawling figure vanished from sight.

"That," Piet mused, "is quite a girl. Going to be a

formidable woman, too," he added. In a whisper: "*Tot siens . . . for a while.*"

Ilona's teeth flashed white in the darkness of the gully; she dug idly at the wall with one of her warsticks, bringing a sharp scent of damp earth. "Not *another* dynastic marriage, Piet?"

"It's a possibility," he shrugged. "No more. Jealous?"

"No, scarcely." She touched her face. "I . . . life is complicated, isn't it, my friend.?"

"Ja."

Jan waited sourly with the shuttered light. "*Magtig, Kapetein,*" he grumbled. "*I still don't like leaving the serious fighting to those yokels; better if we kicked some behinds, hey?*"

"*Sun Tzu maintained that you should always leave your enemy a line of retreat,*" Piet answered. "*This leaves them a route to surrender without feeling beaten. Nearly time . . .*"

"*Ja.*" The ex-sergeant raised the light, flashed it twice. There was a single answering blink from the wall, repeated after an interval. About the interval needed to haul one light person up the four-meter rampart.

"*Gut genoeg,*" he breathed. "And Jan Marais always said you couldn't trust a coolie, even if he's been dead a long time."

"So, you like her too, man, eh?"

He snorted, stowing the light in his pack. "Reminds me of my little sister, a long time ago," he said shortly. "Now we wait, hey?"

Piet nodded. The assault parties were ready, the plans laid. "Now we wait."

"Piet," Ilona said.

"Ja?"

"What were you exiled for, originally, on Frystaat?"

He stared, then laughed; she flinched from his expression.

"I was a socialist," he said.

*   *   *

Boaz slept lightly. In the third watch of the night he awoke with a start, pulling at the sweat-damp collar of his nightshirt. Careful not to wake the girl that, like David who was beloved of the Lord, he had taken to warm his age, he slid from the bed. There was no need for a light as he knelt, and the thick adobe of his house was good insulation.

"Oh, Lord," he began, whispering, "Hearken to Your servant . . ."

It was then that the door burst open. Light speared his eyes, and Elder Geraldson staggered back into the room. Boaz had just begun to open his mouth on a question when there was a rattling stutter, a sharp smell of explosive; the guard-Elder was jerked off his feet and shaken, as if struck by invisible hammer-blows. The girl shrieked once from the bed behind him, and his daughter stepped over the body into the room. He could see only her face, the rest of her body was enveloped in a *something* that merged impossibly with the background. A submachine gun was cradled in her arms.

"Hello, Father," she said. Boaz's mouth made silent writhings. "And cousin Sarah."

Joshua shouldered his way into the room, and others followed behind. There was blood and hair plastered on the sledge in his hands.

"Now, old man," he said, stepping forward and raising it.

"Joshua!" Ruth said sharply.

"Stand aside, Ruthi," he said.

Ruth turned and jabbed the muzzle of the weapon into the spot Jan had showed her, just below the floating rib. The tall young man doubled over, turning an incredulous expression on her.

"Oh, Joshua, don't be more of a . . . a . . . *bliddy ful* than you can help!" she snapped. "This is *politics*, we have to *think*." She turned to the others. "Nehimiah, get your squad to the main gate. We have to secure the armory, and . . ."

The others shifted their gaze to Joshua, back to Ruth, then to each other. They moved to obey.

The prophet made no sound.

"Well," Piet said. He sat his horse in the main gate of Strong-In-The-Lord, still scarred and smoking from the satchel charge that had blown it in. The bodies had been few, and were now cleared away, but the fecal stink of violent death still lingered. "Light casualties. As light as we could hope."

Ruth stood by his stirrup and let her weapon drop on its sling. "Yes," she said, scrubbing a hand across her face. "Does it get easier, talking about people you knew that way?"

Piet reached down and ruffled the damp brown hair. "Unfortunately," he said, "yes, it does." After a moment: "Things are under control, it would be better if I weren't here for a while; Jan will stay. I'll be at the Matherville camp. We should discuss things, uniting the peoples."

"Yes, we should," she said, exhaustion in her voice. "*Tot siens.* For a while."

"*Tot siens,*" he replied, and spurred away.

There was a clatter behind her; she turned to see Jan Marais riding up, prodding the former prophet of Eden before him. The man's expression was still fixed in that first frozen stare, and he had spoken no word since the door of his bedroom burst open. Joshua followed, and the others.

"Ruthi—" he began. She lifted a hand for silence.

"Well, Jan?"

The thickset man jabbed with the muzzle of his assault rifle. "Kapetein says you're in charge of this, miss," he said.

Ruth looked at her father for a long while. She remembered; her mother, and this last night, and other things. She looked at Joshua and considered necessity, and what might have been.

"Ilona," she said. "I need to talk to Piet again, after all. Give me a lift?"

She extended a hand, and Ruth grasped its callused strength to swing herself up pillion. "Nehimiah," she continued. "You're deputy, cooperate with Jan here. I'll be back later . . . no, maybe tomorrow. We'll have an assembly then, there are some things the people should hear. Announcements."

"Ruthi," Joshua began again, in a whisper this time.

"Then, I think I may be away for a while," she said, in a carefully neutral tone, to the group. "It's . . . necessary."

"Miss?" Jan prompted. Boaz stared without recognition. Ruth looked down for a minute longer. When she spoke, her voice was flatly calm.

"Crucify him," she said.

From *The Marine Recruiter's Manual* 23rd Edition (Sparta, 2417).

In spite of their many excellent military qualities, the Havener descendants of earth's Turkic and Mongol nomads have preserved certain customs that adversely affect their adaptability to modern military organizations:

(1) A rigid code of hospitality, enforced with little regard to financial constraints.

(2) The custom of the blood feud for violation of the code of hospitality and many other kinds of offenses.

(3) An acceptance of what would normally be considered "treachery" to avenge "dishonorable" conduct by persons considered enemies under (1) and (2).

These people are best recruited for ethnically and culturally homogeneous units of their own tribesmen or for special-forces units. In small, elite units, pride in displaying their superior skills and general esprit de corps will minimize disciplinary problems. Mixing Havener Mongols with Deccan Moslems in the Grunberg Expeditionary Force was a contributing factor to the Mutiny of 2380 (see Senger and Schmidt, *Mutiny Most Foul*, Sparta, 2411).

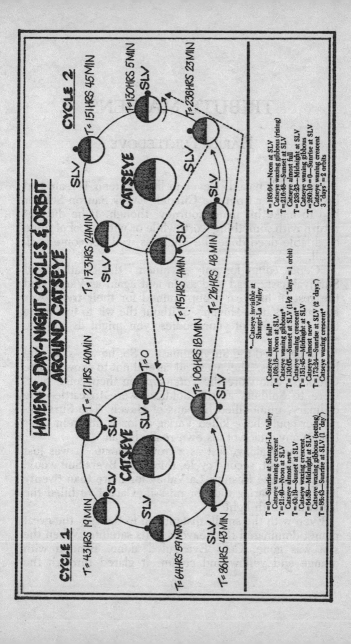

HAVEN'S DAY-NIGHT CYCLES & ORBIT AROUND CATSEYE

CYCLE 1

T= 43HRS 19MIN

T= 21 HRS 40MIN

T=0

CATSEYE

SLV

T= 64HRS 59MIN

T= 86HRS 43MIN

T= 108HRS 18MIN

*—Catseye invisible at Shangri-La Valley

T=0—Sunrise at Shangri-La Valley
    Catseye waning crescent
T= 21:40—Noon at SLV
    Catseye almost new
T= 43:19—Sunset at SLV
    Catseye waxing crescent
T= 64:59—Midnight at SLV
    Catseye waxing gibbous (setting)
T= 86:43—Sunrise at SLV (1 "day")
    Catseye waxing crescent*

CYCLE 2

T= 130HRS 5MIN

T= 151HRS 45MIN

T= 173HRS 24MIN

CATSEYE

SLV

T= 195HRS 4MIN

T= 216HRS 48 MIN

T= 238HRS 23MIN

Catseye almost full*
T= 108:18—Noon at SLV
    Catseye waning gibbous*
T= 130:05—Sunset at SLV (1½ "days" = 1 orbit)
    Catseye waning crescent*
T= 151:45—Midnight at SLV
    Catseye waning crescent new*
T= 173:24—Sunrise at SLV (2 "days")
    Catseye waxing crescent

T= 195:04—Noon at SLV
    Catseye waxing gibbous (rising)
T= 216:48—Sunset at SLV
    Catseye almost full
T= 238:23—Midnight at SLV
    Catseye waning gibbous
T= 260:10 = 0—Sunrise at SLV
    Catseye waning crescent
    3 "days" = 2 orbits

TRIBUTE MAIDENS

HARRY TURTLEDOVE

Variag felt naked. Never in his eighteen T-years had he been so far from the Citadel. Every Sauron Soldier had to make his man's journey, though. If he did not return with something worthwhile or with proof of some creditable deed done, he might as well not come back at all.

"Genes count for only so much," the Death's-head Survivalmaster had said again and again as Variag and the rest of his year-group trained for their treks over the steppes over Haven. "Without the wit to live up to the capabilities of your bodies, you might as well be cattle."

Variag hated the Survivalmaster. So, he was sure, did his classmates. They were all careful not to show it. The Cyborgs, who wore the *Totenkopf* on their collar tabs, were to Soldiers as the Soldiers were to cattle—the ordinary, unmodified humans of Haven. The Survivalmaster could have killed Variag a dozen different ways before any attack of his own really began.

He loped along, fast as a trotting horse. It was just past midnight, second cycle, third day. Byers Sun would not rise in the Shangri-La Valley for more than twenty hours, but Variag did not miss it. Cat's Eye filled the landscape with light.

Even with the small, distant sun in the sky, the great planet dominated the heavens of its satellite. When the sun was gone. Cat's Eye ruled alone. Banded with orange and yellow and cream, it glared through the night-mist. The eternal storm system that gave the gas giant its name peered balefully down at Variag.

Cat's Eye was gibbous, but to the Soldier, the part Byers Sun did not illuminate was bright as the rest. His eyes reached farther into the infrared than a normal man's, and in the infrared, Cat's Eye glowed brilliantly: It was close to being a star in its own right.

How many times, he wondered, had he tried to explain the two inf colors he saw to his human servants? All Soldiers tried that, until they learned better.

For all his altered genes, for all his Spartan training, he was boy enough to worry about his man's deed. Seven stobor skins swung at his belt; bringing the hides of twenty of the nasty little predators back to the Citadel would be acceptable to the Council. But the notion was as tasteless to him as refectory porridge. He dreamed of bigger things.

He thought of the legendary Khamul, who had wiped out a clan of nomad warriors with a cleverly engineered avalanche. Khamul was a Death's-head by the time he had 25 T-years, the youngest since the *Dol Guldur* arrived on Haven two Terran centuries before. Variag wondered what it would take to beat his record.

A distant snort of complaint from a horse, somewhere up ahead—Variag's daydream disappeared as battle-alertness surged through him. He took the safety off his rifle, made sure his fighting knife was loose in its sheath. Silent as a ghost, he moved forward.

The horse snorted again. Variag changed direction slightly. He topped a low swell in the steppe, saw the disabled yurt ahead.

His lips skinned back from his teeth in a humorless smile. The nomads loved to set such traps. They would gladly give up three men to take out a Sauron Soldier; only in an ambush were they likely to get away so cheap.

Variag's first instinct was to go no closer. He had started to turn about when he remembered one of the injunctions the Survivalmaster had drilled into him:

"Never leave a situation unexamined." He peered towards the spots where ambushers would likely post themselves. He saw no one, and it was not easy to hide from a Soldier, not with the way men's bodies showed in the infrared.

He looked at the yurt again. It had a broken axle. He rubbed his chin, considering. That was really *too* obvious for a lure.

He checked again. As far as he could tell, no plainsmen were lurking nearby. He moved a hundred meters to one side, in case the yurt was screening them from his earlier position. No, he decided.

Maybe the plainsmen waited inside the black felt tent. If so, they were idiots for not having sentries out. They deserved to have the tables turned on them. That yurt would burn hot and hard, and he carried a butane torch—

His field-grey cloak made him a piece of the steppe as he drifted closer. Soon he could hear voices inside the tent. He froze again. One of them belonged to a woman, a young woman.

Once more he nearly withdrew, for fear of a trap. The *Dol Guldur* had been a nearly all-male ship. Even after so long, the Soldiers needed women from among the cattle-folk to replenish their kind. They took tribute maidens as part of the price they exacted for letting the nomads graze the fertile valley the Citadel dominated, and still did not have enough.

All Haven knew women were the perfect bait to catch a Sauron. Yet Variag still found himself moving forward. His genes held imperatives millions of years older than the ones the Breedmasters had fixed in them. If this was no trap—or if it was, and he found a way to beat it—here was a man's deed in truth!

"Roll the dice?" Bala pleaded, and his twin sister Baigi echoed him a second later. They each had four T-years; in their boots, leather trousers, and baggy sheepskin jackets, no one who did not know them would have guessed they were not identical. Both were round-faced and almond-eyed, with greasy black hair that looked as if it had been cut under a bowl (it had).

"No," Dokuz said. The twins screamed at their older sister together. Their shrill voices echoed inside the cramped confines of the yurt. "Be quiet," she told them. They yelled louder.

"Let them have the dice," Tekudar said to Dokuz. He was wincing, not so much from the racket itself as from fear of what it might attract. Being forced to halt alone on the steppe at night, even with the Eye of the Cat in the sky, tore at his nerves.

"Yes, father," Dokuz sighed. She rummaged in one of the leather sacks that sat by the wall of the yurt, handed a pair of red transparent cubes to Bala. "Be careful not to lose them under the rugs now, do you hear? They're very old and precious—see, they're plastic, not bone or wood."

The twins made almost as much noise playing with the dice as they had demanding them. Dokuz looked accusingly at Tekudar. Her father sighed and grimaced.

She felt guilty; she did not like seeing him so somber. "It will be all right," she said. "Uncle Ibrahim will tend our flocks well, and we'll have caught up with the rest of the clan by noon, first cycle, first day."

"Forty-two hours," Tekudar said gloomily. "It is too long. Too many things can go wrong. We would be helpless against a pack of stobor—"

"Not so." Dokuz shook her head; her long straight black hair rippled around her. She was slender and wore the same costume as her little sister, but no one with eyes in his head would have mistaken her for a boy. She went on, "The stobor will give cry and warn us. We can ride the horses, each of us with a twin behind."

"Aye, and lose all we own here. My brother Ibrahim is a good man, but only if one does not try his goodness too far. I would not care to be in debt to him. And not everything that hunts the steppe gives cry before it strikes." Tekudar reached for his toolchest.

"What are you doing?" Dokuz fought to hold her voice steady so she would not frighten the twins.

"I am going to try again to fix the axle, at least enough to get us moving at a walk." Tekudar methodically checked to make sure his revolver was on a loaded chamber. "I should have given it another try long before this—I was a fool, to think to sit out the night. Neither Allah nor the spirits forgive a man his errors."

"Let me help," Dokuz said.

"And me!" Bala shouted. "And me!" Baigi echoed, not to be outdone.

Tekudar smiled. "You see, elder daughter? The most help you can give is to keep my herd here from running wild." He opened the flap at the front of the yurt. "I will not be long. If I can make the repair at all, I think I can do it quickly. If not, well, we are no worse off."

He slid down into the night. Dokuz had to grab Bala to keep him from going after his father. She cuffed him, hard enough to make him remember. He bore punishment in silence, as a warrior should. Dokuz turned her head so he would not see how proud she was.

Clankings and bangings came from under the yurt. Baigi giggled to hear Tekudar's voice floating up through the floorboards of the cart that carried the black felt tent. Dokuz giggled at what her father said when an awl slipped and ripped his hand.

She heard a last thump, different from the ones before, then silence. "Are you done, father?" she asked. Tekudar did not answer, but Dokuz relaxed at the soft sound of boots on the yurt's wooden steps.

The flap opened. Dokuz screamed. It was not her father there, but a stranger, a warrior, staring at her from behind his rifle. He was a tall lean man, young, with a long pale caucasoid face, a nose thin and straight as a swordblade, eyes blue and cold and pitiless. His cloak was open, but she did not need to see the Lidless Eye embroidered on the pocket-flap of his tunic to know him for what he was. "Allah and the spirits!" she cried. "A Sauron!"

Ignoring the gun that pointed at her, she dove for the yurt's second pistol. The worst that could happen, she thought, was that the Sauron would kill her and everything would be over. She was wrong. Despite the endless tales, she had not really believed how *fast* he could move.

His body struck hers the instant before her straining fingers reached the pistol. He bore her to the floor. She fought back with all her strength. She might as well have been battling a rockfall, for all the good her struggles did. Her father was a hard-muscled man, but the Sauron seemed made of boulders and cables. He blocked her karate blows as fast as she thought of them.

She shrieked—he had her wrist behind her back and bent it upward with calculated strength. "Enough of this," he said. He spoke the Turkic dialect of the steppe rovers with an Americ accent so thick Dokuz would have found it funny under other circumstances. It was not funny now, not with her shoulder about to come apart in his hands. When he said, "I will break it if I must, to make you obey," she believed him absolutely.

Then the Sauron flung her aside, for Bala was grabbing for the rifle he had dropped when he went after her. The Sauron effortlessly lifted him away from the weapon with one hand, snatched up the rifle with the other. Bala twisted, tried to bite. The Sauron threw him down, hard. He lay stunned on the floor of the yurt.

The whole incident lasted only a moment. Baigi's cry still hung in the air, Dokuz had barely begun to move toward the pistol. "Do we go through this again?" the Sauron said. "All right, we do." He subdued her as easily as he had before.

He slung her over his shoulder, carrying her as if she weighed nothing. Dazed with disaster, she thought she had no room left for more anguish. The unmoving shape under the yurt showed her she was wrong. "Father!" she cried.

"I did not kill him," the Sauron said. "I merely made certain he would not interfere." He paused, added, "One of your brothers is very brave."

"One of—" Dokuz snapped her mouth closed. If her captor learned Baigi was a girl, likely he would go back for her. Tekudar was still alive—Dokuz had to make herself believe that. Even mutilated by her loss, her family could go on, and go on in freedom.

The Sauron trotted west, untiring as a muskylope. He leaned a little to the right to compensate for the burden he bore. Otherwise, Dokuz could not see that carrying her affected him at all. "Where are you taking me?" she managed to gasp out; the pit of her stomach was over his collarbone, and every third jounce knocked the wind from her.

Surprise made his face seem human to her for the first time. "Why, to the Citadel, of course." He was not even breathing hard. She lowered her head in despair.

Inside the yurt, Tekudar rocked back and forth, back and forth, his face in his hands. There was a great swelling at the nape of his neck, but physical pain had nothing to do with his motion. It was made only of grief.

Baigi had not stopped wailing since Dokuz was stolen. She pressed her red, swollen face into her father's dirty coat.

Bala was dry-eyed. "I will kill that Sauron," he said. The determination in his voice gave the lie to its piping tone.

Byers Sun began turning the eastern sky from black to gray more than three hours before it rose. Dokuz hardly believed it when the Sauron slowed. They had halted twice before, when she begged him to let her relieve herself. Each time she tried to escape, and each time he recaptured her in less than a minute. No wonder, she thought bitterly, he had not bothered to ask for her parole.

Now, though, he stopped of his own accord, set her down. Was he tired? She could no more imagine him wearing out than one of the river pirates' steam engines.

He waited dispassionately until she caught her breath. Then he said. "I have a choice to offer you."

Something was in his voice at last. Dokuz took a few seconds to recognize it: not fatigue, nervousness. The Sauron, she realized, was only a little older than she. "What is this choice?" She spat the final word.

"In the Citadel you will breed Soldiers." Dokuz already knew her doom, but having the Sauron speak it was as much as she could bear. She heard his next words faintly, through the roaring in her ears: "Here is your decision: You may enter the Citadel as my woman and bear my children. Or, if you do not choose that, you will enter unassigned, and a mate will be picked for you by lot."

As *your* woman, she started to scream—I'd sooner die. That would hurt him, she was certain, as no blow she could strike would. But so what? He would only take her to the Citadel anyhow, and she would be forced to take whatever Sauron fate chose. This one, at least, was not wantonly cruel. Better the devil she knew—

"Tell me your name," she said suddenly.

He blinked—he *was* young. "Variag," he said. It took him a minute to have the wit to ask for hers.

Dokuz gave it to him, then whispered, "I will go into the Citadel as your woman, Variag."

He still stood straight and stiff, but his eyes lit. "I thank you," he said, almost as quietly as she had. "May we have many sons." He undid the clasp of his cloak, spread the garment on the ground. "If you are to enter the Citadel as my woman, it must be so in fact," he explained.

She nodded; she had expected as much. She shrugged out of her sheepskin jacket, pulled her tunic off over her head. Her nipples shrank and stood in the chilly predawn air. She drew her shoulders back to make her small breasts rise.

She could find no fault with Variag's expression, nor in the alacrity with which he approached. He reached out to take her in his arms. She stumbled slightly as she stepped towards him.

Her hand flashed to the tiny knife hidden in her boot. It darted upward, a thin steel needle long enough to reach the Sauron's heart.

The blade was scant inches from Variag's chest when he caught her wrist. Again she felt the strength that could crush her bones, felt the discipline that kept it from doing so. He took the knife from her with his right hand, threw it away. Then, to her vast surprise, he let her go.

"Do you care to change your mind?" he asked tonelessly.

She was silent a long, long time. "No."

The Breedmaster's assistant palpated Dokuz' swollen abdomen. "The baby is moving down very nicely," he said.

Variag nodded. He sponged cool water onto Dokuz' forehead. "You have a navel again," he told her; as the infant's head lowered, Dokuz' umbilicus, which had been everted through the last third of her pregnancy, regained its normal look.

Variag was conscious of the effort his light tone took. In the two T-years since he brought Dokuz to the Citadel, his face had lost the last vanishing traces of childishness; all planes and angles, it might have been carved from some fine-grained wood. Even the scar seaming the side of his jaw only added to his grim dignity.

He had seen countless battle injuries, and was trained to accept them. Dokuz' travail was something else again, something strange and frightening. She had not heard his feeble jest; her face was red and contorted as she pushed with all her might. Her breath came harsh and quick; not long before, she had shrieked. The hand that clutched his arm seemed to have a grip as strong as his own.

Some endless while—probably less than half an hour—later, the Breedmaster's assistant held up a small, wet, wriggling form. "A boy—a Soldier," he said, proud as if he had borne it himself. The baby squalled.

"Should it be so purple?" Variag and Dokuz asked in the same breath.

"Perfectly normal." The Breedmaster's assistant clamped the cord in two places, offered Variag a pair of long-handled scissors. "Cut between the clamps."

"Me?" Variag was mortified to hear his voice come out a startled squeak.

"Aye, you, Soldier. Don't worry about the little spurt of blood. It'll be the best wound you ever deal." Was that faint contempt in his voice? The Breedmaster's assistant, unlike his superior, was not genetically modified. At another time, Variag might have made an issue of it. Now he hardly noticed. He cut the cord. The blood was dark, but the baby was already growing pinker.

"Give him to his mother, while I tend to the afterbirth and such," the Breedmaster's assistant said.

Trained to wield any weapon with sure confidence, Variag almost dropped his newborn son. He was glad to set him on the now-slack skin of Dokuz' belly. She stroked the baby as it scooted forward. Its toothless mouth worked, searching for the breast. It reached its goal and began to suck.

Variag looked down proudly at his woman and son. Then ice walked up his back—what was that dark patch at the base of the baby's spine? With much of their technology lost, the Saurons on Haven had to deal ruthlessly with defective infants. But setting the baby out for stobor to take, Variag knew, would kill forever the fragile bond growing between Dokuz and him.

The Breedmaster's assistant might have been reading

his mind. The man chuckled, saying, "The spot's normal, too, for Terrasians. Your genes aren't the only ones there, you know."

Variag nodded, too relieved to speak. An orderly stuck his head in the birthing room, called to the Breedmaster's assistant, "We have another one ready for you."

"None for three cycles, and now two at once," the fellow grumbled. "All right, I'm done here anyhow." He washed his hands and hurried after the orderly.

"You are a Soldier yourself," Variag said to Dokuz. He knew no higher praise.

"Hush," she said wearily. Now that her ordeal was done, she had gone pale, save for black smudges beneath her eyes. Sweat and exhaustion left her long black hair a forest of tangles.

Variag's eyes kept returning to the baby at Dokuz' breast. He wondered what sort of Soldier it would make, whether it might someday earn the *Totenkopf*. Dokuz was watching the infant, too. With a rare burst of empathy, Variag realized thoughts such as his were the furthest thing from her mind. The baby was there and it was healthy, and for her, for now, that was enough.

He reached out awkwardly to touch the baby's scanty dark hair. The motion made Dokuz more than peripherally aware of him. She nodded toward a jar and cup on the table by her bed. "Some water, please?"

He poured for her. She drained the cup twice in quick succession. "On the steppe it would be kumiss—fermented mares' milk."

He shrugged. "On the steppe, the water might be bad. On the steppe, you would have to hope your yurt was in the lowlands when your time came, or risk losing the child—or yourself."

"I know." Dokuz bit her lip. "My mother died so, when the twins were born." She spoke of them that way from habit now, not to protect Baigi from Variag.

"So you've said," he nodded. "The air pressure is

safely high at the Citadel, and our doctors more skilled than any the nomads have." That was beating around the bush, and he knew it. By breeding, by temperament, by training, he was unemotional. Even for such a man, though, the birth of his first son crumbled barriers. He asked what he needed to learn: "Is it so bad here? With me?"

He could see her thinking it over. "The Citadel? I tell you truly, living forever in one place still seems wrong to me. I miss opening the flap of my yurt after a sleep and seeing a new horizon."

She paused again with the second part of his question. "You? What would you have me say? I've seen Saurons are men like any others, in most things, not the monsters our tales tell of. And marriages are always arranged for women—one way or another." She gave the tired ghost of a chuckle, remembering. "It could be worse. See what your wonderful doctors have for me to eat, will you? With the baby gone, I feel all empty inside."

As children will, those of the nomads mimicked their elders. When the clansmen practiced their archery, the boys followed suit, with lighter bows to match their strength.

Bala was a Cat's Eye year old—almost eight T-years. Like the other boys of his clan, he had a favorite target that he would tie to a babi yaga bush to give him a mark to shoot at. Some painted stobor on the cowhides, others tamerlanes or horsemen.

Bala's target was a face. Baigi had painted it for him. Though so young, she had a gift. It looked very much like the face Bala still saw in his nightmares: fierce, scowling, pale, the eyes that harsh blue so unlike those of his clansfolk. As they had on that terrible night half his lifetime ago, they stared malevolently at him.

In a single quick, fluid motion, he drew the arrow back to his ear and let fly. He leaped with glee to see the shaft pierce the left cheek of the image. He was hitting so regularly these days that arrow holes were making the painting look poxed.

He would have to get Baigi to do a new one for him, he thought. He wanted the image of the Sauron to match its model.

Horses neighed; muskylopes grunted; yurts rumbled and squeaked as they jounced through the narrow opening into the valley the Citadel warded. An icy wind whistled down from the mountains. Watching the nomads drive their flocks into the valley, Variag was glad of his heavy cape and fur hat. He could take more cold than an unmodified man, but that did not mean he enjoyed it.

A yurt slowed, halted. Several Saurons descended from it, began walking back toward the Citadel's frowning walls.

The Soldier next to Variag nudged him in the ribs. "There's a duty I'd like to have."

"Assessing the new batch of tribute maidens?" Variag pointed. His keen eyes could pick out the many stars and bars, the fancy piping, on the distant men's collar tabs. "Look for yourself, Grima. That's a job they reserve for the officers, the Chief Assault Group Leaders and Chief Assault Leaders."

Grima chuckled. "I suppose so. Us, we get to count goats, instead." His collar tabs, like Variag's, bore a Section Leader's single star and bar, and had no enbroiderywork. He was close to twice Variag's age, though: a career NCO.

"We have to eat, too. Here comes another flock." Two plainsmen, one riding a horse, the other lying atop a muskylope, were guiding the bleating animals. Variag turned businesslike. "Let's see how closely our counts match."

They were so intent on keeping track of the goats that they did not notice the muskylope rider's left arm was out of sight. He sat up suddenly, brought that left arm across his body, and opened fire on the Soldiers with a long-barreled pistol.

Variag and Grima were on the ground before the nomad's second shot. He never got off a third; a Gatling in a concealed firing pit chewed him and his mount to pieces. The other plainsman screamed in terror and flung his hands in the air to show he had no weapon ready. Only the enhanced reflexes of the Soldier in the gunpit saved him—the stubby nose of the Gatling had already swung his way.

So had Variag's rifle. A few meters away, Grima was cursing. Blood soaked the veteran's cape, and once he had cast it aside, the left sleeve of his tunic. "Bad?" Variag called, not yet daring to take his eyes off the nomad, who was trying to control his frightened mount with his knees because he did not dare lower his arms.

"Tell you in a minute." Grima unbuttoned his sleeve, rolled it up. He whistled in relief. "Through the muscle, nice and clean." He wiped away the blood. It welled up again, but not nearly so quickly: Soldiers clotted faster than ordinary men.

"You're lucky," Variag said. "A few centimeters to the right and it wouldn't matter how fast you healed. Go on back inside and get it seen to."

Grima had already slapped a field dressing on the wound. "I won't argue. And I'm lucky twice, because I'm not going to have to chase those damned goats all over the landscape."

Variag thumped his head with the heel of his hand. "I hadn't thought of that."

The officers who had been in the yurt were just outside the Citadel's gates when the trouble broke out, but came dashing back, sidearms at the ready. "All under control?" demanded an Assault Group Leader.

"Yessir," Variag said, saluting. "I can handle it from here."

"Very good. Carry on." The officers turned back.

" 'Very good. Carry on,' " Grima mimicked in a mocking whisper as he joined them. Variag felt himself flush.

Still, he thought as he advanced on the nomad out ahead, looking good under the eyes of the brass never hurt.

"Take your reins," he told the plainsman, gesturing with his rifle.

The fellow obeyed gratefully. "I knew nothing of what Jalal planned, nothing!" He was practically babbling. "By Allah and the spirits I swear it! He must have been a madman, to think to foully murder—"

"Yes, yes. Just a moment, please." Variag walked around so he could see the nomad's pistol. If he had meant to join the late Jalal's attack, likely he would have had his hand on the grip . . . and if so, it would still be glowing in inf-one.

It was not. "Very well. I believe you," Variag said. He sighed. "Let's get after the goats, shall we?"

The nomad girls huddled together in a fearful group. They kept sneaking glances up at the ceiling, as if waiting for it to fall on their head and crush them.

They were so young, Dokuz thought. Had she been that young herself when she came to the Citadel, a Cat's Eye year ago? She had, she realized with some surprise. She had had only two Cat's Eye years then, fifteen T-years. Already her older son Bereg spent most of his time in the Boys' Barracks and on the practice field, well into the training that would make a Soldier of him.

One of the girls pointed to a fluorescent panel. "Forgive me, Dokuz Khatun," she said timidly, giving Dokuz the plains title of respect, "but is that light—is it from atoms?"

"No, my dear, it is only electric, from a water-powered turbine generator. There are no atomics on Haven, not since—"

Not since the Saurons wrecked the fusion plants, she thought. But she did not judge them so harshly as she once had. A defeated force, in flight from its foes, did what it had to do to make sure its tracks stayed covered. Enough steppe tales told of the like.

"—Not for many years," she finished. "Now come along, and I will show you more of the Citadel, so you will come to feel at home here in your new lives."

She led the tribute maidens through the communal refectory, took them to the top of an observation tower for a panoramic view. "There past the walls you see the dam on the river, where it comes swiftly down from the mountains. The electricity you wondered about is made there, Saljan. And there close by it you see the fields that help feed the Citadel."

"Farmers," murmured a girl, putting into the word all the scorn the nomads felt for those forced to spend their whole lives in one spot. "I never thought to be given to farmers."

"Who on the plains would yield his daughter to farmers, Chichek?" Dokuz asked sharply. "You were given to the masters of farmers. Never forget it."

To drive the point home, she took her charges down the tower's spiral stair and across the outer ward of the Citadel to the practice field. The sight of boys half their age running fast as men, throwing each other with as much deadly savoire faire as a belted master among the yurts, and stripping weapons blindfolded reminded the tribute maidens why their clans had surrendered them. They were thoughtful and quiet as they walked on.

One of the boys finished reassembling his rifle, raised his blindfold. Dokuz's heart lifted—it was Bereg. He saw her, grinned, waved.

Grima hit him hard enough to knock him down. The veteran had been taking more turns as instructor in the T-year since his wounding. "You little fool," he growled. "When you're on this field, you pay attention to what you're doing here, nothing else but. Do you understand me?"

Bereg nodded stiffly.

"All right, then. Carry on."

Bereg did, carefully not looking at his mother. Dokuz

bit her lip, but knew Grima had been right to punish her son. Even among the plainsmen, warriors needed to be alert on campaign if they wanted to live to grow grey. With the Saurons, who depended on fighting ability rather than numbers, constant readiness was all the more imperative.

Sighing, Dokuz brought the tribute maidens to her own quarters, to show them how they would live once they had been partnered. The colorful carpets, woven from the wool of goats and muskylopes, gave the front room something of the familiar look of a yurt. So did the selection of Variag's weapons mounted on one wall. Few nomads, though, boasted an automatic assault rifle. Smokeless powder and precisely machined cartridges were hard to come by on the steppe.

Most of Dokuz' charges sat crosslegged on the floor, avoiding the chairs and sofa. She hid a smile; she had done the same herself, her early days in the Citadel. Mats and cushions served for furniture in the yurts: anything more would have been too heavy for beasts to haul about.

Saljan's face was puzzled. "Dokuz Kahtun, where is your chamberpot? I don't see it anyplace."

"I almost burst before I asked that question." Dokuz laughed, remembering. "Here, come with me."

Not all the girls fit in the little lavatory. They exclaimed in such wonder at running water that they crowded in by turns to see. The shower was an ever greater marvel than the water closet.

"Truly, you live in luxury to match a fairy tale princess'," Chichek said when everyone was finally back in the front room. "But what is it like to—to live with a Sauron?" Her eyes flicked nervously towards the bed that was partly visible through a side door.

Now at last we come down to it, Dokuz thought—the tribute maidens' attention was riveted on her. And this was an unusual group, she recalled: "You all chose to enter the Citadel unassigned, didn't you?"

One by one, the nomad girls nodded.

"How disappointed the officers who chose you must have been," Dokuz said drily. She hesitated. "Much depends on the Soldier with whom you are joined, of course. But that is true on the steppe as well as here."

Saljan shuddered. "But on the steppe, Dokuz Khatun, we are not given to bloodyhanded war machines."

"Nor will you be here," Dokuz said at once. "Aye, the Soldiers show Haven only that face, and they are geared to it by training and breeding as other men are not. But they are men, and inside the walls of the Citadel they can show it: they drink, they joke, they gamble . . . and they treat their women, from all I have seen, much as other men do."

Chichek was the boldest of the group. She asked, "Are you happy with your partner, then? Would you not rather be in a yurt?"

"Had you asked me that when I first came here, I would have given anything to go back to the plains. You at least knew for some time this might be your fate. I was taken unawares."

The tribute maidens hissed in sympathy. Dokuz shrugged. "Variag was leading his life by his own customs, as was I. He was not wicked for wickedness' sake—he could have killed my father and the little twins, but he did not. He has treated me with all courtesy and kindness since he brought me to the Citadel. Allah and the spirits know, that is better than many women ever see on the plains."

"But—" Chichek glanced at the bed again. She paused, unsure how to go on.

"There is no privacy in a yurt. You all know what passes between man and woman," Dokuz said. The tribute maidens nodded. "Sometimes a woman has pleasure; sometimes, sadly, not. Whether it is so has more to do, I think, with what she feels for the man with her than for what he does. And that, again, is as true on the steppe as in the Citadel. Do you doubt it?"

The girls shook their heads, though some were hesitant.

"Very well, then. I will say one thing more, and have done: If you do come to care for your partner and have pleasure from him, he will give you more than an ordinary man, for the same reasons the Soldiers are better fighters."

She heard one of the girls whisper, "What does she mean?" "'Saurons never get tired, ninny," another replied. The tribute maidens giggled. Dokuz let them. In essence, the second girl was right.

A servant stuck his head in the doorway. "I'm sorry, my lady. I thought you would be finished by now. Uldor has been wanting you."

"My fault—I'm running late here."

Before Dokuz could tell the servant to let in her younger son, he self-importantly pushed past the man. The tribute maidens watched him as he strutted across the room to his mother. He was younger than Bala had been when Dokuz left the steppe, but carried himself with nearly adult coordination and confidence.

In some ways, though, he was still very much a three-year-old. "Pick me up," he demanded.

Dokuz did. Uldor cuddled against her. She looked over his shoulder at the tribute maidens. "It's also difficult to hate one's own children," she said quietly.

"Father!" Baigi cried early one morning, waking Tekudar and Bala both. "My courses have begun!"

"What's that?" Still half-asleep, Tekudar rubbed his eyes. Then the import of what she had said hit him. He leaned over to hug her. "My little girl has become a woman!"

He shook his head in wonder. "Sometimes I think I should have married again after your mother died. What do I know of such women's mysteries? Let me take you over to old Ayesha's yurt. She will teach you the proper rituals."

Tekudar dressed quickly, turned to Bala, who was still lying under warm layers of sheepskin. "Do you think to be a slugabed? Build up the fire, set the kettle going. We'll want hot glasses of tea when we come back."

"Yes, father." Bala rose, threw on clothing, began adding dried dung to the fire in the iron pan just below the yurt's central smokehole.

"Better," Tekudar said. He opened the flap for Baigi to precede him. She chattered excitedly. Tekudar followed her down, shutting the tentflap to keep the cold air outside.

But Bala was chilled regardless. So long ago he had lost one sister, to the Sauron who still haunted his dreams; now, suddenly, his twin might also draw such interest, for she had reached the age of breeding.

He clenched his fist until his nails bit into his palms. "They will not take her!" he whispered fiercely. "No matter what I have to do, they will not!"

"Isn't that tunic ready yet?" Variag asked for the third time in fifteen minutes.

Dokuz set it down, looked at him with a raised eyebrow. "Almost. It would have been, some little while ago, if you hadn't kept butting in." Ignoring his fidgeting, she finished sewing the new tab to his collar. When she was done, she threw the tunic at him.

He plucked it out of the air with the abrupt flick of his arm that still sometimes surprised her, even after a dozen T-years in the Citadel. Voice muffled as he pulled the tunic down over his mouth, he said, "I don't suppose you'll ever have to put the *Totenkopf* on for me."

"You've done very well," she said when he re-emerged. "You're young, for a Chief Assault Leader." She made a face at him. "I know why you're so eager to get the three stars and bar: to impress the tribute maidens with the honor of being chosen by such an exalted officer."

He snorted. "*They* can't read my rank. But the kham out there can, and he'd be insulted if I didn't have that bar to go with the stars. If it can make things smoother, I'd be a fool not to let it."

"You're no one's fool," she said seriously, then added,

"Be gentle when you sample the maids. Had you not been with me, that first time, I doubt I could have made a home of this place."

"I think your doing well here is one reason I've drawn this duty so soon," he said. "Some Soldiers can't make themselves see the nomad girls as allies to be won, not enemies to be conquered."

"I know. It's one of the reasons the plainsfolk shrink from the Citadel. You be careful, too, come to that. The clan chiefs won't know you for what you are until you show them."

"So long as I behave myself, the clan chiefs will hardly notice me, which suits me fine. I'll be junior man there, not out to draw attention to myself." A servant knocked on the door. Variag laughed. "And I'm also about to be late, which doesn't help."

"My fault," Dokuz said.

"No, mine for bothering you—you're right, you would have been done if I hadn't pestered you." He hugged her for a moment; she felt her ribs creak. Then he hurried out into the corridor.

"Enjoy yourself," Dokuz called after him, but he was gone.

Bala had all he could do to sit impassive at his father's left. He wished Tekudar had never become a subchief. Then, at least, he would have been spared seeing at firsthand the humiliation of his clan by the Saurons. The nomads needed the good grazing in the Citadel's Valley, needed to spend time in the lowlands to ensure safe births to their women.

But the cost, the cost—

The lookout stuck his head into the kham's yurt. "They're coming," he said. Bala watched the tribute maidens shudder. Thirteen girls had come to womanhood since the clan last passed the Citadel. Four would vanish into the Saurons' fortress, never to return.

Baigi shivered with the rest; she was too pale for her fine brocaded robe. Unlike most of the girls, she wore her hair just short of shoulder length, about as long as her brother's. If Baigi looked like a man, Bala reasoned, she was less likely to catch a Sauron's eye.

The first Soldier came into the tent. Kham Emren did not rise from his crosslegged seat on a mound of cushions, but inclined his head to the Sauron. "I greet you, Leader of the Standards Brodda."

"I greet you, mighty kham," Brodda said. No longer young, the Leader of the Standards was growing stout, but he sat nomad-style, limber as any stripling. "My comrades here this day: Chief Assault Group Leader Ulfang, Chief Assault Group Leader Gorthaur, Chief Assault Leader Variag."

Emren bowed to each entering Soldier, as did the men who flanked the kham. Bala paid scant attention to Brodda and his senior officers: to him they were ciphers in field-grey. But when the one called Variag came in, ice and fire ran through the young plainsman. Here was the face that had tortured him so long in his sleep, returned at last!

Was it? Once the first shock passed, Bala studied the Soldier more closely. He had to be sure. Soon he was. Aye, the Sauron had aged, but even his younger self had been gaunt below strong cheekbones, had had that wide, thin-lipped mouth. And the eyes . . . Bala would have known those eyes on his deathbed.

He nudged his father. "That's the one," he hissed behind his hand. "The one who stole Dokuz from us." He no longer remembered what his older sister looked like, which made him want to weep.

"I would not know, son," Tekudar said. "I was struck from behind and never saw him. I do know it was long ago, and you hardly more than a baby."

"I'm certain!"

"You may be certain, but are you right? And if you are, what of it?" Tekudar took a long pull at the skin of kumiss in front of him, not setting it down until it was half empty. Then he sighed, went on, "We would not need to spend any less time in the Valley."

"Father, I've waited all my life to avenge Dokuz. By Allah and the spirits, I will!"

Suddenly, Tekudar's whisper had iron in it. "Not if you harm the clan. Here, leave us now, so the sight of the Sauron does not inflame you further."

"But—"

"Leave us, I say. Obey, or it will be the worse for you!"

His face like thunder, Bala stalked from the tent. Tekudar's eyes swung to the Sauron. He shook his head helplessly. How could he ever tell if Bala was right? He lifted the skin again, began the serious business of getting blind drunk.

Variag hardly noticed the angry young nomad who strode past him. Emren was making every effort to be lavishly hospitable towards his powerful guests. The girls from whom the tribute maidens would be chosen fetched them fermented mares' milk and beer. The latter was an expensive luxury, because the plainsmen had to trade with farmers to get it.

"I thank you," Variag said, nodding to the girl who filled his goblet. She blushed and turned her head away. He smiled. Except for her short hair, she reminded him of Dokuz as she had been when he first brought her to the Citadel.

Food followed drink: roasted lamb, goat, and muskylope; dried Finnegan's figs and tennis fruit; cheeses. The fare was different from what Variag usually ate in the Citadel refectory. The plainsmen used spices, both Terran and local, with a more lavish hand than the Citadel cooks, and had some Variag had never tasted before.

One in particular he liked. He asked the girl who made him think of Dokuz what it was. "*Chesnok,*" she answered: a word he did not know. He shrugged. Whatever it was, it went well with lamb.

Gorthaur felt the thigh of one of the girls as she walked past. She flinched back, her face a frozen mask.

Variag caught Brodda's eye, glanced toward Gorthaur. The Leader of the Standards leaned over, spoke to the other Soldier. Gorthaur muttered something even Variag's ears could not catch, but afterwards kept his hands to himself.

Some of the plainsmen noticed the byplay. Smiling, they pressed drink on Variag. Refusing would have been rude, and cost him the goodwill he had won. He downed skin after skin of kumiss. He could feel it, but did not let that worry him. Drunk or sober, he thought, a Soldier was more than a match for one of the cattle-folk.

These days, he realized, blinking, he meant only nomads by that name, not lesser men. Living with Dokuz had taught him a great deal about the harsh life the plainsmen wrung from the steppe. In their way, they were Soldiers, too, though natural selection shaped them more slowly than the Breedmaster's arts.

He knew better than to speak that thought out loud. Few of his comrades would understand; to most, it would smack of heresy.

With his enhanced breath control, Leader of the Standards Brodda raised a belch that had Emren goggling in admiration. The kham nearly ruptured himself trying to match the compliment.

"Most polite, most polite indeed," Emren said after another gulp from his mug of beer. "No one may deny that the folk of the Citadel are mannerly."

"I thank you, mighty kham," Brodda replied, "and thank you also for the openhandedness with which you have guested us here. Truly we are pleased to see your clan return to graze our lands once more."

"And truly we are delighted that you allow us this boon," Emren said. The stately phrases rolled on, almost a ritual to make more palatable the chief reason the Soldiers had come to the kham's yurt. At last Emren said, "As is his right, let the junior officer among you choose."

All attention swung towards Variag. He inclined his head—yes, he thought, he had drunk a good deal. But he had known for hours which girl he was going to take. "I thank you, mighty kham. If it please you, I shall lead that maiden back to the Citadel." He pointed at the short-haired girl.

Her almond eyes went wide. She dropped the tray she was carrying and bolted from the yurt.

"I pray your pardon, Chief Assault Leader," Emren said. "I will have her fetched back so you may ask her to share a mat with you." Variag heard how nervous the kham was: He was new here, and might take offense at the girl's reaction.

He spoke quickly, to ease Emren's mind: "Let her have some time before you send anyone after her. Her life will change very much before long: only natural for her to need a while to take that in."

"You are most gracious." Unlike a lot of Emren's speeches, that one sounded sincere. He went on, "Let it be as you say, then. Chief Assault Group Leader Gorthaur, which is your choice?"

Bala had been prowling around Emren's yurt like a cliff lion ever since his abrupt dismissal. He thought of firing the tent, but even without guards to stop him, he could not, not with his father and sister inside.

He prayed as he had never prayed before, calling on Allah the compassionate, the merciful, and on the spirits of wind and steppe, rain and mountains, to keep Baigi safe. Surely the boyish cut of her hair would make the Saurons think her less desirable than the other maids.

But what if it did not? No plainsman who wanted to grow old took anything for granted. Bala did not care about growing old, not if he could take that blue-eyed Sauron with him. How, though? He rubbed his beardless chin as he paced. A plan began to form. He prayed he would not have to try it.

Someone burst from the kham's yurt—Baigi! Dread blanketed Bala as he rushed over to his sister. He took hold of her hands; they were cold as ice. "Tell me it is not what I fear!" he cried.

"It is," she said. Her voice was still dreamy with shock. "I have been chosen."

"Which one?" he demanded.

A wind spirit might have whispered the answer in his ear before Baigi spoke: "The youngest." She hesitated, went on, "He did not seem unkind, for a—"

"He is the one who stole our sister from us," Bala broke in. "By Allah and the spirits, I swear it!"

"You cannot be sure—"

"So our father said. I am."

"His face is much like the one you had me paint for your target," Baigi admitted. She began to tremble all over. "What will we do?"

"This . . ."

The tentflap opened. Variag was pleased to see the girl come back of her own accord. Emren started to berate her: "Stupid little jade, you shame me, you shame the clan before our guests! You—"

"Let her be," Variag said. "She has returned, and that is all that matters."

"You are better to her than she deserves," Emren said, but his eyes held gratitude that Variag was not making an issue of it. The kham rounded on the girl: "How will you repay the Soldier for his forbearance?"

Without looking up, she said, "Let him give me a few minutes, to prepare myself, and then he may visit me in the yurt of my father—" she glanced at a nomad near Emren, one lying sodden on the rug—"and I will do my best. It is the third yurt from the left, in the second row of the encampment."

"Why, you lucky bastard," Gorthaur whispered to Variag. The Chief Assault Group Leader had picked the girl he had fondled before, then seemed indignant when she chose to go to the Citadel unpartnered.

Variag made a hushing motion. The nomad girl was wearing perfume, which she had not been before. To her, he said, "You know this is not required of you. Do it only if it is truly your wish."

She raised her head then. He thought again how much she looked like Dokuz. "Truly it is my wish," she said. Her voice rang surprisingly firm. "As I said, though, do allow me time to make ready."

"Of course." Variag dipped his head to her. She nodded, once, and left Emren's yurt once more.

The kham rose and poured beer into Variag's cup with his own hand. "Were all your people like you, the plainsfolk would like the Citadel better," he said softly.

"Tell such things to the Leader of the Standards, not to me," Variag chuckled. "I'll see no mercy from him if he thinks you've turned my head with such flattery." Brodda's sharp ears let him pick up the conversation, though Emren had thought to keep it private. He grinned like a tamerlane at his underling.

Variag felt himself flushing. He slowly drank his beer, making it last as long as he could. When the bronze cup was finally empty, he set it down and got to his feet. The nomads who were still conscious called bawdy advice after him as he descended from the kham's yurt.

Plainsmen walked back and forth through the encampment on their own errands. They looked through the Soldier as if he did not exist. That saddened him. In the distance, a nomad pony was galloping straight north, onto the wider steppe. Variag wondered why its rider was in such a hurry. He shrugged. He would never know.

As he came up to the yurt the girl had named, he scanned the area to make sure no one was lurking close by. The automatic action gave him a curious sense of *déjà vu*: he had checked the ground around the yurt from which he had taken Dokuz in just the same way.

That sense grew as he climbed the three wooden steps to the entranceflap. Emren's tent, being bigger and carried on a larger platform with taller wheels, had had four, each as high as the next. Here, the last step was a short one, as it had been before. He wondered whether all ordinary yurts were made so. Maybe it was a peculiarity of this clan.

He pulled the tentflap open, went inside. There, at least, was a change from what had happened years ago, for the interior of the yurt was almost dark. Only a single tallow dip burned. The smell of hot fat mingled with the scent the girl had put on.

Variag's eyes rapidly adjusted to the gloom. The shape under the blanket, back to him, was slim as a boy's. That did not much matter, he knew; Dokuz's curves were hardly more opulent, but she had no trouble bearing his sons.

A hand beneath the blanket patted an invitation. Variag stripped quickly, slid under the lambs' wool. The face so close to his own was so startlingly like Dokuz', the perfumed body he embraced lithe and well-muscled. He had a moment to feel annoyance it was still clothed. Then the knife was in his back.

Caught drunk, caught napping, caught like a fool, he screamed to himself. He knew at once it was very bad. Through his agony, he remembered the joke he had once made with Grima—put a wound in the right place and no healing was fast enough. The nomad girl had found the right place.

Crazily, she was speaking in a young man's voice: "Not content with one of my sisters, were you, Sauron? You thought you had to have them both. Well, by Allah and the spirits, I am avenged for Dokuz."

How did this plains—man?—know of Dokuz? No time to wonder, not now. Through the blood in his mouth, Variag choked out, "Avenged, is it? So am I." He still held his assailant, as if they were lovers in truth. Summoning what was left of his Soldier's strength, he focused it in his arms.

He felt the other's spine part, smelled the death smell. He tried to rise. He could not. He tried to call out. He could not do that either.

*   *   *

Empty inside, Dokuz walked slowly out to the Grand
Gate of the Citadel to meet the new group of tribute
maidens. It was something to do, better, she told herself, than staying in her rooms and staring at the walls.
Not much better, though. Nothing was much better,
not with Variag gone.

Only three girls waited for her. They had better
reason to look afraid than most who entered the Citadel. Had their kham not swallowed truthweed to prove
he knew nothing of the plot to murder Variag, the clan
would have lost Valley grazing rights, and probably
would have perished. He knew that, and had volun-
teered to send out riders to hunt down the girl who was
part of the scheme.

As if the thought of her was enough to conjure her
up, here she came, frogmarched along by nomads who
seemed as frightened as the maidens. Her hands were
tied behind her, but she walked with chin high. She,
who had reason to fear the Citadel's wrath, was not
afraid.

Gorthaur led the party that went out to take charge
of her. As he passed Dokuz, his gaze hungrily traveled
her up and down. She shivered; she was not yet past
childbearing age. But with Gorthaur . . . even through
her grief, the notion chilled her.

She eyed the girl. Young, rather pretty—why was
her hair cut short? The girl was looking at her, too. Her
lip curled to see a woman of the steppe wearing the
Citadel's field-grey.

The girl said, "How can you stand to serve them? I
was tiny when they stole my sister, but Bala and I had
our requital."

"Bala?" The next question emerged as a thread of
whisper: "So you—you are Baigi?"

"Yes, I am Baigi. How do you know my name?"

"Oh, Baigi." Thinking nothing could hurt worse was
wrong, wrong—she had found that out the night Variag

took her. Something always came along that did. "Oh, Baigi my sister, I am Dokuz."

They looked at each a long moment. Then Gorthaur growled, "Move, you," and led Baigi away.

From *The Chronicle of the Norskuna: The Year of the Coming of the Dinneh*

The Dinneh are of the blood of the Terran Apache Indians. Their forefathers were White Mountain Apaches, Navajos, San Carlos Apaches, and a few Yavapai and Tonto Apaches. Their own tongue mixes all these. They also speak pidgin Terran.

The Dinneh were driven into exile by the CoDominium, which wanted their reservation. They fought well and many died, as did no few soldiers. Others fled underground. Some three thousand came to Haven. They were landed on a mesa in the Badlands between the Streltsy Plateau and the Tierra del Muerto desert.

Few were desert-wise. None had proper clothing or equipment. Also, they were too many to live in such a harsh land. So the men left the women and children camped by springs and trekked to the plateau. Many of the men died from poisonous plants, exposure, exhaustion, hunger, and despair.

By night, the survivors attacked the nomadic Turks and Mongols. Many more Dinneh fell, but those who lived won livestock, weapons, and mounts. In time the surviving warriors returned to their families. All now trekked to the Land of Death.

They found grazing, browse, game, and water in some places. They relearned desert-wisdom. In time, they ambushed a punitive expedition from the nomads. More Dinneh fell, but afterwards all who lived were mounted and armed.

Now they scouted the Land of Death for a better home. They found it in the south and settled there. Two standard years later the dry season ended. By then only one in three of the original shipload yet lived. Mothers and infants died in great numbers, from the low pressure of oxygen. Their fathers had been highland people, however, so in time they acclimated. Also, the trekking and fighting of the first years left the survivors strong and resourceful.

The Dinneh became partly nomadic, and divided into clans. The clans were divided into households, each with its grazing territory. They had little metal except tools and arrowheads, but much practical wisdom in the breeding of plants and animals. Their herds grew faster than the herds of their neighbors.

The Dinneh did not call themselves a tribe, but fought as one. Any clan attacked by an enemy was aided by all the other clans. Enemies soon learned that to attack any Dinneh meant war with all. The Dinneh were most often left in peace.

Their numbers grew slowly. Metal poisoning shortened life. Also, they did not choose to travel to the lowlands for birthing. When their numbers grew enough, new clans were formed. Each new clan would trek to the edge of Dinneh land and take its own territory from neighboring peoples.

When the Saurons came, the Dinneh numbered some four thousand. In the river valley south of the Land of Death, the Saurons built a fort and demanded a tribute of young women. The Dinneh fought, but were beaten in every battle and outfought in every way. When the elders learned that these strong foes wanted only tribute, they chose to give it.

Four hundred years the Dinneh lived, paying tribute to the Saurons. In time the treaty was changed, so that a Sauron warrior would live with each clan, as a sign of war-luck. The Dinneh valued luck even more than they did strength, skill, and intelligence, and as much as they did courage.

The Dinneh also sought to mix Sauron blood with theirs. They did not value purity of the blood, so their women set about enticing Sauron warriors and bearing children to them. Generations passed, in which the Dinneh came to have much Sauron blood, so that they grew stronger yet in war.

At last the peace was broken. A Sauron warrior in a tribute party was too arrogant for the pride of a young warrior to endure. He sent an arrow into the Sauron's unprotected throat. The commander of the tribute party sought to make an example of the young man's kin. Many Dinneh fell, but so did all but two of the Sauron warriors.

These two fled and reached their fort, to warn the commandant. It is said that he was angry at the tribute party, for breaking the long peace with the Dinneh. They had been good tributaries and now would die hard.

The clan that had fought the battle warned all the others. Warriors moved to the canyon leading up from the valley. They were to hold it while the herds and people were gathered for flight.

The Saurons came swiftly, but they had to fight all the way. The Dinneh ambushed them in front, then fled to attack them again in the rear. By the time the Saurons reached the desert, the clans had fled to the western mountains and split up.

The Saurons followed even more swiftly than before. The rearmost clans were overtaken and slaughtered, with few losses to the Saurons. Those Dinneh who reached the mountains had a better chance. The mountains offered many trails and their seaward side was forested. The Dinneh hunters also knew the land better than any Sauron commander. . . .

A LION TO THE SEA

JOHN DALMAS

A trio of Dinneh scouts, of the Cliff Lion Clan, crept from thick mountain jungle onto a rocky point about a hundred feet above a beach. The tide was rising, but a kilometer-wide tidal flat still lay exposed to the strong light of the morning sun. The sun had been up only an hour, and the breeze was still chill after the long semi-night's sixty hours of net radiation loss.

Cats-Eye, slowly approaching the zenith from the west, was a pale white crescent, its apparent diameter seven and a half times that of Luna seen from Earth, its dully glowing nightside hardly visible in the dominating light of the new day.

A brook flowed from the adjacent small canyon to snake its way across the tidal flat toward the sea, eroding newly through sediments that refilled its course with sand in each 130-hour tidal cycle.

The Dinneh stared. They had heard only vague reports of the sea until, a few standard days previous, they'd seen it distantly from a high mountain to the east. Of tides they knew nothing; to them, the water's edge might have been immutable, although to these desert people, bodies of water came and went with the seasons.

At any rate, the scouts gave their attention only briefly to the sea, for on the flat near the most recent high tide line they saw something of more immediate interest: four strange artifacts—log rafts of about seven meters on a side, each holding numerous large leather sacks, fat and rounded. On each raft a pair of long poles—sculls—lay across the deck mats, with a spar removed from its housing, its sail furled, ropes coiled.

Seven men in serapes, with short beards and short, rough-chopped blond or sun-bleached hair, were filling more sacks with water at the brook. The pace of their work was leisurely, even lethargic. The last high tide had left them there more than one hundred hours previously. Most of their work was done, but they could not leave until the tide returned to lift their rafts free.

The Dinneh scouts, of course, saw only the physical realities. The functions and meanings were mysteries to them. To their eyes, the strange men somewhat resembled Sauron soldiers physically, but their manner was far different. For one thing, they did not seem to be keeping any sort of military security. In fact, the Dinneh warriors could not even see a bow or spear among the strangers—only shortswords and knives.

Quick Spirit had never seen a raft before. Even the concept was unfamiliar. But lying on his belly on the bluff, he nonetheless began to suspect what the rafts were for, and that the driftwood row and scattered strands of seaweed marked a recent water level.

He was not called Quick Spirit without good reason. To the Dinneh, intelligence was a function of the spirit.

Even the novelties on the beach, however, did not long hold their attention. The early sun was low behind them, the angle perfect for distant seeing westward, and from their elevation, their eyes, sharpened by life-style and generations of the infusion of stolen Sauron genes, saw a vast floating something well out to sea. And gradually Quick Spirit realized what this must be, too, though he had no name for it.

Then the Dinneh scouts slithered back from the cliff's brink and trotted to their clan, which had broken camp at sunrise and was picking its hurried way down the bouldery canyon bottom, in the creek bed, which was the best, if difficult, track through the mountain jungle.

They had seen worse—broken mountains so rugged that the Dinneh had abandoned most of their mounts, converting some into meat for the trail. They had actually hoisted or lowered the remainder with rope slings in several more difficult places, a terribly slow and arduous task, for even the muskylope, even the desert variety, is a large animal. These were their best breeding stock, used now to carry small children and such pregnant women as were nearing full term.

The pace had been especially hard lately. One had to keep up or fall behind; the clan could no longer wait or even slow down for stragglers. They assumed that the Saurons still tracked them, for the Saurons were relentless in all things.

For centuries, the Dinneh had been a careful tributary people to the Sauron soldiers, giving up the demanded periodic tribute of young women without protest, that the supermen might not destroy them, until it had become a natural part of life.

They had even had a covert victory to assuage their pride. Their distant ancestors had been American livestockmen on Terra, with both a practical and a theoretical knowledge of genetics learned in the universities there. The Dinneh had not forgotten the principles. And they had long since succeeded in obtaining an honor unique among the tributary peoples of the Suarons: they had succeeded in having a Sauron warrior-in-residence assigned to each clan. No one else had ever asked such a thing. The Dinneh had requested it on the stated rationale that luck was contagious, and surely the Saurons were the luckiest of all people.

The Sauron commander found this so amusing that he granted it.

And Dinneh women would entice the Suaron stationed with their clan and had numerous children by Saurons, thus stealing genes from the supermen, and this had gone on for more than a dozen generations. This alteration of the Dinneh genetic pool in no way disturbed them, for they regarded the essence of the

Dinneh not as genetic, but as a matter of culture and tradition.

Meanwhile, the Dinneh had not ceased to be a warrior people. On this moon of Cat's-Eye it had been necessary from the beginning—since their forced relocation from their reservations in the state of Arizona, on Terra, most of a millenium before. The coming of the Saurons had not changed that. It had simply added a force, the only force, that the Dinneh avoided fighting with.

And then one day a youth, enraged by some more flagrant Sauron offense, had put an arrow through the neck, the spine of the offender, an officer of a tribute party. The chiefs had given up the youth immediately, with disclaimers of any tribal responsibility, and with offers of restitution. The tribute party in turn had demanded that the young man's entire extended family, numbering more than twenty, be brought to them. Then the Saurons began to shoot them all. In an eruption of fury, the clan had responded by massacring the tribute party.

Four of the Saurons had escaped unwounded into the desert savannah. The warriors had pursued them, but Sauron endurance and speed, sensory acuity and reflexes and commando skills, had allowed two to lose themselves and return to their distant fortress.

When the pursuing warriors had lost the trail, they'd gone back at once to the village. And there was no question in any mind how the Saurons would react. So riders had been sent out to notify all the clans. War parties had been dispatched to set ambushes in the long and rugged defile up which any Sauron force must come, to delay it, while the clans began an exodus, dispersing into the mountains. They knew not where they were going, nor had they any illusions that the Sauron superman would not run them down and butcher them. But some, they hoped, would escape to keep the Dinneh alive on this world.

For four days—fifteen Terran standard days—the Lion

Clan had pushed westward without sight or report of Saurons. Then two warriors of the Bear Clan had come upon the camp of the Lion Clan in a high mountain meadow where the people of the Lion had thought to rest awhile. And they told that a force of Saurons had found the Bear Clan, which had hoped itself safe after so many days; had attacked it by surprise, and with its terrible weapons killed almost all the people of the Bear.

The Lion Clan had cut short its rest and pushed on.

And now came Quick Spirit to the chief and his council, with this report of strange men and their stranger structures of logs and mats, and their water bags. The story brought a new expression to the chief's face. Before had been only grim determination, the look of a man who expected to be killed but would never quit. Now he and his council looked like men with—not hope so much as something explicit to attempt. Men with a positive action to take, not simply flight.

The Lion Clan had with it families from three other clans—families that had failed to reach their clan assembly ground in time and had attached themselves to the Lions—and with these additions, the clan numbered more than three hundred, even after their losses on the trail. And now it seemed truly possible that the entire Dinneh might not perish to leave only their spirits crying on the wind.

First, the chief dispatched some older warriors, men who could no longer run fast, to watch at intervals along the back trail, giving them the clan's signal horns. As they trotted off, they knew they would never see their people again, but they said nothing. Next, he sent the scouts trotting ahead down the creek with a small party of warriors, under Quick Spirit's leadership. At the canyon's mouth, Quick Spirit stopped the others within the canebrake that curtained it, and slipped ahead to look again. What he had not been able to see from above was an armed lookout squatting on a very large boulder at the foot of the bluff. The man's unstrung bow still could not be seen, it lay on the rock beside him, but Quick Spirit knew it must be there, for he could see a quiver of arrows.

The lookout, his back to the bluff, scanned from his small prominence casually up and down the beach, not expecting to see any hostiles, or any other men at all, on this wild and isolated stretch of coast. The real hazard was not ashore, he thought, but at sea, where an occasional corsair could be found that, if he had numbers and daring enough to take on the raft clansmen, could easily catch their clumsy craft. Corsairs were the reason his people, the Norskuna, ordinarily stayed far out to sea, avoiding the continent's proximity.

Quick Spirit observed the lookout for a moment, then turned his attention to the small rafts—about fifty meters distant—and the foreign men who were almost done with their work. Besides the lookout, there were only the seven he had seen before.

The direct approach would be to shoot the lookout, then rush onto the beach and capture or kill the other strangers. But Quick Spirit often grasped what others did not, and he saw a problem. He could swim, a little, for during the rainy season, streams flowed in the canyons of home, and pools formed. And sometimes hunters crossed flooded playas by holding a length of dead wood, to splash their way across by kicking when the water became too deep to wade. But how to move these unfamiliar and ungainly objects to the much larger one which he could not even see from where he now crouched?

The obvious solution was to make the strangers take them, and negotiation, or perhaps trickery, seemed the most hopeful approach. Assuming the strangers could understand the pidgin Angli that the Dinneh, like many backcountry people, used for communication with foreigners.

And if negotiation failed, then they could attack.

Physically the strangers looked formidable. Except for the lookout, they had removed their serapes as the sun warmed the air, and the Indian was impressed by not only their size but their brawniness. In fact, these men had been oar pullers, net pullers, rope pullers from childhood, and if they lacked the athletic litheness of the Saurons, or of the Dinneh, their bodies nonetheless looked very, very strong.

But his warriors had their bows, if it came to that, and could easily kill them all. He hoped it would not come to that. The Dinneh had enemies enough with the Saurons; what they needed now were allies. Slipping back into the canebrake, Quick Spirit briefed his warriors, then walked openly out onto the beach, open hands forward at the height of his head, palms out.

He walked out twenty meters onto the sand before even being noticed. Then the lookout saw the Apache and shouted, matching up his heavy bow as he rose to his feet, hurrying to bend and string it. The other Norsku* also straightened, staring. Quick Spirit didn't pause, didn't change his open, vulnerable approach, didn't even keep his attention on the lookout, but watched instead the man whom he judged to be the leader of the strangers.

But there was one warrior who was perhaps quicker than he should have been. He stepped from the canebrake as the lookout nocked an arrow, and sent one of his own into the man's upper back. The lookout didn't cry out, just toppled forward off the tall rock with his heart pierced.

The man's fall caught the corner of Quick Spirit's eye, and he turned for a moment, shouting angrily at the warrior who had shot. Possibly the lookout would have shot Quick Spirit, but his instructions to the warriors had been to shoot only if he, Quick Spirit,

---

*The raft people called themselves by the collective term *Norskuna*. The singular noun was *Norski*, the plural *Norsku*. The singular adjective was *Norsk*, the plural *Norska*. The language evolved from a patois of Norwegian and Swedish, as influenced by the variant usages of Finnic and Balt minority speakers.

was attacked. Now he had become a man bringing violence.

Meanwhile, the other strangers had taken up their swords, and one of them held an object which could only be a weapon. It had the look of a very small bow attached to a piece of wood. And he stood with one foot holding it down to help him draw the cord; obviously the bow was extremely stiff.

But Quick Spirit went on, hands still raised and open. "Me no want fight!" he called. "Me friend!" Then an impulse took him. "Me people run away from Saurons!" Surely these strangers knew of the Saurons. And surely they also feared and hated them.

The one he'd guessed was the leader shouted back. "You fella stop there!" Quick Spirit stopped. The stranger was glowering, speaking to his companions in a language Quick Spirit had never heard, a language that had a tonality a little like that of the Dinneh.

"You say you friend?" the man demanded. "What kind friend you? One fella you killed one fella us. What kind friend kill us?"

Quick Spirit still held out his empty hands as before. "Me fella think you fella gonna shoot me. Me fella shoot first. Maybe you fella shoot me if he not be killed."

The other didn't answer at once. His burly body stood straight, sword in one large fist, his expression one of chagrin laid over with thought. His little group had one crossbow, and their longbow lay out of reach atop the boulder. And at any rate, he didn't know how many of the dark people watched from the jungle, or how many of them had bows, while he and his men were exposed out here on the beach.

"What you want?" he asked.

"Saurons come behind, want kill us. Us want go away over water, you take. Saurons not follow over water."

"How many fella you?"

Quick Spirit answered without hesitation. "Fifteen." He splayed his fingers—two hands, then one. "All got bow. Not want kill you fellas. Want you take us to . . ."

He stopped. "To big thing same you stand on." He pointed at the raft on which the large blond man stood, then out to sea. "To big thing far out on water."

The Norski pursed his lips thoughtfully. If Saurons were following these people, they would come here, and meanwhile the rafts were effectively stranded until the next high tide, which would not be until midmorning some time. The raftsman didn't think in terms of hours—the Norskuna had long since ceased to have clocks. But in Haven's long days it would be about seven more hours to midmorning—seven hours until high tide would float their rafts off the beach.

"How close Saurons?" he asked.

"Don't know. Mebbe soon, mebbe not till sun that place." Quick Spirit pointed at the zenith.

It might be long then, the Norski thought, for it would take nearly twenty slow hours for the sun to climb so high.

"We can no take you till Cats-Eye that place," the Norski said, and pointed a little short of the zenith. For this high tide would come higher than the last, he knew, and reach the raft a little before the tidal peak. "Then water come to rafts. Rafts too much big to pull to water." He made a decision. "But me fellas can take canoe, go to clan raft. Other me fellas come back plenty canoes, take you fellas away this place."

Quick Spirit didn't know the word 'canoe,' but before he could ask, the Norsk leader turned and gave an order to the others. These moved quickly, trotted the few meters to a log lying beside the creek, and turned it over. It was hollow!—a beautifully made dugout canoe with a close-set outrigger. Its sides were no thicker than a carvel-built skiff's. In a moment its bow was in the creek, and the men stood waiting.

While Quick Spirit stared, the Norsk leader started for it. Seven men were about three more than it was built to carry—it was a light work boat for use around rafts—but in a pinch . . . and this was a pinch.

Quick Spirit raised a quicker hand. "Wait! You no go

'way from us," he said, shaking his head firmly. "Me think you go 'way from us, you no come back this place. You stay or me fellas shoot."

The Norsku all stopped, stood motionless. "Okay," the leader said. "Eight too many fellas one canoe, but we take you 'long. You anyway not big fella."

Quick Spirit's thoughts raced. If they took only him, they could overpower him later and kill him. They'd never come back for any of the others if the raftsmen all left now, no matter how he parleyed. But it was undeniable that the canoe could hold no more than eight, if that many.

"You right," he said. "Eight too many. You take three me fellas, two you fellas. Other you fellas stay this place. You, me, come back later, get other me fellas, you fellas."

He turned, calling to the other warriors, and all fifteen, lithe and sinewy, trail-hardened, came loping from the jungle with bows strung, arrows nocked but pointed groundward.

The big Norski raised his hand and shook his head, talking faster this time. "Two me fellas not 'nuff—not make canoe go 'nuff fast. Take too much long get to clan raft, too much long come back this place. Me take two you fellas. Two you fellas, four me fellas. Four us make canoe go very much fast to clan raft. Then come back this place, get others."

He ignored the semicircle of near-naked warriors around them, looked expectant as if assuming Quick Spirit's agreement. Behind his eyes he was thinking that if the Saurons came too soon, at least only three of his people would be left behind.

Quick Spirit frowned for only a moment. The difference was trivial: three hostages would probably serve to bring the raft people back if five would. As for himself and his warriors, they had little desire to survive if they could not bring some of their clansfolk with them, some women at least to continue the people. He himself would willingly stay and let another ride the canoe in his stead, but he was the leader, and he was Quick Spirit; it was up to him to gain the help of the raft people if it could be done.

He nodded, then surprised the big Norski by reaching out a hand. They shook, and the raftsman was surprised at the hard strength of the smaller hand in his own beefy fist.

And with that handclasp, something changed in big Arvo Olassøn.

He turned to his men and gave more orders, as did Quick Spirit. Three warriors stepped from the semi-circle, coming up to their leader. To one called Knife Lizard, the smallest of them all, he spoke only a few words. For the other two he had more: they were to run to the clan chief and tell him what had happened. The clan should come to the beach at once.

Meanwhile, one of the Norskuna had taken the stern of the canoe and pushed it the rest of the way into the little creek, hopping into the stern as he did so. Then, alone, he guided it down the current with a paddle; the creek was too shallow to carry the craft with more than one or two men. The whole mixed assemblage followed, the Dinneh warriors watching with great interest beneath their apparent stoicism.

Where the creek met the light surf, two of the Norskuna waded out a few steps, holding the canoe. Avro turned to Quick Spirit and gestured at it. "You and that fella get in, sit on bottom."

For the briefest moment, Quick Spirit and Knife Lizard held back, staring as a small breaker raised, then dropped the canoe. Then, hiding their misgivings, they waded out to their knees with Arvo and one other, and the two warriors, gingerly in spite of themselves, stepped over the side and sat down. Two Norsku followed quickly, one from each side, into the front, to kneel instead of sitting, and took up paddles. Arvo and the fourth Norski pushed then, a few running steps, through another small breaker, and jumped into the stern. Quick Spirit felt the craft settle deeper with their weight, and heard the cry of the warriors behind them on the shore, half shout and half groan. Paddles dug, and spray from another breaker wetted them. Apprehensively, he looked about him. They were under way.

It felt good! The apprehension fell away and he grinned, then licked some drops of spray from his lips. Salty! He dipped a hand over the side, catching a bit of sea in his palm and licking it. The sea was bad water; the Dinneh, desert people, knew about poisonous water holes. Now Quick Spirit understood why the raft people, living on a great water, sent men ashore to get water from a creek.

They were well beyond any breakers now, the canoe surging with the paddlers' powerful strokes. Then Quick Spirit heard a distant sound, a short pattern of them, the hooting of a single horn, and he almost tried to stand up, twisting to look back. On the beach, the others were waving to their leader to come back.

Quick Spirit's eyes went to Arvo in the stern, digging hard with his paddle. "Back!" shouted Quick Spirit. "We go back! Saurons coming!"

The Norski straightened, his halted paddle dripping. "Canoe not hold more fellas," he said.

"All me people come to beach. Very many fellas and they woman, they chillun. 'Nuff they take rafts to water before Saurons come this place."

Arvo knelt dumbly for a moment, sandbagged by the two pieces of new information: the Saurons were near, and the damned landsmen had a whole clan coming! If they could get the rafts to the water, he could get all his men off the beach. He gave orders in his own tongue again. The dugout turned as one low swell let it down and the next lifted it, then the paddlers drove it toward the beach where it slid to a stop on rasping sand.

This time Quick Spirit moved with the speed of a threatened cat, splashing through ankle-deep backwash to his warriors. Arvo followed him out of the surf. "What place you people?" asked the Norski.

Quick Spirit pointed at the canyon. "Up that place. They come." He snapped an order, and one of his warriors sprinted away. "You hear horn? That me people." It sounded again. "Horn say enemy seen. That be Saurons. Me people leave fellas back to watch for Saurons. Some back fella him see Saurons, blow horn. 'Nother back fella hear, not so far, him blow horn. Horn we hear, it horn belong chief. Me people not so far, Saurons much more far. But Saurons coming."

Arvo chewed his lips for a moment, then, mostly in pidgin so the Indians would understand, snapped instructions to his men, who had pulled the canoe above the surf. Two stayed to pull it up the creek. The rest, with the warriors trotting beside them, ran to the four rafts and began to open and empty the big waterbags, throwing the empties into piles on the raft. The Apaches, seeing this, followed suit.

Arvo snapped more orders, and the men gave their full efforts to one of the rafts, leaving the others till the first was done. He frowned absently at the coarse deck matting beneath his feet. Though this raft was only a small section of the clan raft, and the logs were paperwood, it still was massively heavy. Could enough men take hold of it to drag it? They'd have to, he decided, untying the mouth of another waterbag, but the thought remained gnawing at the edge of his mind.

Also it irked him to dump the water. But he had no choice: the tide's edge was still more than half a kilometer away, its progress slow, and while he knew the Saurons only through the stories told around night fires, they were described as ruthless killers who ran faster than other men, had weapons which show arrowheads very fast and very straight, and killed at a distance farther than the strongest bow.

Arvo raised the heavy bag and felt the rush of water from it. Long ago his people had dwelt on the shore, going to sea only to fish and to haul. It was the demands of the Saurons for women and for fish, along with their general arrogances, that had caused the

Norskuna to make the first sea rafts and leave, to dwell on the ocean in peace. That had been long ago, well before the time of the grandfathers of grandfathers.

Two rafts had been cleared and work begun on a third when the rest of the Lion Clan began to emerge from the canyon. The first out was a party of warriors, followed by muskylopes led by women and bearing children, or women big with child. Quick Spirit ran over to one of the newly arrived warriors, Sees Far, chief of the Lions, and talked urgently to him. The chief, a sinewy man of middle years, asked certain questions which Quick Spirit answered urgently. Sees Far nodded curtly, then began to bark orders to those around him.

Quickly the children and women were unloaded from the muskylopes. Light-footed warriors holding braided leather ropes led the ungainly muskylopes toward the rafts, other warriors following, and women. As more animals arrived, they, too, were dismounted, or in the case of unrideable bulls, unloaded. Within a few minutes, all of the clan's remaining twenty-six animals were attached to the seaward side of an unloaded raft by ropes of varying lengths. Makeshift harnesses and collars were used, left over from hoisting in the broken lands, to prevent the animals from choking when they pulled. Warriors, too, prepared to pull with shorter ropes over their shoulders. Other Indians braced themselves against the landward side, some with hurriedly cut pry poles.

The Norskuna, however, continued to unload a third raft, all but Arvo, who braced a pry pole beneath a timber while wondering what had become of his authority. The foreign chief had taken over.

Then Sees Far shouted an order in the Dinneh tongue, stout sticks descended sharply on the flanks of muskylopes, and grunts emerged from human throats, Avro's included. The raft moved. The sticks struck again, muscles strained; once more it moved. By now they knew they could do it, and beasts and men kept it moving almost continuously in a series of jerks, until halfway to the surf they paused to rest. But briefly. Then they pulled and pushed again till the muskylopes approached the surf.

Quick Spirit called to Sees Far, who shouted at the muskylopes to halt, and Arvo walked over to the two Apaches. "This 'nuff far?" asked the Apache.

Arvo nodded. " 'Nuff far," he said. Sees Far shouted to the warriors and women, and the humans and beasts, sweat-covered despite the breeze, went back to get a second raft. When they got to it, Sees Far noticed the stack of empty water skins on it, which added weight, and asked Quick Spirit about that. Quick Spirit repeated the question to Arvo, who explained that the waterskins were precious to the Norskuna; that on the ocean they must carry all their drinking water; that it was very far between places safe to land for more. And on the sea they could get no more bags. The chief scout nodded and turned to Sees Far.

"This great water is a great desert," he said to his chief, "for its water is poison. I have tasted it." And now he saw that many of the waterbags on the third raft had not been emptied, but piled on deck mats laid on the beach. He did not have to ask why. And when he took his rope over his shoulder to pull, he saw that now all the Norskuna, with their thick raftsmen muscles, were behind the raft with pry poles.

The second and third rafts seemed easier. When they came to the fourth raft, all of its waterbags were still on it, full, and the body of the dead lookout. But this raft too they moved, by sheer determination. By the time they reached the surf with it, the tide had reached the first three, each breaker sending water washing entirely around them. They had the muskylopes drag the fourth until the breakers nearly washed the animals' chests. Then Quick Spirit sent men with the muskylopes to drag the mats of filled waterbags.

Now was a time for decision. Warriors sat on the rafts, and it was clear they would not give them up. Arvo looked glumly at them, then turned to Quick Spirit and Sees Far, and several of the chief's council who stood looking back at him.

"Now time you fellas got to say what fella go and what fella stay. But all me fellas go. We know how make rafts go to clan raft. What fellas you go?"

Sees Far called his council—Quick Spirit plus four other warriors—and briefly they conferred. Water surrounded the rafts now, through not yet enough to float them. The muskylopes were arriving with the filled waterbags, and men—warriors and Norsku—were loading the bags on the three rafts that had none.

"Children go," the chief announced loudly to his people. He'd already lost some of the younger on the trek and would not willingly leave any. "I will also name certain young women and certain young warriors, that more children may be born, and to teach the children in the ways of the Dinneh." He turned to Quick Spirit. "And Quick Spirit shall go, to council with the yellow hairs."

He looked around and began to name names, ten young men, twenty young women. When the young men and women had climbed on the rafts, the preadolescent children were handed up or climbed on by themselves. Some were crying because their mothers were being left behind.

When the children were on board, the rafts still were not too crowded; Sees Far named more names, and some of the older survivors boarded. Then he scowled at Quick Spirit, who still stood in the surf wash. "And you! Now!" Reluctantly the scout climbed on a raft, feeling somehow traitorous for doing so, despite the logic of it.

The rafts were now packed with people, and several of the Norskuna were speaking concernedly to Arvo; the rafts were too crowded, they said. There was not even room to manhandle the small masts into place when the time came. And the rafts were starting to lift now with the breakers.

"You will have to manage," he answered, then turned to Sees Far. "You fellas go 'long beach that way," he said, pointing south. "Me fellas come back, get more you fellas."

If there is time, he added inwardly. *And if our council agrees*. He would do his best to convince them. But some would be angry that he brought even these, although he'd had little choice.

Then the warriors and women who would stay behind pushed the rafts, which dragged bottom between breakers for a little, while the Norsku seated their sculls between sculling posts, helped by the young adults among their passengers. Then the rafts were free, and warriors pushed until the water reached their chests; perhaps one in four of them could swim.

As the raftsmen sculled, the men in the surf waded back to the beach to watch the ungainly craft move slowly away, one towing the dugout by its side. One of the rafts had only Arvo to operate it, from among the Norskuna, for the lookout had been his partner. But his was the raft that Quick Spirit had climbed onto, and the Apache, watching him, had picked up a scull when Arvo did, seated it, and was imitating the Norski's action with the second twelve-foot sweep.

Then Sees Far must have given another order, for all the Dinneh left behind began trotting toward the high tide line where their gear and weapons lay. The rafts were some two hundred meters offshore when, near the distant bluff, Arvo could see some of the Dinneh beginning to run south along the beach.

A minute later the Norski heard a distant inland sound, and looked at Quick Spirit. The brown man's expression almost didn't change; only the lips had tightened, very slightly. Another horn blast: the Saurons had been sighted farther along.

He shouted a command to the other rafts, then quickened his stroke with the scull. There was no way to make the rafts go fast, but they could make them go less slow.

* * *

It didn't take terribly long to reach the clan raft; it only seemed to. Masts struck, it lay sprawled, structured but flexible, some five kilometers offshore, held approximately in place by men working casually at sculls. Closer than five kilometers the raft's "skippari," her skipper, did not care to take her. If this unconscionable drought should break, a strong onshore breeze was distinctly possible, and that would mean hard work to keep from being driven shoreward.

The clan raft had been driven ashore once in a storm, when Skippari Janssøn was a little boy, and had broken up with a loss of much iron goods and other valuable material. Fortunately, that had been on an uninhabited island, one where paperwood grew, and rope vine. But many of their hand tools had been lost, and it had taken ten of Haven's long days, about thirty-six standard (Terran) days, to repair and rebuild, while the children had searched the beach and raked the shallows to recover what they could of the implements lost.

Actually, Hansi Janssøn would have preferred to have his raft at least two hundred kilometers out, beyond any reasonable likelihood of meeting landbased fishers or merchantmen, and especially corsairs. But the dry season had been much drier than usual at sea, and considerably longer. On the islands to which the Norskuna usually sent water parties, the streams had dried up, and the occasional waterholes they'd found were too small, too thick with algae, too fouled by animals. They'd had to come to the mainland to seek it, and traveling on short water rations at that.

No, the skippari did not like this proximity, and looked forward to loading the waterbags and leaving. Now and again he glanced at Cats-Eye's slow progress up the sky. About the time the glowing gas giant reached the meridian, the rafts would float. After that it would not be long.

His musing was interrupted by a shout. A lad doing lookout on the maerstoppi, the masthead, called that the water rafts were coming, which was hard to believe; they should still be high and dry. But other boys quickly scaled masts too, to peer and point, so there could be no question, and the skippari sent a dugout to meet the water-rafts. Swiftly the canoe returned, the paddlers digging hard, and in it was Arvo Olassøn, in place of one of the canoe's original paddlers. When it had come alongside, Olassøn had scrambled quickly aboard the clan raft, where Skippari Janssøn had been joined at the edge by Stamchef (clan leader) Oska Egolfssøn and two of the *"størsmennu"*—the clan council.

"How have you come back so early?" asked Janssøn.

"Saurons were coming to the beach, sooner than the tide. And there were *landmennu* there, who dragged the rafts to water for us."

"*Landmennu!*?" The stamchef's mouth was slightly open in his astonishment. "But the scouts we sent ashore said there was no sign of people there! And what *landmennu* are they that would help?"

Arvo's stomach tightened; now, he thought, the trouble would begin. "They call themselves 'Dinneh,'" he answered. "You will meet some of them soon. We have their children on the rafts, and some of their young women. And a few of their men and their old. The Saurons were following them to kill them, had been following them for more than five days [Haven's nearly 87-hour days—about twenty Terran days]. And the Dinneh men, after helping us drag the rafts to the water, insisted we save at least these few from the Saurons, who will kill all the rest when they catch them."

Stamchef Egolfssøn and the listening størsmennu stared at Arvo Olassøn, while Skippari Janssøn bunched blond brows above blue eyes.

"You are bringing foreigners, *landmennu*, to the clan raft?" Egolfssøn said incredulously. Such a thing was utterly unprecedented. And unthinkable. To the raft clans, *landmennu* had long meant trouble. They included the Saurons, of course, but also others told of in the rich and colorful oral tradition of the Norskuna. And the corsairs, who had decimated more than one raft clan in slave-raids.

Even those Norskuna who, after the exodus from the continent, had settled as farmer/fisherfolk on the green island of Nyttheim, were considered *landmennska* foreigners, and thought poorly of. It was they the raft clans visited to trade with occasionally—but no more often than necessary.

The hard feelings had begun at once, those generations ago, when some of the people had chosen to settle ashore. For the choice had split families: wives had reluctantly followed husbands, leaving parents; or wives had left husbands; or . . . While on almost every trading visit, one or a few of the younger raft folk would run away to live a life ashore, and it was scarce consolation that an occasional Norsk *landmani*, struck by the idea of raft life, or perhaps by a raft girl, was accepted by the raft.

And their kin ashore had an advantage over the raft clans. For with the ore-bearing surface formation they had found in the hills of Nyttheim, the furnaces they had built, their clever but greedy ironsmiths, their water-driven sawmills, they had what the raft folk needed very much. But what the raft folk had to exchange—fish—the Norska *landmennu* caught for themselves.

So the exchange seemed always unfair to the raft clans: bales of dried but delicate coldwater laex, which they must sail far to catch, in trade for a score of planks; bales of hard-to-find sprotfisku from the distant coral reefs for a few bundles of iron rods to be smithed, a simple sheet of iron on which to set a stove, and maybe a kettle or two. And the prices for grain and vegetables were as bad. Thus the raft folk looked on their *landmennska* cousins as extortionists and cheats, and at other landsfolk as actual threats.

And now this Olassøn was bringing four water rafts full of *landmennu*, who would not even speak the language!

"They cannot stay!" the stamchef said.

Arvo Olassøn glared at him, a thing startling in itself. "If you insist on that," said Olassøn, "I will ask for a *størsmotti*—a *folkmotti* if necessary. It was the Dinneh who dragged our rafts to water before the Saurons could come."

Slowly the indignation drained from the stamchef. The young man had the right to both of those: *størsmotti* and *folkmotti*. In such a matter, a meeting of the council, a *størsmotti*, was his for the asking, without risk. But for a common *flottkarli*, an ordinary citizen, to demand a folk meeting in an effort to overrule the council—if that went against Olassøn, then Olassøn would be shunned. And on the raft, in those narrow confines, that was an intolerable punishment.

Clearly the young man must feel that those foreigners were deserving of sanctuary. But to receive them on the clan raft . . . ? Impossible.

"Well," said the stamchef, "I suppose these people must know Angli, else you would not know what you do of them. I will speak with them. But you—remember the cost to you of a *folkmotti*, should it go against you, which it surely would."

He moved as if to turn, to walk away, but Olassøn spoke again, stopping him. What Olassøn had to say, he felt, should not wait for the water rafts. "*Min Herri*," he said respectfully, "Torval Benssøn is dead."

"What! How?"

The young man told him how the sentinel had died, stressing the peaceful approach of Quick Spirit. The stamchef was not as upset as Olassøn had feared. Benssøn had been a blusterer, had as a child even been something of a bully, although he'd been broken of that. He was a kind neither frequent nor welcome in a raft clan, where people live close, and he probably would have shot the *landmani*. But still he'd been one of theirs, and now was killed by the hand of the foreigner, maybe even one of those coming on the water rafts.

Oska Egolfssøn turned away tight-mouthed. He did

not want to say anything to Olassøn that he might later regret; the young *flottkarli* had been his protege, whom he'd thought of as one day becoming a *størmani*, possibly even stamchef. And he reminded himself as he walked away that it was no fault of Olassøn's that Torval Benssøn was dead. Even, he admitted to himself, the foreigners seemed not severely culpable.

Walking to a nearby shed, the stamchef climbed atop it to see what he could of the human cargo on the rafts, still the better part of a kilometer distant. They were covered with people. Shaking his head, he climbed back down.

What Arvo Olassøn had told of the happenings ashore had swiftly spread. So when the water rafts arrived, virtually every member of the raft clan was on hand to see the foreigners. The raft folk were markedly quiet at the sight of such dark people. Not that they weren't themselves sunbrowned, but many of the desert-dwelling Apaches were tanned nearly black. And although no few of the Dinneh had brown hair, an occasional child verging on sandy blond, the hair of most was very dark, even raven black. And all wore it long, including the men.

There was also interest in the Dinneh physique. Most of the warriors were barrel-chested, but their sinewy limbs were mostly more slender than those of the raftsmen, especially now after weeks on the trail, fleeing the Saurons.

For their part, the Indians felt utterly exposed and vulnerable. This was another people's territory, a medium utterly foreign and unknown to them, only a few could swim at all, and the strangers far outnumbered them. And the great clan raft itself was intimidating. The small rafts rode about as high—they were of course sections of it—but just now they were free-floating, and moved differently on the coastal swell. Leads would open between the clan raft and their own, then close with a heavy bump.

And the edge of the clan raft was almost solid with the large foreigners.

Thus the Apaches did not move from the water rafts until Arvo Olassøn told them to. Then a few of the Norskuna reached out hands to help, taking first the smaller children. In a few minutes all the Dinneh were across.

Only when the rafts were mostly cleared did Oska Egolfssøn realize that but two of them bore filled waterbags. The muscles in his strong jaw tightened, for this upset him more than the death of Benssøn. His people had been on short water rations for days, had run very low on the vital fluid. Now his water party had returned with less than half what they should have brought, and dozens of new people to help drink it.

But the time to speak of these things was in meeting. Now he voiced only orders: the *størsmennu* should gather in the privacy of the *størshusi*, the council house, along with Arvo Olassøn and the chief of the foreigners. He turned and walked away between the low, dowel-fastened wooden dwellings, sheds, and work shops which, along with drying racks, strewed most sections of the great raft.

He had taken his place in the *størshusi* when the others arrived, and after a stern glance at Olassøn, his eyes went to the foreigner. Nothing was said until the others were seated.

"You talk Angli?" he asked.

Quick Spirit nodded. "Me talk Angli. All people on land talk Angli; Saurons make talk Angli."

Oska Egolfssøn looked then at Olassøn, still talking "Angli"— pidgin—so the foreigner could follow what was said. "Why you fellas not bring more water?" he demanded. "You there 'nuff long, bring very much water."

"Water make rafts too much heavy, very hard drag so heavy raft. Us much hurry, Saurons come."

The Saurons again. Oska Egolfssøn pursed his lips, preparing to speak, but Olassøn wasn't done. He gestured with his head to the Apache. "This fella name Quick Spirit. The rest him people go south now, 'long shore. Saurons come after, mebbe catch. If us send more rafts, mebbe save him people from Saurons—fellas, women. No save, Saurons kill. If us gonna save 'em, us gotta hurry, not sit talk-talk long time."

The stamchef flushed. It was not this young man's place to tell him to hurry. He replied in their own language, in which he could express himself more exactly. "There are things to ask before we decide. How many would die if you hadn't been there? All of them, apparently. We have already saved many of his people. And we have no room for more on the raft. Also we would have to feed them." He paused. "And we don't have water for any more; we will be hard pressed even for these."

Somewhat to Egolfssøn's embarrassment, Olassøn interpreted his words for the foreigner. The brown man's expression did not change, and he made neither comment nor sign. Then Olassøn turned to his chief.

"*Min Besta Høyherri*," he said, using the ceremonial term of highest respect, "what you have said is all true. But let us save the rest of this people if we can! If we were in their situation, surely we'd hope they would save us. Can we not at least try? In the old days, in the time of the valley wars, the Norskuna had heroes. Their deeds are recited around the night fires. Surely the rescue of these people would be another for our grandchildren to tell theirs.

"Our people can be crowded for a little, and with the water we have brought back, if we ration it . . . The rains are already overdue, and surely they will not hold off much longer. Ask the people if they are willing. Now, while there may still be a chance."

The stamchef shook his head slowly. The sagas included also stories of the Norskuna's experience of the Saurons, and little of that was even remotely heroic. It would be sweet to take away the Saurons' prey, but there were certain hard realities.

"You ask us to trust that the rains will come soon," he said, "and that is not wise. And even if we had more water . . . I do not criticize you for bringing back so little; I understand now why you couldn't. But the fact remains that we are short of it. Also . . ." He turned to Quick Spirit. "How many you people—fella, women, *bahnu* . . . chillun?"

"All mebbe three hundred. Mebbe three hundred twenty."

Oska Egolfssøn pursed his lips, unconsciously shaking his head. His own clan numbered, at last count, four hundred thirty-eight. Three hundred *landmennu* would more than crowd them; they would constitute a danger. But before he could say it, Arvo Olassøn spoke again, almost as if he'd read his stamchef's mind.

"*Min Besta Høyherri*, the Dinneh do not know how to sail the raft, or handle it at all. They do not know the ways of the sea. Did you not see how they looked about them, as if afraid that the sea would eat them? They would never try to take over the raft.

"Ask the people if they are willing to be crowded. And if they are willing to have water rationed again. Ask if they wish to show that the Norskuna can still do great acts. Ask now, while there may still be time. The chance will soon pass. We can . . ."

A *størsmani*, Matts Janssøn, interrupted. "Did you see any Saurons? How do you know the Saurons were coming?" He stared hard at Olassøn. "You have taken the word of these *landmennu* for it! The Saurons don't chase anyone for five days; they catch them and kill them long before five days. Those people lied; they fooled you! They have some plot. . . ."

"No," interrupted Egolfssøn, "that is improbable. They would not have sent all their children and so many women, with so few fighting men, unless they were in great danger."

He shifted his big body on the high seat. "The *størsmotti* will prepare to vote now," he said. Then, to

Arvgo and the Apache: "You two must leave the *størshusi*. I will tell you the decision."

Arvo Olassøn got up. Quick Spirit with him, and they left. Outside, Olassøn said, "Boss fellas much soon done talk-talk. Them. . . ." He paused, having no Angli word for "vote," and finished lamely. "Them say yes or no much soon."

Quick Spirit nodded without speaking, not indifferent but resigned, and Arvo led him to a nearby bench, where they sat down to wait. Actually, the Apache had brought no expectations with him, and not much hope. Their wait was short; in less than five minutes, Oska Egolfssøn, followed by his *størsmennu*, ducked out of the *størshusi*. The stamchef, with Skippari Janssøn, came over to Olassøn.

"The vote was three to three. Therefore, this is what I will do. I am calling a *folksmotti* to vote on the issue; it will be when Cats-Eye is there." He pointed up at a meridian about two hours away. "Meanwhile we will set sail southward* while manning the sweeps, and approach nearer to shore, so that, should the vote be favorable, we will not have far to go. I will also send canoes out to see what is happening. While we are doing those things, the *størsmennu* can talk on the matter to the people, who will of course talk to each other." He pointed at the sky again. "Then, when Cats-Eye is there, we will learn what we must do."

Sees far had just slung his pack onto his back and turned to look at the diminishing water rafts when he heard the far off horn hoot. The distance, he thought,

---

*Due to Haven's slow axial rotation, its Coriolus Force is much weaker than on many planets. Thus the prevailing winds are largely north or south, depending on latitude and, in the equatorial zone, season. At the location of the clan raft, about two degrees north latitude, with Byers' Sun about four degrees south latitude on that date, the prevailing surface winds were northerly, often with an on-shore vector during the long mornings and an off-shore vector at night.

might be a kilometer, but the horn would be passing on the signal from watchers farther back.

But Saurons were swift.

At once he had shouted orders. Eight of the older warriors, again men who could no longer run so fast, separated from the group and disappeared into the jungle to set ambushes. Like the watchers, these men would almost surely be killed. Sees Far had no illusions that eight men with bows would kill many Saurons; considering Sauron senses, reflexes, torso armor, and especially weapons, the ambushers would do well to kill two or three. Their purpose was more to distract, delay, buy a little time.

The rest of the people began to hurry, most loping southward along the beach, the pregnant and some of the other women scrambling or being helped onto muskylopes. Sees Far himself was rather old for Haven— forty-seven years in Terran terms. But considering the Haven ecology, and particularly the chemistry of its desert waters, he was in unusually good health for his age, marvelously trail-toughened, and in his youth had been known as much for his speed as his eyesight. And as clan chief, he belonged near the front of the column, so he speeded up accordingly to get there.

For a little while now they might excel the Saurons in speed, for the beach was level and unobstructed, and its sand yet firm from the long night's dew, while the Saurons would still be trotting slowly among the boulders and fallen trees that littered the canyon. But when the Saurons reached the beach, a footrace would begin that the Lion Clan could only lose, and that fairly quickly, unless something intervened.

Nor could those on muskylopes long outspeed a Sauron. Even the better distance runners among the Dinneh, though initially left in the dust, could catch and pass a rider over the course of perhaps two days. And these muskylopes all carried more than one rider.

Nor did the chief have any illusions about the raft people coming to rescue them. But until his people were dead, they would try to save themselves, in flight and then in battle. The adolescents were the final hope for a continuance of the people. When battle was imminent, they were to take the muskylopes and run them to collapse, then scatter into the jungle in mated pairs. Perhaps the hunting Saurons would overlook some or decide they were not worth the time and trouble. But that was problematical, a hope rather than an expectation.

Occasionally the chief took a hard piece of jerky from his belt pouch and bit off a piece, running steadily as he chewed. When he had mastered the tough dry meat, he slowed enough to take a swallow of water from the section of boiled-out muskylope gut which, slung over his shoulder, served as canteen.

He was grateful to the north breeze, which cooled him, and thought his thanks to it.

With the passage of one hour and then another, the tide continued to rise, somewhat narrowing the beach. In places, Sees Far could see that, at its peak, the water reached the bluffs. By now the Saurons, too, would probably be on the beach, coming swiftly behind, closing the gap.

The coast, remarkably regular here, began to curve westward, and bluffs gave way to progressively gentler, jungled hills. The Dinneh waded a small, slow-flowing river that came to their chests, their armpits, the clan's surer swimmers crossing first to test the depth, dragging ropes with them to help the smaller cross without being drowned. It was a short break from running, but briefly it slowed them.

So for a little they trotted faster than they had, to make it up.

As runners, Sees Far's people were less inferior to the Saurons than he knew. The Dinneh policy of genetic infusion from the Saurons had had more influence than they'd realized. No people of, say, nineteenth or twentieth century Terra were as genetically gifted, physically, as these descendants of the White River and San Carlos and Navajo Apache. And though the Saurons gained steadily on them now, the gaining was not as fast as Sees Far believed.

But not all of the Dinneh were warriors, nor all the warriors young, and the sand, drying in the sun, was beginning to be looser, harder to run on. Some of his people had begun to lag. Perhaps, thought Sees Far, it was time to slow for a bit, to rest by slowing to an easy jog.

It was then that someone shouted, and the old chief turned to look. An arm was pointing, and there, driven by sails and paddles, were three canoes, not more than three hundred meters away. He had not seen them, had not been looking seaward, hopeward. Sees Far ordered the slowdown and, waving the others on, himself angled toward the water's edge and slowed to a walk. One canoe changed direction and slanted to meet him.

As Sees Far watched, he could make out other sails far off, out to sea and farther back, and he felt a cautious quickening of hope. Looking back along the beach then with his Sauron-enhanced vision, he also saw, minute in the distance, what could only be Saurons, pursuing. The canoe came in on one of the small breakers, and grounded, the paddlers jumping out as it did so, to pull it farther up on the sand. He recognized one of them as a man who'd been with the rafts.

"Rafts come!" the man said urgently. "You fellas hurry, that place!" He pointed at a headland. "Go in water that place, rafts take you fellas 'way?"

Then he pointed back in the direction of the pursuing Saurons; his eyes too, though unenhanced, saw far. "Me think them fellas Saurons, run fast. You fellas gotta run fast too."

Sees Far nodded but said nothing for a moment. His eyes measured the distance to the Saurons, then to the headland, and he estimated speeds. Again he nodded; he knew what he needed to do next.

"Me fellas, them be that place for rafts," he answered. The chief reached out, as Quick Spirit had to

Arvo, and gripped the Norski's beefy hand before turning to lope off after his people. The Norski stared after him for just a moment before turning to push the dugout back into the surf. He was glad he had voted as he had.

As Lieutenant Shtenuk loped tirelessly along the beach, his Sauron eyes had picked out the canoes, had even seen one land, seemingly to contact the Dinneh. He didn't know what that was all about, but supposed that the canoe people were responsible for the disturbed beach where the canyon emerged from the hills.

Still, what could primitive fishermen do that would make a difference?

He had not taken the time to examine the marks, had assumed they'd been made independent of the Dinneh, who then had simply paused to look them over. More pertinent to his mission, he'd thought, were the tracks of the fleeing Dinneh leading southward along the beach. Without stopping, he'd led his platoon on their trail. Later, near the horizon, he had seen—something. From his sea-level viewpoint there had been small sails and something low in the water, but it did not seem significant. Coastal fishermen.

And finally there was something he'd failed entirely to notice—a number of Dinneh warriors had, individually, slanted a few strides to the jungle's edge, to backtrack in the cover of its fringe, out of sight even to Sauron eyes at that distance.

A kilometer ahead he could see a river emerge from the jungle, carrying brown water out into the ocean. To the lieutenant the river was no problem. Nor was the fact that his platoon was now sixteen short of its normal complement of sixty-four. Eleven of his losses had come in the hard-fought march up the long and rugged defile that led to the desert basin which had constituted the Dinneh's territory. The several skirmishes and ambushes since then had cost him only five more. He and his men wore light torso armor, sufficient to stop arrows. You were all right unless you took one in the face or neck, or in a limb. In that case, you were in trouble; the damned Dinneh had coated their arrowheads with something quick and nasty.

He didn't think of them by the name "Dinneh," of course. To the Saurons, except for a few of those who'd been stationed among the Dinneh before the revolt, they were referred to simply as "cattle," like the rest of Haven's non-Sauron populations.

The cattle would no doubt fight when cornered. But Shtenuk took no particular pleasure from the thought; they were too few, their warriors outnumbering his men only perhaps two or three to one. And they would have seen him coming by now—even cattle could see that well. They were probably shitting in their pants.

He'd have preferred to be chasing a much larger force, or perhaps approaching them in some mountain fastness—something to make things interesting. Like the fight up the defile to the basin; that had been more worth a soldier's time!

The Saurons had been spoiled by centuries of dominance—of few challenges in their zone of interest. Thus Shtenuk's mind was in part on these other matters, and not totally on business. Had there been a cyborg with his platoon, Shtenuk would have been more alert, or been relieved of command by it, or perhaps summarily executed for poor attitude on a combat mission. But the cyborgs had declined in numbers over the centuries; only three had accompanied the entire battalion on this campaign. Of course, cyborgs were seldom really necessary in battle on this world. They served their function now mainly in training Sauron youth to the required keen edge of physical and military prowess. Or as keen as you could get without fighting worthwhile enemies.

Shtenuk had reviewed the old maps of this territory, had looked at the map for this particular quadrangle only that morning while he ate. The shore here curved westward into a small and narrow peninsula. But the cattle wouldn't know it was a peninsula. To them it could easily be simply a curve in the coastline.

He should overtake them somewhat before they reached the point, he decided, even allowing that these particular cattle had shown themselves surprisingly tough and fast. So, depending on how much energy they had in reserve, they might conceivably reach the point first. In that case he would send a squad through the jungle to cut them off—waylay them when they fled down the beach on the peninsula's other side. He smiled inwardly at the prospect. It would be amusing to let them reach the point, just to do that, and salvage something entertaining out of this pursuit. But Shtenuk would never do something as unprofessional as that. A Sauron always closed a pursuit with utmost dispatch, holding back only for good operational reasons.

His three-point men had reached the river bank and paused momentarily to scan the other side. The shore here was indented, scoured by the river's current, and the tide had reached within twenty meters of the jungle. Crossing the river, they'd be relatively vulnerable to ambushers in the undergrowth. Seeing none, they started across, rifles held overhead, the water rising to their chests, then emerged from the other side. The rest of the platoon prepared to follow them by squads.

The first squad was past the middle, up almost to their necks, the second starting watchfully down the bank, when the arrows began to fly. The first squad disappeared at once, submerging. The second ducked back into cover, but three had been hit and collapsed in the brush to die. The third and fourth squads knelt in the underbrush where they'd taken cover at the first arrow shot, and immediately began to fire their rifles into the growth on the other side—aimed fire at any movement, into any favorable cover, their practiced hands operating the bolts with sufficient speed that they could smell hot wood on the forepiece. Within a minute, their gatling gun had been set up and began to rake the other side systematically. Then Shtenuk saw the heads of the first squad emerge one by one under the overhanging growth of brush along the far bank. As far as he could tell, only one of them was missing. He shouted the order to cease fire.

From where he lay now, he couldn't see the point men. But in the instant before diving into the jungle, he'd glimpsed two of the three lying on the beach with arrows in them. Presumably the third had made it into the jungle, but it would be surprising if he'd made it unwounded.

Shit, he told himself, not angrily, *things are getting interesting after all*.

There was no sign of further enemy activity. They could easily all have been hit and out of action now, for the Sauron rifleman used his weapon with an accuracy grown of inborn talent and long practice, while their gatling gun pumped out bullets at a sustained rate of three per second. Or the display of firepower might simply have shocked the survivors into stunned stillness. If so, his men would probably see signs of their movement when they tried to crawl away.

Shtenuk never missed the firepower the Saurons had brought to Haven centuries earlier. The old weapons had long since worn out, and among the Saurons, with their deliberately now-oriented culture, the past was barely even folklore. The systems of the fugitive transport which, crippled, had landed them there, had early ceased to function. And Sauron armorers had neither the facilities nor the precision engineering skills to tool parts for things like automatic rifles.

The basic problem was that, through selection, indoctrination, and training, the Sauron culture had culled, quashed, and failed to develop the potentially skilled engineer in its single-minded emphasis on the skilled and utter warrior. Like the smilodon, the Sauron was a highly specialized killer.

Of course, genus *Smilodon*, despite or because of specilization, had lasted some thirty million years, to succumb eventually to primitive man. So far the Saurons had shown no sign of succumbing. Personal warrior skills, highly flexible and foot-mobile combat tactics, unit coordination, and ruthlessness, all intensively drilled, along with rifles, grenades, and the primitive gatling gun, had long been more than adequate—with only occasional help from pack artillery.

Now Schtenuk shouted harsh Sauron gutturals and watched the first squad crawl out of the water into the underbrush on the other side. Then he sent the second squad out of the vegetation on this side, down the slick bank into the water, also to submerge. No more arrows flew. The third squad he sent through the jungle to cross upstream a hundred meters, just in case. He'd hold the fourth here as a reserve, to lay down aimed rifle fire if needed. It seemed highly unlikely that it would be.

A shout reached him, via a relay man on the other side. They'd found a body, then another, and a third and fourth. The second squad was crawling out of the water now, and upstream, Sergeant Burkha's third squad should be crossing or about to cross.

It was precisely then that a brief flurry of shooting occurred in the jungle on the other side, followed by a pause and more shots. Meanwhile, the second squad had disappeared, melted into the thick vegetation. Shortly two more flurries of gunfire were heard, and a minute later another. Moments later there were two more. After that it was quiet until Sergeant Bezhut, in charge of the first squad, sent a runner to report. One of the cattle had shot at them with a rifle, and a private had been lungshot. They'd returned the fire, but hadn't seen the target, and as far as they could tell, hadn't hit anyone. They'd quickly found his trail and begun to follow him. Also at once Bezhut had sent men to the beach, assuming that the enemy had gotten his rifle from the point men, who presumably had been killed in the ambush. They would track from there.

Eventually the situation sorted itself out. The enemy body count came to nine. Corporal Langruf was dead and the lungshot man was dying. All rifles had been recovered. Two more enemy had fled, separately, one of them leaving blood flecks. He'd let them go, Shtenuk decided; this had already taken too long.

He gave the order to reassemble at once on the beach beside the river, then took the fourth squad across and waited briefly for the third squad to get there. Meanwhile, the fourth squad had broken down the gatling gun into its constituent parts for carrying, a twelve-second job done before crossing, and the lungshot man had been given the coup de grace. The Sauron dead came to eight.

Shtenuk hated to leave Sauron bodies for vermin to feed on, but he'd have to for now. They'd carry them to the beach later and make a funeral pyre for them, after they'd caught and finished off the cattle.

While he waited, the lieutenant reviewed the skirmish. They'd been delayed for more than twelve minutes, which, though Shtenuk didn't realize it, was all that Sees Far had intended the action for, and died for.

The Sauron platoon reassembled and started off again on the trail of the cattle. But now it had ceased to be a recreation for them, a wilderness hunting expedition. Sauron troops were proud as well as ruthless, fearless, and unmatched in competence. They resented Saurons killed, and also, each of them felt embarrassed by losing eight to an ambush.

Now, as they loped along the beach, the new point men were absolutely alert to any sign of movement in the jungle's edge. And of course, anyone any distance back from the edge would be in no position to shoot arrows at them. They could only move in after the Saurons were past, to shoot from the rear. To guard against that, Shtenuk had assigned four men as a rear guard, two of them loping along at the very edge of the jungle, finger in the trigger guard, thumb on the safety. Two others followed a little farther back and near the gentle surf, eyes left.

There was, of course, some wind movement of the

edge vegetation, but trained Sauron eyes would recognize the difference.

These precautions slowed their pace from about three minutes per kilometer to something approaching four. And while they still gained steadily, it was clear to Shtenuk now that the cattle would reach the point before he caught them. So before then he would have two squads shortcut across the peninsula and waylay them on the other side after all—take them between the guns in front and those behind.

When the shooting stopped from across the river, Swift Feet and his grandfather had gotten to their feet. But not Laughing Man. He lay dead. One of the three Sauron point men, though shot in the neck, had snapped off a shot as he'd darted into the jungle and hit the ground. Like Laughing Man, the Sauron would never get up, and it was to him that Swift Feet and his grandfather had gone. His grandfather had handed Swift Feet the pistol and belt, keeping the rifle for himself.

He also gave the youth some hurried instructions, then Swift Feet had left, running the first five hundred meters through jungle, dodging trees, ducking lianas, hurdling fallen trunks. For one so fleet, this was slow going. But it was important that he escape unseen, if possible, for even he could not long outrun a Sauron if it came to a footrace.

When he'd come out on the beach again, there'd been another flurry of shooting, and briefly he'd ducked back into cover. But it repeated when he was out of sight, so he decided it was not at him, and came out onto the beach again where he could run faster. Over the next few minutes he heard gunfire several more times, increasingly distant as he sped from the site.

Only once did he slow to look back, some two kilometers beyond the river, and his keen eyes, with their hawk-like magnifying central vision, saw no sign of Saurons on the beach. As for himself, though he kept to the heavily-tracked trail of his people, he kept to that part of it closest to the jungle fringe, where the visual background of tangled vegetation would render a single runner next to invisible at a distance.

He did not slow to examine the handgun or cartridge belt. He was already familiar with Sauron handguns, crude, heavy, long-barreled revolvers whose cylinder advanced by thumbing. Every Lion warrior had at least a little familiarity, for man and boy, they had never failed to observe when Saurons among them had used or handled arms, as they often did to impress the people.

But Swift Feet had a closer familiarity. His father had been a Sauron officer assigned to the Dinneh, and his mother, too, carried Sauron genes. This ancestry was reflected in Swift Feet's brown hair and blue eyes, the lighter tan of his skin, and, more importantly, in his Sauron-like strength and speed and quickness of reflexes. And the fifth-from-last Sauron officer to live with the Lion Clan (the assignment was for one standard Terran year) had been less arrogant than most; he had been friendly to the chief's grandson, who looked so much like a Sauron child. Grinning, the man had shown him his pistol, even shown him how it worked, and let him touch it though not hold it.

Oska Egolfssøn could work a scull like any other Norski, though he didn't do nearly as much of it as he once had—enough to keep his strength. A stamchef acted as referee, consultant, and occasional judge, and he was also the raft's executive director. However, all these tasks together were only moderately time-consuming, and in the populist societies of the raft clans, a stamchef was expected to stay moderately busy like everyone else, putting his hand to ordinary duties.

Just now he was sculling one of the section rafts—a module, so to speak, calved off like seven others from the clan raft to serve not for fetching water but for rescue. And he was not sculling today because it was expected of him. It wasn't.

But he'd laid his reputation on the line when he spoke in support of Arvo Olassøn's proposal. Despite the clan wives' captivation by the smaller Dinneh children, and the appeal to old Norsk heroism, the practical and conservative raftsmen would not have approved the rescue proposal without his support of it. And even that would not have sufficed without his last minute solution for what to do with the foreigners. With that, the margin of approval had been substantial.

Beyond that, no fewer than twenty-four scullsmen were placing their lives at unusual risk. For the mission required eight rafts, and this time each raft had three sculling posts manned.

So he felt a sharper responsibility, and almost compelled to take an active role in the rescue mission. Besides, he ascribed to the viewpoint that the best way to see something difficult done right was to do it or direct it yourself, or more often, simply be on hand and available.

And beyond that, it felt—exciting. Once he'd decided to support the mission, juices flowed in him that he hadn't felt since boyhood. Excitement seldom came his way.

Peering southeastward across light-spangled, jade green water, he could see not only the point for which he steered, but a distant train of people running toward it along the beach. The sight amazed him: his own people never ran farther than a few steps. Even the Nyttheim Norskuna, living on land, didn't run such distances, so far as he knew. No wonder the Dinneh warriors had such sinewy legs!

He continued the powerful movements of his heavy torso and legs, thick callused hands gripping the sweep solidly, his practiced mind judging wind and currents without conscious attention. He knew exactly where he wanted to go, and together his body and subconscious constituted a marvelously sophisticated servo-mechanism to carry out command intention. Meanwhile, he kept track of the seven rafts that followed him, and the three dugouts, sails furled now, that sat lightly grounded on the still distant point.

Only with a telescope—and they'd lost all but memory of such an instrument—could he have seen the smoothly running Saurons against the backdrop of jungle, but he did not doubt they were coming. A canoeman, Jøssi Mikkissøn, had seen them early on, had signalled word to him.

This was more than a simple race he'd gotten his little flotilla into, the stamchef told himself. For it would not be enough just to get off the shoal ahead of the Saurons. Quick Spirit had told him frankly that the Saurons had weapons which could kill across a distance much longer than arrow flight, and indeed, Norsk tradition said the same. So they needed to be well away before the Saurons got there. That's what made the peninsula's point essential as a loading place, or the shoal that was an underwater extension of it. Load there, raise sail, and the north wind, freshening now, would move even such clumsy craft quickly away from shore.

His sense of urgency surged, reinforced by fear, and he called out to the other rafts to hurry, then speeded the cadence of his sculling.

The people were still perhaps two kilometers ahead when Swift Feet, glancing back, spotted the distant file of Saurons coming. For him to continue running on the beach was to risk being seen. Perhaps, he thought as he entered the jungle, they had seen him already. But if he were them, he would be watching for another ambush, perhaps glancing at the fleeing clan now and then, if they could see them from that far, examining the intervening beach only occasionally, if at all.

Spying a large fallen tree not far within the jungle's edge, he went to it. He would lie behind it to attack, up where the trunk separated into thick branches between which he could shoot. They would make him harder to see and give him some protection from bullets.

But first he would crouch where he could watch the Saurons coming.

Stationary now, Swift Feet watched them rapidly closing the gap. Then, to his surprise, about half of them left the beach, disappearing into the jungle, while the rest came on. For a moment he almost panicked and fled, for it seemed to him that they must have seen him, that the soldiers had gone into the jungle to flank him. But he rejected the thought: surely they would have come farther before they did that.

It would not be long now, so he took his ambush position and practiced sighting down the top of the long weapon—twenty-five centimeters, receiver and barrel. Both hands, the Sauron had told him; use the sight, *squeeze* the trigger. "But not you, little Dinneh," he'd added with a laugh. "Gun for Sauron only."

The Saurons were getting near, and Swift Feet released the safety. He would shoot the leader first, if he could recognize him. Not the man in front necessarily. In the tribute parties, the officers had worn shiny metal sunbursts or crossed metal swords on there collars; he would look for those. And shoot low, he reminded himself; Saurons wore torso armor.

The lieutenant was not more than fifty feet distant when Swift Feet squeezed the trigger, his front sight on Shtenuk's thighs, and the Sauron's momentum took him sliding along the sand. Swift Feet was startled by the revolver's recoil, but nonetheless remembered to thumb the cylinder ahead one click.

The soldiers had swerved, darting toward the jungle and the as yet unseen Swift Feet. But his reflexes were scarcely slower than theirs. Again he fired—once, twice, now with wrists and hands more firm, as a return flurry of rifle bullets slapped and sang in his vicinity, some hitting the fallen tree. Yet he rose to his knees for better shots, snapping off two more quickly before three bullets struck him almost together, killing him instantly.

The Saurons crouched in the undergrowth for a moment, only their hard eyes moving, alert for any further enemy. After half a minute, one of them slowly stood, trigger finger ready, deliberately exposing himself to draw fire, but there was none. He slipped forward and found their attacker, whose feet would run no more.

Only one! thought Sergeant Bezhut. *These cattle are dangerous when they have guns!* But maybe there *was* another, lying low, waiting quietly for them to turn their backs. So he left the first squad there, rifles ready, fingers on triggers, eyes alert for any movement, and he himself took the second squad back onto the beach.

Shtenuk was dead, Bezhut found, a bloody hole in his chest. Swift Feet's first shot had been high, but the Saurons light torso armor was intended to stop arrows, not high velocity bullets. Another Sauron lay dead at the jungle's edge, while a third sat bleeding in the undergrowth, swearing now.

Bezhut ordered the first squad back onto the beach then, and they began to run again. But for the moment more slowly than before, albeit faster than any other human soldiers would have run. They were trying to see more deeply into the undergrowth now; an enemy with a gun might lay farther back from the beach than a bowman would, like the one they'd just killed.

The third and fourth squads had stopped dead in their tracks at the sound of shooting, and for a long moment Sergeant Burkha held them there with an up-raised hand.

It was quiet again. All he could hear now was his own heavy breathing and that of the others nearest him. The first and second squads couldn't be shooting up the cattle this soon; there must have been another ambush. And the fourth squad, with the gatling gun, was with him. The question was whether to continue or to go and back up the others. But he'd been given his orders, and the others could handle anything the cattle might try.

He waved his hand forward, and they began running through the jungle again, toward the other side of the narrow peninsula, where they would set up an ambush of their own.

Bezhut had sent the sails before, but thought them simply a fleet of canoes. They'd gotten a good look at some canoes a while earlier, and dismissed them as too small to be meaningful to them—curious coastal fisherman hanging about to see what was going on.

But now he realized that these new craft were larger, and moving toward the point, and it occurred to him that they might possibly intend to interfere. He shouted a sharp order, and his men speeded up.

The first of the Dinneh reached the ultimate point of land and, shouted on by canoemen, waded into the water. The first three rafts were waiting for them, sails down. Each was held more or less in place against the breeze by two scullsmen who, as the raft drifted into position, had quickly switched their sculls from the sculling posts at one end to those at the other. The third raftsman stood ready to hoist the sail again.

Gunfire sounded at a distance rearward, impelling stragglers to greater speed.

The water was hip deep to the warriors who reached the nearest raft, but its deck stood shoulder high, rising and falling gently. Quickly the first several were boosted aboard. Then, with help from above and behind, Indians began to board en masse, while canoemen shouted and waved more to other rafts. Some Dinneh women were on muskylopes, two and even three to an animal, and the now nervous beasts were dragged and cudgeled by warriors out to a raft with their burdens.

The first raft was quickly loaded. Its scullmen lifted their sweeps from the sand while their partners hoisted the sail, and the clumsy craft began to move sluggishly ahead of the breeze, its crew shouting now at the crowding Indians to let them through with their sculls. A few Apaches had tried to pass it on the downwind side and found the raft pushing them ahead of it. Shouting, in some cases choking and sputtering, they were hauled aboard by others. One was overridden and drowned.

A fourth raft, its sail down too now, was being wind-pushed toward the mob; its scullsmen dug blades into the sand to stop. The second raft left with its load, and then the third, to the sound of renewed gunfire.

Sergeant Bezhut had abandoned any doubts about the intentions of the raftsmen, and himself leading, had increased the pursuit to a speed almost too fast to sustain. In another hundred meters they would commence firing. At that moment, the final ambush struck, while his men were straining, their attention on speed instead of the undergrowth. Arrows streaked, and several men fell while others felt the hard blows of arrows on torso armor. The remaining Saurons dispersed instantly, the several foremost hitting the sand, firing their rifles in the direction of the ambush, while those behind them darted for the jungle's edge. More arrows struck into and around the men on the sand as guns continued to slam, aimed now at seen targets, bullets ripping into the jungle. The arrows ceased. The Saurons who'd reached cover quickly moved through the vegetation, weapons ready, occasionally firing. They found seven Dinneh dead, and five wounded whom they killed.

Sergeant Horsht of the second squad trotted back out onto the sand, saw Bezhut lying with an arrow in one eye, then looked along the beach again. He could not see the very point, for in the final four hundred meters the beach curved southwest, and the jungle, though scrubby there, screened it. But Horsht *knew* what had to be happening. He knew. With a sharp shout, he ordered his men on again. Those with a clear line of fire paused at will to shoot at the still-distant rafts standing off the shoal waiting for a place.

Bullets, their energy more or less spent, had thudded into the seventh and eighth rafts, but their crews hadn't realized what the sounds meant. The fourth raft was just beginning to move away, its scullsmen crowding their way through the pack of Indians when, on the seventh raft, starting now to move in, a raftsman went down, struck in the temple by a Sauron round.

Indians still were climbing onto the fifth and sixth rafts. It was a canoeman who realized what had happened, and what to do. Shouting, he waved the two off-lying rafts to move to the shoal, out of the line of fire. They did, farther out, and Indians breasted the water past the fifth and sixth to get to them.

A moment later, the Saurons appeared around the curve of the beach and slowed, the leaders emptying their magazines at the rafts and Indians less than a half kilometer away. People began to fall. The fifth raft, a scullsman down, swung slowly around, uncontrolled, and began to drift away, mostly loaded. The raftsman by the sail quickly raised it; one of the warriors had grabbed the fallen scullsman's sweep and placed it between two scull posts, then imitated as best he could the actions of the other scullsman. The raftsmen on the sixth, swearing mightily for haste, held her there until she was pretty much loaded, then lifted their sculls. As they traded ends, the sail was raised and the raft moved away, the scullsmen quickly sculling for dear life. Then one of them fell too.

By now the Saurons were near enough for greater accuracy. On the seventh raft, both scullsmen went down and the sail up with the raft less than half loaded. One, not badly wounded, still gripped his scull, though, and got back up, cursing, to add his strength as the craft began to move downwind under fire. The eighth lost both scullsmen with not more than a dozen Indians aboard; the third raftsman raised the sail, then hit the deck among the prostrate Apaches as it too began to move away.

Fortunately, the first three rafts had taken on more than their share of the people, but still some thirty of the Dinneh were left in the water. Some began to swim after the rafts, some who'd never swum before and never would again. Most turned to wade toward the beach, trying for the scrub growth on the point.

Briefly, moving south ahead of the wind, the rafts were again out of the line of fire, all but the last picking up speed. Meanwhile the bowman in one canoe picked a fallen scull from the water, and the other paddlers started after the raft, digging hard, closing quickly on it. The man with the salvaged scull transferred to the derelict raft, swearing its prone crewman to his feet; together they manned their sculls and picked up speed.

But several of their dozen Indians aboard were dead or wounded.

The Saurons rounded the point, knelt, and began to fire again at the retreating rafts. Three of the rafts were within easy range, though their Indians were mostly lying flat. On the hindmost raft the riflemen saw both scullsmen go down at once, presumably shot; they'd hardly have had time to hear the renewed gunfire and hit the deck deliberately. Several other men fell into the water in the first volleys of gunfire, as far ahead as the fourth raft. But all the remaining targets flattened themselves, providing low profiles, the hindmost shields for the rest. And the distance continued to widen. After emptying a pair of magazines each at the retreating rafts, a thin-lipped Sergeant Horsht ordered a cease fire; their ammunition was not inexhaustable.

The Saurons turned to the jungle; there still were the cattle who'd missed the rafts.

Epilogue

Time passed. Before the clan raft had headed for the mid-ocean reaches, another mission had gone to a mainland stream for water. This time canoes took in the empty water bags only two hours before high tide, and their crews worked rapidly, filling and pilling them.

Then the rafts came to quickly load and leave, minimizing the danger of shore attack.

Later, a corsair had seen the outward-bound clan raft and approached to examine it as a possible victim. But the lean and hungry ship had veered off and disappeared, no doubt because of the large number of armed males to be seen on the raft.

The Dinneh learned to eat fish and help catch them, pulling on nets and long hand lines, and to gather and cook the seaweed that floated here and there in beds larger than the rafts. And some of their women birthed children.

There had been no conflict between the two peoples. To some degree they tended to keep to themselves, and their leaders quickly handled such potential conflicts as occurred. The raft folk, used to living together on a small floating island, had long since learned to handle trouble and its causes before they became a source of serious upsets.

But the Dinneh desired greatly to live ashore again in a land of their own, while the Norskuna wished to be what they considered uncrowded once more.

So when at last the forested bulk of Grønøy—"Green Island"—rose above the horizon, both Dinneh and Norshkuna went about grinning, one at the other as well as among themselves. The island was uninhabited; now it would be the country of the Dinneh, far from the landbound Saurons.

Two days later, the clan raft lay a few kilometers offshore while the Dinneh disembarked onto section rafts, taking with them a few bales of dried fish and seaweed, enough to start with. Nor would they depart alone. Besides the raft crews, who would return, four Norska men and their families went with the Dinneh—two with Norska wives and two with wives from among the Dinneh, for the Dinneh had a considerable surplus of women. The three older Norsku had been *landmennu* on Nyttheim; they had gone to the raft clan because they had fallen in love with raft girls. One knew the smelting of iron, and on an earlier visit to Grønøy claimed to have seen a vein of iron ore in a cliff. Another, since widowed, had been apprenticed to a millwright on Nyttheim, and on the raft had been a master smith. The third had been a farmer lad.

They were to teach the Dinneh what they knew—help them to make their own iron and to grow gardens. Just now, the warriors were more interested in the game to be hunted on Grønøy, but Quick Spirit, who had become chief of the Lion Clan, knew that here, where they could not trade for iron goods, some of the Dinneh must learn to do other things than hunt.

The raft clan, of course, looked forward hopefully to trading with the Dinneh for the goods they could only get on land.

To the two clans involved—the clan of the Cliff Lion, and that of the raft—all this was a matter of getting along, of surviving as well as the circumstances allowed. Neither people realized consciously that what they had done and were doing would prove significant in the civilizing of Haven.

DISCOVERY

"For God's sake, give them a break."

Harvey Blaine Barton, Commander, Imperial Navy Reserve, frowned at his superior. "Give *Saurons* a break?"

"You don't know they're Saurons," Captain Lavrenti Berendtson said. "All you have is some printout pages from a book that may never have been published, about a place we don't have any record of. You don't know if the place exists, much less if they got any of the details right."

"There are lots of places we don't have any record of, sir. I just want to do a search," Barton said. "Sir, if there are live Saurons, the Admiralty will want to know. It's my job—"

"They won't be live Saurons," Berendtson said. "Not after all this time. Grandchildren, maybe. And scared enough to hide." He took the notebook from his subordinate's hands. The pages were ordinary printout, carefully sheathed in transparent plastic and inserted into a looseleaf book. "Ever hear of this Bar-Lev?"

"No, sir, but a lot of books were lost in the raids on Dayan. I expect this was one of them, probably never printed, just put on the electronic net. And someone in the New Jerusalem University library thought enough of it to make a printout. This claims to have been written right in the middle of the Secession Wars—the Imperial Historian will want to see it if nobody else does."

361

"And then what? It gets to the Court, and some hothead from Ekaterina will talk the Navy into looking for this place. Haven. I never heard of the place. God knows what it will take to find it. We don't have enough ships now!" Berendtson said.

"So that's what you're really worried about—"

"Damn right! Harv, I can't order you to forget about this, but I sure wish I could. It can't do a damn bit of good, and it sure could cost us."

"Well—"

"We've got real enemies," Captain Berendtson said. "We don't have ships to waste looking for shadows. Look, I'll make you a deal. You send it Eyes Only to your uncle. I'll add a cover letter. Dyan's in Crucis Sector. Let the Marquis decide.'"

Barton looked thoughtful. Finally he nodded. "I'll send him a copy," he said. "I want to keep the original."

From Bar Lev, *A Traveler's Tales of Twenty Worlds* (Dayan, 2618)

From Bar Lev, *A Traveler's Tales of Twenty Worlds*
(Dayan, 2618)

Viewed from above the plane of the ecliptic, Byers' Star bathes its inner worlds in warmth and solar wind. For those members of its family, their places in the biosphere are an unnecessary luxury, for none of them bear life.

Farther out, in the harsh area called the Tolerable Zone, little of Byers' life-sustaining light and heat penetrate. In most other systems of its type in known space, these worlds also would be lifeless.

But here, nature has allowed life to maintain its reputation for ubiquity. The first world in the Tolerable Zone is a gas giant, a swirling morass of orange-brown gasses, blighted with a sepia-hued elliptical storm region along its equator. The storm's dark, elongated oval against the bright orange sphere instantly earned the giant the name "Cat's Eye," despite the protests to Captain Byers from the first expedition's scientists. They held out for the more romantic designation of G-MA-11-797-Ag.

No matter. A titanic cat's eye it resembled, and Cat's Eye it has been called ever since. Like most gas giants, this one has several moons. It is on the largest of these ten bodies that life made its place. Cat's Eye is far enough from Byers' for her moons to be cold, but the giant herself produces light and energy.

So the moon is warmed. Not enough to give life a niche, exactly; one expedition scientist described it as more of a loophole. But it is enough. The CoDominium government that had funded the discovery wanted worlds, even moons, with life, any life.

For where life could exist at all, men could follow.

The moon was named Haven. A dark jest, by some unknown clerk in the Bureau of Relocation, for it was nothing of the sort, not yet. The irony of that name was as yet several centuries in the future. But to the New Harmony Church and countless other persecuted minorities on crowded Earth, the name of the distant and isolated frontier world shone like a beacon.

The CoDominium used Haven as it had so many other low-value worlds, as a dumping ground for all sorts of undesireables from Earth and the other, more settled worlds. Hundreds of thousands of refugees and "troublemakers" were sentenced to Haven, never to return to Earth.

Godlike, the CoDominium charged the exiles with the reclamation of Haven, a world no one could have wanted in the first place. Godlike, that same CoDominium promptly ignored its charges' struggle for existence on the moon. The system was valued more for the refueling station orbiting Cat's Eye than for the millions of souls on the largely ignored lesser body nearby. Haven entered no one's thoughts until the next batch of exiles from the Bureau of Relocation needed disposition.

And yet, godlike, the Haveners (as they soon came to call themselves) did exactly as they were told. The plants and animals of Haven were given names like shark's fin, wireweed, land gators, hangman bush. They fought the colonists and their Terran plants as, eons ago, they had fought for survival on the harsh surface of Haven. They nearly won.

In time, the CoDominium devoured itself. The Haveners survived, and after a fashion, even flourished, long beyond the death of the State that had created them. The Empire arose and grew to greatness. When its ships arrived to annex the system and its by-now respectable moon, it found strong communities of tough, independent-minded people. Their admission to the Empire was as much their choice as it was the Imperial Will.

The Haveners' hardy and pugnacious spirit was soon recognized by the Empire. In time, they composed the core of several Imperial Guard units. Under the influence of successive Imperial viceroys, Haven waxed and waned variously as a quaint tourist trap, a renowned outworld fleshpot, and finally just another Imperial backwater, as the fortunes of the Empire of Man fluctuated.

In time, the Empire has come to its final crisis. The death throes of such a vast and advanced organism will be long and violent. The Haveners would say: "The healthier the beast, the harder to kill it."

They would know, too. Haven has many healthy beasts, most of them two-legged. . . .

The petty tyrannies that have sprouted all over the Empire would have been of little consequence by themselves. They are not alone. They have rallied under the banner of the Saurons.

The Saurons are a race of specially bred soldiers, warrior-eugenicists, whose genetic science is far beyond the Empire's. Sauron Soldiers are to elite human troops what those elite troops are to civilians. Beyond even the Soldiers lies the Saurons' greatest triumph and greatest weapon, the Cyborgs.

Genetically and chemically enhanced, the Cyborgs are living machines of human/Sauron origin and superhuman capabilities. With a genetic code based on synthesized RNA, they often breed true. Their own society holds them in awe, and barely in check. Ultimately the Cyborgs have come to dominate their own people—which we must hope will be their doom.

The Cyborgs exist only to fight, and they fight like no other creatures in the universe. As victory piled on victory, the Saurons formed the Coalition of Secession. Disaffected worlds of the Empire have gathered under their rubber-stamp council, to be ruled and wielded in the Sauron bid to topple the Empire and bring all known space under Sauron rule.

To meet this threat, the Empire has rallied totally. It may be the Empire's last rallying—but it should be more than the Saurons can face.

Yet the Saurons can be only the last link in a long chain. The first link in that chain was the early experiments in human eugenics, under the CoDominium. Illegal and underfinanced, they needed a hiding place—a world of outcasts, far from Terra or other unfriendly eyes. It was fitting that the CoDominium chose Haven.

The first cycle is now closed. New ones begin.

ROBERT A. HEINLEIN

"Heinlein knows more about blending provocative scientific thinking with strong human stories than any dozen other contemporary science fiction writers."
—*Chicago Sun-Times*

"Robert A. Heinlein wears imagination as though it were his private suit of clothes. What makes his work so rich is that he combines his lively, creative sense with an approach that is at once literate, informed, and exciting."
—*New York Times*

Seven of Robert A. Heinlein's best-loved titles are now available in superbly packaged new Baen editions, with series-look covers by artist John Melo. Collect them all by sending in the order form below: